Dreadnought

Tor Books by Cherie Priest

Dreadnought

Cherie Priest

A Tom Doherty Associates Book *New York*

DREADNOUGHT

Copyright © 2010 by Cherie Priest

Edited by Liz Gorinsky

A Tor Book
Published by Tom Doherty Associates, LLC
175 Fifth Avenue
New York, NY 10010

www.tor-forge.com

Tor® is a registered trademark of Tom Doherty Associates, LLC.

ISBN 978-0-7653-2578-5

First Edition: October 2010

Printed in the United States of America

0 9 8 7 6 5 4 3 2 1

To Jerry and Donna Priest

I used to joke that they could come home and find a bus full of first-graders crashed on the front lawn, caught in the cross fire of a bank robbery, in the midst of an alien invasion... and they'd have the situation under control in under a minute. But for the record, I was only kind of joking.

This is a work of fiction, featuring impossible politics, unlikely zombies, and some ludicrously incorrect Civil War action. I hope you enjoy it! And I'd like to thank you in advance for not sending me e-mail to tell me how bad my history is. I think we all know I've fudged the facts rather significantly.

(Except the zombie parts.)

Acknowledgments

At the risk of sounding redundant, my first paragraph of thanks and warm kudos goes to the usual suspects: my husband, Aric Annear, for not yet admitting that he's sick to death of hearing about these stories, bless his heart; my editor, Liz Gorinsky, for saving me from many a prose misstep and being my in-house champion over at Tor; my agent, Jennifer Jackson, for making all the hard phone calls and letting me periodically stomp around like a tiny Godzilla; and to my publicity team at Tor—Patty Garcia and Amber Hopkins—for meeting me in strange cities and booking my travel so I don't have to.

And I can't have a thanks page without a nod to my day-job chief, Bill Schafer. Thanks for helping me keep the lights on without crowding out the writing work, dude; and thanks to Yanni Kuznia, because she seriously does manage to do it all, and I don't know *how*—but I sure am glad for it.

Thanks also to Andrea Jones, she of the copious Civil War knowledge—for always answering dumb questions with intelligent, interesting, sometimes wacky (but always cool-as-hell) speculation. She and her usual suspects at the Manor of Mixed Blessings have become my go-to crowd for obscure trivia and strange guesses. Thanks be likewise to Christina Smith at the Texas Ranger Hall of Fame and Museum for her input on "Ranger" usage and treatment. Because honestly, I just didn't know.

Likewise, thanks to Louisa May Alcott for writing letters home when she was working at a Washington, D.C., hospital during the Civil War. Her collection of "Hospital Sketches" was immensely helpful in imagining and re-creating a fictional version of the Robertson facility in Richmond.

Epic gratitude and much love go to everyone in the secret clubhouse that serves the world; and to Warren Ellis for being Warren Ellis; and to Wil Wheaton for being Wil Wheaton. Also I send it out to Team Seattle—Mark Henry, Caitlin Kittredge (even though she's leaving us for Massachusetts), Richelle Mead, and Kat Richardson—for giving me a posse of writer peeps with which to hang; to Duane Wilkins for helping manage the signed cargo at the University Book Store; and to the crew at Third Place Books (hi Steve and Vlad!) for their continuing support as well.

More hearty thanks go to Greg Wild-Smith, my original and forever webmaster (unless I eventually drive him off with my crazy); to Ellen Milne and Suezie Hagy for the brunches, company, the organizational skills, and the cat-sitting services.

And finally, thanks to my dad and stepmom—Jerry and Donna Priest, both of them retired from the U.S. Army. Dad was a medic in Vietnam who went on to become a nurse, then a CRNA; Donna was an ER nurse for decades, and now she teaches. Back in the day, she went around the world a time or two on the hospital ship USNS *Mercy*—which may or may not be a coincidence regarding any characters appearing in this book.

Anyway, Dad, thanks for everything. Donna, thanks for everything . . . and the boots.

Then bring me here a breastplate,
And a helm before ye fly,
And I will gird my woman's form,
And on the ramparts die!

—FELICIA HEMANS, *from the poem "Marguerite of France"*

I want something to do.
—LOUISA MAY ALCOTT, *upon announcing her intention to serve as a nurse at the Washington Hospital during the Civil War. To be filed under, "Be careful what you wish for."*

 **One**

Down in the laundry room with the bloody-wet floors and the ceiling-high stacks of sheets, wraps, and blankets, Vinita Lynch was elbows-deep in a vat full of dirty pillowcases because she'd promised—she'd sworn on her mother's life—that she'd find a certain windup pocket watch belonging to Private Hugh Morton before the device was plunged into a tub of simmering soapy water and surely destroyed for good.

Why the private had stashed it in a pillowcase wasn't much of a mystery: even in an upstanding place like the Robertson Hospital, small and shiny valuables went missing from personal stashes with unsettling regularity. And him forgetting about it was no great leap either: the shot he took in the forehead had been a lucky one because he'd survived it, but it left him addled at times—and this morning at breakfast had been one of those times. At the first bell announcing morning food, against the strict orders of Captain Sally he'd sat up and bolted into the mess hall, which existed only in that bullet-buffeted brain of his. In the time it took for him to be captured and redirected to his cot, where the meal would come to *him,* thank you very kindly, if only he'd be patient enough to receive it, the junior nursing staff had come through and stripped the bedding of all and sundry.

None of them had noticed the watch, but it would've been easy to miss.

So Nurse Lynch was down in the blistering hot hospital basement, dutifully fishing through laundry soiled by injured and greasy heads, running noses, and rheumy eyes in hopes that Private Hugh Morton would either be reunited with the absent treasure, or would be separated from it long enough to forget all about it.

Upstairs, someone cried out, "Mercy!"

And downstairs, in the hospital basement, Vinita Lynch took a very deep breath and let it out slowly, between her teeth.

"Mercy! Mercy, come up here, please!"

Because that's what they'd taken to calling her, through some error of hearing or paperwork, or because it was easier for a room full of bed-bound men to remember a common word than call her by her given name.

"Mercy!"

It was louder this time, and insistent, and bellowed by Captain Sally herself somewhere up on the first floor. Captain Sally sounded like she meant business; but then again, Captain Sally always meant business, and that was why she was the captain.

The nurse angled her head to cast her voice up the stairs and shouted, "Coming!" though she continued to rifle through the laundry, because something sharp had tapped against the nail of her thumb. And if she could just snare one long finger around the smooth metal plate of the watch's back—yes, that *had* to be it—then she'd be only a moment longer. "I'm coming!" she said even more loudly, to stall for those extra seconds, even though the summons hadn't come again.

She had it. Her fist closed around it and wrested the palm-sized device, ticking and intact, up through the folds of cotton bedding and out of the vat. The watch was cool in her hand, and heavier than it appeared—not an expensive piece, but one with thumb-spots worn into its finish from a lifetime of use and appreciation.

"Found it," she said to herself, and she shoved it into her apron's pocket for temporary safekeeping.

"Mercy!" Again from upstairs, and impatient.

"I said I was coming!" she responded as she hiked the hem of her skirts and bolted up the stairs, less ladylike than swiftly, back into the hall behind the kitchen. Moving sideways, she squeezed past the orderlies, one of the doctors, and three of the elderly women who were hired to perform mending but mostly bickered amongst themselves. Her way was briefly blocked by one of the retained men who was carrying a basket full of bandages and wraps; they did a brief and awkward dance, back and forth, each trying to let the other pass, until she finally dashed by with an apology—but if he replied, she didn't hear him, because the main ward was now immediately before her.

She entered it with a breathless flourish and stood panting, squeezing at the pocket watch in her apron and trying to spot Captain Sally in the sea of supine bodies lying on cots in varying states of health and repair.

The rows ran eight cots by fifteen in this ward, which served as admittance, triage, and recovery room alike. It should've held only two-thirds that number, and the present crowding served to narrow the aisles to the point that they were nearly impassible, but no one was turned away. Captain Sally said that if they had to stitch them standing up and lash them to the closet walls, they'd take every Confederate boy who'd been carried off the field.

But she could make such declarations. It was *her* hospital, and she legally outranked everyone else in the building. The "Captain" bit was not a nickname. It was a commission from the Confederate States of America, and it had been granted because a military hospital must have a military commander, but Sally Louisa Tompkins would accept no superior, and she was too wealthy and competent to be ignored.

The din of the ward was at its ordinary hideous level; the

groaning patients, creaking cot springs, and hoarse requests combining to form the usual background hum. It was not a pretty noise, and it was sometimes punctuated with vomiting or cries of pain, but it was always there, along with the ever-present scents of dirty bodies, sweat, blood, shit, the medicinal reek of ether, the yellowy sharp stink of saltpeter and spent gunpowder, and the feeble efforts of lye soap to combat it all. Mere soap, no matter how finely scented, could never scour the odors of urine, scorched flesh, and burned hair. No perfume could cleanse away the pork-sweet smell of rotting limbs and gangrenous flesh.

Mercy told herself that the reek of the hospital wasn't any worse than that of the farm in Waterford, Virginia. That was a lie.

It was worse than the summer when she'd gone out to the back twenty and found their bull lying with its legs in the air, its belly distended with the bloat of rot and a crawling carpet of flies. This was worse than that because it wasn't the decomposition of beef lying in the sun, flesh dripping away gray and mushy. This was worse because after a while the bull had faded and gone, its smell washed away by the summer rains and its remains buried by her stepfather and brother. After a while, she'd altogether forgotten where the creature had fallen and died, and it was as if it'd never happened.

But that never happened here.

Not even at the cleanest hospital in all the Confederacy, where fewer men died and more men recovered to return to the front than in any other in the North or South or even Europe. Not even in the wake of Captain Sally's strenuous—almost maddening—insistence on cleanliness. Enormous pots of water boiled constantly, and mops were pushed in two-hour shifts by legions of retained men who were healed enough to help but not enough to fight. Paul Forks was one of these men. Harvey Kline was another; and Medford Simmons a third, and Anderson Ruby a fourth; and if she knew more of their names, Mercy Lynch could've listed another dozen maimed and helpful souls.

They kept the floors from staining red, and helped carry the endless trays of food and medicines, tagging along in the wake of the doctors and helping the nurses manage the unruly ones who awoke afraid.

And even with the help of these men, and two dozen nurses like herself, and five doctors working around the clock, and a whole contingent of laundry and kitchen women, the smell never, ever went away.

It worked itself into the wrinkles in Mercy's clothes and lurked in her hair. It collected under her fingernails.

She carried it with her, always.

"Captain Sally?" Mercy called out, and as soon as the words were spoken, she spied the woman standing near the front door, accompanied by another woman and a man.

Sally was small and pale, with dark hair parted severely down the middle of her head and a plain black dress buttoned tightly from waist to chin. She was leaning forward to better hear the other woman speak, while the gentleman behind them shuffled back and forth on his feet, moving his gaze left to right.

"Mercy." Captain Sally wended through the maze of cots to meet the young nurse. She had stopped shouting. "Mercy, I need a word with you. I'm very sorry, but it's important. Would you join us?" She indicated the anxious-looking man and the stoic woman with a New Englander's ramrod posture.

"Who are those people?" she asked without agreeing to anything.

"They have a message for you."

Mercy didn't want to meet the man and woman. They did not look like people with good news to pass along. "Why don't they come inside to deliver it, then?"

Sally said, "Dearest," and she pressed her mouth close to Mercy's ear. "That's Clara Barton, the Red Cross woman, and no one'll bother her. But the fellow beside her is a Yankee."

Mercy made a little choking sound. "What's he doing here, then?" she asked, though she already had a very good idea, and it was horrible.

"Mercy—"

"Ain't they got their own hospitals, hardly a hundred miles away in Washington? He doesn't look hurt none too bad, anyhow." She was talking too quickly.

Sally interrupted. "Mercy, you need to talk to that man, and Miss Barton."

"That Red Cross woman, what does she want with me? I've already got a job nursing, and it's right here, and I don't want to—" Sweat warmed the inside of her collar. She tugged at it, trying to give herself some air.

"Vinita." The small woman with the big rank put her hands on Mercy's shoulders, forcing the younger nurse to stand up straight and meet her eyes. "Take a deep breath now, like we talked about before."

"I'm trying," she whispered. "I don't think I can."

"Breathe deep now. Let it out, and take your time. Hold yourself up. And come, let's have a talk with these people." Her tone softened, dipping from commander to mother. "I'll stay with you, if you like."

"I don't want . . . ," she began, but she didn't know what she wanted, so when Sally took her hand and squeezed it, she squeezed back.

"Someplace private," the officer said. Sally nodded at Clara Barton and her nervous companion, indicating that they should follow; and she led Mercy through the remaining rows of cots and out the back, and down a corridor swiftly—urging their followers to hasten—and then they were in the courtyard of what used to be Judge Robertson's mansion. Tents peppered the yard and bustling officials came and went from flap to flap, but they ignored the nurse and her party.

Back between the trees, where the chilly, sun-dappled grass moved with shadows from the leaves overhead, Captain Sally led all three to a picnic area where the ground was cleared and a set of benches was placed for lovers, or lunches, or rest.

Mercy was still squeezing Sally's hand, because the moment she let go, someone was going to speak.

When everyone was seated, Sally pried Mercy's fingers off her own, then held the shaking hand and patted it gently as she said, "Miss Barton, Mr. Atwater. This is Vinita Lynch, though around here, most everyone calls her—"

"Mercy," said Mr. Atwater. He'd been good-looking once, but was almost haggard now, with dark hair and brown eyes, and a thin body that seemed on the rebound from the very cusp of starvation.

"Mrs. Lynch," he tried again. "My name is Dorence Atwater, and I was in the camp at Andersonville for six years." He kept it low, soft. Quiet. Not wanting anyone to hear.

He wasn't fighting anymore, and he wasn't in uniform, but the cadence of his speech marked him as a northern boy—a *real* northern boy, not a border-state boy like Vinita's husband. He didn't have an accent that could go either way: Kentucky or Tennessee; Virginia or Washington, D.C.; Texas or Kansas.

"Mr. Atwater," she said, more curtly than she meant to. But all her words were clipped, and her grip on the matron's hand was leaving crescent moons where her nails were digging deep. "That must've been . . . difficult."

It was a stupid word, and she knew it. Of *course* the camp had been difficult; everything was difficult, wasn't it? Marrying a border-state Yankee was difficult when her Virginia home stayed gray. Missing him for two years now was difficult, too, and folding his letters over and over again, reading them for the hundredth time, and the two hundredth time, that was difficult. Nursing the injured was difficult, and so was wondering with each new wound if it'd been inflicted by her very own spouse, or if her very own spouse was somewhere else—maybe a hundred miles away in Washington—being nursed by a woman much like herself, dutifully tending her own cannon fodder lads on sagging cots.

But he wasn't in Washington.

She knew that. She knew it because Clara Barton and Dorence Atwater were sitting on a low stone bench facing her, with serious eyes and sad news on their lips—because, bless them both, they never brought any other kind.

Before either of the visitors could say anything else, Mercy nattered on again. "I've heard of you, both of you. Miss Barton, it's wonderful work you're doing on the battlefield—making it safer for the lot of us, and making it easier for us to comfort the wounded, and patch them up—" She nearly spit that last part out, for her nose was beginning to fill, and her eyes were blinking, slamming open and shut. "And Mr. Atwater, you made a . . ."

Two things rampaged through her brain: the name of the man not four feet in front of her, and why she'd heard it before he ever entered the Robertson Hospital. But she couldn't bring herself to make these two things meet, and she struggled to hold them apart, so the connection couldn't be made.

It was futile.

She knew.

She said, and every letter of every word shook in her mouth, "You made a list."

"Yes ma'am."

And Clara Barton said, "My dear, we're so very sorry." It wasn't quite a practiced condolence. It wasn't smooth and polished, and for all the weariness of it, it sounded like she meant it. "But your husband, Phillip Barnaby Lynch . . . his name is on that list. He died at the Andersonville camp for prisoners of war, nine months ago. I'm terribly, terribly sorry for your loss."

"Then it's true," she burbled, not quite crying. The pressure behind her eyes was building. "It'd been so long since he sent word. Jesus, Captain Sally," she blasphemed weakly. "It's true."

She was still squeezing Sally Tompkins, who now ceased patting her hand to squeeze back. "I'm so sorry, dear." With her free hand, she brushed Mercy's cheek.

"It's true," she repeated. "I thought . . . I thought it must be. It'd been so long. Almost as long as we were married, since I'd got word of him. I knew it went like that, sometimes. I knew it was hard for the boys—for you boys—to write from the front, and I knew the mail wasn't all kinds of reliable. I guess I knew all that. But I was still dumb enough to hope."

"You were newlyweds?" Clara Barton asked gently, sadly. Familiar with the sorrow, if not quite immune.

"Been married eight months," she said. "Eight months and he went out to fight, and he was gone for two and a half years. And I stayed here, and waited. We had a home here, west of town. He was born in Kentucky, and we were going to go back there, when all this was done, and start a family."

Suddenly she released Sally's hand and leaped forward, making a grab for Dorence Atwater's.

She clutched his wrists and pulled him closer. She demanded, "Did you know him? Did you talk to him? Did he give you any message for me? Anything? Anything at all?"

"Ma'am, I only saw him in passing. He was hurt real bad when they brought him in, and he didn't last. I hope that can be some comfort to you, maybe. The camp was a terrible place, but he wasn't there for long."

"Not like some of them. Not like you," she said. Every word was rounded with the congestion that clogged her throat but wouldn't spill out into hiccups or tears, not yet.

"No ma'am. And I'm very sorry about it, but I thought you deserved to know he won't be coming home. They buried him in a grave outside of Plains, unmarked with a dozen others. But he didn't suffer long."

He slouched so that his shoulders held up his chest like a shirt on a hanger. It was as if the weight of his message were too much, and his body still too frail to carry it all. But if he didn't carry it, nobody would.

"I'm sorry, ma'am. I wish the news were kinder."

She released him then, and sagged back onto her own bench, into the arms of Sally Tompkins, who was ready with an embrace. Mercy let the captain hold her and she said, "No. No, but you came all this way, and you brought it to me anyway."

Mercy Lynch closed her eyes and put her head on Sally's shoulder.

Clara Barton and Dorence Atwater took this as their cue to leave. They left silently, walking around the side yard rather than cutting back through the hospital, toward the street and whatever transportation awaited them there.

Without opening her eyes, Mercy said, "I wish they'd never come. I wish I didn't know."

Sally stroked her head and told her, "Someday you'll be glad they did. I know it's hard to imagine, but really, it's better knowing than wondering. False hope's the worst kind there is."

"It was good of them," she agreed with a sniffle, the first that had escaped thus far. "They came here, to a Rebel hospital and everything. They didn't have to do that. They could've sent a letter."

"She was here under the cross," Sally said. "But you're right. It's hard work, what they do. And you know, I don't think anyone, even here, would've raised a hand against them." She sighed, and stopped petting Mercy's wheat-colored hair. That hair, always unruly and just too dark to call blond, was fraying out from the edges of her cap. It tangled in Sally's fingers. "All of the boys, blue and gray alike. They all hope someone would do the same for them—that someone would tell their mothers and sweethearts, should they fall on the field."

"I guess."

Mercy loosed herself from Sally's loving hold, and she stood, wiping at her eyes. They were red, and so was her nose. Her cheeks were flushed violently pink. "Could I have the afternoon, Captain Sally? Just take a little time in my bunk?"

The captain remained seated, and folded her hands across her lap. "Take as long as you need. I'll have Paul Forks bring up your supper. And I'll tell Anne to let you be."

"Thank you, Captain Sally." Mercy didn't mind her roommate much, but she could scarcely stand the thought of explaining anything to her, not right then, while the world was still strangely hued and her throat was blocked with curdled screams.

She walked slowly back into the house-turned-hospital, keeping her gaze on the ground and watching her feet as she felt her way inside. Someone said, "Good morning, Nurse Mercy," but she didn't respond. She barely heard it.

Keeping one hand on the wall to guide herself, she found the first-floor ward and the stairwell that emptied there. Now, two different words bounced about in her mind: *widow* and *up*. She struggled to ignore the first one and grasp the second. She only had to make it up to her bunk in the attic.

"Nurse," a man called. It sounded like, *Nuss*. "Nurse Mercy?"

One hand still on the wall, one foot lifted to scale the first step, she paused.

"Nurse Mercy, did you find my watch?"

For an instant she was perplexed; she regarded the speaker, and saw Private Hugh Morton, his battered but optimistic face upturned. "You said you'd find my watch. It didn't get all washed up, did it?"

"No," she breathed. "It didn't."

He smiled so hard, his face swelled into a circle. He sat up on the cot and shook his head, then rubbed at one eye with the inside of his arm. "You found it?"

"I did, yes.' Here," she said, fumbling with the pocket on her apron. She pulled it out and held it for a moment, watching the sunlight from the windows give the brass a dull gleam. "I found it. It's fine."

His skinny hand stretched out and she dropped the watch into the waiting palm. He turned it over and over, and asked, "Nobody washed it or nothing?"

"Nobody washed it or nothing. It's still ticking just fine."

"Thank you, Nurse Mercy!"

"You're welcome," she mumbled, though she'd already turned back to the stairs, scaling them one slow brick at a time as if her feet were made of lead.

Two

Mercy Lynch would've liked to take a second afternoon of solitude if she'd been able, sitting on the foot of her narrow bed and reading and rereading the letters Phillip had sent while he was still in a position to write them. But the hospital didn't slow enough to let her grieve at her leisure.

By the second afternoon, everyone knew that she was a widow.

Only Captain Sally knew she was a widow of a Yankee.

There was always the chance it wouldn't have mattered if everyone knew. Kentucky was a mixed-up place, blue grass and gray skies, split down the middle. Virginia was nearly the same, and she suspected she'd find proof enough of that in the Washington hospital where the boys in blue were brought when they'd fallen. All along the borderlands, men fought on both sides.

Phillip had fought for Kentucky, not for the Union. He fought because his father's farm had been attacked by Rebs and halfway burned; just about the same as how Mercy's own brother fought for Virginia and not for the Confederacy because her family farm had been burned down twice in the last ten years by the Yanks.

Everyone fights for home, in the end. Or that was how she saw it. If anyone anywhere was fighting for state's rights or abolition or anything like that, you didn't hear about it much anymore. Those first five or six years, it was all anyone had to talk about.

But after twenty?

Mercy had been a small child when the first shots were fired on Fort Sumter and the war had begun. And as far as she'd ever known or seen since, everything else had been a great big exchange of grudges, more personal than political. But it could be that she'd been looking at it too closely for the last fourteen months, working at the Robertson Hospital, where they sometimes even treated a Yankee or two, if he was caught in the wrong place at the wrong time, and especially if he was a border-stater. Likely as not, he was kin or cousin to someone lying on a cot nearby.

Likely as not, he hadn't been born when the war first broke out anyway, and his grievances were assigned to him, same as most of the other lads who moaned, and bled, and cried, and begged from their cots, hoping for food or comfort. Praying for their limbs back. Promising God their lives and their children if only they could walk again, or if only they didn't have to go back to the lines.

Everyone prayed the same damn things, never mind the uniform.

So it might not've mattered if anyone knew that Vinita May Swakhammer of Waterford, Virginia, had married Phillip Barnaby Lynch of Lexington, Kentucky, during the summer of her twentieth birthday—knowing that they'd been born on the wrong sides of a badly drawn line, and that it was bound to come between them some day.

And it had.

And now he was on the other side of an even bigger line. She'd catch up to him one day; that was as certain as amputations and medicine shortages. But in the meantime, she'd miss him terribly, and take a second afternoon off her shift to mourn, if she could.

She couldn't.

She'd have to miss him and mourn for him on her feet, because no sooner had she ignored the lunch Paul Forks brought and left than another round of casualties landed hard in the first-floor ward.

She heard them arrive, all of them drawn by the cramped, dark little ambulances that were barely better than boxes. Retained men and doctors' assistants unpacked them like sandwiches, sliding their cots into the daylight, where the men who were strong enough to do so blinked against the sun. Out the small window in her bunk, she could see them leaving the ambulances in impossible numbers; she thought dully that they must've been stacked in there like cordwood, for each carriage to hold so many of them.

Two . . . no, three of the soldiers came out wrapped from head to toe, still on a cot, but needing no further assistance. They'd died making the trip. A few of them always did, especially on the way to Robertson. Captain Sally had a reputation for healing even the most horribly wounded, so as often as not, the most horribly wounded were sent to her.

Only three men hadn't survived the transport.

That made it a good load, unless there was another ambulance someplace where Mercy couldn't see it.

She'd been given permission to stay cloistered upstairs, but two nurses were already down with pneumonia, and one had packed up and headed home in the wee hours of the night without saying anything to anybody. One of the doctors had been commandeered by a general for field surgery, which Mercy didn't envy in the slightest. So this hospital, which was low on beds and high on chaos under the best of circumstances, was now shorthanded as well.

Two suitcases sat at the foot of Mercy's bed. They were both packed. She'd been living out of them since she arrived. There weren't any drawers in the bunks; so you made do, or you kept your belongings on the floor, or under your bed if it was hitched up high enough.

Mercy's wasn't.

She unfastened the buckle of the leftmost case and slipped a locket back inside an interior pocket, where it was always kept. She buckled the case again and stood up straight, pinning her apron into place against her collarbones. A slab of polished tin served as a foggy mirror. Her cap was crooked. She fixed it, and used a pin to secure it while she listened to the cacophony swell on the floors below.

Yes, she was taking her time.

For those first frantic minutes, she'd only be in the way. Once all the men were inside and the ambulance drivers had finished their hasty paperwork, and once the mangled soldiers were lying in bleeding lines, then she could be more useful.

There was a note to the chaos that she'd learned—a pitch achieved when the time was right, when everyone who'd fit inside the walls of the judge's old house was crammed within, and all the doctors and all the retained men were barking clipped instructions and orders back and forth. When this very particular note rang up to the attic, she left her bunk and descended into the carnival of the macabre below.

Down into the thick of it she went, into the sea of unwashed faces turned black with bruises or powder, through the lines of demarcation that cordoned off the four new typhoids, the two pneumonias, and a pair of dysenteries who would need attention soon enough, but could wait for the moment.

There were also two "wheezers"—hospital slang for the drug addicts who'd magically survived on the front for long enough to land in a hospital. Their substance of choice was a yellowish muck that smelled like sulfur and rot; and it went through their brains until they did little but stare, and wheeze softly, and pick at the sores that formed around their mouths and noses. The wheezers could wait, too. They weren't going anywhere, and their self-inflicted condition made them a bottom-rung priority.

Around the nearest hastily cleared lane, doctors bustled back-to-bottom with shuffling nurses who squeezed through the corridor as swiftly as if it were a highway. Mercy stood there, only for a moment, triangulating herself among the dilapidated patriots who lay wherever they were left by the medics—either on their stretchers upon the floor, or against the cots of earlier patients who'd not yet vacated them.

She was overrun by two chattering surgeons; battered by a set of coal hods, water pails, medicine trays; and run into by one of the small boys who ran messages from floor to floor, physician to physician. Mercy counted four of them, scuttling in different directions, delivering scraps of paper with all the speed of a telegram service, if not the accuracy.

Deep breaths. One after another. Work to be done.

Shoving through the narrow artery, she emerged on the far side of an intersection where the entrance to the old judge's ballroom had become a filthy pun, since the worst of the gunshot patients were assembled there. Ball shot was unpredictable and messy, always. Sometimes gruesome lacerations, sometimes blown limbs left connected only by stray fragments of bone and gristle. Sometimes pierced cheeks, hands, and feet, or a crater where an eye had been. Sometimes a punctured lung or a splintered rib.

Never anything but awful.

Thirty beds were already occupied, with half a dozen other ragged men lying on the floor, muddy to the knees and covered with bandages so dirty that it was difficult to tell what dark stains were blood and which were only the filth of the field. Most of their faces were as pale as death already, from loss of bodily fluids or from the shock of what they'd seen, and what they continued to see.

They waited in relative silence, too exhausted even to moan. One or two called hoarsely for water, or begged for a doctor, or cried out for a distant mother or wife. More than a handful had lost their coats somewhere along the line; they were wrapped in blankets and huddled together pitifully, sometimes sharing the covers for warmth even though the room was kept from freezing by the billowing fires that were constantly stoked by two retained men at either end of the room.

A new nurse, a girl younger than Mercy by several years, stood immobilized by the urgency of it all. Her hands fluttered at her sides and her eyes welled up with tears of frustration. "Where do I start?" she whispered.

Mercy heard her, and she could answer.

She swept past a table piled with lone socks, slings, splints, bandages, discarded holsters with weaponry still in them, and shirts that were missing sleeves. From the next table down, she retrieved a basin the size of a small sink, plus a fistful of washrags and a kitten-sized bar of ugly brown soap that smelled like a cheap candle.

"Nurse," she said, and she would've grabbed the girl's arm if she'd had a free hand to do so.

"Ma'am?"

"Nurse. What's your name?"

"Ma'am? It's . . . it's Sarah. Sarah Fitzhugh."

"Sarah, then." Mercy foisted the basin into Sarah's not-quite-ready arms. Warm water sloshed up against the girl's apron, dampening her breasts in a long wet line. "Take this."

"Yes ma'am."

"And this, and these." She handed over the soap and the rags, which Sarah was barely capable of balancing. "You see those men over there?" Mercy pointed at the end of the row, where a sad-looking collection of as-yet-unprocessed newcomers were waiting their turns at paperwork and a doctor's inspection.

"I see them—yes ma'am."

"Start at the end of the line. Take off their shoes if they've still got them, and then their socks, coats, and shirts. Scrub them down and do it fast. There are clean shirts in the corner behind you, against the wall, and a small pile of socks to the left. Dress them in the clean shirts and socks, toss the dirty ones into the laundry vats in the next room, and then move on to the next row of soldiers."

"Scrub . . ." Sarah was stuck on that one word. "Scrub them? The soldiers?"

"Well, I don't mean the doctors or the rats," Mercy told her. "Be quick with it. The surgeons'll be along in less than half an hour, and if Captain Sally sees dirty men on her floor, she'll throw a hissy fit."

The poor girl's face went nearly as white as her first and nearest charge. But she said, "Yes ma'am," with only a small wibble in her voice, and turned to do as she'd been told.

Mercy would've helped her, but Mercy was the nursing superintendent of the first ward and had more important things to do. Granted, she was now in the ballroom ward instead of the first ward, but the nursing superintendent of the ballroom ward was bedridden, and no one else had been ready to step up to the task, so Mercy had swooped onto the scene to assist with pressing matters at this end of the marble-floored room. A curtain had been hung to wall off a portion of the ballroom ward—not for the sake of modesty or decorum, and certainly not to shield the sensibilities of the soldiers. Most of them had heard and seen plenty.

Someone authoritative cried out, "Nurse!"

Mercy was already on her way. The surgeons liked her, and asked for her often. She'd begun to preempt them when the pace was wicked like this and a new batch of the near mortally wounded was being sorted for cutting.

She drew the curtain aside, stifled a flinch, and dropped herself into the seat beside the first cot—where one of the remaining doctors was gesturing frantically. "Mercy, there you are. I'm glad it's you," he said.

"That makes one of us," she replied, and she took a bloody set of pincers from his hand, dropping them into the tin bucket at her feet.

"Two of us," croaked the man on the cot. "I'm glad it's you, too."

She forced a smile and said teasingly, "I doubt it very much, since this is our first meeting."

"First of many, I hope—" He might've said more, but what was left of his arm was being examined. Mercy thought it must be god-awful uncomfortable, but he didn't cry out. He only cut himself off.

"What's your name?" she asked, partly for the sake of the record, and partly to distract him.

"Christ," said the doctor, cutting away more of the man's shirt and revealing greater damage than he'd imagined.

The injured man gasped, "No, that's not it." And he gave her a grin that was tighter than a laundry line. "It's Henry. Gilbert Henry. So I just go by Henry."

"Henry, Gilbert Henry, who just goes by Henry. I'll jot that down," she told him, and she fully intended to, but by then her hands were full with the remains of a sling that hadn't done much to support the blasted limb—mostly, it'd just held the shattered thing in one pouch. The arm was disintegrating as Dr. Luther did his best to assess it.

"Never liked the name Gilbert," the man mumbled.

"It's a fine name," she assured him.

Dr. Luther said, "Help me turn him over. I've got a bad feeling about—"

"I've got him. You can lift him. And, I'm sorry, Gilbert Henry"—she repeated his name to better remember it later—"but this is gonna smart. Here, give me your good hand."

He took it.

"Now, give it a squeeze if we're hurting you."

"I could never," he insisted, gallant to the last.

"You can and you will, and you'll be glad I made the offer. You won't put a dent in me, I promise. Now, on the count of three," she told the doctor, locking her eyes to his.

He picked up the count. "One . . . Two . . ." On three, they hoisted the man together, turning him onto his side and confirming the worst of Dr. Luther's bad feelings.

Gilbert Henry said, "One of you, say something. Don't leave a man hanging." The second half of it came out in a wheeze, for part of the force of his words had leaked out through the oozing hole in his side.

"A couple of ribs," the doctor said. "Smashed all to hell," he continued, because he was well past watching his language in front of the nurses, much less in front of Mercy, who often used far fouler diction if she thought the situation required it.

"Three ribs, maybe," she observed. She observed more than that, too. But she couldn't say it, not while Gilbert Henry had a death grip on her hand.

The ribs were the least of his problems. The destroyed arm was a greater one, and it would certainly need to be amputated; but what she saw now raised the question of whether or not it was worth the pain and suffering. His lung was pierced at least, shredded at worst. Whatever blast had maimed him had caught him on the left side, taking that arm and tearing into the soft flesh of his torso. With every breath, a burst of warm, damp air spilled out from amid the wreckage of his rib cage.

It was not the kind of wound from which a man recovered.

"Help me roll him back," Dr. Luther urged, and on a second count of three, Mercy obliged. "Son, I've got to tell you the truth. There's nothing to be done about that arm."

"I . . . was . . . afraid of that. But, Doc, I can't hardly breathe. That's the ribs . . . ain't it?"

Now that she knew where to look, Mercy could see the rhythmic ooze above his ribs, fresher now, as if the motion of adjusting him had made matters worse. Gilbert Henry might have a couple of hours, or he might have a couple of minutes. But no longer than that, without a straight-from-God's-hand miracle.

She answered for the doctor, who was still formulating a response. "Yes, that's your ribs."

He grimaced, and the shredded arm fluttered.

Dr. Luther said, "It has to go. We're going to need the ether."

"Ether? I've never had any ether before." He sounded honestly afraid.

"Never?" Mercy said casually as she reached for the rolling tray with the knockout supplies. It had two shelves; the top one stocked the substance itself and clean rags, plus one of the new-fangled mask-and-valve sets that Captain Sally had purchased with her own money. They were the height of technology, and very expensive. "It's not so bad, I promise. In your condition, I'd call it a blessed relief, Mr. Gilbert Henry."

He grasped for her hand again. "You won't leave me, will you?"

"Absolutely not," she promised. It wasn't a vow she was positive she could keep, but the soldier couldn't tell it from her voice.

His thin seam of a grin returned. "As long as you'll . . . be here."

The second tray on the rolling cart held nastier instruments. Mercy took care to hide them behind her skirt and apron. He didn't need to see the powered saw, the twisting clamps, or the oversized shears that were sometimes needed to sever those last few tendons. She made sure that all he saw was her professional pleasantness as she disentangled her fingers and began the preparation work, while the doctor situated himself, lining up the gentler-looking implements and calling for extra rags, sponges, and a second basin filled with hot water—if the nearest retained man could see to it.

"Mercy," Dr. Luther said. It was a request and a signal.

"Yes, Doctor." She said to Gilbert Henry, "It's time, darling.

I'm very sorry, but believe me, you'll wake up praising Jesus that you slept through it."

It wasn't her most reassuring speech ever, but on the far side of Gilbert Henry were two other men behind the curtain, each one of whom needed similar attention; and her internal manufacturer of soothing phrases was not performing at its best.

She showed him the mask, a shape like a softened triangle, bubbled to fit over his nose and mouth. "You see this? I'm going to place it over your face, like so—" She held it up over her own mouth, briefly, for demonstrative purposes. "Then I'll tweak a few knobs over here on this tank—" At this, she pointed at the bullet-shaped vial, a little bigger than a bottle of wine. "Then I'll mix the ether with the stabilizing gases, and before you can say 'boo,' you'll be having the best sleep of your life."

"You've . . . done this . . . before?"

The words were coming harder to him; he was failing as he lay there, and she knew—suddenly, horribly—that once she placed the mask over his face, he wasn't ever going to wake up. She fought to keep the warm panic out of her eyes when she said, "Dozens of times. I've been here a year and a half," she exaggerated. Then she set the mask aside and seized the noteboard that was propped up against his cot, most of its forms left unfilled.

"Nurse?" Dr. Luther asked.

"One moment," she begged. "Before you start napping, Gilbert Henry who'd rather be called just Henry, let me write your information down for safekeeping—so the nurse on the next shift will know all about you."

"If you . . . like, ma'am."

"That's a good man, and a fine patient," she praised him without looking at him. "So tell me quickly, have you got a mother waiting for you back home? Or . . . or," she almost choked. "A wife?"

"No wife. A mother . . . though. And . . . a . . . brother, still . . . a . . . boy."

She wondered how he'd made it this far in such bad shape—if he'd clung to life this long purely with the goal of the hospital in mind, thinking that if he made it to Robertson, he'd be all right.

"A mother and a little brother. Their names?"

"Abigail June. Maiden . . . name . . . Harper."

She stalked his words with the pencil nub, scribbling as fast as she could in her graceless, awkward script. "Abigail June, born Harper. That's your mother, yes? And what town?"

"Memphis. I joined . . . up. In Memphis."

"A Tennessee boy. Those are just about my favorite kind," she said.

"Just about?"

She confirmed, "Just about." She set the noteboard aside, back up against the leg of the cot, and retrieved the gas. "Now, Mr. Gilbert Henry, are you ready?"

He nodded bravely and weakly.

"Very good, dear sir. Just breathe normally, if you don't mind—" She added privately, *And insofar as you're able.* "That's right, very good. And I want you to count backwards, from the number ten. Can you do that for me?"

His head bobbed very slightly. "Ten," he said, and the word was muffled around the blown glass shape of the mask. "Ni . . ."

And that was it. He was already out.

Mercy sighed heavily. The doctor said quietly, "Turn it off."

"I'm sorry?"

"The gas. Turn it off."

She shook her head. "But if you're going to take the arm, he might need—"

"I'm not taking the arm. There's no call to do it. No sense in it," he added. He might've said more, but she knew what he meant, and she waved a hand to tell him no, that she didn't want to hear it.

"You can't just let him lie here."

"Mercy," Dr. Luther said more tenderly. "You've done him a kindness. He's not going to come around again. Taking the arm would kill him faster, and maim him, too. Let him nap it out, peacefully. Let his family bury him whole. Watch," he said.

She was watching already, the way the broad chest rose and fell, but without any rhythm, and without any strength. With less drive. More infrequently.

The doctor stood and wrapped his stethoscope into a bundle to jam in his pocket. "I didn't need to listen to his lungs to know he's a goner," he explained, and bent his body over Gilbert Henry to whisper at Mercy. "And I have three other patients—two of whom might actually survive the afternoon if we're quick enough. Sit with him if you like, but don't stay long." He withdrew, and picked up his bag. Then he said in his normal voice, "He doesn't know you're here, and he won't know when you leave. You know it as well as I do."

She stayed anyway, lingering as long as she dared.

He didn't have a wife to leave a widow, but he had a mother somewhere, and a little brother. He hadn't mentioned a father; any father had probably died years ago, in the same damn war. Maybe his father had gone like this, too—lying on a cot, scarcely identified and in pieces. Maybe his father had never gotten home, or word had never made it home, and he'd died alone in a field and no one had even come to bury him for weeks, since that was how it often went in the earlier days of the conflict.

One more ragged breath crawled into Henry's throat, and she could tell—just from the sound of it, from the critical timbre of that final note—that it was his last. He didn't exhale. The air merely escaped in a faint puff, passed through his nose and the hole in his side. And the wide chest with the curls of dark hair poking out above the undershirt did not rise again.

She had no sheet handy with which to cover him. She picked up the noteboard and set it facedown on his chest, which would serve as indicator enough to the next nurse, or to the retained men, or whoever came to clean up after her.

"Mercy," Dr. Luther called sharply. "Bring the cart."

"Coming," she said, and she rose, and arranged the cart, retrieving the glass mask and resetting the valves. She felt numb, but only as numb as usual. Next. There was always another one, next.

She swiveled the cart and positioned it at the next figure, groaning and twisting on a squeaking cot that was barely big enough to hold him. Once more, she pasted a smile in place. She greeted the patient. "Well, aren't you a big son of a gun. Hello there, I'm Nurse Mercy."

He groaned in response, but did not gurgle or wheeze. Mercy wondered if this one wouldn't go better.

She retrieved his noteboard with its unfilled forms and said, "I don't have a name for you yet, dear. What'd your mother call you?"

"Silas," he spit through gritted teeth. "Newton. Private First Class." His voice was strong, if strained.

"Silas," she repeated as she wrote it down. Then, to the doctor, "What are we looking at here?"

"Both legs, below the knee."

And the patient said, "Cannonball swept me off my feet." One foot was gone altogether; the second needed to go right after it, as soon as possible.

"Right. Any other pains, problems, or concerns?"

"Goddammit, the legs aren't enough?" he nearly shrieked.

She kept her voice even. "They're more than enough, and they'll be addressed." She met his eyes and saw so much pain there that she retreated just a little, enough to say, "Look, I'm sorry, Mr. Newton. We're only trying to get you treated."

"Oh, I've been treated, all right. Those sons of bitches! How am I going to run a mill like this, eh? What's my wife going to think when I get home and she sees?"

She set the noteboard down beside the cot. "Well, all God's children got their problems. Here . . ." She pulled a filled syringe off the second tier of the rolling cart and said, "Let me give you something for the pain. It's a new treatment, but the soldiers have responded to this better than the old-fashioned shot of whiskey and bullet to bite on—"

But he smacked her hand away and called her a name. Mercy immediately told him to calm down, but instead he let his hands flail in every direction, as if he desperately needed someone to hit. Dr. Luther caught one hand and Mercy caught the other. This wasn't their first unruly patient, and they had a system down. It wasn't so different from hog-tying, or roping up a calf. The tools were different, but the principle was the same: seize, lasso, fasten, and immobilize. Repeat as necessary.

She twisted one of his beefy arms until another inch would've unfastened the bones in his wrist; and then she clapped a restraining cuff from the tray down upon it. With one swift motion, she yanked the thusly adorned wrist down to the nearest leg of the cot, and secured the clip to hold him in place. If Dr. Luther hadn't been performing pretty much the same technique on the other wrist, it wouldn't have held up longer than a few seconds.

But the doctor's restraints were affixed a moment after Mercy's. Then they were saddled with one violently unhappy man, pinioned to a cot and thrashing in such a manner that he was bound to injure himself further if he wasn't more elaborately subdued.

Mercy reached for the mask, spun the knob to dispense the ether, and shoved it over Silas Newton's face, holding him by the chin to keep him from shaking his head back and forth and eluding the sedation. Soon his objections softened and surrendered, and the last vestiges of his refusal to cooperate were overcome.

"Jackass," Mercy muttered.

"Indeed," said Dr. Luther. "Get his shoe off for me, would you, please?"

"Yes sir," she said, and reached for the laces.

Over the next three hours, the doctor's predictions were borne out. Two of the remaining three men survived, including the disagreeable Silas Newton. In time, Mercy was relieved by the severe and upstanding Nurse Esther Floyd, who hauled the young Nurse Sarah Fitzhugh along in her wake.

Mercy left the bloody beds behind the curtain and all but staggered back into the main ballroom grounds, where most of the men had at least been seen, if not treated and fed quite yet. Stumbling past them and around them, she stopped a few times when someone tugged at her passing skirt, asking for a drink or for a doctor.

Finally she found her way outside, into the afternoon that was going gold and navy blue at the edges, and would be nearly black before long.

She'd missed supper, and hadn't noticed.

Well. She'd pick something up in a few minutes—whatever she could scavenge from the kitchen, even though she knew good and well it'd be pretty much nothing. Either you ate as soon as you were called, or you didn't eat. But it'd be worth looking. She might get lucky and find a spare biscuit and a dab of butter, which would fill her up enough to let her sleep.

She was almost to the kitchen when Paul Forks, the retained man, said her name, stopping her in the hallway next to the first-floor entry ward. She put one hand up on the wall and leaned against it that way. Too worn out to stand still, she couldn't hold herself upright anymore unless she kept moving. But she said, "Yes, Mr. Forks? What is it?"

"Begging your pardon, Nurse Mercy. But there's a message for you."

"A message? Goddamn. I've had about enough of messages," she said, more to the floor than to the messenger. Then, by way of apology, she said, "I'm sorry. It's not your fault, and thanks for flagging me down."

"It's all right," he told her, and approached her cautiously. Paul Forks approached everyone cautiously. It could've been a long-standing habit, or maybe it was a new thing, a behavior acquired on the battlefield.

He went on to say, "It came Western Union." He held out an envelope.

She took it. "Western Union? You can't be serious." She was afraid maybe it was another message repeating the same news she'd received the day before. The world was like that some-times. No news for ages, and then more news than you can stand, all at once. She didn't want to read it. She didn't want to know what it said.

"Yes ma'am, very serious. The stamp on the outside says it came from Tacoma, out in Washington—not the one next door, but the western territory. Or that's where the message started, anyhow. I don't know too well how the telegraph works."

"Me either," she confessed. "But I don't know anybody in Washington."

"Are you sure?"

"Pretty sure." She turned the envelope over in her hand, still unwilling to open it, reading the stamped mark that declared the station in Tacoma where the message had been composed.

"You . . . you going to open it?" Paul Forks asked, then seemed to think the better of it. "Never mind, it's no business of mine. I'll leave you alone," he said, and turned to go.

She stopped him by saying, "No, it's all right." A laundry boy bustled past her, prompting her to add, "Let me get out of the hallway, here. No sense in blocking up the main thoroughfare." She carried the envelope to the back scullery stairs, where no one was coming or going at that particular moment.

Paul Forks followed her there, and sat down beside her with the stiff effort of a man who hadn't yet learned how to work around his permanent injuries. He was careful to keep a respectful distance, but the naked curiosity in his face might've been mirrored in her own, if she hadn't been so fiercely tired.

"Washington," she said aloud to the paper as she extracted it from the light brown envelope and unfolded it. "What's so important out in Washington that I need to hear about it?"

"Read it," he encouraged her. Paul Forks couldn't read, but he liked to watch other people do it, and he liked to hear the results. "Tell me what it says."

"It says," she declared, but her eyes scanned ahead, and she didn't say anything else. Not right away.

"Go on."

"It says," she tried again, then stopped herself. "It's my . . . my daddy."

Paul frowned thoughtfully. "I thought your kin came from Waterford?"

She gave a half nod that ended in a shrug. Her eyes never peeled themselves off the paper, but she said, "I was born there, and my momma and father live there now, working a farm that's mostly dairy."

Paul might've been illiterate, but he wasn't stupid. "Father? Not your real pa, then?"

Though she didn't owe him any explanation, she felt like talking, so she said, "My daddy ran off when I was little. Went West, with his brother and my cousin, looking for gold in Alaska—or that was the plan as I heard it. For a while he sent letters. But when I was about seven years old, the letters just . . . stopped."

"You think something happened to him?"

"That's what we always figured. Except, it was strange." Her voice ran out of steam as she read and reread the telegram.

"What was strange?" Paul prompted.

"One day Aunt Betty got a box in the post, full of Uncle Asa's things, and Leander's things, too. Leander was my cousin," she clarified. "And there was some money in there—not a lot, but some. There was also a note inside from somebody they didn't know, but it said Asa and Leander'd died on the frontier, of cholera or something. Anyway, when I was about ten, the justice of the peace said that my momma wasn't married anymore on account of desertion, and she could marry Wilfred. He's been my father ever since. So I don't know . . . I don't know what this means."

The tone of her voice changed as she quit relating ancient history and began to read aloud from the sheet of paper, including all the stops.

"To Vinita May Swakhammer stop. Your father Jeremiah Granville Swakhammer has suffered an accident stop. His life hangs by a thread stop. He wants you to come to Tacoma in the Washington territory stop. Please send word if you can make it stop. Sheriff Wilkes can meet you at station and bring you north to Seattle where he lies gravely wounded stop."

The letter sagged in her hands until it rested atop her knees.

"Is that all?" Paul asked.

"That's all." She stared at the letter, then looked up at Paul. "And all this time, I figured he was dead."

"It looks like he ain't."

"That's what it looks like, yeah," she agreed. And she didn't know how to feel about it.

"What're you going to do?"

She didn't shrug, and didn't shake her head. "I don't know. He left me and Momma. He left us, and he never sent for us like he said he would. We waited all that time, and he never sent."

They sat in silence a few seconds, until Paul Forks said, "He's sending for you now."

"A little late."

"Better late than never?" he tried. He leaned back and braced against the stairwell in order to help push himself back to a standing position. "Sounds like he might be dying."

"Maybe," she agreed. "But I'm not sure if I give a damn. He left us . . . Jesus, fifteen, sixteen years ago. That son of a bitch," she mumbled, and then she said it louder. "That son of a bitch! All this time, he's been out West just fine, just like he said he was going to be. And all that time, we sat at home and wondered, and worried, and finally we just gave right up!"

"He might've had his reasons," Paul said, awkward as he stood there, uneven on his one real foot and one false one, and unsure exactly who he was defending.

Glaring down at the paper, she said, "Oh, I'm real sure he had his reasons. There are about a million reasons to leave a woman and a little girl behind and start a new life someplace else. I guess he just picked one."

He said quickly, "Don't you want to hear it?"

"Why would I want to hear it?" She wasn't quite shouting, but she was warming inside, like a furnace catching its coals. The heat spread up from her belly to her chest, and flushed up her throat to her cheeks. "A million reasons, goddamn him, and I don't need to hear even one of them!"

"Because you don't care?"

"Damn right, because I don't care!" Except that she *was* shouting now, and nearly on fire with anger, or sorrow, or some other consequence of her tumultuous week. "Let him die out there, if that's where he wanted to be all this time!"

Paul Forks held out his hands, trying to halt her, or just defend himself—even though it wasn't his fight, and he wasn't the man with whom she was so furious. "Maybe he's where he wants to be, or maybe he's just where he ended up. Either way, he wants to see his little girl."

Mercy gave him a look like she'd kill him if he blinked, but he blinked anyway. And he continued: "Someday, you'll wish you'd gone. If you don't do it now, like as not, you'll never get another chance—and then you really *will* spend the rest of your life wondering. When you could've just . . . *asked*."

She clenched the telegram in her fist, crumpling the paper. "It won't be as simple as that," she said. "If he was dying when this was sent, he's probably dead by now."

He fidgeted. "You don't know that for sure."

"It'd take *weeks* to make the trip. A month or more, I bet. You know as well as I do what the train lines are like these days. Everyone talks about transcontinental dirigible paths, but nobody's making it happen. Maybe I could hop, skip, and jump it by air—but that'd take even longer than going by train. Forget it," she said, stuffing the wad of paper into her apron pocket.

Paul Forks stepped out of the stairwell and shook his head, "Yes ma'am. I'll forget it. And I'm sorry, it wasn't my place to bother you. It's only . . ."

"It's only *what*?"

"It's only . . . when I took that hit on the field, and when they brought me here . . . I sent for my wife and my boy. Neither one of them came. All I got was a message that my boy had died of consumption six months after I went to war, and my wife went a few weeks behind him."

She said, "I . . . Paul. I'm real sorry."

He shifted uncomfortably in his clothes. "Anyway, that's why I stayed on here. Nothing to go home to. But I don't mean to pry. It just hurts like all get-out when you think you're meeting your Maker, and there's no one there to send you off."

With his left hand, the whole one, he touched her shoulder in a friendly way. And he left her alone there, in the stairwell with the message she couldn't stand to read again, and no idea how she was going to answer it.

Still pondering, she went back up to her bunk, and opened her cases to retrieve the stationery she'd taken from Captain Sally's stash down in the hospital office. Not knowing what else to do, or what else to think about, she sat on the edge of the bed and started writing.

Mercy's handwriting wasn't any good, because she'd never been schooled long enough to make it smooth, but it was legible. And it said:

Dear Mrs. Henry,

My name is Vinita Lynch and I am a nurse at the Robertson Hospital in Richmond, Virginia. I am very sorry to tell you that your son, Gilbert Henry, died this afternoon of February 13, 1879. He was a good soldier and a nice man, and he made jokes while we tried to save him. He had been wounded bad but he died peaceful. I stayed with him until he was gone. He spoke fondly of you and his brother. His last thoughts were of home.

When she was finished, she sealed it up and set it on the nightstand beside her bed, to be mailed on Monday, when the post came.

Three

Mercy Lynch told Sally, "Thank you. For everything."

She'd already said the rest of her good-byes, though they'd been few: to the other nurses, a couple of the doctors, and to Paul Forks, who'd worked beside her for six months and would have guessed why she was leaving, regardless.

No one had mentioned her departure to any of the patients. It was better not to, she'd decided. She'd seen other women leave before, going down the rows and receiving impassioned pleas, promises of future remembrance, and the occasional marriage proposal; and she wasn't interested in any of it. She'd learned, by watching other employees come and go, that it was best to simply leave at the ordinary time, and fail to return.

If she made any declarations, she'd cause a scene.

If she merely went away, it would probably be days before any of the bedridden men noticed. They had their own problems and pains to distract them, and the absence of one nurse out of thirty meant little to most of them. Eventually someone would look up, scratch his head, and wonder, "What ever happened to Nurse Mercy?" and then Captain Sally would say, "She left. Last week." At which point, the invalid would shrug.

Mercy figured it was easier to ask forgiveness than permission. They'd forgive her for leaving. But they might not give her permission to go.

Sally was different, though, and she understood. She lowered her voice, even though they were in the woman's office and there was no one lurking nearby. "I'm glad you've got your widow's papers, and the scraps of Union pension. That'll take you most of the way, I expect. Their money's worth more than ours."

Mercy said, "Ma'am, if anyone sends for me here, you'll give them the address in Waterford?"

"Of course I will. Did I forget anything? You've cleaned out your bunk upstairs . . . and you've tucked away the nursing papers, I hope? My recommendation letter will mark you as one of ours, and that'll be good for the first legs of your trip, but there's no telling what you'll find out West."

She promised, "I'm going south, then up the river and west. I have a plan."

"You'd better. It's a long trip, darling. I'll worry for you, and pray."

Mercy hugged her. Then she made one last walk through the first-floor ward, past the entry to the ballroom, out through the corridor that would take her through the kitchen, and into the backyard grounds . . . so that no one but the staff would see how she carried a suitcase and a large shoulder bag stitched with a distinctive red cross. The suitcase she was taking had come with her from Virginia; the other one had been the property of the hospital, so she was leaving it behind. But the shoulder bag was a gift from Captain Sally. In it, Mercy carried the basics of her profession, as well as her papers, her money, a few small books, letters, pencils, and other useful objects that made her feel prepared.

At the curb to the side of the Robertson house, she stood squeezing her luggage and wondering where to begin, and how. The entirety of her planning process amounted to little more than what she'd told Captain Sally.

But first things first: She went to the Western Union office.

The clerk at the counter took the envelope with her father's message and read it, and while he perused the marks, Mercy said, "I need to send a message back. To . . . to Sheriff Wilkes, I guess. Wherever this telegram came from. I need to tell him that I'm coming."

The small man in the striped vest peered at the paper through a pince-nez and told her, "I can certainly do that. And I'm sorry to hear about your father," he added politely.

He quoted her a price, which she paid from the cash that Sally had offered, an immediate severance payment, plus a bonus. And with the help of the clerk, she composed a response to send back across three thousand miles.

TO SHERIFF WILKES: PLEASE TELL JEREMIAH SWAKHAMMER THAT HIS DAUGHTER WILL COME TO JOIN HIM STOP THE JOURNEY MAY TAKE SEVERAL WEEKS STOP WILL SEND ANOTHER TELEGRAM WHEN MY ARRIVAL IS NEARER STOP

She couldn't think of anything else to add, so she watched while the clerk transcribed her message and placed it into a box on his desk. He explained that the telegraph operator was out of the office, but that when she returned, the message would be sent out across the lines.

Mercy thanked him and left, emerging on the street again with her bags in hand and an intense nervousness in her heart—a steady fear that this was the wrong thing to do, and her father would probably be dead by the time she arrived, anyway.

"But it'll be an adventure," she said to herself, not so much believing it as clinging to it.

Slinging her pack over one shoulder, she stepped down off the Western Union's wooden porch and into the street, where she dodged one speeding cab and leaned backwards to avoid a lurching wagon. In the distance she could hear shouting, and warnings of incoming something-or-others headed for the hospital; she heard "Robertson" above the din, and her chest ached.

She should drop this ridiculous mission.

She should go back, where she was needed.

Even if she made it all the way West, and even if she made it to her father's bedside, would they know each other? Her memories of him had distilled over sixteen years, down to blurs of color and a rumbling voice. When she thought of him, if she tried to push aside her anger at his leaving, she could recall glimpses of a wide-shouldered, brown-haired man with arms as thick as logs. But she remembered little of his face—only a scratchiness, from when she'd rubbed her cheek against his.

Maybe, then. Maybe she'd know him.

But would he know *her*? It'd been a lifetime between knee-high childhood and Robertson nurse. She'd grown several feet, to a height that was just shy of "quite tall" for a woman, and the corn-tassel blond hair of her youth had grown to a darker shade that was closer to unpolished gold than to baby yellow. The willowy limbs of her formative years had given way to a frame that was sturdy enough for farm work, or hospital work. She was not dainty, if in fact she ever had been.

She hesitated at the edge of the street, recoiling from the traffic and wondering if she shouldn't go back to the office to send another telegram to let her mother know what she was doing. But then she came back to her senses and resolved to write a letter and post it from the road.

Always easier to ask forgiveness than permission.

On the street corner, a little boy in ill-fitting pants cried out the daily news. He hefted a stack of papers up like a Roman shield and declared the latest known troop movements, wins, losses, and points of interest. "Yankees rebuffed at Nashville!" he declared. "Maximilian the Third calls for Texian investigation into missing peace force!"

She took a deep breath, picked the appropriate direction, and got walking. The boy's bellowing voice followed her. "Mystery surrounds northwestern dirigible disappearance in Texas! Terrible storm strikes Savannah! Rebs take heavy losses in Bowling Green!"

She shuddered and kept moving, four blocks past the narrow three-storied hotels and boardinghouses and the wider, lower shapes of banks and dry goods stores. On the steps of a big white church stood a man with a big black Bible, urging people to come inside and repent, or join him for fellowship, or some other thing in which Mercy was not interested. She stuck to the edge of the crowd and ignored him, and did her best not to look at the giant steeple the color of bone.

She passed another set of churches, lined up shoulder to shoulder with one another despite their dogmatic differences, then came to a stockyard, then a large foundry populated by soot-covered men in clothes filthy with sweat and tiny burns. One of them called out to her, opening his mouth to say something dirty or childish.

But when Mercy turned his way, the man closed his mouth. "Pardon me, Nurse. Ma'am," he said upon seeing her cloak and the cross on her satchel.

"Consider yourself pardoned, you lout," she grumbled, and kept walking.

"I'm sorry," he said after her.

She didn't answer him. She adjusted her bag so the cross was more visible against her shoulder blade. It was not a foreign emblem, or a Yankee emblem, or even a Confederate one. But everyone knew what it meant, pretty much, even if once in a while it got her mistaken for one of those Salvation Army folks.

In the distance, over the tops of the mills, factories, and shipping warehouses down in the transportation district, she could spy the rounded, bobbing domes that indicated the tops of docked dirigibles.

Before long a sign came into view, announcing, RICHMOND REGIONAL AIRSHIP YARD. Beneath it, two smaller signs pointed two different directions. PASSENGER TRANSPORT was urged to veer left, while MERCHANTS AND CARGO were directed to the right.

She dutifully followed the signs, head up and shoulders square, as if she knew exactly where she was going and what she needed. Another sign pointed to ROWS A & B while one next to it held another area, indicating ROWS C & D. But finally she spotted something more immediately useful—a banner that read, PASSENGER TICKETS AND ITINERARY. This banner was strung over a wood-front shack that was shaped like a lean-to, with no glass in the windows and no barrier in the front except a cage like those used by bank tellers.

The nearest available attendant was a crisp brunette in a brown felt hat with an explosion of colored feathers on the side. Mercy approached her and said, "Hello, I need to buy passage west."

"How far?"

"How far west can you take me?"

The woman glanced down at a sheet of paper Mercy couldn't see. "That depends."

"On what?"

"On a number of things. Right now, the war is the number one deciding factor in precisely how far you can travel. We've had to trim some of the northernmost lines, and redirect traffic south."

Mercy nodded. "That's fine."

The clerk said, "Good. Because as of this morning, Charleston, West Virginia, is about as far west as we're going along our present estimated longitude. We're trying to reroute anything headed for Frankfurt down through Winston-Salem or Nashville. But Nashville's a little uncertain right now, too."

Recalling what she'd heard from the young crier, she said, "There's fighting out that way?"

"That's what they tell us." The clerk pointed at a miniature telegraph set.

While Mercy stared at it, the fist-size device hiccupped and spit out a long thread of paper covered in dots and dashes.

The clerk explained, "Latest news from the fronts. It comes in filtered through headquarters."

"What does that say?" Mercy asked.

"It says Nashville's still uncertain. Sometimes they update us like that, and it's useless. Anyway, you want to head west, and you never said how far."

"I hope to wind up in Washington—all the way on the other coast. But if I understand it right, you can only get me to the river."

The clerk didn't ask "Which river?" because everyone knew that the Mississippi was where everything stopped. She pursed her lips thoughtfully and then said, "That is correct, and you can pick it up at Memphis. It ought to be safe enough, that far down from the border skirmishes. If you can get to Fort Chattanooga, you can hop a train there, and make it the rest of the way in no time flat."

"That sounds fine." It sounded terrifying, but she swallowed the lump in her throat and stood up straight.

Having now gleaned enough information to begin pressing the protuberant buttons in front of her, the brunette woman peered down at her console as she spoke. "It won't be a straight flight, you understand. I'm going to send you through Winston-Salem, and then down to Charlotte, and then over to Fort Chattanooga." She looked up from the buttons and said with a note of apology, "Ordinarily I'd send you down through Knoxville instead, but you know how it goes."

"Oh, yes," Mercy said. "I know how it goes."

"This'll add another hour or two to the flight, but it's safer in the long run, and it won't cost you any more. Here, let me stamp you out a ticket," she offered, and something pinged in readiness behind the counter. The clerk braced herself and pressed hard on a lever, using almost her full weight, and a punched card popped up through a slot between the buttons at her waist level.

Mercy traded some money for the ticket, and the clerk pointed toward Row B, Slot Two.

The airship yard was laid out much like a train station—at least, that was Mercy's impression. She took a seat near the end of the row, where she could keep an eye on the airship comings and goings, but also watch for the dirigible that would carry her down to Tennessee. It hadn't yet arrived, but she could gather much about it from the other passenger ships that came and went while she observed. All of them were minimally marked, with names like *Papillion, Helena Mine,* and *Catie James.* Most had a label across the rear that marked them as CIVILIAN TRANSPORT, to differentiate them from the military ships.

According to everyone who kept track of such things, travel by air was infinitely safer than travel by train (what with the bandits and rail pirates), and even safer than simple carriage (given the highwaymen and unscrupulous checkpoints between regions and war zones). But when the *Zephyr* drifted into Row B, Slot Two, Mercy felt something in her chest clench with anxiety.

It moved so quietly for something so big; it docked with nothing but the tug and stretch of hemp lines and the creak of metal joints settling, then finally the clack and lock that affixed the great machine to the pipework dock. When the claws were all fastened and the hull had quit bobbing like a child's toy in a tub, a seam along the hull's underside cracked and then descended, followed by a folding set of stairs that tumbled down like a dropped accordion.

Down these stairs came the handful of passengers from Raleigh, if Mercy had overheard correctly. None of them looked bruised, battered, frightened, or otherwise shaken by their experience, though several were visibly relieved to have earth beneath their feet again.

Mercy tried to take this as a good sign.

The *Zephyr*'s captain descended last. He was short, wide, and younger than she'd expected, and seemed cheerful as he met the teams of maintenance men who greeted every new arrival. Mercy lingered by the benches with her five fellow passengers-to-be as he discussed the hydrogen levels and how they were holding, and how much of a topping-off he needed here in Richmond. When his landing duties had been completed, he wandered over to his next batch of passengers and introduced himself with a round of handshakes and a tip of his hat.

"Captain Curry Gates, at your service, ladies and gentlemen," he said.

Mercy was one of only two ladies present, and the other woman was elderly, accompanied by her equally aged husband. Another two passengers had arrived when the airship came to port, bringing the total number of riders and crew to nine.

"It'll be about two hundred miles to Winston-Salem, where we'll stop for more fuel, then another seventy or so to Charlotte, and not quite three hundred more along the Tennessee line to Fort Chattanooga; then on to Atlanta for our final stop. Does that sound right to everyone? Check your tickets, and make sure this is the ship you're looking for. The next one on this route won't be along until tomorrow."

While he spoke, the remaining two members of his crew were descending behind him, toting equipment and inspecting the work performed by the dock crew, making sure everything satisfied their personal standards. Then they stepped to the side of the ship and behind it, where they began gesturing to something down at the end of the row.

Mercy craned her neck and spied the thing they motioned toward the ship.

It moved on a narrow rail that ran the length of the dock between the rows and was roughly the size of a small train engine, with a taller, rounder shape confined by riveted bands of metal. It looked like a great steel-crusted loaf of bread, and it came up on the *Zephyr* smoothly, with only the soft ratcheting sound of segmented wheels on a carefully fitted track. A series of hoses was toted in a rear compartment, like a caboose. The men on the dock unfurled the hoses and locked one end onto the metal canister, one end to some port on the backside of the *Zephyr*. The biggest man present—a tall fellow in an undershirt, with arms like an ape—climbed up to the top of the canister and turned a valve there, which prompted the hose to puff like an elongated marshmallow as it unloaded the canister's contents into the ship's tanks.

One of Mercy's fellow passengers leaned toward her and said, "Hydrogen."

She replied, "I know."

"It's a marvel, isn't it?" he pressed, until she turned to regard him.

He was well dressed, and the details would've betrayed his foreign origins even if his voice had not. The shoes were a brand and shape Mercy rarely saw; likewise, his suit had a cut that was a few lines distant from contemporary American styles. His hair was dark and curly, and his hands were long, soft, and unmarked—they were the hands of a scholar, not a man prone to labor.

Mercy said, "A marvel, sure. We're living in an age of them, aren't we? Practically swimming in them." She turned again to watch the dirigible refuel.

"You don't sound too pleased by it."

"By what?"

"By this age of marvels."

Mercy looked his way again and he was grinning, very faintly. "You've got me there," she told him. "Most of the marvels I've seen are doing a marvelous job of blowing men to bits, so you'll have to pardon me if, if . . ." Something large clicked with the sound of small arms fire, and she gave a little jump.

"You view these marvels with some trepidation," he finished for her. "Have you ever flown before?"

"No." Surrendering to the demands of politeness, though somewhat reluctantly, she tore her attention away from the ship and its tanks long enough to ask, "What about you? You ever been flying before?"

"A few times. And I always consider it a grand adventure, because we don't have such ships yet in England—at least, not in the numbers one finds here."

"Is that where you're from?"

"More or less," he said, which Mercy thought was a strange answer, but she didn't ask about it. He continued. "But I understand ships like these are becoming more common in Australia these days, as well."

"Australia?"

He nodded. "So progress must come easier to nations of such tremendous size. Thousands of miles to be traveled in any direction . . . it's not so surprising that newer, more comfortable methods of long-distance travel might become more commonplace."

"I doubt it. It's a side effect of war, that's all. These ships were first built for the fronts, but the damn things can't go more than a few hundred miles without refilling, and they can't hardly carry any weight at all."

If he minded her profanity, he didn't say anything. "Give it time," he said instead. "The technology improves every day. It won't be long before people are crossing from coast to coast in machines like this. Or greater machines, built on a similar template."

"People already go coast to coast with them, but it's all merchants moving goods here and there, not people. Did you see the armored dirigibles earlier? The ones that came and went from the commerce docks?"

"No, I only just arrived."

"They're war machines, and there are only a handful of them—for a real good reason," she informed him. "The hydrogen's as flammable as the devil's knickers, and that don't work so good with live ammunition flying all over the place. Not a month after the first dirigibles took to the front, antiaircraft guns were up and running, shooting them down like carnival balloons." She was parroting someone now, and she wasn't certain whom. One of the soldiers at the hospital? One of the doctors?

"But they're such impressive instruments. And armored, like you said."

"Yeah, but the more armor that covers them, the less weight they can carry. The trade-off makes them a losing bet on the field. Though I heard from one of the retained men that a CSA dirigible was stolen a few years ago, and that people sometimes talk about seeing it out West, flown by a pirate and outfitted for his trade. Maybe it'll be the frontier pirates, after all, who will show the East how to make them into proper riding vessels."

"Pirates *do* tend to be an innovative lot," he murmured. "By the way, I fear I haven't introduced myself properly. I'm Gordon Rand, lately of the good Queen's service, but recently discharged to my own recognizance."

She almost responded with "Vinita Lynch," but instead opted for, "I'm Mrs. Lynch."

"Mrs. Lynch?" He glanced at her hand, which was covered in a tight leather glove and therefore hiding the wedding ring she still wore. "It's a pleasure to make your acquaintance." He took her hand and gave it a perfunctory kiss.

She let him do it, then reclaimed the hand and asked, "What business of the Queen's takes you west, Mr. Rand?"

"I believe I'm going to write a book," he informed her. "And the subject matter takes me west. It might take me farther south later on, and maybe even into Mexico, if time and health permit. But we shall see."

Mercy gave him a noncommittal, "Hmm," and gazed again at the ship, which heaved gently back and forth in its moorings as bits of luggage were loaded up through a rear hatch with a retracting ladder.

The indefatigable Mr. Rand asked, "Keeping an eye on your bags?"

"No. I'm holding my bags."

"Traveling light. That's an admirable trait in a woman."

She was on the verge of saying something rude when the captain came strutting by like a fat little game hen in his tailored uniform.

"My fair passengers!" he addressed them, opening his chubby arms to indicate the group. "I've just been informed by headquarters that we'll be taking off in less than a quarter hour. If you would all be so kind as to board at this time, find the seat that's marked on your ticket, and make yourselves comfortable. If you have not checked your luggage for rear-well storage, then please stash your items at your feet, or secure them in any empty seats that might present themselves. We're traveling at only two-thirds capacity today, so there should be plenty of room for everything."

"Oh, this is so *exciting*," the older woman cooed in an upper-class accent that Mercy thought might come from farther east, maybe on the coast, or maybe she only thought that because the woman's companion was wearing a jacket that reminded Mercy of an ocean trade. But she would've made a bet that they hailed from Savannah, or Charleston.

"Exciting!" repeated the husband, who was entirely too thin for his clothing. He rattled around inside it when he took his wife's arm and let her lead him over to the accordion stairs.

Mercy couldn't shake the impression that the poor old gentleman wasn't all there. But his wife was still plenty sharp, and she guided him to the places where she wanted him.

One by one they filed aboard the craft, Mercy refusing to allow Mr. Rand to help hoist her baggage up the stairway, and the little old man babbling happily to his wife. The other two passengers, a pair of students from Atlanta named Larsen and Dennis, were working their way home to family after studying in Richmond for the year. On the way on board, the captain asked one of them if he'd learned anything interesting, and the baby-faced lad said something about how very *fascinating* he found the war. Mercy assumed that he found the engagement *fascinating* because he'd never be bound to fight it. A clubfoot interfered with walking, stair-climbing, and even settling into a seat. He'd never be drafted, even in the Confederacy's darkest hours of desperation.

His seat was next to his scholarly friend's, opposite the aisle from Mercy's. He gave her a shy smile that might have been less earnest if she'd removed her gloves.

Mr. Rand was forward a few rows, to the nurse's idle relief. The elderly couple sat behind her. Two of the crew members fastened themselves to a belted rack built into the dirigible's interior walls, at the rear of the craft; the remaining donned another hat and joined the captain in the cockpit—presumably to serve as copilot, or first mate, or however these things worked. Mercy's curiosity was dampened by her nervousness, and by the frittering patter of artillery fire she could swear she heard, even from inside the ship.

Something about the look on her face prompted the lame student to ask, "Ma'am?"

And she replied, "Do you hear that? Or is it only me?"

"Hear what?"

"That sound, like gunfire."

Mr. Rand turned around to meet her eyes, barely, over his

shoulder and over his seat back. "Don't worry about that sound, Mrs. Lynch. It's the sound of a pneumatic hammer working on rivets somewhere. We're miles from the nearest fighting, you know."

"I know," she said without conviction.

Captain Gates made a rambling, chipper series of announcements over a speaking tube that was all but superfluous. The passenger cabin was so small, and so close to the cockpit, that he could've simply turned around and given his announcements in an ordinary speaking voice and everyone would've heard him just fine.

He concluded by informing them that, "The claws have been unlatched, the tanks are topped off, and our course is set. We're ready for takeoff." With that, the sounds of machinery aligning, clicking, adjusting, and correcting filled the chamber.

But then the lifting of the ship was accompanied by a strange silence, as if all that preparation had been for something imaginary. And now nothing was happening at all, except the belly-moving rise of the ship as it drifted vertically above the trees to dangle below the low-lying clouds.

Mercy's stomach lunged in slow motion, along with the sway of the craft. She placed one hand there as if to hold her belly in place, and gripped the arm of the seat with her other hand. She wasn't going to vomit. That wasn't in the cards. But she could hardly bring herself to look out the round portal to her right, at least not for the first few minutes. She gave it only the barest glance until the ride seemed secure and steady and she was convinced that Captain Gates wouldn't kill everyone on board with an incorrectly pressed button or lever. Then her gaze slipped sideways to the reinforced glass and she peered down and out as far as the curve of the ship allowed. Below, the trees shivered in the breeze and the people at the airyard grew small, as small as mice, and then as small as beetles.

"We're flying!" declared the old man.

"Indeed, love," said his wife.

The students tittered to each other, quietly whispering and pointing out landmarks below; and for a moment, Mercy wondered what was wrong with the one who appeared able-bodied. Why hadn't he been fighting? Why had he been studying in Richmond? Half the schools were more than half empty. The study of anything but war had become a tricky thing, almost a socially prohibited thing. Still, someone had to read the books, she figured. She'd never been much of a reader herself, but she wouldn't begrudge anyone else the privilege. God knew the Confederacy needed doctors and military tacticians as surely as it needed mechanics and oilmen, engineers and pilots. Rationally she knew that no one learned these things spontaneously, and that few people even learned them as apprentices. But still, all the young men she'd known for the last few years had been soldiers, and rarely anything else before or after.

As the *Zephyr* continued to fly without incident, Mercy relaxed enough to close her eyes from time to time, even dozing off. She only realized the ride was changing when the dirigible settled in Winston-Salem for a fuel refill.

The captain told them they were welcome to stay aboard or disembark in the Carolina airyard, so long as they returned to their seats within half an hour. The students and Mr. Rand did just that. But the elderly man was asleep with his head on his wife's shoulder, so she remained.

Mercy decided to stay, leaning her head against the cool surface of the window and watching and listening as a tank on a rail just like the one in Richmond approached, docked, and began the hissing pump of hydrogen into the tanks above their heads.

When the students climbed back aboard, they were chattering, like always; their patter was a background hum, blending into the whir and wheeze of the gas flowing from tank to tank through the rubber-treated hoses with heavy brass fittings.

Mercy ignored them, leaving her eyes closed until she heard one of the students say, ". . . farther south, around Nashville by a wider berth."

She blinked to awareness, enough to interrupt and ask, "The troops?"

"Beg your pardon, ma'am?"

"The troops? Are you talking about the troops?"

Dennis, the one with the unmarred feet, was a brunet with watery blue eyes and a young man's mustache. He told her, "We overheard a bit, that's all. They're saying the Yankees have made a push to the southeast, so we'll have to fly out of our way to dodge a battle. I almost hope we don't," he added, and the words were tickled by a flutter of excitement.

"Don't talk that way," Mercy said. "We end up over a battle-field, and we're all of us dead as stones."

"What makes you say that?" he asked.

She shook her head, either sad for him or amazed that he simply didn't know. Before she could answer, Gordon Rand's head popped up into the cabin, followed by his torso and a trailing string of gossip.

"The fighting's going on clear out over the Appalachians, that's what they're saying," he contributed.

Mercy said, "Jesus."

The young brunet wanted to know more. "Do you think we'll see fighting?"

To which Mr. Rand said, "We won't see any, or we'll all see en-tirely too much. Mrs. Lynch is right. The moment this little pas-senger rig brushes up against a hit or two of antiaircraft fire, we're doomed."

"Your hearing must be quite remarkable," she observed, since he hadn't quite been present when she'd made her observation.

He beamed, and in his near lisp of an accent he continued, "I wouldn't worry about it too much, if I were you. The captain is presently taking note of the very latest telegraph information from the front, and he'll adjust our course accordingly. I have the utmost faith in this. In fact, so utmost is my faith that I plan to stay aboard and ride on to Fort Chattanooga in the civilized comfort of this very fine ship."

"That's confidence for you," piped up the old woman, with enough cool sarcasm to surprise them all.

The captain rejoined them before anyone could comment further, and he led the first mate back to the cockpit while urging everyone else to be seated. He must've heard something of their conversation himself, for as he got situated he said, "It seems as if you've heard about the movement in the front. I want you all to know, it's to be expected, and it's something we deal with regularly. There's nothing to be concerned about, for I've got the freshest of all possible coordinates right here." He indicated a slip of paper covered in dots, dashes, and someone's handwriting. "We'll leave within the next five minutes and have you all safely in Fort Chattanooga within a few hours."

With that, he donned an aviator's hat and a pair of goggles that were largely for show. He waved at the two crew members who'd latched themselves against the back wall, signaled to the passengers that the ship was ready to disengage, and flashed a big thumbs-up before smiling and taking the controls.

Four

The next leg of the journey took them over low mountains—crushed green and brown hills, brittle and dry with the season, revealing crags, cliffs, waterfalls, and enormous rocks. Toward evening, Mercy could pick out fires between the trees and on the intermittent peak. She wondered what they might be—troops or travelers or homesteaders—until the captain clarified through his overly loud speaking tube.

"Down below us—oh! There's one, just to the right. You see those little sparks? Those fires that look so tiny from our prodigious height?"

The passengers mumbled assent.

He said, " 'Shiners, the lot of them. They do their distillations in the evening, and in the rural parts between the county lines, where they aren't likely to be bothered."

"Their distillations?" asked Mr. Rand.

The old lady spoke up. "Busthead. Red-eye. Mountain dew. They're brewing alcohol, Mr. Rand," she informed him, and likewise informed the group that there might be more to her sophisticated-looking soul than they'd previously assumed. "The South would like to tax it for revenue, but the folks who produce it often lack any other source of income; so I trust you can see the difficulty."

"Absolutely," Mr. Rand nearly purred. "Though I don't suppose the CSA has the time or resources to devote to pursuing boot-leggers."

This time it was the clubfooted lad who contributed. "The local authorities—sheriffs, policemen, constables, or however the cities and townships are organized—they're given leave by the capital in Danville to pursue the moonshiners at a personal profit, provided they collect the unpaid taxes. It's been compared to privateering, and is approximately as popular as that old practice." He sounded as if he were reciting some passage of a newspaper's article, or a textbook's chapter.

Gordon Rand smiled. "Which is to say, both very popular, and very dangerous, to both sides of the law. Yes, I understand."

Mercy seethed a moment, then told him—and, by proxy, the rest of the passengers, "You know, not everyone does it to dodge the law. Some folks brew up batches for reasons of their own, and you might as well tax the chickens for making eggs as try to shake folks down for the pennies they might or might not earn." Then, because everyone was looking at her strangely, she added, "Yes, my father brews up a barrel or two, every so often. Ain't nobody's business if he does."

She straightened in her seat and fluffed up her smaller bag, preparing to use it as a pillow. She jammed it between her shoulder and the increasingly chilly window.

The student named Dennis said to the one named Larsen, "It *does* raise questions about the invasion of the private sector by the public office, and where those lines ought to be drawn. To what lengths can a society reach in order to maintain order?"

The other student's response could've been cribbed from the same manual on politics. Soon the two were engrossed and ignoring her. The other passengers retreated to their newspapers, novels, or naps.

Between dozing and the inevitable tedium, Mercy was uncertain how much time had passed when she heard the popping noise again—the one that, she'd been assured, was only the result of a pneumatic hammer. But this time, when she looked out over the now-black mountains and valleys below, she knew she was well above any hammers or other tools. And down there, in broken lines and in sparkling flashes, she could see more fires in the distance.

All the other passengers were awake already and watching in utter silence, except for the elderly man, who still rested his head upon his wife. But even she strained to see over his head and out the window, wondering, like the rest of them, how close they were to the fighting.

The captain, ordinarily ebullient and talkative, was quiet. Mercy could see him through the gap in the curtain that separated the cockpit from the passenger cabin; in the glow of the low-lit cockpit lamps, she could tell that his knuckles were white on the steering column. He shot a nervous look at the first mate, but the other man's attention was occupied by something down below, and then with something in the passenger cabin. He hissed back at the crew members in the rear. "All the lights. Every last one of them, off—now!"

The sound of unbuckling was loud in the otherwise empty space, and the two men in the back went from corner to corner, unplugging the strings that gave a dim electric glow to the *Zephyr*'s interior.

Gordon Rand asked, in his quietest and calmest voice, "Surely they can't see us, all the way up here?"

"They can see us," the captain replied, equally quiet but only half as calm. "All they have to do is look up. Problem is, they won't see our civilian paint job. We thought we were far enough from the fighting that we could leave the heavy exterior lights back at the station."

"Are they likely to notice us?" Against all logic, but keeping with the mood, Larsen was whispering.

"Hopefully not," the captain was quick to say. "I'm going to take us higher, so they won't hear us if we run the engines. We need to get out of their immediate airspace."

"What are we doing *in* their immediate airspace?" Mr. Rand demanded.

The first mate replied, "We aren't there on *purpose,* you limey bastard. The Yanks must've made a *serious* push between this morning and this evening. Carter said there's no way they'd swing this far, unless we've gone off course—"

"I know what Carter said," the captain growled. "And we haven't gone off course. We're brushing the south end of the Smokies, for God's sake. If there's fighting, it must've gotten here faster than the telegraph got to Richmond."

The students were pressed with their noses against the glass like little boys examining a store display at Christmas. They were actually smiling, as excited as Mercy was nauseated. She'd never been to a front—the CSA's, or anybody else's—and knowing one was immediately below made the sides of her head hurt.

In front of her, the old man awakened and asked loudly, "What's going on?"

Mercy resisted the urge to shush him, but Gordon Rand was nervous enough to wave his hand and say, "Sir, *please.*"

One of the crew members said, "They can't hear us all the way up here."

Everyone knew it was true, but no one wanted to push any of the luck that held them aloft.

It was nearly as black as the inside of a cave, there inside the *Zephyr.* Only the peeping glow of moonlight bouncing off the clouds lit the scene. The passengers could hardly see one another, though they traded nervous stares, looking from face to face for signs of comfort or confidence and finding nothing but the weak, pale frowns of ghosts.

Down on the ground, the world was bumpy and black, except

where artillery flared, fired, and coughed thick plumes of smoke that looked white against the stark pitch of the night around the lines.

If Mercy looked long enough, she could almost see the battle lines themselves, or imagine them, letting her mind fill in the blanks. There, along the nubs of the Smoky Mountains, she could see a strip cut across the earth; it was a fragile thing from such a height, only a dim break in the trees where a railroad ran. It snaked, but not sharply, around the prohibitive geography; and in front of this line, she saw the big guns fanning forward, away from the train tracks, and into the forests.

She leaned out of her seat and asked the cockpit, "Captain, how far are we from Fort Chattanooga?"

"Thirty miles or so. We're nearly on top of Cleveland, a little town outside it," he replied without taking his eyes off the windscreen. From inside that tiny rounded space, blinking green and yellow lights flashed against the faces and hands of the men who worked them. "Worst comes to worst, we'll make it to Cleveland and we can set down there and wait things out."

Gordon Rand nearly sneered, "Worst comes to worst? We'll crash and die, isn't that closer to the worst end of the possibility spectrum?"

"Shut your mouth," Mercy ordered him. "Have a little goddamned faith, would you?"

"Everyone stay calm!" The captain wasn't quite breaking the veil of muffled conversation that stayed below the level of ordinary chatter, but his voice was rising. "No one even knows we're up here."

"How do you know that?" Dennis asked, sounding anxious for the first time.

"Because no one's shooting at us yet. Now, all of you, please stay calm, and keep the chatter to a minimum. I need to concentrate."

Their jolly little leader had turned out to be made of sterner stuff than he looked. That was fine by Mercy, who hadn't initially pegged him as a man who was accustomed to handling an emergency. His hands worked the controls with familiarity, and there was a set to his jaw that inspired optimism, if not outright confidence. But she heard the first mate say, "We can't go too much higher; these cabins aren't pressurized for that kind of altitude."

And the captain responded, "Yes, Richard. I know. But if we can just spin it up, we can give ourselves an arc and a boost outside their hearing."

"It looks hot down there. They won't hear a damn thing. And if we don't shoot the boosters now, we'll—"

"I'm doing the best I can. You see over there?" He pointed at something no one could see, but all the eavesdropping passengers craned their necks to spy at it regardless. "That's the northern line. It's got to be. And the southern one is back this way. Other than that, I can't make heads or tails of what's going on down there. But it's either south or north for us—the fighting's running east and west. I'll take my chances with my own kind."

"Your own kind can't read in the dark any better than the boys in blue," Richard countered. "They won't see that we're private and licensed until after they shoot us down, for all the good that'll do us."

"They're *not* going to shoot us down. They don't even know we're here," Gates repeated.

This was the moment fate chose to make a liar out of him.

Something struck them, a glancing blow that winged the outer edge of the *Zephyr*'s port side. The ship rocked and steadied, and the captain took the opportunity to gun the boosters hard— sending everyone slamming back in their seats. "Oh, God," said one student, and the other gripped his friend's arm as hard as he gripped the seat's arm. Neither one of them was smiling anymore.

Mercy grabbed her seat and took a deep breath that she sucked in slow, then let out all at once.

"I thought you were taking us higher!" hollered Richard.

The captain said, "No point in that now, is there? They damned well know we're—"

Another loud clang—like a brick hitting a cymbal, or a bullet hitting a cooking pot—pinged much louder and much closer, somewhere along the ship's underbelly.

"Here. They know we're here," he finished as he leaned his full, copious weight back, drawing the steering column with him. From her tense position a few rows away, Mercy could see him digging his feet into a pair of pedals beneath the control panel.

"Then what's the plan?" the Englishman asked, his words snapping together like beads.

The old woman asked, "Who's shooting at us? Our boys, or theirs?"

And Mercy answered shrilly, "Who cares?"

"I don't know!" the captain said through clenched teeth. "Either side. Both. Neither one has any way of knowing who we're flying for, and it's too dark to see our civvy designation."

"Can't we shine a light on it or something?" Mercy asked.

"We don't *have* those kinds of lights," the captain said. "We left them in Richmond for the next crew flying border territory." But something in the hesitation between the words implied he was still pondering them.

A series of hits, small but more accurate, peppered the undercarriage.

The old man started to cry. His wife clutched him around the shoulders.

The students were out of their seats, and the two crewmen from the back came forward, urging them to sit down.

One of these crewmen held out his hands, standing between

the cockpit and the passenger area. He said to the captain, though he was watching the passengers, "We have the dual-light torches. If we could hook a few to the hull, we could show our boys we're on their side. Get at least one set of shooters off our case."

The captain snapped back, "Are you joking? Those things are barely lanterns, and if you unhook them from the power source, they'll burn for only a few—" He swung the ship hard to the right, responding to some threat Mercy couldn't see. "—minutes."

"It's better than nothing, ain't it?" the crewman pressed. "It'll get us behind our own lines. They'll see we're one of theirs, and let us land."

"Do you want to be the man who climbs outside and tries to hang them, like a row of goddamned Christmas candles?" The captain was shouting now, but the crewman didn't flinch.

He nodded. "I'll do it. I sailed before I took to the air. I've dangled from less than our outer hull, sir."

Every face was turned to him, except for the man who steered the dark and bouncing ship through the night. They looked at him with hope, and with bewilderment. Even Mercy wanted to tell him he was mad, but she didn't. Instead she prayed that he was serious.

"You'll get yourself shot," the captain told him.

"Or we'll all of us go down in flames. I don't mind taking my chances, sir," he said. Without waiting to be dismissed, he ducked back into the recesses behind the seating area. His fellow mate swung his eyes back and forth, from the authority to his friend.

"Ernie," he called into the dark place behind the back nook's curtain. "Ernie, I'll come with you. I'll help out."

Ernie's head popped back out, splitting the curtains. His shoulders and torso followed, and his right hand appeared toting a cluster of strangely shaped lanterns that glowed like lightning bugs.

Their gleam cast a yellow green glow around the cabin, not so bright that it could be seen from the ground, surely.

The old woman said crossly, "Those things don't have near enough light. They'll never reveal our sign from the field."

But Ernie said, "Ma'am, they're turned down low, on purpose. For now. I'll spark them up when I get outside—and they'll stay real bright for four or five minutes. They run on an electrical charge, and a static liquid on a set of filaments," he explained, as if anyone present had the faintest clue what it meant. "When I flip the switch, it'll light up the whole damn sky, plenty enough for the Rebs to spy us and let us down. Captain," he said as he changed direction, "get us as far behind our own lines as you can, sir."

Mercy fidgeted with the seat back in front of her. "Is there anything we can do to help?" she finally asked.

She could hardly see Ernie's face, even in the ambient ooze of the lanterns.

He said, "No ma'am. Just hold on tight, I'll take care of this. Or I'll do the best I can, anyhow."

"Ernest," the captain said, making some token attempt to stop him or sway him. But he had nothing else to add, so he turned his attention forward. The dirigible swayed again, making Mercy wonder if he could see some of the threat as it fired up at them through the sky. "Ernest," he finally finished. "Be careful out there. What are you wearing?"

"Sir?"

"Wearing—," he said again, and looked very fast over his shoulder. "I see. You're sporting your grays. Throw on something darker. Robert, give him your jacket. Yours is black, isn't it?"

"Yes sir," said the other crewman. He pulled it off and tossed it to Ernie, who set the lamps down only long enough to don it.

Ernie nodded his thanks and retrieved the lamps, then mounted a ladder that Mercy hadn't seen until just that moment.

He leaped up it like a small boy scaling an oak. She'd never seen a man climb like that before, as if he were born in a tree.

He was gone, his feet disappearing up a hatch.

Another strip of rounds banged against the ship's underside, casting a horrible noise into the otherwise stone-silent cabin. Mercy leaned against the window and tried to keep from looking out at the blackness and height that horrified her whether she admitted it or not. Consumed by feelings of uselessness and doubt, she clung to the edge of the seat in front of her.

Above and beyond, she could hear Ernie climbing, scuttling out some portal in the hull and balancing—she could hear it, or imagine it, the way he stood and gripped and held his breath to keep his angles upright—then half-slipping, half-crawling along the exterior. She could hear the way his hands and feet found handholds and footholds, and the stomp of the toe of his boots hitting horizontally against the hull. She tracked it.

Around. Sideways. Down. Over. Down some more.

Soon he was underneath them, holding on to God knew what.

Under her feet she could feel him, swinging like a monkey from hook to hook, or metallic outcropping to outcropping. The ship ticked, ever so slightly, left to right and forward and back. Ernie wasn't a heavy man—Mercy thought maybe he was 150 pounds, soaking wet with rocks in his pockets—but his gravity was enough to change the flow of the dirigible's progress, and the passengers could feel the faint jerk to the flow through the floor at their feet. It was the tapping pull of his body, slinging from point to point.

Every once in a while, despite the dimming of the lights and the silence of the folks within, a stray antiaircraft bullet dazzled the darkness with a shattering spray of sparks and sound. It was only by luck, all of them knew, that nothing hit harder, or penetrated the hull underneath.

All it would take, Mercy anxiously believed, was one round

that entered the cabin and proceeded farther, up into the hydrogen tanks above. One round, and it was over; all of them were burning, and the ship was falling. One round would change everything with its precision, or its blind chance.

Underneath them, Ernie was swinging above the earth, hanging from his hands and firing up lanterns to show the Confederacy that this transport was not intended for target practice, but at the same time drawing the attention and fire of anyone within range.

Mercy lifted her head and asked the captain, "Sir, are we behind southern lines?"

"I think so," he told her without looking at her. "It's hard to tell down there. Very hard to tell. And if the Union has any anti-aircraft power on its side, it might not matter. We might still be in range. Goddammit, Ernest," he said with a growl.

As if in reply, three sharp raps banged against the outer hull—not shots, but knocks from a human fist.

Gordon Rand asked, "What does that mean?"

The captain answered, "That he's done and coming back, I assume. Robert, poke your head out and see if you can help him."

"You think he needs help?" The second crewman fidgeted over by the ladder.

"Three raps might mean help, or hurry, or go to hell, for all I know. Just check!"

Robert attempted to follow orders, scaling the ladder not quite so smoothly as Ernie. He reached the top just in time to hear another spray of fire, a wildcat's yowl of tearing sheet metal. "What was that?" he demanded. No one answered him.

Everyone knew exactly as much as he did—that they'd been hit again, though heaven knew where or how badly. And then the captain knew, and probably the first mate also, for both of them made unhappy noises and yanked at the controls. Finally the first mate wanted to know, "What have we lost?" and the captain said back, "One of the rudders. Let's just pray we're over our own lines now, because there's no way we're doing anymore turning, unless it's in circles."

Above her head and to the right, Mercy heard Robert call, "Ernie! Where you at? You need a hand?"

Mercy joined the rest of the passengers in listening, perched on the very edge of their seats, breathing shallowly while waiting for a response. None came.

Robert called again: "Ernie? You out there?" His phrasing raised the possibility that he wasn't out there, that he'd fallen or been picked off by the puncturing line of fire.

But then, to everyone's relief, they heard the faint scrape of boots against steel, and Ernie called back, "I'm still here. Hold on." Then they all heard more scuttling. "Getting down is easier than getting up."

When Robert helped pull him back inside, everyone could see precisely why. His left hand was covered in blood, and the sailor-turned-dirigible-crewman was as pale as death in the unlit cabin. He announced, "One of the lanterns busted in my hand while I was trying to hang it. But the other two are up and holding. I placed 'em by the 'civilian' end of the sign. That's where the CSA logo is tamped on, anyway. Hopefully they'll see it all right."

"It might've worked," Gordon Rand posited. "No one's shooting at us. Not right this second."

The first mate said, "Maybe someone's planning to make the next shot count. Or maybe they can't see the paint job yet and they're trying to get a good look."

Rand added, "Or perhaps they're slow readers."

Mercy was out of her chair now, invigorated by the prospect of having something to do. She told Ernie, "Come sit over here, by me. And give me your hand."

He joined her at her seat and sat patiently while she rummaged through her sack.

"Everybody hang on to something. We're losing altitude," the first mate announced.

The captain amended the announcement to include, "We're going down, but we aren't *crashing*. Brace yourselves as you can, but I repeat, *we are not crashing*. The steering's all but gone out, that's all, so I can raise or lower us, but not point us in any direction."

"Are we behind southern lines?" someone other than Mercy asked, but she didn't see who'd raised the question again.

"Yes," the captain's tone of certainty was an outright lie, but he stuck to it. "We're just setting down, but we might take a tree or two with us. Estimated time to landing, maybe two or three minutes—I've got to take her down swift, because we're drifting back the other way."

"Oh, God," said the old lady.

"Don't holler for him yet," Mercy muttered. "It might not be as bad as all that. Ernie, let me see your hand."

"We've only got a couple of minutes—"

"I only need a couple of minutes. Now hold still and let me look." By then, she'd found her bandage rolls. She tore off a portion of one, and used it to wipe the area clear enough to see it better. It wasn't all cuts, and it wasn't all burns. In the very dim light that squeezed in through the windows, she could see it was a blending of both. Mercy would've bet against him ever having proper use of his mangled index finger again; but the wound wouldn't be a killing one unless it took to festering.

"How bad is it?" he asked her, both too nervous too look, and too nervous to look away. He blinked, holding his head away so he couldn't be accused of watching.

"Not so bad. Must hurt like the dickens, though. I need to wash it and wrap it up."

"We only have—"

"Hold it up, above your shoulder. It'll bleed slower and hurt less that way," she urged, and dived back into the bag. Seconds later, she retrieved a heavy glass bottle filled with a viscous clear liquid that glimmered in the moonlight and the feeble glow from the lanterns outside.

He said, "We're going down. We're *really* going down."

He was looking out the window beside her head. She could see it, too—the way the clouds were spilling past. She tried to ignore them, and to ignore the throat-catching drop of the craft.

"Don't look out there. Look at me," she commanded. Meeting his eyes she saw his fear, and his pain, and the way he was so pallid from the injury or the stress of acquiring it. But she held his eyes anyway, until she had to take his hand and swab it off with a dampened bandage.

The *Zephyr* was not falling, exactly. But Mercy could not in good conscience say that it was "landing" either. Her stomach was up in her mouth, nearly in her ears, she thought; and her ears were popping every time she swallowed. If she didn't concentrate on something else, she'd start screaming, so she focused on the bleeding, burned hand as she cleaned it, then propped Ernie's elbow on the headrest to keep it upright while she fumbled for dry bandages.

The old man leaned forward and threw up on the floor. His wife patted at his back, then felt around for any bags or rags to contain or clean it. Finding none, and lacking anything better to do, she returned to the back-patting. Mercy couldn't help them, so she stayed with Ernie, wrapping his still-bleeding hand and doing it swiftly, as if she'd been mummifying hands for her whole life. She did it like the world was ending at any minute, because for all she knew, it might be.

But things could be worse. No one was shooting at them.

She told Ernie, "Hold it above your heart and it won't throb so bad. Did I tell you that already?"

"Yes ma'am."

"Well, keep doing it." She gasped then as the ship gave a lurch and a heave as if its own stomach were sinking and rising. The captain told everyone to "Hang on to something!" but there was no something handy except for the seat.

Ernie went for chivalry, flinging his right arm over Mercy's shoulder and pulling her under his chest; she ducked there, and wrapped her left arm around his waist. She closed her eyes so she couldn't see the ground rearing up out the window, not even out of her peripheral vision.

The next phase was not as sudden as she'd expected. It sneaked up on her, taking her breath away as the *Zephyr* sliced through tree-tops that dragged it to a slower pace, then snagged it and pulled it down to the ground with a horrible rending of metal and rivets. The ship sagged, and dipped, and bounced softly. No one inside it moved.

"Is it—?" asked the old woman whose name Mercy still didn't know. "Are we—?"

"No!" barked the captain. "Wait! A little—"

Mercy thought he might've been about to say *farther,* because something snapped, and the craft dropped about fifteen feet to land on the ground like a stone.

Though it jarred, and made Mercy bite her tongue and somehow twist her elbow funny, the finality of the settled craft was a relief—if only for a minute. The ship's angle was all wrong, having landed on its belly without a tethering distance. From this position, they lacked the standard means of opening the ship to let them all go free. A moment of claustrophobic horror nearly brought tears to Mercy's eyes.

Then she heard the voices outside, calling and knocking; and the voices rode with accents that came from close to home.

Someone was beating against the hull, and asking, "Is everybody all right in there? Hey, can anybody hear me?"

The captain shouted back, "Yes! I can hear you! And I think everyone is . . ." He unstrapped himself from his seat—the only seats with straps were in the cockpit—and looked around the cabin. "I think everyone is all right."

"This a civvy ship?" asked another voice.

"Says so right on the bottom. Didn't you see it coming down?"

"No, I didn't. And I can't read, nohow."

Their banal chatter cheered Mercy greatly, purely because it sounded normal—like normal conversation that normal people might have following an accident. It took her a few seconds to realize that she could hear gunfire in the not-very-distant distance.

She disentangled herself from Ernie, who was panting as if he'd run all the way from the clouds to the ground. She nudged him aside and half stepped, half toppled out of her seat, bringing her bags with her. The crewman came behind, joining the rest of the passengers who were trying to stand in the canted aisle.

"There's an access port, on top!" the captain said to his windshield.

That's when Mercy saw the man they were speaking to outside, holding a lantern and squinting to see inside. He was blond under his smushed gray hat, and his face was covered either in shadows or gunpowder. He tapped one finger against the windshield and said, "Tell me where it is."

The captain gestured, since he knew he was being watched. "We can open it from inside, but we've got a couple of women on board, and some older folks. We're going to need some help getting everyone down to the ground."

"I don't need any help," Mercy assured him, but he wasn't listening, and no one else was, either.

Robert was already on his way up the ladder that he and Ernie had both scaled earlier, though he dangled from it strangely, so tilted was the ship's interior. He wrapped his legs around the rungs and used one hand to crank the latch, then shoved the portal out. It flopped and clanged, and was still. Robert kept his legs cinched around the ladder and braced himself that way, so he could work his arms free.

He reached down to the passengers and said, "Let's go. Let's send some people up and over. You. English fella. You first."

"Why me first?"

"Because you ain't hurt, and you can help catch the rest. And Ernie's got his hand all tore up."

"Fine," Gordon Rand relented, and began the tricky work of climbing a ladder that leaned out over his head. But he was game for it, and more nimble than the tailored foreign clothes let on. Soon he was out through the portal and standing atop the *Zephyr,* then sliding down its side, down to the ground.

Mercy heard him land with a plop and a curse, but he followed through by saying to someone, "That wasn't so bad."

That someone asked, "How many are there inside?"

"The captain, the copilot, and half a dozen passengers and crew. Not too many."

"All right. Let's get them down, and out."

Someone else added, "And out of here. Bugle and tap says the line's shifting. Everybody's got to move—we might even be in for a retreat to Fort Chattanooga."

"You can't be serious!" ·

"I'm serious enough. That's what the corporal told me, anyway."

"When?"

"Just now."

"Son of a *bitch*. They're right on top of us!"

Mercy wished she could see the speakers, but she could see only the frightened faces of her fellow passengers. No one was moving yet; even Robert was listening to the gossip outside. So she took it upon herself to move things along.

"Ma'am? Sir?" she said to the older couple. "Let's get you up out of here next."

The woman looked like maybe she wanted to argue, but she didn't. She nodded and said, "You're right. We'll be moving slowest, wherever we go, or however we get there. Come along, dear."

Her dear said, "Where are we going?"

"Out, love." She looked around. "I can make it up on my own, but he'll need some assistance. Captain? Or Mr. . . . Mr. First Mate?"

"Copilot," he corrected her as he climbed into the cabin. "I'd be happy to help."

Together they wrested and wrangled the somewhat reluctant old man and his insistent wife up the concave ladder and out the hatch. Then went the clubfooted student; and then Ernie, with a little help from Robert; and then Mercy, who couldn't get off the thing fast enough. Finally, the other student and the rest of the crew members extracted themselves, leaving the *Zephyr* an empty metal balloon lying tipped and steaming on the ground.

Five

A message had come and gone to someone, somewhere, and two more gray-uniformed men came running up to the group, leading a pair of stamping, snorting horses and a cart. The man holding the nearest horse's lead said to the group, "Everyone on board. Line's shifting. Everybody's got to go while the going's good."

"*Where* are we going?" demanded Gordon Rand even as he hastened to follow instructions.

He was helping the elderly woman up the back gate and into the makeshift carriage when the second newcomer replied. "Fort Chattanooga."

"How far away is that?" he inquired further.

"Better part of thirty miles."

Larsen exclaimed, "We're going to ride thirty miles in *that*?"

And the first man answered, "No, you're going to ride *two* miles in this, and then the rail will take you the rest of the way."

"We're outside Cleveland? That's what the captain said," Mercy said, fishing for confirmation of anything at all.

"That's right." The second Reb had hair so dark, it gleamed blue in the light of the lanterns. He gave her a wink and a nod that were meant to be friendly. "But come on, now. Everybody aboard."

The captain lingered by the *Zephyr* while the elderly couple settled in. The students climbed over the cart's edge behind them. "I need to reach a telegraph. I'll have to tell my dispatcher that the ship is down, and give them coordinates to retrieve it," the captain said plaintively.

But Mercy saw the artillery flashes and heard the earsplitting pops of gunfire through the trees, and she answered with a guess before anyone else could say it. "There won't be anything left of her by morning."

"One bullet," Gordon Rand said softly from his spot in the cart. "That's all it'll take, on her side, with her tanks exposed like that."

"Damn straight," said the blond who'd first communicated through the windshield. "All the more reason to hit the road, sooner rather than later. We don't want to be anywhere near her when she goes up in flames. She'll take a quarter mile of forest and everything in it."

Ernie gave a yelp when he was hauled onboard, prompting the dark-haired private—Mercy thought he was a private, anyway—to ask if anyone else was hurt. "Does anyone need any help? Is this everybody?"

"This is everybody," the captain confirmed. "We weren't traveling full. And the line wasn't supposed to move this far south; they told me at Richmond that it hadn't come this far," he complained even as he climbed aboard to join the rest of his passengers and crew.

The private reached for the reins and held on to them as he climbed up onto the steering seat. His companion leaped up to take a spot beside him, and with a crack of the reins, the cart was turning around to go back the way it had come. The private continued, raising his voice to make himself heard over the background roar of fighting, "We were holding 'em back real good, up until tonight. We'd cut 'em off from their cracker line, and the Chatty trains were keeping us in food and bullets, while they were running low on both."

Mercy didn't see the blond soldier who'd been first on the

scene—he had either stayed on the scene or gone in some other direction. The other blond had left the driving to the private, and was scanning the trees with a strange scope layered with special lenses, the nature of which Mercy could only guess.

The captain asked, "Then what happened, man? What turned the tide so fast that the taps couldn't catch up?"

Over his shoulder, the driver said, "They brought in an engine. That thing tore right through our blockades like they were made of pie dough. Killed a score every half a mile. Eventually we just had to let them have it."

Mercy said, "An engine? Like a train engine? I don't understand."

The blond lowered his scope and said, "The rail lines around here, they run crisscross, all over each other, every which-a-direction. We commandeered the switches and posted up our lads to keep the Yanks' cracker line squeezed off shut. But then they brought—"

The private interrupted him. "The *Dreadnought*. That's what they call it."

"My CO said he thought the damn thing was back east, over in D.C., watching over the capital after our rally there last month. But no! Those bastards brought that unholy engine all the way out here, and it mowed us right down. They took back their line in under an hour, and now they're pushing us back. They're pushing us back *good*," he emphasized, and drew the lenses back up to his face. "Veer us left, Mickey," he said to the driver. "I don't like the look of the smoke kicking up to the east."

"We're going to run out of road."

"Better that than running into artillery, eh?"

The *Zephyr*'s copilot was sour looking, squatting next to the captain. He asked, "How do you know it's artillery? I can't see a damn thing past the lanterns on the cart."

The navigator gave the copilot a look like he must be the

stupidest man alive and waggled his scope, with its myriad jingling lenses. "They're the latest thing. They ain't perfect, but they do all right." One more glance through the lenses, and he said, "But we gotta get rid of our lights or they'll spot us over there. Mickey, the lanterns. Kill 'em. Kill all of 'em."

"Clinton, I swear to God—"

"I'm not asking you a favor, you nitwit, I'm telling you—"

"I'm working on it!" Mickey cut him off. "Who's holding the other one?"

"I am," the captain said. "And I'm trimming the wick right now."

"Not enough," insisted Clinton. "Turn it off. Damp the whole thing down."

Mickey's lantern had already been snuffed, so when the captain reluctantly killed the light he held, the forest swallowed them whole. The horses slowed without being told, whinnying and neighing their displeasure and their nervousness. Mickey told them, "Hush up, you two." Then, to the people in the back, he said, "Down, all of you. Get as low as you can go. Cover your heads."

The old man, who had been silent against his wife thus far, instead asked, in a voice far too loud for anyone's comfort, "Why did it get so dark and quiet?"

Gordon Rand slapped his hand firmly over the old man's mouth and whispered, "Because none of us want to die. Now contain yourself, sir."

The old man did not so much contain himself as begin to giggle, but it was a quiet giggle, and no one chided him for it. All of them crouched down low, hunkering as deeply as possible against the floor of the cart as it rattled, jostled, and bounced them along the nearly invisible road between the trees . . . then off to the left where the road was less distinct, and rougher. It was also harder to bear for the folks whose knees, elbows, and ribs battered against the wood-slat bottom.

Nearby, a tree exploded, casting splinters as large as arms and legs through the darkness. The old woman muffled her own scream, and everyone else flattened even lower, as if they could meld themselves with the floor of the cart.

Mickey groaned. When Mercy looked up, she could see something dark and shiny all over his face and side, but he stayed upright and flipped the reins at the horses, yelling "Yah!"

The elderly man, absent Gordon Rand's hand over his mouth, exclaimed, "I thought we were supposed to be quiet!"

But there was no being quiet anymore; it wouldn't do any good at this point, and the horses and cart were barreling—kicking back to the main road where travel was faster, if more exposed. Another tree nearby was blown to bits with a sound like the whole world falling down. As the echo of it faded, Mercy's ears were ringing, and there was a tickle in her nose, of sawdust or vibration, then a knock against her head as a rock in the road launched the cart higher, then dropped it to the ground again with a clap that fractured the back axle.

"Oh, Jesus!" Mercy gasped, not that she thought He might be listening. Beneath her body, she could feel the sway and give and tug of the weakened wheels, and an added quiver to the cart's retreat.

"Mickey!" Clinton cried.

Mercy looked up just in time to see him wobble back and forth to the rhythm of the fleeing horses, and begin to fall. Clinton grabbed him and jerked him back onto the seat, but couldn't hold him steady; so the nurse leaped from her crouch and snagged the driver, pulling him back into the cart and right on top of herself, since there was no chance to maneuver him and no steady spot to put him down.

Clinton seized the reins.

With the help of Gordon Rand and the students, Mercy rolled Mickey over and patted him down in the darkness. She could see almost nothing, but she could feel a copious, warm dampness. "Captain!" she said. "Bring that lantern over here!"

"We're supposed to keep it turned off!"

"Turn it up, just a spark. I need to see. And I don't think it matters now, nohow." She took the lantern from his hand and twisted the knob just enough to bring it up to a pale glow, barely enough illumination to help. The light swung wildly back and forth from its wire handle, and the whole scene looked unreal, and hellish, and rattled. "He's bleeding bad."

"Not *that* bad . . . ," he slurred, and his eyes rolled up in his head.

Black-haired Mickey had lost a chunk of that pretty mane, exposing a slab of meat that Mercy prayed didn't show any bone, but couldn't get a stable enough look to see if it went as deep as that. His left ear was gone, and a terrible slash along his jawline showed the white, wet underpinning of his gums.

The Englishman said, "He must've gotten hit by a bit of that last tree."

"Must've," Mercy said. She pulled Mickey's head into her lap and daubed the wound until it was mostly clean.

Ernie asked, "Can you help him?"

"Not much," she confessed. "Here, help me get him comfortable." She adjusted his body so that his oozing head rested against the older woman's thigh. "Sorry," she told her. "But I've got to get inside my bag. Give me a second."

The woman might've given the nurse a second, but the line wouldn't.

A cannonball shot across the road in front of them, blasting a straight and charred zone through the woods, across the two wheel ruts, and into the trees on the other side, where something was big enough to stop it. A second followed the first, then a third.

The horses screamed and reared, and Clinton wrestled with the reins, begging them with swears, threats, and promises to calm themselves and for God's sake, keep *pulling*. One after another the horses found their feet and lunged, heaving the damaged cart forward again. But the axle was creaking dangerously, and Mickey wouldn't stop bleeding, and in the empty spaces between the trees, gunfire was whizzing and plunking against trunks.

"We're too heavy," the copilot said, and withdrew to the farthest corner, away from the damaged axle. "The cart isn't going to make it!"

"One more mile!" shouted Clinton. "We're halfway to the rail lines; it only has to make it one more mile!"

"But it's not *gonna*," Mercy cried.

"Holy Jesus all fired in hell!" Clinton choked, just loudly enough for the nurse to hear him. She looked up to see where he was staring, and glimpsed something enormous moving alongside them, not quite keeping pace but ducking back and forth between the thick trunks of the trees that hid almost everything more than twenty yards away.

"What was that?" she asked loudly, forgetting her manners and her peril long enough to exclaim.

"They didn't just bring the engine," Clinton said to her, half over his shoulder while he tried to watch the road. "Those bastards brought a walker!"

"What's a—?"

Another rock or a pothole sent the cart banging again, then the axle snapped, horrifying the horses and dragging the back end down to the ground, spilling out passengers and cargo alike. Mercy wrapped her torso around Mickey and her arm around the old woman who held him and stayed that way, clinging to a corner under the driver's seat until the horses were persuaded to quit dragging the dead weight and let the thing haul to a stop.

Half off the road and half on it, the cart was splayed on its side much like the *Zephyr* had wound up, only open and even more helpless looking.

"Goddammit!" Clinton swore as he climbed down from the cart in a falling, scrambling motion. He then set to work unhitching the horses. A swift hail of bullets burst from the trees. One of the horses was struck in a flank, and when it howled, it sounded like some exotic thing—something from another planet. It flailed upward onto two legs again, injured, but not mortally.

Mercy set to work directing the old couple, who had remained in what was left of the broken cart; and with a grunt she hefted Mickey up and slung him over her shoulder like a sack of feed. He was bigger than her by thirty pounds or more, but she was scared, and mad, and she wasn't going to leave him. He sagged against her, nothing but weight, and blood soaked down the back of her cloak where his earless scalp bounced against her shoulder blade.

She staggered beneath him and hoisted him out of the cart's wreckage, where she found one of the students—Dennis—standing in shock, in the middle of the road. "Good God Almighty!" She shoved him with her shoulder. "Get out of the road! Get down, would you? Keep yourself low!"

"I can't," he said as if his brain were a thousand miles away from the words. "I can't find Larsen. I don't see him. I . . . I have to find him. . . ."

"Find him from the ditch," she ordered, and shoved him into the trees.

The captain was missing, too, and the copilot was helping with the horses, who were reaching shrieking heights of inconsolability. Robert was on point; he went to the elderly folks and took the woman's hand to guide them both into some cover, and Ernie popped up from around the cart—looking more battered than even ten minutes previously, but in one piece, for the most part.

Mercy said, "Ernie," with a hint of a plea, and he joined her, helping to shoulder Mickey. Soon the private hung between them, one arm around each neck, his feet dragging fresh trails into the dirt as they took him off the road.

"Where's . . . ," she started to ask, but she wasn't even sure whom she was asking after. It was dark, and the lanterns were gone—God knew where—so a head count was virtually impossible.

"Larsen!" Dennis hollered.

Mercy snapped out with her free hand and took him by the shoulder. She said, "I'm going to hand Mickey over to you and Ernie right now, and you're going to help carry him back into the woods. Where's Mr. Clinton? Mr. Clinton?" she called, using her best and most authoritative patient-managing voice.

"Over here . . ."

He was, in fact, over there—still wrestling with the horses, guiding them off the road and doing his damnedest to assure them that things were all right, or that they were going to be all right, one of these days. "We can't leave them," he explained himself. "We can't leave them here, and Bessie's not hurt too bad—just winged. We can ride them. A couple of us, at least."

"Fine," Mercy told him. She also approved of assisting the horses, but she had bigger problems at the moment. "Which direction is the rail line?"

"West." He pointed with a flap of his arm that meant barely more than nothing to Mercy.

"All right, west. Do the horses know the way back to the rails?"

"Do they . . . what now?"

"Mr. Clinton!" she hollered at him. "Do the horses know the way back to the rails, or to the front? If I slap one on the ass and tell it to run, will it run toward safety or back to some barn in Nashville?"

"Hell, I don't know. To the rails, I suppose," he said. "They're draft horses, not cavalry. We rolled them in by train. If nothing else, they'll run away from the line. They ain't trained for this."

"Mr. Clinton, you and Dennis here—you sling Mickey over the most able-bodied horse and make a run for it. Mrs. . . . Ma'am"— she turned to the old woman—"I'm sorry to say it, but I never heard your name."

"Henderson."

"Mrs. Henderson. You and Mr. Henderson, then, on the other horse. You think she can carry them?" she asked Clinton.

He nodded and swung the horses around, threading them through the trees and back toward Mercy. "They ain't got no saddles, though. They were rigged for pulling, not for riding. Ma'am, you and your fellow here, can you ride 'em like this?"

Mrs. Henderson arched an eyebrow and said, "I've ridden rougher. Gentlemen, if you could help us mount, I'd be most grateful."

"Where's Larsen?" Dennis all but wailed. "I'm supposed to look out for him! Larsen! Larsen, where'd you go?"

Mercy turned around to see Dennis there, standing at the edge of the road like an enormous invitation. She walked up to him, grabbed him by the throat, and pulled him back into the trees and down to a seated position. "You're going to get yourself killed, you dumb boy!"

On the other side of the road, somewhere thirty or forty yards back, things were going from bad to worse. What had started as intermittent but terrifying artillery had grown louder and more consistent, and there was a bass-line undercurrent to it that promised something even worse. Something impossibly heavy was moving with slow, horrible footsteps, pacing along the lines on the other side. She spotted it here and there, for a moment—then no more.

She forced herself to concentrate on the matters at hand.

One problem at a time. She could fix only one problem at a time.

Prioritize.

"Dennis, you listen to me. Get on that horse with Mickey, and hold him steady. Ride west until you hit the rails, and get him to some safety. You can ride a horse, can't you?"

"But—"

"No *but*." She jammed a finger up to his nose, then turned to Clinton. "Clinton, you're an able-bodied man and you can walk or run the rest of the way, same as me. Ernie, can you still walk all right?"

"Yes ma'am. It's just the hand, what's all tore up."

"Good. You, me, Clinton, and . . . where's Mr. Copilot—?"

"His name is Richard Scott, but I don't see where he's gone," Robert interjected.

"Fine. Forget about him, if he's gonna run off like that. Has anyone seen the captain?"

"I think he fell out when the cart broke," Ernie said.

"Right. Then. We're missing Larsen, the captain, and the copilot. The Hendersons are on Bessie." She waved at Mrs. Henderson, who was tangling her hands in the horse's mane and holding her husband in front of her. She could barely reach around him, but she nodded grimly. "The Hendersons are riding Bessie, and Dennis will be riding the other horse, with Mickey. Is that everyone?" She began her litany again, pointing at each one in turn. "That leaves me, Ernie, Robert, Mr. Rand, and Clinton to find our own way to the rails, but we can do that, can't we, gentlemen?"

"Larsen!" Dennis called once more.

This time she smacked him, hard across the face. He held his breath.

She said, "If you open your mouth once more, I'll slap it clear into next Tuesday. Now hush yourself. I'm going to go find Larsen."

"You are?"

"I am. You, on the other hand, are heading west, so help me God—if only to get you away from us, because you're going to get us shot. Clinton, kindly help this fellow get on that horse and then the rest of us can get moving, too."

Clinton nodded at her like a man who was accustomed to taking orders, then hesitated briefly, because he was not accustomed to taking orders from a woman. Then he realized that he didn't have any better ideas, so he took Dennis by the arm, led him to the horse, and helped him aboard. The student did not look particularly confident in the absence of a saddle, but he'd make do.

"Don't you let him fall!" Mercy commanded.

Clinton slapped both horses on the rear, and the beasts took off almost cheerfully, so delighted were they to be leaving the scene. The remaining members of the ragtag party had no time to discuss further strategy. No sooner had the horses disappeared between the trees, headed generally west, than the southern side of the fighting line met them at the road.

The soldiers rushed up with battle cries, leading carts with cannon, and crawling machines that carried antiaircraft guns modified to point lower, as necessary. The crawling machines moved like insects, squirting oil and hissing steam from their joints as they loped forward; and the cannon were no sooner stopped than braced, and pumped, and fired.

On the other side of the road, the northern line was likewise digging in. Soldiers were hollering, and in the light of a dozen simultaneous flashes of gunpowder and shot, Mercy saw a striped flag waving over the trees. She saw it in pieces, cut to rags by shadows and bullets, but flying, and coming closer. All around Mercy, soldiers cast up barricades of wood or wire, and where cannon felled trees, the trees were gathered up—by the men themselves, or with help from the crawling craft, which were equipped with retracting arms that could lift much more than a man.

Some of the soldiers stopped at the strange band of misfits beside the road, but not for long. A wild-eyed infantryman pointed at the ruins of the cart and hollered, "Barricade!"

In thirty seconds, it was hauled out of the road and then was further dissected for dispersing along the line.

Clinton was back in his element, among his fellow soldiers. He took Gordon Rand by the arm, since Gordon seemed the least injured and most stable male civilian present, and said, "Get everyone to the back of the line, and then take them west! I've got to get back to my company!"

Everyone was shouting over the ferocious clang of the war, now brought into the woods—which compressed everything, even the sound, even the smell of the sizzling gunpowder. It was like holding a battle inside someone's living room.

Gordon Rand replied, "I can do that! Which way is west again?"

"That way!" Clinton demonstrated with his now-characteristic lack of precision. "Just get to the back of the line, and ask somebody there! Go! And run like hell! Their walker is getting closer; if ours don't catch up, we're all of us fish in a barrel!"

Most of the party took off running behind Rand, but Ernie hesitated. "Nurse?" he said to Mercy, who was looking back down the road, the way they had come.

"We're still missing the captain, and the copilot, and Larsen." She looked at Ernie. "I told Dennis I'd try and find him, and I mean to. Go on," she urged. "I'll be better off by myself. I can duck and cover, and I've got my red cross on."

She mustered a smile that was not at all happy.

Ernie didn't return it. He said, "No way, ma'am. I'm staying with you. I'm not leaving a lady alone on a battlefield."

"You're not a soldier."

"Neither are you."

It was clear that he wouldn't be moved. Mercy sized that up in a snap; she knew the type—too chivalrous for his own good, and now he felt like he owed her, since she'd done what she could to take care of his hand. Now he was bound to take care of her, too, or else leave the debt to stand. Yes, she knew that kind. Her husband had been that kind, though she didn't take the time to think about it right then.

"Suit yourself," she told him. She lifted up her cloak, pulling the hood up over her head and adjusting her satchel so that the red mark stood out prominently. It wasn't a shield, and it wasn't magic, but it might keep her from being targeted. Or it might not.

"Behind the barrier—we can't jump it, not now," she said. It was amazing, how the thing had gone up while they stood there, piecemeal by rickety piecemeal, made up of logs and metal shards, and strips of things meant to tear human flesh beyond repair. Even if she could've fit through it, that would've left her in the middle of the worst of the cross fire, and that wouldn't do. Especially not with Ernie tagging along.

So they wound their way through the soldiers, getting sworn at, shouted at, and shoved toward the safety they didn't want every step of the way until they'd gone far enough east, away from the relative safety of the rails, that the barricade hadn't yet found purchase and the road was not quite the highway of bullets that it had become farther up the way.

Mercy dashed into the road, crying out for Larsen—wondering if she'd passed him already in the turmoil, and wondering if he'd even survived falling out of the swiftly moving cart. "Captain? Mr. . . . Mr. Copilot? What was his name again? Scott something? Mr. Scott? Can anyone hear me?"

Probably more than a few people could hear her, but it sounded like the fighting was heating up back where the cart had crashed and been disassembled, and no one was paying any attention to the cloaked nurse and the bandaged dirigible crewman.

"Anyone?" she tried again, and Ernie took up the cry, to as much effect.

Together they tried to skirt the line of trees and keep their heads low as they walked up and down the strip where they concluded the cart had most likely come apart. And finally, off to the side and down a rolling culvert, into a cut in the earth where spring rain had carved a deep *V* into a hill, they got a response.

"Nurse?" The response was feeble but certain. It called like the men called from the cots, back at the hospital. *Nuss?*

They scarcely heard it over the battle, and it was all Mercy could do to concentrate on the sound—the one little syllable—over the clash a hundred yards away. The footsteps were still stomping, too, and stomping closer with every few steps; she shuddered to imagine what kind of machine this might be, that walked back and forth along the front and sounded much larger than any gun . . . maybe even larger than the *Zephyr* itself. Whatever it was, she didn't want to see it. She only wanted to run, but there came that voice again, not quite crying, but pleading: "Nurse?"

"Over here!" Ernie said. "He's down here!" And he was already sliding down there, toward the rut in the earth where Larsen had landed.

"I thought it was you," Larsen said when Mercy reached him. "I thought it must be. Where's Dennis, is he all right?"

"He's fine. He's on his way to the rail lines, where the train'll pick him up and run him to Fort Chattanooga. We had to *make* him go, but he went. I told him I'd come looking for you."

"That's good." He closed his eyes a moment, as if concentrating on some distant pain or noise. "I think I'm going to be just fine, too."

"I think you might be," she told him, helping him sit up. "Did you just crash here, or roll here? Is anything broken?"

"My foot hurts," he said. "But it always hurts. My head does, too, but I reckon I'll live."

She said, "You'd better. Come on, let me get you up."

"I remember there was a big snapping sound, and everything came apart. And I was *flying*. I remember flying, but I don't recall anything else," he elaborated while the Mercy and Ernie pulled him upright and to his feet. His cane was long gone, but he waved away their attempts to assist him further. "I can do it. I'll limp like a three-legged dog, but I can do it."

"I don't suppose you've seen the captain, or the copilot, have you?" asked Ernie.

"No, I haven't. Like I said, I went flying. That's all."

"You're a lucky son of a gun," Mercy told him.

"I don't feel real lucky. And what's that noise?"

"It's the line. It's caught up to us. Come on, now. Other side of the road. Get down low, and make a dash for it—as much as you're able. You landed on the Yankee side, so don't go thanking your lucky stars quite yet."

But soon they were ducking and shuffling, flinging themselves across the road and back to gray territory, and not a moment too soon. The barricade-makers were shouting orders back and forth at one another, extending the line, setting up the markers along the road. They ordered Mercy and the men to "Clear the area! Now!"

Larsen yelled back, "We're civilians!"

"You're going to be *dead civilians* if you don't get away from this road!" Then the speaker stopped himself, getting a good look at Mercy. "Wait a minute. You a nurse?"

"That's right."

"You any good?"

"I've saved more men than I've killed, if that's what you want to know." She helped hoist Larsen down over the drop-off at the road's edge, leaving herself closer to the dangerous front line. She stared down the asker, daring him to propose one more stupid question before she kicked him into Kansas.

"We got a colonel with a busted-up arm and chest. Our doctor took a bullet up the nose and now we've got nobody. The colonel's a good leader, ma'am. Hell, he's just a good man, and we're losing him. Can you help?"

She took a deep breath and sighed it out. "I'll give it a try. Ernie, you and Larsen—"

"We'll make for the rails. I'll help him walk. Good luck to you, ma'am."

"And to the pair of you, too. You—" She indicated the Reb who'd asked her help. "—take me to this colonel of yours. Let me get a look at him."

"My name's Jensen," he told her on the way between the trees. I hope you can help him. It's worse for us if we lose him. You, uh . . . you one of ours?"

"One of yours? Sweetheart, I've spent the war working at the Robertson Hospital."

"The Robertson?" Hope pinked his cheeks. Mercy could see the flush rise up, even under the trees, in the dark, with only a sliver of moonlight to tell about it. "That's a damn fine joint, if you'll pardon my language."

"Damn fine indeed, and I don't give a fistful of horseshit about your language."

She looked back once to see if Larsen and Ernie were making good progress away from the fighting, but the woods wouldn't let her see much, and soon the cannon smoke and barricades swallowed the rest of her view.

Jensen towed her through the lines, guiding her around wheeled artillery carts and the amazing crawling transporters. She gave them as wide a berth as she could, since he told her, "Don't touch them! They're hot as hell. They'll take your skin off if you graze them."

Past both good and poorly regimented lines of soldiers coming, going, and lining up alongside the road they dashed, always back—to the back of the line—following the same path as the wounded, who were either lumbering toward help or being hauled that way on tight cotton stretchers.

Back on the other side of the road, on the other side of the line, she heard a mechanical wail that blasted like a steam whistle for twenty full seconds. It shook the leaves at the top of the trees and gusted through the camp like a storm. Soldiers and officers froze, and shuddered; and then the wail was answered by a returning call from someplace farther away. The second scream was less preternatural, though it made Mercy's throat cinch up tight.

"It's only a train, out there," she breathed.

Jensen heard her. He said, "No. Not only a train. That metal monster they got—it's talking to the *Dreadnought*."

"The metal monster? The . . . the walker? Is that what they called it?" she asked as they resumed their dodging through the chaos of the back line. "One of your fellows told me they have one, but I don't know what that is."

"Yeah, that's it. It's a machine shaped like a real big man, with a pair of men inside it. They armor the things up and make them as flexible as they can, and once you're inside it, not even a direct artillery hit—at real close range—will bring you down. The Yanks have got only a couple of them, praise Jesus. They're expensive to make and power."

"You sound like a man who's met one, once or twice."

"Ma'am, I'm a man who's helped *build* one." He turned to her and flashed a beaming smile that, for just this once, wasn't even half desperate. And as if it'd heard him, from somewhere behind the Confederate lines a different, equally loud and terrible mechanical scream split the night across the road with a promise and a threat like nothing else on earth.

"We got one, too?" she wheezed, for her breath was running out on her and she wasn't sure how much longer she could keep up this pace.

"Yes ma'am. That-there is what we like to call the *Hellbender*."

She saw its head first, looming over the trees like a low gray moon. It swiveled, looking this way and that, the tip of some astounding Goliath made of steel and powered by something that smelled like kerosene and blood, or vinegar. It strode slowly into a small clearing, parting the trees as if they were reeds in a pond, and stood up perfectly straight, before emitting a gurgling howl that answered the mechanized walker on the other side of the road—and sent out a challenge to the terrifying train engine, too.

Mercy froze, spellbound, at the thing's feet.

It was approximately six or seven times her height—maybe thirty-five or forty feet tall, and as wide around as the cart that had carried her away from the *Zephyr*. Only very roughly shaped like a man, its head was something like an upturned bucket big enough to hold a horse, with glowing red eyes that cast a beam stronger than a lighthouse lamp. This beam swept the top of the trees. It was searching, hunting.

"Let's go." Jensen put himself between her and the mechanized walker, flashing it a giant thumbs-up before leading her toward a set of flapping canvas tents.

But she couldn't look away.

She couldn't help but stare at the human-style joints that creaked and bent and sprung, oozing oil or some other industrial lubricant in black trails from each elbow and knee. She had to watch as the gray-skinned thing saw what it was looking for, pointed itself at the road, and marched, spilling puffs of black clouds from its seams. The mechanized walker didn't march quickly, yet it covered quite a lot of space with each step; and each step rang against the ground like a muffled bell with a clapper as large as a house. It crashed against the ground with its beveled oval feet and began a pace that could best be described as a slow run.

A cheer went up behind the Confederate line as the walker went blazing through it. Everyone got out of the way. Hats were thrown up and salutes were fired off.

Back in the woods, somewhere on the southern line, an explosion sent up a fireball so much bigger than the tree line that, even though it must've been a mile away, Mercy could see it, and imagine she felt the heat of it.

Jensen said, "You got here on that dirigible, the one that went down?"

"That's right," she told him. "And it just went up in flames, didn't it?"

"Yup. Hydrogen'll do that."

"What about that thing? The *Hellbender*?"

"What about it?" he asked.

"What does it run on? Not hydrogen?"

He shook his head and then ducked under a tent flap, indicating that she should do likewise. "Hell no. Texas done developed it, so it runs on processed petroleum. Can't you smell it?"

"I can smell *something*."

"*Diesel*. That's what they call it, and that's why our *Hellbender*'s gonna take down their . . . whatever they call theirs. Theirs just run on steam. They move all right, but they run so hot, they can't keep pace with ours, not for very long. Not without cooking the men who ride inside 'em." He paused his exposition to salute a uniformed fellow in the tent's corner. Then he said, "Chase," to acknowledge a second man who was sitting on a camp stool beside a cot. "Ma'am, this is George Chase—he's been looking after the colonel. And there, that's Colonel Thaddeus Durant. You can see he's not doing so good."

"I can see that," she said, and went immediately to the colonel's side. She dragged a second camp stool to the cot's edge and tugged a lantern out of George Chase's hand.

He gave clear consideration to mounting a protest, but Jensen shushed him by saying, "She's a nurse from the Robertson joint, George. Dropped right out of the sky, she did. Give her some breathing room."

George scooted his stool back and said, "I don't know what to do. I fix machines; I don't know how to fix things like this!"

She swung the lantern over the pulp of the colonel's face, neck, shoulder, and ribs, and guessed that he'd taken a close prox-imal blast of grapeshot, or something messier. Peeling back the blanket they'd thrown across him, she followed the damage like it was a trail marked out on a map. The blanket stuck to him where the makeshift bandages had bled clean through. Everything was beginning to dry to a sticky, wet paste of cotton, wool, and shred-ded flesh.

"Gentlemen, I'm not entirely sure what to tell you—"

"Tell us you can save him!" George Chase begged.

She wouldn't tell them that. Instead she said, "I need all the clean rags you can get your hands on, and your doctor's medical bag if you can scare it up for me. Then I'm going to need a big pot of clean water, and if you find some that's good and hot, so much the better."

"Yes ma'am." George saluted her out of habit or relief on his way out of the tent, thrilled to have been given a task.

The uniformed officer fretted in place, looming beside Jensen. He said, "There's nothing to be done for him, is there?"

She said, "Maybe if I clean him up, I'll get an idea of how bad it is." But she meant, *No.*

"He's going to die, isn't he?"

Jensen clapped the other man in the side and said, "Don't you put it like that! Don't talk about him like that, he's right here and he can hear you. He's going to be all right. Just damn fine, is how he's going to be."

Mercy very seriously doubted that the colonel could hear anything, much less any studied critique of his likely survival. But when the requested items arrived, she dived into exploratory cleansing, peeling away the layers of clotted fabric and gore as gently as possible to get at the meat underneath. She soaked the rags and dabbed them against the colonel's filthy skin, and he moaned.

It startled her. She'd honestly thought he was too far gone for pain or response.

Inside the doctor's bag, she found some ether in a bottle, as well as needles and thread, some poorly marked vials, tweezers, scissors, syringes, and other things of varying usefulness, including another fat roll of bandages. She whipped these out and unrolled them, saying, "The first thing is, you've got to stop his bleeding. The rest of this . . . god*damn,* boys. There's not enough skin to stitch through here, or here—" She indicated the massive patches where his flesh had been blasted away. "You need to get him out of this field. Ship him up to Robertson, if you think you can get him that far. But right here, right now . . ."

She did not say that she did not think he'd ever survive long enough to make it to the nearest hospital, or that any further effort was damn near futile. She couldn't say it. She couldn't do that to them.

Instead she sighed, shook her head, and said, "Mr. Chase, I'm going to need you to hold this lantern for me. Hold it up so I can see."

She retrieved the dead doctor's tweezers.

"What are you going to do?"

"The poor bastard's got so much scrap and shot in him, it's probably added ten pounds. I'm going to pick out what I can, before he wakes up and objects. I need you to help me out with this water."

"What do I do?"

"Take this rag with your free hand, here. Dunk it and get it good and wet. Now. Wherever I point, that's where I want you to squeeze the water out to clear the blood away, so I can see. You understand?"

"I understand," he said without sounding one bit happy about it.

Outside, somewhere beyond the small dark tent, two enormous things collided with a crash that outdid all the artillery. Mercy could picture them, two great automatons made for war, waging war against each other because nothing else on earth could stop either one of them.

She forced herself to focus on the shrapnel that came out of the colonel in shards, chunks, and flecks. There was no tin pan handy, so she dropped the bloody scraps down to the dirt beside her feet, directing George Chase to aim the light over here, please, or no—farther that way. Occasionally the colonel would whimper in his sleep, even as numb with unconsciousness as he was. Mercy had kept the ether bottle handy just in case, but he never awakened enough to require it. Still she tweezed, pricked, pulled, and tugged the metal from his neck and shoulder. Nothing short of a miracle held his major arteries intact.

An explosion shook the tent, illuminating it from outside, as if the sun were high instead of the moon. Mercy cringed and waited for the percussion to pass, waited for her ears to pop and her hands to stop shaking.

Down, then. Down his shoulder, to his chest and his ribs.

Never mind what's happening outside, on the other side of a cotton tent that wouldn't stop a good thunderstorm, much less a hail of bullets—and the bullets were raining sideways, from every direction. Men were yelling and orders were flying. Perhaps a quarter of a mile away, two monstrous machines grappled with each other for their lives, and for the lives of their nations. Mercy could hear it—and it was amazing, and horrifying, and a million other things that she could not process, not while she had this piece of bleeding meat soaking through his cot. Somehow over the din she detected a soft, rhythmic splashing, and realized that his blood had finally pooled straight through the spot where he slept, and it was dribbling down on her shoes.

She did not say, *He'll never make it. All of this is for show. He'll be dead by morning.* But the longer she kept herself from saying it, the less inclined she was to think it—and the more focused she became on the task at hand, and her borrowed tweezers, and the quivering raw steak beneath her fingers.

When she'd removed everything that could reasonably be removed (which probably left half as much again buried down in the muscles, somewhere), she dried him and wrapped him from head to torso in the doctor's last clean bandages, and showed George Chase how to use the opium powders and tinctures that the good doctor had left behind.

As far as Mercy could tell, the colonel had stopped bleeding—either because he'd run out of blood, or because he was beginning to stabilize. Either way, there wasn't much else she could do, and she told George so. Then she said, "Now, you've got to keep him clean and comfortable, and make him take as much water as he'll swallow. He's going to need all the water you can get inside him."

George nodded intensely, with such earnest vigor that Mercy figured he'd be taking notes if he'd had a pencil present.

Finally, she said, "I wish him and you the very best, but I can't stay here. I was on my way to Fort Chattanooga when my dirigible . . . well, it didn't precisely crash."

"How does a dirigible not precisely crash?" he asked.

"Let's just say that it landed unwillingly, and well ahead of schedule."

"Ah. Hmm." He pulled his small wire-rimmed glasses off his nose and wiped at them with the tail of his shirt, which probably didn't clean them any. But when he replaced them, he said, "You'll need to catch the rails, over in Cleveland. We're not far. Probably not a mile."

"Can you point me that way? I've got a pretty good sense of

direction; I can walk a straight line, even in the middle of the night, if I can trouble you for one of your lanterns."

George Case looked aghast. "Ma'am, we certainly can't allow anything like that! I wish you could stay and lend us a hand, but we've already sent for another surgeon and he'll be here within the night. I'll call back Jensen, or somebody else. We'll get you a horse, and a guard."

"I don't need a guard. I'm not entirely sure I need a horse."

He waved his hand; it flapped like a bird's wing as he rose and went to the tent's panel, pushing it open. "We'll see you to the rail yards, ma'am. We'll send you there with our thanks for your time and ministrations."

She was too tired to argue, so she just pushed her camp stool back away from the cot and cracked her fingers. "As you like," she said.

As he liked, two horses were swiftly saddled. Jensen rode one while Mercy rode the other, away from the camp and into the trees once more, between the trunks, between the bullets that sometimes whipped loosely past, having flown too far to do much but plunk against the wood. The roar of battle was still loud, but fading into the background. She could see, in hints and flashes, the two giant monsters wrestling, falling, and swinging.

She drew her cloak up over her head and gripped the reins with hands that still had dried blood smeared into the creases. Her luggage was long gone—lost with the cart, and the people who were lost with it—and she could mourn for it later, but her professional bag with its crimson cross stitched boldly on the side banged against her rib cage, where it was firmly slung across her chest.

The rail yard was not the same as a station; there was no major interchange, but several smaller buildings planted amid the maze of tracks. One of them had a little platform, and on this platform huddled a dozen people, milling about together and tapping their feet.

Jensen led her over a walkway that crossed four rows of tracks and went around three giant engines with boilers clacking themselves cool. He paused to dismount at the platform's edge. By the time he'd reached the reins of Mercy's horse, she'd already climbed down without assistance.

Someone on the platform called her name, and she recognized Gordon Rand, who looked delighted to see her. The other known survivors of the *Zephyr* were there also, having waited the better part of the night for the train that presently pulled in with a raucous halt, spraying steam in all directions, covering the stragglers on the platform in a warm cloud of it. The horses stamped unhappily, but Jensen held their reins firmly and said to Mercy, "Ma'am. George said you were headed for Fort Chattanooga, and it looks like you're traveling alone." The horse took half a step forward and backward, shuffling to keep from stepping off the walkway and onto a narrow metal rail.

"Both of them things are true," she admitted.

"You're all by yourself, headed west from Richmond?"

"My husband died. In the war. I just learned a week ago, and now I'm going home to my daddy's." She did not add that her trip was going to take her another couple thousand miles west of Fort Chattanooga, because she had a feeling she knew where this conversation was going.

She wasn't perfectly correct. Jensen—and whether that was his first name or last, she'd never asked and would never know— pulled a small cotton satchel off his chest and handed it to her. "George thought maybe you ought to take these with you. They belonged to the doctor, who was a Texan by birth, and he traveled like it."

She took the satchel and peered inside. The light from the platform's lamps cast a yellow white square down into the khaki bag, revealing a gunbelt loaded with a pair of six-shooters, and several boxes of bullets. Mercy said, "I don't know what to say."

"You ever fire a gun before?"

"Course I have. I grew up on a farm. But these are awful nice."
She looked up at him, and back at the guns. "These must be worth
a lot of money."

Jensen ran a hand through his hair, shifted, and shrugged. "I
reckon they probably are. He was a good doctor, and he'd made
good money before joining us out in the fronts. But our colonel is a
good man, too, and he's worth more to us than these guns. The doc
won't be needing them anymore, anyway. George just thought . . .
and I thought so, too . . . that you ought to take them."

"You don't have to do this."

"You didn't have to stop and pick all that iron out of poor
Colonel Durant. So you take these, and we'll call it even. So long
as you take care of yourself, and have a safe trip to Fort Chattanooga." He touched the front of his hat with a polite little bow
and swung himself back up over his horse's back. Still holding the
reins of the one who'd toted Mercy, he gave his beast a tap with
his heel and rode back over the tracks, back to the trees, and back
to the front.

A large, nervous man in an engineer's uniform and cap ushered everyone on board the train—a lean vehicle for all its size,
identified by gold-painted script that said *Birmingham Belle*. It
towed only two cars. One was heaped with coal, and the other
was a passenger car that had seen better days, and had clearly
been scared up for the occasion at the very last moment.

"Everyone on board, please. Quickly—we need to leave the
yards. Let's get all of you to town before we're closed off for
good."

Mercy didn't know what he meant by that, so when she finally
hauled herself up the steps—the very last of the passengers being
evacuated—she asked. "What could close off the yard?"

"Ma'am, please move along," he said stiffly.

But she didn't move from the top step.

He looked her up and down, this woman covered with someone's blood, smudged with gunpowder from hair to gore-flecked boots, and thought it might be less trouble to tell her than to fight with her. So he said, "Ma'am, the rail junction was sewed up tight till the *Dreadnought* came through, carrying that mechanized walker up to the line. And they didn't recall that miserable machine back to Washington—it's still here, crawling the tracks. Prowling around, tearing up everything it meets. So we've got to get out of its way."

"It's coming here? Now? For us?"

"We don't know!" He sounded almost frantic. "Please, ma'am. Just get aboard so we can fire up the engine and take you someplace safe."

She allowed herself to be ushered into the car and down to a seat that was really just a bench bolted into the floor. Her head fell slowly against the window. She didn't sleep, but she breathed deeply and crushed her eyes shut when someplace, far too close, a train whistle pierced the coming dawn.

Six

The *Birmingham Belle* rolled into Fort Chattanooga as the sun rose over the green-covered Appalachian ridges that welled up around the Tennessee River. The motion of the train must've lulled Mercy more than she'd imagined, because she didn't remember much of the getting there—only the rollicking lurch of the vehicle's progress, clipping along the rails.

There was a station there—a proper station, with rows of platforms and a café, and porters and patrons and clocks—out on the south side of the city, in the shadow of Lookout Mountain. Mercy lowered her window and leaned her head out to catch the morning air and refresh herself, inasmuch as possible. She smelled soot, and more diesel fuel. She whiffed coal dust, ash, and manure; and over the clatter of the arriving train, she heard the lowing of cattle and the natterings of goats, sheep, and the people who ushered them along.

The *Birmingham Belle* stopped with an exhausted sigh, seeming to settle on its rails. A few minutes later, the engineer himself drew out the passenger steps and opened the doors to release them.

All of them, from the *Zephyr* folks to the strangers who'd likewise required evacuation from Cleveland or the railyards, stumbled into the light and blinked against the steam that clouded the platform like battlefield smoke.

The Fort Chattanooga Metropolitan Transit Station looked unaccountably normal.

Laborers moved luggage, supplies, and coal in every direction—some carried right along the platforms, and some pumped by hand-moved carts that clung to the rails, darting between the trains at every switch and junction. Scores of dark-skinned men in red uniforms did most of the toting and directing, guiding the flow of everything that must come and go from a train, including people.

None of them were slaves anymore, and most hadn't been for years. Like Virginia and North Carolina, Tennessee had ratified an amendment abolishing the practice back in the late 1860s, over the grumbles and general disapproval from the deeper Confederacy. But preaching states' rights was only talk if a nation wouldn't uphold its own principles, so these three upper states got their way. Over the next ten years, most of the others followed suit, and now only Mississippi and Alabama held out . . . though there were rumors that even these two bastions of the Peculiar Institution might crack within the next year or two. After all, even South Carolina had caved to English abolitionist pressure in 1872.

Like so many things, in the end it had come down not to a matter of principle, but a matter of practicality. The Union had more warm bodies to throw at a war, and the Confederacy needed to harness a few of its own or, at the very least, quit using them to police its vast legions of imported labor.

It was Florida that first got the idea to offer land grants as added incentive to settle or sign up and fight. Texas caught on shortly thereafter, inviting the former slave population to homestead for almost precisely the same reason as Florida—an enormous Spanish population that had never quite come to terms with its territory loss. Besides, Texas was its own republic, with plenty of farmland available, and its informal allies in the Confederacy had an army to feed. In 1869, the governor of Texas said to a local newspaper,

"Looks like easy math to me: We need people to grow food, and we've got nothing but room to farm it, so bring in the free blacks and let them break their backs on their own land for a change."

Florida was already sitting on a large free colored population, mostly courted from the Carolinas by the Catholic missions in the previous century; and besides, Texas was nursing a war on two fronts: against the Union to the northeast (though not, of course, officially) and with growing ranks of dissatisfied Mexican separatists from the south and west. These two states had the most to gain from claiming the ex-slaves as their own, inviting them to make themselves comfortable, and calling them citizens. This was not to say that things were egalitarian and easy for the free blacks, but at least they were employees rather than property throughout much of the CSA these days.

There in Tennessee, a great number of freed slaves had found themselves welcoming their brethren from Alabama (only a few short miles to the south) to a place with few occupations that did not feed the wartime economy. Competition for employment was fierce, even when many jobs were available. So they worked at the train station, and in the factories; they worked on the river, in the shipping districts. There was even one school teaching young negro and mixed men to become mechanics and engineers. The school was rumored to be one of the best in the nation, and there were rumors that once in a blue moon, a *white* boy would try to sneak in.

One man, a tall colored porter with high cheeks and a crisp Pullman uniform, asked if he could take Mercy's bag or direct her to a train. His words trailed off when she looked up at him; he saw her smudged skin, filthy hair, and blood-covered clothes.

"I beg your pardon?" she said. Tired, and not even certain what she ought to ask him.

"Do you need any help? Assistance?"

She looked back at the train, a gesture that turned her shoulder and showed her bag.

He noted the cross, and in an effort to gently prompt her, he said, "Back from the front, are you?"

"As it turns out," she muttered, meeting his eyes again. "I'm . . . I need to . . . I'm on my way to Memphis," she finally spit out.

"Memphis," he repeated. "Yes, there are trains going that way—one this evening, departing at seven fifteen, and one much later, at eleven twenty," he said from memory. "And there's another at ten seventeen tomorrow morning. If you don't mind my saying so, I think you ought to consider the morning train."

"I don't mind you saying so," she assured him. "I'll just . . . I think that's a good idea. I'll go head inside, and ask about a room."

"The transit hotel is all full up at the moment, ma'am. But the St. George Hotel is right across the street. Rooms are reasonable, and there's board included. Supper and breakfast, at six thirty sharp, both a.m. and p.m."

"Thank you. For your help," she told him, though she said it as though she weren't really awake, and wasn't really thinking about it. She wandered away from him in the same dazed fashion. Mercy was so tired, she could hardly stand, but "across the street" didn't sound far. She climbed up and down stairs that took her across platforms and around busy carts and porters and restless passengers. She ignored the stares of the well-dressed folks waiting for their transport, if she even saw them gaping at her; but she tugged her cloak a little tighter, trusting the dark blue to hide more of the dried blood than the beige linen of the apron that covered her brown work dress. If the rest of her was distractingly dirty, then the world would just have to deal with it.

Immediately across the street, as promised, a gray brick building called itself the St. George Hotel. Mercy let herself inside and found a place that wasn't beautiful, but was spacious—three

stories and two wings, with a big lobby that had a bright lamp
hanging overhead and a threadbare carpet leading straight up to
the front desk. A man there was scribbling something down in a
ledger, and he didn't look up when she approached; he only said,
"Need a room?" and tapped the tip of his pen against his tongue
to moisten it.

Mercy said, "I do, please." She retrieved her handbag from inside the satchel, praising Jesus quietly for her habit of keeping it
there. It could easily have been lost with the rest of her luggage.

The man looked up at her. He was wearing a headband with a
magnifying lens attached to it that hung down over his right eye.
His face was shaped like a potato, and was approximately as
charming.

"Where's your husband?"

"Dead, in a field someplace in Georgia," she answered flatly.
"I'm on my own."

"A woman traveling alone," he observed, and lifted the edge
of his nose in a distasteful sneer. "We don't cotton to those, too
much. Not here. This ain't that kind of establishment."

She said, "And I ain't that kind of client, so we don't have a
problem. I'm a nurse, passing through to Memphis. I'm on my
way from the Robertson Hospital in Richmond," she tried, since
that place had opened doors for her before.

"Never heard of it."

"Oh, for heaven's sake . . ."

"You got any paperwork?"

"Course I do." She rummaged through the satchel, with its
logo that did nothing to melt the heart of the hotelkeeper, and
found the letter from Captain Sally. She showed it to him, and he
made a show of reading it.

"All right, then, I guess. But you pay up front."

"Here."

"Fine." He counted it, taking his time with every coin and bill. He handed her a key. "Room eleven. First floor. The hallway to your right."

She forced herself to say, "Thank you," and went immediately to her room.

The room was bare but clean, with a bed, a dresser, a basin in the corner, and, attached to one wall, a slab of polished tin for a mirror. A note on the back of the door told her where the pump was located, so before she settled in, Mercy went out into the center courtyard to the public pump and filled the basin, then carried it back to her room and pulled off everything except her underclothes.

A slim bar of butter-colored soap rested under the mirror.

She used it to scrub down everything, rinsing the worst of the blood and muck out of her apron, and out of the dress beneath it where it'd soaked through. When she was done, she hung everything up around the room to dry, then dropped herself down onto the bed, which caught her with a puff of cheap, flattened feathers.

By the time she awoke, it was late afternoon, and very, very bright. The mountain's shadow lay long and sharp across the south side of the city, which churned and rolled with trains from every part of the Confederacy.

Mercy was fiercely hungry. She couldn't remember when she'd last eaten, except that it must've been in Richmond. After reassuming clothes that were mostly dry, if not quite, she went out into the lobby and found a different man behind the counter. The new fellow's face was shaped more like a radish than a potato, and the pinched expression he wore conveyed nearsightedness more than malice.

"Excuse me," Mercy asked him. "Could you tell me what time it is?"

"That way, ma'am." He pointed over her head, and when she followed his finger, she saw an enormous clock. He didn't try to call out the time, which reinforced her suspicion.

So she said aloud, "Ten minutes until six. I understand there's a supper included at six thirty?"

"That's right, ma'am. It's served in the ballroom, down the west wing. Second door to the left." He lowered his voice. "But if I were you, ma'am, I'd wait until six thirty on the nose. Mr. and Mrs. Ferson don't take too kindly to those who 'vulture,' as they're keen to put it."

"Thank you, then. For that information, I mean. And could I ask you another question?"

"By all means, ma'am."

"Could you please direct me to a notions store, or a general goods establishment? I'm afraid my—well, most of my luggage was lost, and I'll need to replace some things."

He said, "Absolutely. On the next block over, to the left around the corner, you'll find Halstead's. If you can't find everything you need there, I'm certain that a clerk can point you someplace else."

She thanked him and turned away from the counter, finding her way back out the front door and into the street, where the city looked strangely sharp—filed that way against the long, lingering rays that cut past the mountain and the ridges. Fort Chattanooga was a bustling place, filthy and disorganized. And the fort was furthermore augmented by the addition of city walls where the natural boundaries failed to provide adequate protection against incoming marauders.

Halstead's was the promised block away.

It had a cut-stone front with the establishment name chiseled therein in roman block letters, and a window with printed script scrawled from corner to corner, detailing the day's specials.

Mercy pressed the door open and let herself inside.

She found rows of goods precisely ordered and carefully stacked, divided into all the expected categories. She picked up a basket from the door's entrance and a few of the essentials she'd lost: a comb, some gloves, a bar of soap that wouldn't make her skin dry and itchy, a toothbrush and some baking soda to mix into a paste, some fabric for sanitary rags, a small sewing kit, a spare pair of stockings, and a handful of other small items that would fit in the large medical satchel—since she didn't feel the need for another portmanteau and she probably couldn't afford it, anyway. What she was carrying would have to suffice. If she had enough money left over for new clothes, she'd see about getting some in Tacoma.

After paying the man behind the counter, she returned outside to the busy street with its narrow wooden walkways—or, sometimes, no walkways at all.

When she emerged into the street again, it was almost thoroughly dark, though the sky was still orange around its western edge. Low, tree-smattered mountains, jagged ridges, and the man-made corners of walls had cut off the last of the winter afternoon light, and lamps were coming up everywhere. They popped and fizzed into a white, incandescent glow as a pair of small brown boys in clean gray uniforms took an *L*-shaped key and removed a panel at the base of the light, then flipped a switch therein. One by one they lit the street this way.

On the nearest corner, a stack of the morning's leftover newspapers was being gathered up for disposal, and a stand for periodicals was closing up and being disassembled. Mercy approached the newspaper stack and the red-haired teenager who was lifting the remaining bundles onto the waste cart. She asked, "Can I buy one off you?"

He said, "It's late. May as well wait for the next edition; it'll come up in a few hours."

She looked back and forth between him and the round-bellied man who was hefting the magazines and street literature into his cart. Then she asked, "Will you be here in a few hours? It looks like you're leaving."

The kid shifted his eyes sideways, and brought them back to her, but he wore them lidded and wary. He told her, "I don't rightly know. Things are about to get messy, I think."

"You think?"

"Well, that's what I heard."

The fat man on the waste cart caught just enough of this to join the conversation. "Ma'am, I don't know what you're doing here—if you missed a train or if you're just passing through, or whatever reason you're lingering on the southside all by your lonesome—but wherever you're going, you might want to head there sooner rather than later."

"The line," she guessed.

He nodded. "It's coming, one way or t'other. Our boys is gonna hole up here, set up the city for siege and response. Don't you worry, though. They won't take Chatty down. I think they know it, too. I don't know what they's trying to prove by bumping up against us like this, but it's all right if they want to get theyselves killed."

"I heard they brought a walker to the fight last night," Mercy fished.

He snapped, "And we brought ours, and brought theirs down. They think they got a foothold, though, so they sneaking in around Raccoon and lining up behind Signal," he said, meaning that the Union was creeping around from the mountains to the west and north.

"I heard they took the *Dreadnought* out of play," said the boy as he went back to discarding his papers. "I heard they took it back north, or maybe east, to feed another cracker line. Maybe they won't come no closer, not without their big old engine to beef 'em up."

She said, "*Dreadnought*. That's the engine they used to move the walker, ain't it?"

The magazine man said, "Yeah, they use it to tote around their biggest war toys." He sat on the back of the cart, dipping it lower on its axle. "You see, miss, what they done is, they built themselves the biggest, meanest engine they could imagine, and then they trussed it up with enough armor and artillery to be a real war machine. Ready to go from place to place, easy as anything else that rolls along a line." He made a little gesture, like a man playing with a child's cars on a carpet railway.

"It's a monster," said the boy.

"It's a fine piece of engineering," the man countered. "But it's only an engine—and just *one* engine, at that. Even if they brought it here, to Fort Chattanooga, and used it to try and rout the lot of us straight back across the Georgia state line, it wouldn't do no good."

Mercy asked, "And why is that?"

He pointed a finger at her and said, "Because I don't give two pebbles of squirrel shit how awesome the *Dreadnought* is. This-here is the proper rail exchange for everything east of Houston and north of Tallahassee. We got enough engines here to run it out on a rail." He chuckled at his own joke. "It can't take on all of us, not all at once. Not here. This-here city is *made* of rails, miss. It's made of steel, and coal, and sweat, and no one train is going to come here and change *nothing*. 'Sides," he added. "Monster or no, it can't run across the street, or waltz up a rock wall and bust a line into a mountain."

"That's what the walkers are for," the boy chimed in.

"Yeah, well." The man spit a gob of tobacco into the street. "They only got a handful of those, and after last night, they're down one. We got half a dozen, and ours are pushed by Texas crude, not by old-fashioned steam. It's the way of the future!" he assured Mercy. "This city, right here. This is where the future puts its feet on the ground and starts kicking Yankee ass. Right here," he emphasized, and waggled his rear end off the edge of the cart. He hit the ground with a whump, and reached for the last pile or two of papers. He pointed his finger back at her one more time and said, "But for now, I think ladies ought to find their way out of the city limits. Things might get worse before they line up again."

Then he brought the gate up on the cart with a satisfied slam, tipped his hat in salutation, and took the reins of the mule who was hitched up to it, leading the whole setup away.

Mercy wandered back toward the St. George and thanked the man at the desk when he indicated that supper was well under way. She settled for what she found there, then returned to the safety of her room.

Once there, she took inventory of what she had left, stacking her money in discrete piles. "Lord Almighty," she said aloud. "This is going to be one hell of a mess, Daddy."

The word startled her. She'd never called her stepfather anything but "Father," and she could hardly remember Jeremiah Granville Swakhammer, except from her mother's disappointment. In the years since he'd left them both, she'd heard more about him than she'd ever personally experienced—and what she'd heard had run the gamut, depending on the speaker.

She knew he was a big man, and uncommonly strong, and not terribly well educated—but none too stupid, either. She knew he was funny sometimes. She remembered laughing. Vividly, it hijacked her. Just a flash, a tiny moment of being a child, and seeing something hilarious, coming from her father. The feeling of warmth, the knee-high grass tickling her legs under her dress, and the primroses she'd tied together and stuck in her hair with a bobby pin. He was showing her something, and making a game of it.

But the game eluded her. The memory stayed sharp, but contained few details.

And it wasn't enough to tell her why she was doing this. Not really.

It'd been a hard enough crawl already, just from Richmond to the bottommost side of Tennessee; and the trip had hardly begun. What on earth was she doing, crossing a whole world by herself to see a man she could barely recall?

"I don't know," she said to the small piles of money, and the new stockings and gloves and toiletries laid out across the bed, "I guess now that Phillip's gone, I just don't have anywhere to go. Or, at least," she amended the sentiment with a catch in her throat, "I don't have anywhere I've gotta *be*."

She repacked everything, rolling the cloth items tightly and arranging the rest carefully, cramming it all into the medical satchel that she hadn't let out of her sight since leaving the hospital. Then she went downstairs and left a note asking to be roused for breakfast, and settled down for a badly needed night of sleep.

She dreamed of Phillip's corpse, friendly and waving a handkerchief from the train platform, seeing her off as she left him for parts unknown. And she awoke in the night with a sob, clutching her chest, her face covered in tears.

Seven

It had been dark when she first entered the Fort at Chattanooga, and she hadn't noticed the gates. She knew she'd dozed, but she must've been damn near dead asleep to have missed them—or so she decided, as the train dragged her through them at a swift crawl, tugging the whole line of cars through a pair of vast steel portals. They rose so far up into the sky that if Mercy craned her neck to see out the window, she could just barely make out the tops of the things—and the guards who paced back and forth there—before the train had successfully threaded through them. Afterwards, the massive hydraulic hinges crushed the mechanical doors shut once more with a grinding of metal and hissing of steam that could be heard even over the engine and the clacking of the wheels being vigorously pumped along the rails.

The engine on Mercy's new train was called *Virginia Lightning*. Its hand-painted letters had caught her eye as she boarded the first car in the line, standing out in green and white against the matte black body of the engine. She'd be traveling in the first class compartment, for all that she hadn't the money to afford it. But it was either that, the colored car, or nothing at all—or so she'd been informed at the ticket counter. It had been dumb luck that assigned her to the Pullman; a pair of ragged soldiers had tottered along, and one of them recognized her as the woman who'd done her best to save the colonel, who still clung to life somewhere, en route to either a proper hospital or a Christian burial. Between them, the two gray-clad boys had rustled through their pockets and pulled out enough money to grant the nurse the upgrade, against her feeble protests.

So she was to ride in the *fancy* Pullman car, all the way to Memphis.

From her semi-comfortable seat in the passenger car, Mercy had witnessed half a dozen tearful partings and one or two solemn good-byes. They reminded her of a man she'd once lovingly seen off to war. She shuddered at the thought of her dream, and closed her eyes when it was too much, trying to remember other things, without much success.

It had been so long since she'd seen Phillip, and now she wouldn't see him again. That ought to make his face, or the sound of his voice, more precious to her mind, but strangely, this wasn't so. What was left in his absence was an empty, sorrowful discomfort. She wondered if it wouldn't eventually grow dull or dim if she worried at it enough, or softened and more palatable. Easier to overlook. Forgotten, or at least smoothed into some pearl-like blandness, if not a thing of beauty.

She looked around her car, which was laden with comfortably middle-class women of many shapes and ages, plus a few surly children who'd had the seriousness of the occasion impressed upon them until they grudgingly held their tongues.

The first two hours on the track between Fort Chattanooga and Memphis passed dully, with all the passengers acting docile and blank, waiting for their destination, and counting on precious little entertainment in the interim. But in the third hour, Mercy was startled by a tap on her shoulder. When she turned around, she gazed up into the face of a mulatto woman, perhaps forty years old or a little more.

She was dressed in clothing nicer than anything Mercy had ever personally owned, and she smelled faintly of gardenias, or some perfume derived therefrom. Her hair had been braided up and back, and a hat was perched on it with such firmness that the nurse doubted she could've knocked it loose with a stick.

"Pardon me," said the woman. "I don't mean to bother you, but I was wondering if you were a nurse. I saw the cloak, and your bag, there."

"Yes, I'm a nurse."

"From the fields?"

"Not on purpose," Mercy said. "But I been in the fields, just the other night."

The train gave a shrug as it changed its velocity to climb a low grade. The woman shrugged with it and asked, "Could I sit here, just a moment?"

Mercy said, "I don't see why not," even though she was pretty sure that plenty of other people in the car could think of a few good reasons. Most of the other women in the car shifted or adjusted their luggage, and either pretended not to look, or made a point of looking. Still, Mercy gestured to the empty seat on the aisle.

But the woman kept standing, and said, "My name's Agatha Hyde, and I'm on my way to Memphis to meet my brother. My son—he's in the next car back—he was tomfooling around this morning as we were getting ready to leave, and I'm afraid he might have broken his foot falling down the stairs. We wrapped him up and headed out because we had a train to catch, same as everyone on board here; but he won't stop crying about it, and it seems like it's swelling up something awful. I was hoping, maybe, that I could ask you if you'd take a look at it."

"Mrs. . . . Mrs. Hyde," Mercy said, "I'm not a doctor or anything, and—"

"I can pay you," she said quickly. "I can appreciate the position I'm putting you in, here like this, but my boy's only a little thing, and I'd hate for him to grow up lame because I didn't know how to fix his bones and we couldn't find a colored doctor till Memphis."

Mercy opened her mouth to say something about how it wasn't about the money, but the money did in fact make it easier for her to say, "I suppose I could take a look. I can't make you any promises, though."

Someone to the rear of the car said, *"Honestly,"* under her breath, but no one else said a word as Mercy collected her bag and followed the older woman back into the next car.

The next car back was emptier than Mercy's. Most of the people in it had skin in shades varying from toffee to ink, and there was a greater spread of passengers represented, from working class to leisure class. Again, she mostly saw women and children; but a few old men gathered at the back, playing chess on a board they balanced on the seat between them. Everyone gazed at her curiously. Mercy stiffened, but said, "Hello."

Some of them said hello back, and some of them didn't.

Mrs. Hyde led Mercy over to a corner row, where two brown children were wearing crisp Sunday clothes. One of them had his arms crossed over his chest, and dried tear-trails marking his cheeks. His foot was wrapped up to such a size that he could've hidden a hatbox under the bandages.

Mercy took the bench across from him and said, "Hi, there, um . . ."

"His name's Charles."

"Charles, all right. Hi, there, Charles. I'm Nurse Mercy," she told him, and gestured at his foot. "Your momma's asked me to take a peek at your foot. Would that be fine with you?"

He ran his forearm under his nose to wipe it, and squinted at her. Charles was seven or eight, and he looked precisely as disgruntled as one might expect from a boy with his foot wrapped so extensively. But he nodded, and Mercy told him, "Good. That's good."

Children had never been her favorite patients, though, as the doctors at Robertson had pointed out more than once, grown men often behaved far worse than little boys. Mercy couldn't argue, but she hadn't had little boys in her care too much, except for a few of the other nurses' children, or the children of the widows or wives of the maimed who came to the hospital to visit. Small *colored* children were even farther out of her realm of expertise, and small colored children with monied parents went right past her threshold of experience.

But all things being equal, she figured a busted-up leg was a busted-up leg, and there was no sense in letting the little fellow suffer from it if there was anything she could do about it.

So she did her best to ignore the inquisitive eyes that followed her every move. Before long, she came to the conclusion that she was not much more out of place in the colored car than in the rich car, where her fellow passengers were high-class ladies who'd never worked a day in their lives, with their trussed-up offspring and upturned noses.

She turned back to Charles, saying, "Here, I'm just gonna pick up your leg and set it on my knees, you see?" as she took the tiny leg and began the process of unwinding the swaths of cloth that bound it.

Mrs. Hyde said, "I do appreciate you taking the time like this. I know you're only traveling, and not working, and as I told you, I don't mind paying for the service. There's not a doctor on this train, and even if there was one, I don't know that he'd bother with us. But I thought maybe another woman . . ."

Mercy said, "I understand," because she did, and because she wasn't sure what else she should say to follow that.

"Do you have any children of your own?"

"No," she said. "My husband died not long after we married. We never had no children."

"I'm sorry," said Mrs. Hyde. "He died in the war?"

Mercy nodded. And suddenly, because she'd wanted to say it

for so long, but had no one to say it to, she blurted out in a hard whisper, "He was from Kentucky. He died at Andersonville."

Taken aback, Mrs. Hyde said, "But you . . . you're—"

"I been working at the Rebel hospital up in Richmond. Patching up the grays."

"Oh my," said the other woman. "It's . . ." She hesitated. "These are complicated times. And I'm sorry about your Yank," she said the word softly. "But I'm glad you're here on board, and I mean every word when I say I thank you."

Mercy reached the end of the winding bandages. The limb she unwrapped had met some terrible event; that much was plain. The top of the foot was swollen far beyond its regular size, and Charles's tears flowed afresh when the nurse prodded it.

Mercy asked, "What'd he do, exactly?"

Mrs. Hyde frowned at the child, who grimaced back with his lower lip puckering. "He fell down the stairs, running after his sister. If he'd had his shoes on like I told him, he might not've slipped."

Charles began, "She took my—"

"I don't care," his mother said, punctuating every word with a firmness that told the boy that the time for arguing was well past. "You knew better."

"Ow!"

"Sorry, sugar," Mercy said. She lifted the foot and peered at it from all the other angles before saying, "Maybe I'm wrong, but . . ." She looked again, and harder, and pressed against the purpled flesh over the boy's protests. "It's not the worst I ever seen by a long shot. I think probably he's cracked a couple of the little bones here on the top of his foot, and maybe broke one outright. But it could be worse. If he'd messed up his ankle, that would've been a lot harder to heal. These little ones over here—" She indicated the spot where the real damage appeared to have occurred. "—there's not much to be done about them. All you can do is wrap his foot up tight and keep him off it, as much as you can. And once it heals up, it won't bother his walking too bad, like it would if it'd broken at a joint."

"Can you show me how to wrap it up?"

She nodded, and reached into her bag. "I've got some willow extract here—let me give you some. It won't speed up the healing, but it'll take the edge off the pain and swelling some." Then she straightened the bandage and tore about half its length off. "If you tie it right," she explained, "you only need about this much."

She straightened the boy's foot out. He whimpered, and chewed on the back of his hand.

Mercy wound the cloth tightly, but not so tightly that she'd cut off all the blood. She braced it back around his ankle to hold it stiff, and finally, when she was done, she asked Mrs. Hyde to hold the end while she rustled around in her bag again. She pulled out a pair of safety pins and fastened it, then put the boy's foot back down.

Mrs. Hyde cooed over him briefly, telling him how brave he'd been, and she reached for a bag that had been tucked under the other child's arm. "Thank you so much, Nurse. . . . Here, let me dip into the travel fund and see—"

But Mercy shook her head, having come to a decision on the matter. "No, please. That's not necessary. All I did was tie up his foot. It's not a big thing, and he'll be all right."

"Please, I insist!"

But Mercy hemmed and hawed, rising to leave, and finally Mrs. Hyde sighed and gave up. "If you won't take any money, that's fine. But listen, dear," she said—which Mercy thought sounded strange coming from a mixed woman, whether or not she was almost old enough to be Mercy's mother—"pretty much everyone here's getting off in Memphis. And you are, too, isn't that right?"

"That's right," she said.

Mrs. Hyde rifled through her bag once more and pulled out a sharp white card with her name printed on it, and the legend, "The

Cormorant: Traditional Cuisine, Soul Food, and Fine Dining for All Types." Beneath that was listed, "Knoxville, Chattanooga, Memphis."

She said, "This is my restaurant. Or, they're my restaurants, mine and my sister's."

"You have your own restaurants? I didn't know . . ." She knew of some free colored men who owned property in Richmond, but she'd never heard of a woman owning anything like this.

Mrs. Hyde shrugged. "There used to be laws about it, but those laws are getting looser. And there's ways around them now. These days."

"Restaurants," Mercy said again, taking the card and reading it. "You've got three of them?"

"The one in Memphis just opened last year. We started in Knoxville and worked our way west," she said proudly. Then a sly look crossed her face. She added, "You're a southern girl, I can see that plain as day. But I bet you never had anyone but your momma cooking for you."

"Yeah. I grew up on a farm. We had farmhands, but nobody to help with . . ." She was beginning to catch on. She said, "You, and your sister—I guess you used to be—" She stopped herself from saying *house niggers* because suddenly it seemed impolite, or maybe she only felt outclassed. She continued, "You used to do all the cooking for the rich ladies, in the plantations."

Mrs. Hyde winked at her. "Some of us didn't feel like sticking around as employees, for what they were talking about paying us. We figured we could do better on our own. My sister Adele, she wrote our first cookbook, and it sold like *crazy*! Then we went into business together, thinking we could make the food ourselves and sell it just as easy."

"Nice!" Mercy exclaimed with genuine admiration. "And it's called the Cormorant? Or all three of them are?"

"Mm-hmm. It's a franchise, that's what it's called. And you listen to me, dear," she said it again. "You take this card, and you show it to the host at the Memphis Cormorant. You tell him I said to let you have anything you want, and I'll take care of it."

Mercy said, "Gosh, thank you—I mean it, thank you very much. I've been eating travel food for the last few days, and I don't mind telling you, that sounds real good right about now."

Mrs. Hyde patted her arm. "Don't you worry about it. And thank you, for fixing up my Charlie."

The nurse left with the card, and returned to her original seat in the forward car.

Memphis was only a few hours more, plus or minus a stop or two where people got off and people got on. The train filled up and emptied out in unequal measure, since more people were headed for Memphis than to Lawrenceburg, Kimball, Selmer, or Somerville.

But eventually the Memphis station rolled into view, a beautiful white beaux arts building that looked like a museum. Mercy thought it was definitely the prettiest thing she'd seen in Tennessee thus far, day or night, city or countryside. Fort Chattanooga was a military garrison, and every stop in between had featured small-town nondescript style. This station, though . . . it made the nurse crane her head around to see out the window again, if only to admire it before she could enter its undoubtedly hallowed halls.

The train pulled into its slot with a squeal of the brakes that pinched the track all along the vehicle's length, and Mercy stepped out into a crowd that flowed riverlike along the platforms, under the overhangs that shaded waiting and debarking travelers from the sun.

Now it was growing late again, and cooler, which the nurse found disorienting. It felt as though her entire life had been lived from dusk to dawn ever since she learned of Phillip, only tiptoeing around the edges of sunset or sunrise, and sleeping or traveling all day.

She stretched, then turned her neck to and fro to let it pop and spring back to its usual position. Her satchel was heavy in her arms, more so now than ever with the added weight of the guns; she slung it over one shoulder, under her cloak. The cloak felt almost too warm, but with night coming on, she'd be glad to have it—she knew that—and, anyway, she didn't want to carry it.

Mercy shuffled along in the crowd until she'd reached the lovely terminal building and filtered inside it. The interior was as lovely as the exterior promised, with marbled floors that shone so brightly, the lanterns' reflections made Mercy squint. Every surface was shined, from the polished wood of the handrails and guardrails to the brass of the fixtures and the glass of the ticket windows.

But although the building was a marvel, Mercy was famished, so she hastily ushered herself out and away from it, pausing only to ask directions to the restaurant called the Cormorant and hailing a buggy cab to take her there. She fondled the card between her fingers and hoped it'd be enough, as promised, and furthermore that she wouldn't find herself embarrassingly underdressed. This latter thought burrowed beneath her outer layer of security and festered there, remembering Mrs. Hyde's fine clothes and her mannered children and comparing them to her own stained dress and gunsmoke-smelling cloak.

The Cormorant looked to be a firmly middle-class establishment, and a popular one. Mercy saw mostly white people coming and going, but there were a handful of colored people (relegated to a separate dining section, she noted when she arrived inside), and even a pair of Indian men wearing matching clothes that may or may not have been some kind of uniform.

A man at a pedestal asked if he could help her, and she handed him the card that by now she'd worn so thoroughly that the corners had curled. "I . . . I talked to Mrs. Hyde, on the train here from Fort Chattanooga. She said if I gave this to you, that—"

"Oh, yes!" he said sharply. "Yes, indeed. Are you alone to-night, Miss—" He spied the ring on her finger. "Missus?"

"Lynch. Yes, I'm alone tonight. Is that all right?" She looked around and saw no one else dining alone, and her sense of conspicuousness grew. She was on the verge of changing her mind altogether and begging the host's pardon before she left when a familiar voice cried out from a table by the far left wall.

"Nurse? Nurse Mercy, wasn't that it? Well look at *you*," declared Mrs. Henderson, from the dirigible and its terrible aftermath. "Dear child, you made your way to Memphis after all." The older woman stood and crossed the room, dodging a serving girl or two and taking Mercy's hand. "I'm so glad you arrived here safely! Won't you join us?"

She gestured toward the table, and to her husband, who was freshly washed and smiling happily at her over his shoulder.

Mercy said, "That'd be very kind, thank you."

The nurse continued to feel out of place, but when seated with the Hendersons, she grew more at ease. Mercy suspected quite quickly that Mrs. Henderson was overjoyed by the prospect of conversation with someone other than her addled husband, and it was hard to blame her. The two of them did most of the talking until supper arrived.

Mercy had chosen the sweet potatoes and pork chops, with apple pie for dessert, and she could scarcely pause between bites to keep up her end of the chatter. When she was finally so full that she thought she'd burst, she leaned back and said aloud, "Well, that was just wonderful! That lady sure knows how to make a pie, I'll tell you what."

Mrs. Henderson's brows knit ever so slightly. "Lady? But I thought you said you met her in the colored car?"

"Yes ma'am."

"Ah." Mrs. Henderson sipped at the tea that had come at the end of the meal, delivering only a tiny glance of reproach at the nurse, who suddenly felt a little stubborn about the whole thing, and outclassed again from another direction entirely.

"Well," she said at the risk of being rude. "She was nice to me, and she can cook like the devil."

The older woman opted to change the subject. "At any rate." She concluded the phrase as if it were a full sentence, and began again. "How long do you plan to remain here in Memphis?"

"Not too long. I need to find a boat that'll take me upriver."

"Upriver?" Mr. Henderson piped up with a voice that declared him to be deeply appalled by the prospect. "Little missy, what would . . ." But then some other thing snared his attention, upending his displeasure and scattering his attention like a child's blocks.

His wife picked up the thread and said, "I'm sure he only means, it's wartime and you're going north? A woman of your skills and abilities? You should stay here, with our lads, and perform your patriotic duties. If not at the Robertson Hospital— that's where you'd been before, correct?—then perhaps one of the Fort's establishments, or even here, in Memphis. A good nurse is always in need."

"My father's gone west, and contracted some illness. I'm not sure what ails him, but I mean to go see to him, all the same." Not so far from the truth, after all. And a daughter's duty might compete with a nurse's.

"West, you say? Off to the Republic, then, are you?"

"No ma'am. Wester than that. I'm going all the way to the coast, to the Washington territory."

"Gracious me, that's an alarming proposition. Going all that way, all by yourself?" she asked, setting her cup down on the saucer with a sturdy clink.

Mercy said, "My husband died. There's nobody left to go with me."

"I suppose no one can fault you for the trouble, but my, how it worries me! In my day and age, young ladies wouldn't *dream* of such travels alone, not even working women like yourself—no offense, of course. Now, more than ever, I fear it's all the worse for the war."

"I'm inclined to agree with you," Mercy said, even though she wasn't, though she wasn't offended either. "But you know what they say about desperate times and desperate measures. I'll be all right. I just need to find a place to sleep and get on a steamer first thing in the morning, to haul me up to St. Louis."

Mr. Henderson revived again, long enough to nod and say, "St. Louis. A fine city."

"Is it?" Mercy asked politely, happy to redirect the topic. "I've never been before."

"Transcontinental," he said. "Lines there'll take you right to the water, clear out to the Pacific."

She nodded. "They'll take me to Tacoma. That's where I'm headed in the long run, so St. Louis is where I'm going for now."

Mrs. Henderson pursed her lips and said, "I might be able to help with the ship you seek, if not necessarily a place to stay for the night."

Mercy understood. The Hendersons were undoubtedly staying somewhere where she couldn't possibly afford to join them. "I'll gratefully take any suggestions you can give me, ma'am."

Satisfied by this much, at least, Mrs. Henderson said, "Very well. If you make your way down to the pier, I believe the steamer *Providence* is still docked there, at least through tomorrow morning. I can't recall precisely when Benham said they'd be setting forth."

"I'm sorry . . . Benham?"

"My brother-in-law. My sister married him. She's gone now, God rest her soul, but he's a good fellow in his way, and the *Providence* is his ship. He has a special dispensation to travel back and forth through the borders and boundaries; he's a Texan by birth, you see, and technically his ship is politically undeclared."

"Technically." Mercy knew what *that* meant. Everybody knew Texas worked with the Confederacy, fueling it and feeding it. Keeping it alive.

"Technically," Mrs. Henderson repeated without a wink or a smile, but with a rush of breath that indicated some tiny mote of clandestine excitement. "If you're bound for St. Louis, he can get you there faster than any certified ship you might otherwise board. Oh, the checkpoints are *dreadful*. They drag the journey out by two or three days sometimes."

"Really? I've never been up or down the river, so I don't know how it works."

"Oh, it doesn't work at *all*. That's the problem! It's an endless, halting parade of inspections, bribes, and nonsense—but if you're aboard a Texas vessel, you'll find less inconvenience along the way."

"It's because of their guns!" declared Mr. Henderson, once more escaping his reverie, bobbing out of it as if to gasp for air.

"Concise, my love." Mrs. Henderson gave him a smile. "And correct. Texans are heavily armed and often impatient. They don't need to be transporting arms and gunpowder to create a great nuisance for anyone who stops them, so they tend to be stopped . . . less often."

"That's good to know," Mercy said, suddenly eager to wrap up the meal and escape the company—which wasn't fair, she thought, but the Hendersons made her feel a little on display, and still quite awkwardly conspicuous. She also still needed to find lodging for the night. She stifled a yawn with the back of her hand. "I thank you for all the kind suggestions, and the company for the meal. But I hope you'll excuse me now. It's getting late, and I've had a rough couple of days."

"Don't we know it!" Mrs. Henderson exclaimed. She exclaimed almost every short thing she said, and now that it'd been noticed, Mercy couldn't unnotice it.

The nurse took her napkin off her lap, wadded it up beside the plate, thanked the couple once more, and gathered her satchel to leave.

Outside, it was dark yet again.

Down the street, Mercy spied a Salvation Army sign swinging beneath a fizzing gas lamp. This seemed like a safe enough place to ask for directions, so she knocked upon the door and was greeted by a small, squat woman in a gray suit that matched her hair. Her face was round and friendly. She asked if she could be of service.

"I'm Mrs. Leotine Gaines," she declared. She looked Mercy up and down, and before the nurse could reply, she asked, "Are you a sister from one of our English offices?"

"Oh, no. I'm sorry, I'm not," Mercy said. Any doubts Mrs. Gaines might've had would surely be buffeted away by the Virginia accent. "I'm from Richmond, and only passing through. But I was looking for a place to spend the night, and I wondered if you might direct me to something safe and quiet. I have to catch a steamer in the morning."

"Ah." Mrs. Gaines said it with a happy snap. "And I'm not mistaken, am I? I recognize it now, the cross you carry. It's not so different from our own. You're a medical woman, yes?"

Mercy grinned, having not heard it put that way before. "I'm a nurse. I have a letter from the Robertson Hospital, anyway."

"Please, won't you come on inside? I have a small proposal for you."

"A proposal?"

"Certainly. An exchange of services, if you will. Come on, Nurse—or, Mrs. . . . I'm sorry, I didn't catch your name."

"Lynch. I'm Mercy Lynch," she said. It occurred to her that she hadn't given anyone her Christian name since she'd taken to the road, though her own motivations in the matter were unclear, even to herself.

"Nurse Lynch. Yes, indeed. Come in, and let me get you some tea."

"But, ma'am, I'm awful run down. I've had . . . too much excitement these last few nights. It's a humdinger of a story. I don't know if you'd even believe me, if I told you. But I'm so worn out."

Mrs. Gaines said cheerfully, "Tea will take the edge off of that! I'll set a kettle on. Here, make yourself comfortable at the table there, in our kitchen area." With a broad sweep of her arm, she indicated a room beyond an open doorway. "I'd see you to the dining area, but it's been cleaned up and sorted for the night, and besides, right now most of the people living here are men— single men, many of them all torn up from the war. We tend to leave the proper dining area for them. The other ladies and I take our victuals back here."

She seized a kettle as promised, filled it with water, and set it to boil while Mercy took a seat at a low wood table set with benches on either side. She dropped the satchel beside her left thigh. As the stove heated and the water within the kettle warmed, Mrs. Gaines sat down across the table from Mercy and continued. "You see, it's as I said: Here at this mission we help the men who've fallen down on their luck, as well as those who've taken to alcohol or other vices. It's our good Christian duty. But right now, our doctor is out at the front, having been called there by none other than General Jackson himself, and we're . . . shall we say . . . between replacements right now. My own nursing skills are minimal at best, and I think I do myself too much credit to even say that much. It's a pity, too, because we have a handful of fellows here in various stages of . . . oh, I can't say what! It's surpassing strange, is all I know. They seem to be dying of . . . not a disease, precisely. But I'd love a professional's opinion on the matter, and if you wouldn't mind giving them an hour of attention, I'd be more than happy to see you settled in one of our officer's suites upstairs."

Mercy didn't take long to think about it. It'd take her a couple of hours to find someplace else to stay for the night, likely as not, and the kettle was nearly boiling. She didn't know what a Salvation Army officer's suite was, but if it came with a bed and a basin, she'd chalk it up as a lucky find.

"All right, Mrs. Gaines. I expect I won't get a better offer tonight, anyhow."

"I expect you won't." She winked, and pulled the kettle from the stove. "Not in this part of town, at any rate."

"It didn't seem so bad," Mercy said, eyeing the china cup. "There's a nice restaurant down the street."

"The Cormorant? Yes, it's a good place with good food, if you can afford it. The neighborhood is beginning to gentrify, in bits and pieces, and the restaurant is pulling more than its fair weight. It's helped by its proximity to the train station, I imagine, and the river isn't so awful far away, either."

When the tea was finally ready to sip, Mercy sipped more extensively than Mrs. Gaines, who was happy to provide most of the chatter.

It turned out that Mrs. Gaines was originally of Maryland, which satisfied Mercy's curiosity about her somewhat un-Tennessee-like accent; and that she was also widowed without any children. She'd been visiting distant cousins in England when she'd learned of the Salvation Army and its intent, and she'd been intensely eager to begin a chapter back in her own land. How she'd wound up in Memphis remained a bit of a veiled mystery, but Mercy didn't pry.

When the tea had been drunk and the china washed and put away, Mrs. Gaines led Mercy back through the building with a lamp in hand to augment the few that had been placed on the walls but turned down low on account of the hour.

"This once was a Catholic school," whispered Mrs. Gaines. "It's suited our purposes well, since it was laid out for dormitories and classrooms. This way, and up these stairs, if you please. I'm afraid we've had to isolate the sicker men from the others," she said as she pulled a ring of iron keys out of a pocket in her suit.

Mrs. Gaines took a particularly pointed key, jammed it into the lock, turned it, and retrieved it. Then she added, "Please don't think less of us for the restraints."

The nurse's voice slipped half an octave out of her usual range. "Restraints?"

Mrs. Gaines pleaded, "Just look at them, and you'll see. And be careful. Don't let them bite you."

"Bite me?"

"Yes, bite. They do that sometimes, I'm afraid. But don't worry—I'm convinced that their ailment is caused by a substance, and not some unaccountable microbe or spore. But the bites *do* hurt, and they are prone to inflammation. Again, I'd beg you not to judge our handling of the matter until you see for yourself."

Finally, she opened the door. She leaned forward, setting the lamp on a shelf to the left of the doorframe, then picked up a candle to light a few other spots as well. The light did nothing to wash away the horror. In fact, the flickering gold, white, and red wobbly beams only added a more gruesome cast to the scene.

Four men lay restrained on pallets, each suffering from the same affliction. All were bone thin, with skin hanging from the peaks and joints of their skeletons like rags on a line, and all were boasting a set of cankerous sores around the mouth and the nose—and almost entirely across one poor man's eyes. It was difficult to see from the diluted light in the windowless room, but it looked to Mercy like their skin had a yellowish tinge, as if the kidneys or liver were the root of the problem. It looked familiar—or, rather, it looked like the logical conclusion of something familiar.

"Wheezers," she breathed.

Mrs. Gaines looked at her strangely but did not ask any questions yet.

One man moaned. The other three simply lay there, either sleeping or dying.

"That's Irvin," Mrs. Gaines said softly of the moaner. "He's the one in the best condition. You might actually get a few words out of him. He's more lucid than the rest."

"And you took him in, like this? With the wounded veterans and alcoholics?" Mercy asked, keeping her voice low and hoping that by lowering her volume, she could diminish the reproach that filled the question.

"The symptoms were gentler when these men arrived. But things deteriorated so badly, so quickly; at first we thought we had a plague on our hands, but it became clear within a few weeks that the ailment is self-inflicted." Mrs. Gaines shook her head. "The best I can ascertain is that there's some form of drug that's becoming common out on the lines—making its way both north and south, amongst the foot soldiers. You know how they trade amongst themselves. They call it 'sap,' or sometimes 'yellow sap,' though I've heard other designations for it, too. Sick sand, grit, and . . . well, some of their names aren't very polite."

Mercy sat down beside Irvin. He did seem to be the least afflicted, though he still presented the very picture of death warmed over in a chamber pot. She'd seen it before, the hue of his skin and dull crust of his sores. But this went well beyond anything she'd encountered in the Robertson. This was something else, or something more extensive.

Mrs. Gaines hovered, wringing her hands. "Have you ever seen anything like it?"

Irvin's head rolled slowly so that he looked at her, without really looking at her at all. He did turn his neck so that he faced her direction, but whether he was curious or simply delirious, it was hard to tell. His lids cracked open, revealing squishy, yellowish eyeballs that had all the life of half-cooked egg whites.

"Maybe," she replied. Then she said, "Hello there, Irvin." She said it nervously, keeping an eye on his mouth, and the oversized teeth that dwelled therein. The warning about the bites had stuck with her like a tick.

It might have been a trick of Mercy's imagination, but she thought the cadaverous lad nodded, so she took this as encouragement and continued. "Irvin, I'm going to . . . I'm going to examine you a little bit, and see if I can't . . . um . . . *help*."

He did not protest, so she brought the lamp closer and used it to determine that his pupils were only scarcely reacting to the light; and he did not flinch or fuss when she turned his head to the side to peer into the canal of his nearest ear—which was clotted like a pollen-laden flower. She took a fingernail to the outermost crust of this grainy gold stuff and it chipped away as if it'd grown there like lichen on the side of a boat.

Mrs. Gaines did her best to keep from wrinkling her nose, and did an admirable job of at least keeping the heights of her discomfort to herself. She observed Mercy's every move closely and carefully, without any kind of interference, except to say, "His ears have been leaking like that for days now. I don't think it bodes well for him. I mean, you can see the other gentlemen have the same problem—it's not mere wax, you can tell that for yourself."

"No, not wax. It's more like dried-up paste." She shifted the lamp, and Irvin obligingly leaned his head back, as Mercy directed. "And it's all up his nose, too. Good Lord, look at those sores. They must hurt like hell."

Mrs. Gaines frowned briefly but outright at her language, but didn't say anything about it. "One would think. And they do pick at the sores, which only makes them worse."

"It looks almost like . . ." She peered closer. "The crust from sun poisoning. Like blisters that have festered, popped, and dried. Mrs. Gaines, I assume these men are regularly turned over and cleaned?"

The other woman's mouth went tight. "We pay some of our

negro washwomen extra to come up here and perform those duties. But this isn't a hospital. We don't have staff that's prepared
or qualified to do such things."

Mercy waved her hand as if none of this was relevant to what
she was asking. "Sure, I understand. But could you tell me if the
yellow grit also manifests below the belt?"

Even in the lamplight, Mercy could see Mrs. Gaines redden.
"Ah, yes. Erm . . . yes. It does soil their undergarments as well. I
realize the poor souls can't help themselves, but I *do* wish I knew
what it was, and how to prevent it. They're cleaned daily, I assure
you, top to . . . well, *bottom*. But you see how the material accu-
mulates."

The nurse sniffed at her fingernail and got a whiff of something
sour and sulfurous, with a hint of human body odor attached. Yes.
She knew that smell, and it filled her with disgust.

"Irvin," she said. "Irvin, I'm Nurse Mercy, and I need for you
to talk to me."

He grunted, and tried to look at her through those runny-egg
eyes. *"Nurse,"* he said. He said it *nuss,* just like the men at the hospital.

She couldn't tell if it was an observation or a response, so
she plowed forward. "Irvin, you've been taking something that's
terrible bad for you, haven't you?"

"Sap." The one word came out relatively clear. The next did
also. *"Need."*

"No, you don't *need* it, you silly man. You don't need it and
you can't have it, either. But I want you to tell me about it. Where
did you get it?"

He rolled his face away, but she caught him by the jaw, keeping her fingers well away from his mouth.

"Irvin, answer me," she said as sternly as any governess, and
with all the command she'd learned when bossing about the surly
wounded veterans. "Where did you get the sap?"

"Friend."

"Where did your friend get it?"

Nothing.

"All right. Well, tell me this: Do you smoke it like opium, or eat it, or sniff it up your nose?" She doubted that last guess, since the gritty substance also came out of his ears, and she doubted he'd been ingesting it *that* way.

"Sap," he said again. Petulant.

"Which friend's been giving it to you? Tell me that much."

Irvin's eyes glittered as he choked out, *"Bill Saunders."*

"Bill Saunders!" Mrs. Gaines cried. "I know the man myself; I've given him blankets and food for these last few months, and this is how he repays me?"

"Irvin." Mercy snagged his attention once more. "Where does Bill Saunders get it? Where does the sap come from? What is it made of?"

"West," he said, drawing out the *s* against his discolored teeth, making the word sound wet and possibly venomous. "Gets it . . . West."

Mercy turned to Mrs. Gaines to ask if there were any men from the western territories present. In the short instant that her gaze was directed elsewhere, Irvin's head leaped up off the striped pillow and his jaw snapped like a turtle's, making a vicious grab for the nurse's lingering fingers.

Before Mercy could even think about her reaction, her reaction caught him upside the face in a hard right hook that split his lip and sent runny, strangely colored blood flying against the wall. His bid for human flesh had failed, and now he was unconscious, but Mercy clutched both hands against her bosom and panted like a startled cat.

Eight

The morning dawned clear and a little cold. Mercy collected her things from the officer's suite and departed the Salvation Army mission as soon as was reasonably polite—or, rather, a little sooner; but she hadn't slept terribly well and was eager to leave the building far, far behind. Her dreams had been plagued by skeletal forms with clacking teeth and a taste for fingers, and with the burned-yellow smell of death from the gritty substance in Irvin's ears and nose. She'd dreamt of a whole hospital full of those biting, corpse-like men with runny eyes.

She shuddered under her cloak, although it was not really cool enough to warrant it, and hustled away from the mission as fast as her legs could carry her.

This might've been a bad area of Memphis, or it might only be that it was dawn, and therefore both too late and too early for much traffic; but she found the city as unthreatening as most places, and less threatening than some. Perhaps Mrs. Gaines had been accustomed to a different standard of living up in Maryland. More likely, it occurred to Mercy as she glanced around, the other woman simply wasn't accustomed to living amongst so many people who weren't white.

Mercy stopped a small newspaper boy, unloading his wares onto the curb and setting up his sandwich board. The little fellow had rich brown skin, plus eyes and teeth that seemed unnaturally vital and white compared to the dying men upstairs a block away.

She said, "Boy, could you tell me how to get to the docks?"

He nodded, pointed the way, and gave her a few quick instructions. Like a good little capitalist, he added, "And you can have a paper for just a couple pence 'federate."

A quick glance at the headlines revealed words like *union lines, Chattanooga, civilian crash,* and *Dreadnought.* Since many of those things had had such a recent impact on her person, Mercy said, "All right," took the paper, and handed the boy some change. She rolled the purchase up and stuffed it into her satchel, then followed the child's instructions down to a river district that startled her with its size and complexity.

Between the boats, the boardwalks, the businesses, and the early-morning bustle of commerce beginning, Mercy could see the river in slivers and peeks. She'd heard stories about the Mississippi. Hadn't everyone? But to see it in real life was to be astounded by the sheer breadth of the thing. By comparison, every other waterway she'd ever passed had been a stone-skip across. This one—and she saw it better when she brought herself across the street, dodging a pair of carts overflowing with cargo—seemed all but endless. Standing as near to the edge as the civilized crust of the city would let her stand, she still could not see the other shore through the morning mists.

She held her hand up to shield her eyes, but since the sun was still rising behind her, the hood of her cloak served the same purpose when she turned around to take in the scenery.

The strip was thick with cotton retailers and distributors, their signs swinging back and forth with every gust of wind coming high up off the water to the bluff where the city was built. Down the street she saw piles of crates with stenciled labels that declared

COCOA, COFFEE, and BULK CLOTH. Men haggled, bartered, and bickered with one another, either arranging for transport for items freshly delivered or seeking a ride to someplace else.

She scarcely knew where to begin, so she asked a woman sweeping a stoop which way she might walk in order to buy passage on the river. The broad-waisted shopkeep thought about it a moment and said, "Go down that way, past the next couple of streets, down the bluff to the port proper, and ask about the Anchor Line. Them's the boats what run up and down the river most often, taking people as much as cargo."

Mercy followed her instructions, and in another twenty minutes found herself standing at the docks for the Anchor Line steamers, only to realize that she couldn't possibly afford to take one. Every boat was a floating palace of white gingerbread with gold trim, red paddles, and polished whistles that glinted in the lifting dawn. But this was just as well, because from Mercy's new vantage point, she could see a big REPUBLIC OF TEXAS RIVER TRANSPORT STATION sign strung up between two huge columns shaped like the pumps that dredged up the wealth of that nation.

The *Providence* was right past the pumps, low in the water, God-knew-what filling its cargo hold and a big Lone Star flag flying beside the topmost whistles above a red-and-blue-painted paddle wheel at the stern. It lacked the gingerbread and polish of the Anchor Line crafts, but its design appeared sturdier, more ready to face a fight with a cannon instead of a gloved hand. Maybe it was the set of the prow, like a bulldog's jaw; or maybe it was the gray paint job and straight, unfrilly lettering on the side that announced the vessel's name.

Mercy pulled her cloak's hood back so that her hair hung almost loose, having halfway fallen from the bun she'd put it in an hour earlier. The breeze off the river felt cool and smelled bad, but it was fresh air, and it didn't carry even a whiff of gunpowder—just the occasional flash of petroleum fuel, which reminded her of the mechanized walker outside Fort Chattanooga.

She approached the dock and stood anxiously, not knowing what to do next. Broad-shouldered colored men in plaid cotton shirts hefted crates to and fro, two men to a crate, and a pallid white man with a stack of papers was bickering with another man who held another stack of papers.

From behind her, a voice asked, "Hey there, ma'am. Can I help you with something?" in a Texas accent that could've stopped a clock.

The speaker wore a hodgepodge outfit that was one part Rebel grays, one part western ranch wear, and one part whatever he'd felt like putting on that morning. His mustache and side-burns were blond once, but had faded on to gray in such a fashion that they grew the consistency and color of a corn tassel.

"Er . . . yes. I think. Thank you, sir," she said. "I'm Mercy Lynch, and I'd like to buy passage aboard this boat."

"This ship in particular? That's right specific of you."

"I was referred to the *Providence* by Mrs. Henderson, who I met on a dirigible from Richmond. She told me the captain was her brother-in-law, and he might treat me kindly if I could pay my way. And I can. Pay my way, I mean."

"Adora? On a dirigible? You can't be serious."

"Her first name's Adora?" Mercy responded.

"It fits her about as well as a glove on dog's ass, don't it?"

"I wouldn't go so far as to say *that*—"

His face bloomed into a smile that stretched the full length of the mustache. "That's all right. You're not family, but I am, and I don't just say it, I *declare* it."

She guessed the obvious. "So that must make you the captain? Captain . . . I'm sorry, she only called you Benham, and I won't presume."

"Captain Benham Seaver Greeley, at your service, Nurse. You

are a nurse, ain't you? I've seen that cross before. Salvation Army, isn't it? Or no." He shook his head. "Something else. But I'll be damned if I can recall just what."

"I'm a nurse, yes. With the . . ." She brandished the ornamented side of her satchel. "With the Red Cross. The organization's very popular in Europe. Miss Clara Barton is trying to establish a solid presence here in the Americas, too." She did not add that she was not strictly a member of this agency, in case it would've mattered.

"But that's a *little* like the Salvation Army, right?" he asked, still trying to get a handle on precisely where the situation stood.

"I guess. I mean, I'll treat anybody who needs treatin', and I try not to look at the uniforms. But," she added quickly, "I've been patching up our boys for the last few years. The Rebel boys, I mean. And a few Texians, too."

He nodded, as if this made sense, or at least it didn't confuse him any. "And now you're moving on, to patch up some other boys? I don't know if Adora told you or not, but our run's between St. Louis and New Orleans." He said *New Orleans* in two syllables: *Norleans.* "Our afternoon run will put us in Missouri by the end of next week, so if you're looking to head down to the delta, you may want to wait for the return trip at the end of the month."

"No, no. I'm headed north. And west."

"West? Out into the Republic proper?"

"No sir," she said, and she gave him the same story she'd given half a dozen times already, about her widowhood, and her ailing father in the Pacific Northwest. "So, you see, I need to reach St. Louis, and from there I'll find myself a transcontinental line out to Tacoma."

He let out a low whistle that rattled the edge of his facial hair. "That's a monster of a trip you're taking, Mrs. Lynch. Another two or three thousand miles from here, depending on the way you go and the trains you catch."

"And the steamers I talk my way on board," she added with a note of hope. "Captain, I assure you, I know what I'm doing. And even if I didn't, I'd still have to find a way. Will you carry me as far as St. Louis at your usual rate? I've some savings, set aside for just such an occasion. Though I don't know if you take . . . you must take Confederate money, don't you?"

" 'Federate money, Yankee money, Republic money—all that and anything else worth a stitch. Got paid in wampum once, and one time I took a horse. Another time, somebody paid me in a crate of books I never did read. So I sure do take your Rebel coin, and I'll be happy to have you aboard. The trip upriver will run us about ten days, if all goes according to plan. We can chug along right about thirty-five knots if nothing stops us, and the trip's about three hundred miles."

"Thirty-five knots?" Mercy repeated, attempting to sound impressed, though she had no idea if that was fast, slow, or standing still. "That's . . . quite a clip," she finished.

"Ain't it though? We could run circles in the water round any one of them Anchor Line boats, I tell you what. You want me to let you know why that is?"

"I'd be tickled to hear it."

"This-here boat's not *strictly* a steamer. She's a two-fuel runner, with fully a ton of diesel on board to give her that added boost."

"That sounds like . . . a lot."

"It *is* a lot! And it's a good thing, too. Otherwise, you'd be stuck on this river with me and my motley crew for two weeks or longer. So let me just get your paperwork in line and get you squared away on board, how does that sound?"

"It sounds just about perfect," she said, relieved to have found a spot so easily after all the tangle and turmoil of the trip's first leg.

"Then come along with me. I'm between activities at the

moment, so I'd be happy to show you around." He held out his bent elbow, and she put a hand on it, not for the sake of assistance but for the sake of the show he was clearly delighted to make. He reinforced her suspicion by adding, "We don't get too many ladies going up or down the water. Mostly we get men, moving from one lost fortune to the next one, or running away from the war or running off to it. Sometimes we get merchants and managers, keeping an eye on their stock, and once in a while we get a few Injuns and even Mexies and whatnot. Don't you worry about it, though. Nobody'll give you any grief; you've got my promise on that. Anyone treats you less than purely gallant, and you tell me about it. I'll toss 'em overboard sooner than they could squeak."

"Thank you, Captain. And I'm glad for the offer, but I hope I won't have to take you up on it. Generally speakin', I done some of my best work surrounded by men—in the Robertson, I mean," she blushed and added quickly, lest he get the wrong impression. "I've learned the hard way how to handle them myself."

"Robertson. That rings a bell."

"The big hospital up in Richmond."

"That's right, that's right. They do good work there, don't they? That's the place where they send all the fellows who got real torn up. And there's a lady what runs it, ain't that right?"

Mercy nodded. "Captain Sally. She runs that place good as any man, and probably better than some."

"I don't doubt it," he said, leading her down the gangplank and waving a dismissive arm at the bickering men with papers, who had stopped to call his name in unison. "Not now, boys! Can't you see I've got a lady on my arm? Rare as it happens, I won't have you spoilin' it for me!"

At the end of the gangplank, they took a small step onto the gently swaying deck of the *Providence,* which bobbed very faintly as the river's waves lapped against its underside and the current tugged against the moorings. The decks were clean but made of hand-planed boards with a grain that scraped against Mercy's boots. She let the captain lead her around the lower deck in a full circuit of the craft, then inside to the first deck, where the galley and its workers managed all the meals, the alcohol was stored and served, and a set of tables was reserved in a lounge for the men who wanted a game of cards.

The captain led her to a narrow wood-slat stairway that went up to the top deck. There, the rooms lined either side of a hall that was scarcely wide enough to accommodate the two of them side by side. "Up here are the cabins. We've only got the nine, including my room up near the pilothouse. When we take to the river, we'll be traveling not-quite-full. But if you feel the need for feminine company, I'm afraid all I've got is the nigger girl who helps the cook. She's a sweet thing, though, and if you need something, you can ask her about it—I'll let her know you're here."

"Which room'll be mine?"

He drew her toward the end of the row, on the left. "How about this one?" He opened the door and held it open for her. "You won't have anybody next door to you, and across the hall is an old oilman headed up to count his money in Missouri, since he's already counted everything he made in Texas. I keep telling him he could afford a better ride, but he don't care. He says he'd rather ride fast in a shitty cabin than take all month on a *la-dee-dah* paddler covered up in frosting like a rich lady's cake."

"Can't say as I blame him," she said.

"Me either, all things being equal. But he's getting on up there, maybe close to eighty. If he gives you any guff, you can probably take him." The corners of his mouth shot up even higher as he said the last bit, lending a comic angle to every facial tuft. "Anyhow, I realize it's a tiny space and none too pretty, but we keep all the rooms straight as possible, and have plenty of fresh water on board for the basins."

"Don't sell yourself short. This is just as big as where I lived at the hospital, almost."

He handed her a key from a ring he carried on his belt, dangling just below his waistcoat. "Here's your security, ma'am, and I'll be pleased to show you the rest of it—what little there rightly is to see. You can set your things down, if you like. Pinch the door up, shut it behind you, and no one'll bother it."

"But my money and my papers—I still have to pay your clerk."

"Don't worry about *him*. He'll be on board, too, and you can sort that out any time. If you don't square up before St. Louis"—which he pronounced *Saint Looey*—"then we'll just keep you here and let you work it off in the galley. Come on. I'll show you the top deck, the pilot's house, the whistles, and anything else I can think of that'll slow that old bore Whipple from cornering me over the cargo weights."

Together they chatted as they walked around the *Providence,* killing time until the last of the cargo was loaded and the final passengers had presented themselves for boarding. By then, Mercy had been treated to the ins and outs of the craft, had met most of the crew—including Millie, who worked in the kitchen—and felt as if she might spend the next ten days quite comfortably and securely in the quiet of her own little room. So when the gangplank was pulled and all the moorings were loosed, she felt practically optimistic about the way her trip was now proceeding. As the *Providence* heaved slowly into the current and began to churn against it, she sat on one of the benches that lined the bottom deck to watch Memphis up on its bluff, sliding away behind her.

Nine

Though Mercy had been warned of the possibility of motion sickness, she did not become ill and was thankful for it. The food was fairly good, the weather remained quite fair—sunny and cool, with the ever-present breeze off the river—and the voyage promised to be pleasant and problem free.

However, by the second day, Mercy was bored beyond belief. It wasn't quite like being bored on a train. Despite the fact that she could get up, and wander through several decks, and lie down or stretch her legs at her leisure, something about being in the middle of that immense, muddy strip of water made her feel trapped in a way that a simple railcar did not. Certainly, it would be easier to dive overboard and swim to safety should trouble present itself than to fling herself from a moving train; and to be sure, the grub down in the galley was better than anything she'd ever packed for herself; and it was a demonstrable fact that this boat was making swifter progress than virtually any of the others it passed going upriver. But even when the paddles were churning and the diesel was pumping so fast and hard that the whole craft shuddered, she couldn't shake the sensation that they were moving more slowly than they ought to be.

The captain told her it was a trick of the water, and how swiftly it worked against them. She forced herself to be patient.

If the sun was out, she'd sit on the benches on the deck and watch the water, the distant shore, and the other vessels that moved along beside them, coming and going in each direction, up and down the river. Bigger, heavier cargo fleets swam along at a snail's crawl, paddling and sometimes towing barges packed with cotton bales, shipping crates, and timber. Lighter, prettier steamers from the Anchor Line piped up and down, playing their organs alongside the whistles to announce themselves and entertain their passengers. Every now and again, a warship would skulk past, the only kind of craft that could outpace the *Providence* as she surged forward into the current. On their decks Mercy saw grim-faced sailors—and sometimes happy ones—waving cloths or flags at the Texian vessel, waiting for the captain to pull the chain and sound his whistle back at them, as he invariably did.

The warships made her think of Tennessee, and of Fort Chattanooga, and that terrible night near Cleveland. They also reminded her of the newspaper she'd stashed in her satchel, so she retrieved it and sat outside reading it while the weather and the light held.

As she read, scanning the articles for interesting highlights, then reading the whole things anyway, she was joined on the bench by Farragut Cunningham, a Texian cargo manager with a shipment of sugar from the Caribbean. He was a great friend of the captain's, and had swiftly become a reasonable and engaging conversation-mate. Mercy was terribly interested in the extensive traveling he'd done for his business dealings, and on their first night aboard she'd interrogated him about the islands. She'd never been on an island, and the thought of it fascinated and charmed her.

On the second day of the journey, he sat beside her on the deck bench and struck a match. He stuck it down into the bowl of his pipe and sucked the tobacco alight with a series of quick puffs that made his cheeks snap.

"Is any of the news fit to read?" he asked, biting the end of the pipe between his teeth so that it cocked out of his mouth at an

angle, underneath the fringe of his dark brown mustache and just
to the right of his chin, where a red streak bisected his beard.

"Some of it, I guess," she replied. "It's a couple days old now,
but I don't have anything else to read."

"No paperbacks? No novels, or assortments of poetry?"

She said, "Nope. I don't read much. Just newspapers, sometimes, when I can get my hands on 'em. I'd rather know what's
happening than listen to someone tell me a story they made up."

"That's a reasonable attitude to take, though it's a shame. Many
wonderful stories have been made up and written down."

"I guess." She pointed at the article about the *Dreadnought*'s
movement out of southern Tennessee, and she said, "I almost saw
that thing, the other night."

"The *Dreadnought*?"

"That's right. I was taking an airship from Richmond to Chattanooga, and we crashed down right in the middle of the lines,
just about. That engine was there, and everyone acted like they
was scared to death of it."

He took another puff, filling the air with a dim, sweet cloud of
grayish blue smoke. "It's a frightful machine, and I mean that in
more ways than one." He lifted the brim of his hat and scratched
a spot on his hairline while staring out into the distance, over the
water.

"How so?"

"On the one hand, it's a machine built to be as mighty and dangerous as possible. It's armored to the teeth, or from the cowcatcher
to the hitch, however you'd like to look 'at it. It's a dual-fuel creature like this ship—part diesel and part coal for steam—and it can
generate more power than any other engine I ever heard of. It's
plenty fast for something as heavy as it is, too." He added softly,
"Faster than any other engine the Union's got, that's for damn sure,
armored or not."

"But not faster than ours?" She didn't bother to differentiate between the Confederacy and the Republic. She'd learned already that aboard this ship the distinction was merely semantic.

"No, not faster than ours. Course, none of ours are half so deadly. We could catch the *Dreadnought,* no problem at all. But God knows what we'd do with it, once we caught it."

Mercy looked back down at the sheet, spread across her lap. "What about the other hand?"

"Beg your pardon?"

"You said 'on the one hand.' What's on the other one?"

"Oh. That's right. On the one hand, the engine is frightful because it's an instrument of war. On the other hand, it was designed quite deliberately to make people afraid. You said you were there, in Tennessee," he cocked his head at the paper. "Did you get a good look at it?"

"No sir, I didn't. I only heard the whistle, back on the battlefield. I heard it brought a Union mechanized walker to the fight."

He said, "I reckon it did. Those walkers weigh so much, there's no other way to move 'em around the map. All powered up, even our petroleum-powered walkers can't run more than an hour or two. The Yanks have those shitty steam-powered jobs. They can hit like the dickens—don't misunderstand me—but no one can stand to drive 'em for more than thirty minutes. But now, you said you didn't see the *Dreadnought.*"

"No sir. You ever see it?"

He nodded. "I saw it once, up in Chicago when I was passing through on my way to Canada to nab a load of pelts. I saw it in the train yard, and I don't mind telling you, it made me look twice. It's a devil of a thing. It's got so much plating that it looks like it's wearing a mask, and they've welded so many guns and light cannon on top of it, it's a wonder the damn thing'll roll at all; but it does. If you came that close to it and never saw it, much less encountered it up close and personal, that's a lucky thing for you," he said. Then he amended the assessment to include, "Airship crash or none."

He sucked at the pipe for a few seconds. Mercy didn't say anything until he pulled the pipe out of his mouth and used it to point at the bottom right of the page. "Now, what's that say? Down there? Can you tell me?"

"Something about Mexico, and the emperor there being up to no good."

Farragut Cunningham snorted. "Well, that just makes it a day ending with a *y*. Can you read me a line or two? I left my magnifiers in my cabin, and I can't hardly see a thing without them."

" 'Emperor Maximilian the Third accuses Texian vigilantes, rangers, and residents in the mysterious disappearance of Mexican humanitarian legion.' "

The Texian sniffed. "I just *bet* he does."

She went on. " 'The emperor insists that the troops were merely a peacekeeping force sent north in order to assist the emigration of Mexican nationals back into undisputed Mexican territory—' "

"Let 'em go. Let 'em all go, we don't want 'em."

" 'Texians have disputed that claim, and insisted that the military presence amounted to an act of invasion.' "

"More or less, damn straight that's what it is. Should've never sent those uniforms over the Rio Grande like that—they sure as hell know that's their boundary, agreed upon by their own people, and years ago now."

Mercy looked up from the paper. "All right, I'm confused. Does this mean there are Mexicans in north Texas?"

Her bench-mate fidgeted as if this was an irritating subject, and stuffed the pipe back in his mouth. "Oh, you know how it is. They done lost their war, and now the nation's ours. But they like to dicker with us about where the northwest lines are."

"That seems . . . imprecise."

"Maybe it is, a little. Problem is, even when we can agree with ol' Max on where the northwest boundaries are, the people who live there sometimes don't. I ain't going to lie to you—it's the middle of godforsaken nowhere, and the homesteaders and settlers and the like, some of them are pretty sure they're citizens of Mexico. But when the lines got redrawn—" He hesitated and clarified. "—when the lines got redrawn this most *recent* time, a bunch of citizens got right peeved about paying taxes to the Republic, when they thought they were Mexicans."

"So now Mexico is helping them . . . move back to Mexico? Even though they already lived in Mexico, as far as they knew?" she asked.

"More or less. But things change, and the map lines change, and people can either go with that flow or go jump, for all I care."

Mercy glanced down and skimmed the rest as quickly as she could. "Then why'd Texas get upset, if the troops were only there to move their own folks back to the right side of their line?"

Cunningham sat forward and used the pipe to gesture like a schoolteacher, or like someone's father explaining the family's political opinion to a child with too many questions. "See, if that's *all* they were doing, that'd be fine. But if all they wanted was to move their own folks back, they didn't have to send five hundred men with guns and uniforms, bullying their way up past Oneida. They could've just sent some of their religious folk from the missions or something—since they got papists coming out the ears—or maybe they could've talked to that Red Cross. Get some people out to help the relocaters relocate, that's fine; but don't send the contents of a presidio and expect everybody to believe they're minding nobody's business but their own."

Mercy nodded, even though there was a lot she didn't really understand. She followed enough to ask, "What happened to the troops, then? Five hundred men don't just disappear into thin air."

He leaned back again, still drawing shapes with his pipe, which was nearly burned down cool. "I don't know if it was five hundred or not. Something like that, though. And I don't know what happened to 'em—could've been anything. That far north and west, shoot . . . could've been rattlesnakes or Indians, or cholera, or a twister . . . or maybe they ran across a town big enough to object to a full-on military garrison sneaking across their property. I'm not saying they ran afoul of the locals, but I'm saying it could've happened, and it wouldn't surprise me none." He put the end of the pipe back in his mouth and bit at it, but didn't suck at it. And he said, "Wouldn't be nobody's fault but their own, neither."

"I'm sure you're right," Mercy said, despite the fact that she wasn't. But she didn't want to be rude, and there were lots of things she didn't know about Texas—and even more she didn't know about Mexico—so she wouldn't open her mouth just to put her foot in it.

"You see anything else interesting in that paper?" Cunningham asked, giving up on the pipe and drawing one leg up over his knee so he could tamp out the bowl's contents against the heel of his boot.

"Most of the rest of it's just stuff about the war."

"No big surprise there, I guess. Does it say anything about what the Yankees were doing, pushing that line down all the way past Nashville? They must've had *some* good reason for a spearhead like that. God knows they went to plenty of trouble to make it happen, bringing that engine and that mech. Then again," he mused, "maybe there's no good reason. Maybe we're just whittling the war down to the end, and this latest back-and-forth is only its death throes. It feels like the end. It feels like something thrashing about before it's done for."

Mercy said, "Naw, it don't talk about why; it just talks about them doing it." She folded the paper over again, halfway rolling it up. She offered it to the Texian, asking, "Would you like it? I've

read it now, top to bottom and front to back, and I'm done with
it."

"Thank you, ma'am, but no thank you. Looks like more bad
and pointless news to me. I'd just as soon skip it."

"All right. I'll just put it in the game room, on one of the poker
tables." She rose, and Cunningham rose with her, touching the
front of his hat.

He then sat back down and refilled his pipe. Once it was alight
again, he leaned back into the bench to watch the river, the boats,
and the occasional fish, turtles, and driftwood sweep on past.

 *Ten*

Supper came and went, what felt like many times over, and the days ran together as the *Providence* dragged itself upstream. It sometimes docked at little spots and big spots between the big cities, loading and unloading cargo, and every now and again losing one or two passengers and taking on one or two new ones. At the Festus stop, the *Providence* picked up another Texian, as if to maintain some balance of them. The nurse was beginning to think they must be as common as brown, to encounter them just about everywhere.

The new Texian was Horatio Korman, and he was polite without being effusive, preferring to keep to himself for the short remainder of the trip. He was of a somewhat indeterminate age (Mercy guessed he might be thirty-five or forty, but with some faces it was difficult to judge, and his was one of them), with an average height and build, uncommonly green eyes, and hair that was quite dark, except where a faint streak of white went tearing along the part. His mustache was a marvel of fluff, each wing as big as a sparrow, and clean but not excessively groomed. Mercy thought he looked rather pleasantly like a Texian on an advertisement she'd once seen for a brand of chewing tobacco, as if he fit some mold that she'd heard about, but never actually encountered.

He came aboard with two handheld luggage cases that appeared to be heavy, even for a man with long, apelike arms such as his; and she noted the enormous pair of guns he wore openly on his belt. They were bigger than her inherited six-shooters by another third, and they hung off his hips like anchors. A long, slim spyglass stuck out of one vest pocket and gleamed a little when he walked.

Captain Greeley saw Mercy watching the new Texian board and find his way to a room. He told her, "That Horatio. He's a real piece of work, as they say."

"How's that?"

The captain shrugged, and lowered his voice just enough to ensure that everyone on deck would listen closely. "You may as well know: He's a Ranger of the Republic."

"That's some kind of lawman, right?"

"That's right." He nodded. "I've known Ratio going on ten years now, and I'm glad to have him aboard. Not that the going's been rough, because it surely hasn't been. It's been a smooth ride, wouldn't you say, Mrs. Lynch?"

She said, "Yes sir."

"But sometimes the trips aren't so easygoing; and sometimes, the passengers aren't so easygoing either. I don't mind telling you, I think that having a woman on board might've had a . . . a *civilizing* effect on some of the lads."

"Now don't you go blaming a boring river run on *me*," she said.

"Wouldn't dream of it! But it's a given: without you there'd have been more drinking, more fussing, and more cardplaying . . . which means more fighting, almost definitely. I know you're leaving next stop, and I won't hold that against you, but I hope Horatio stays aboard awhile. He'll keep me out of trouble. I'd hate to go to jail for throwing a fellow overboard—whether he deserved it or not. I'd rather leave that to the ranger."

The last night's supper was a good one, and the next day's trip was as uneventful as the previous week. When the *Providence* pulled into St. Louis, Missouri, Mercy was itching to debark and pin down the next leg of her journey. The docking and the settling took half the morning, so by the time the boat was ready to let her go, she stayed one last meal to take advantage of the readily available lunch.

Finally she said her good-byes to the captain, and to Farragut Cunningham, and to Ranger Korman, who was cool but polite in return. She stepped out onto the pier and idly took the offered hand of a porter, who helped her to leave before he occupied the gangplank with the loading and unloading of whatever was coming and going from the boat.

Mercy dodged the dockhands, the porters, the sailors, the merchants, and the milling passengers at each stall as she left the commerce piers and went back onto the wood-plank walks of a proper street, where she then was compelled to dodge horses, carriages, and buggies.

She found a nook at a corner, a small eddy of traffic that let the comers and goers swirl past her. From this position of relative quiet, she pulled a piece of paper out of a pocket and examined it, trying to orient herself to Captain Greeley's directions. A fishmonger saw her struggle to pick the right road, and he offered his services, which got her three streets closer to Market Street, but two streets yet away from it. She intercepted a passing soldier in his regimental grays, and he indicated another direction and a promise that she'd run right into the street she sought.

He was right. She ran right into it, then noted the street numbers on the businesses, which got her to the edge of a corner from whence she could actually spot the lovely new train station whose red-roofed peaks, towers, and turrets poked up over this corner of the city's skyline. The closer Mercy drew, the more impressed she was with the pale castle of a building. Although the Memphis station had struck her as prettier, something about the St. Louis structure felt grander, or maybe more grandiosely whimsical. It lacked elaborate artwork and excessive gleam, but made up for it with classic lines that sketched out a medieval compound.

At one end of the platform, there was a crowd and a general commotion, which she skipped in favor of finding the station agent's office. She followed the signs to an office and rapped lightly upon the open door. The man seated within looked up at her from under a green-tinted visor.

"Could I help you?" he asked.

She told him, "I certainly hope so, Mr.—" She glanced at the sign on his desk. "—Foote."

"Please, come inside. Have a seat." He gestured at one of the swiveling wooden chairs that faced his desk. "Just give me one moment, if you don't mind."

Mercy seated herself to the tune of her skirt's rustling fabric and peered around the office, which was heavily stocked with the latest technological devices, including a type-writer, a shiny set of telegraph taps, and the buttons and levers that moved and changed the signs on the tracks that told the trains where to go and how they ought to proceed. Along the ceiling hung a variety of other signs, which were apparently stored there. STAY CLEAR OF PLATFORM EDGE read one, and another advertised that BOARDING PASSENGERS SHOULD KEEP TO THE RIGHT. Another one, mounted beside the door in such a way as to hint that it was not merely stored, but ought to be read, declared with a pointing arrow that a Western Union office was located in the next room over.

When Armistad Foote had finished his transcription, he turned to the telegraph key—a newfangled sideways number that tapped horizontally, instead of up and down—and sent a series of dots and dashes with such astonishing speed that Mercy wondered how anyone, anywhere, could've possibly understood it. When the transmission was concluded, the station agent finally pushed the device to the side and leaned forward on his elbows.

"And what can I do for you today?"

"My name is Mrs. Lynch. I don't mean to interrupt your afternoon, but I'm about to take a real long trip. I figured you could tell me what the best way might be to head west."

"And how far west do you mean to go, Mrs. Lynch?" He was a bright-eyed little man, wiry and precisely tailored in a striped shirt with a black cinch on his right sleeve. He smiled when he talked, a smile that was not completely cold, but was the professional smile of a man who spends his days answering easy questions for people whom he'd rather usher out of his office via catapult. Mercy recognized that smile. It was the same one she'd used on her patients at the Robertson Hospital.

She sat up as straight as she could manage and nodded for emphasis when she said, "All the way, Mr. Foote. I need to go all the way, to Tacoma."

"Mercy sakes!" he exclaimed. "I do hope you'll forgive me asking, Mrs. Lynch, but you don't plan to undertake this trip alone, do you? May I inquire about your husband?"

"My husband is dead, Mr. Foote, and I absolutely *do* intend to undertake this trip alone—seeing as how I don't have too many options in the matter. But I have money," she said. She squeezed at the satchel as she added, "In gray and blue, what with this being a border state and all; and I brought a little gold, too—since I don't know what's accepted out past Missouri. It's not a lot, but I think it'll get me to Tacoma, and that's where I need to go."

He fidgeted, using his heels to kick his own swiveling seat to the left, and then to the right, pivoting at his waist without moving his torso or arms. He asked slowly, as if the question might be delicate, "And Mrs. Lynch, am I correct to assume—by the cadence of your voice, and your demeanor—that you're a southern woman?"

"I don't know what *that's* got to do with anything. Heading west ain't like heading north or south, is it? But I'm from Virginia, if you really must know," she said, trying to keep the crossness out of her voice.

"Virginia." He turned the name over in his mouth, weighing what he knew of the place against the woman sitting before him. "A fine gray state, to be sure. Hmm . . . we have a train leaving very shortly—within the afternoon—for the western territories, with a final destination of Tacoma."

She brightened. "That's wonderful! Yes sir. That's exactly what I'm looking for."

"But there will be many stops along the way," he cautioned as if this were some great surprise. "And the atmosphere might . . . prove . . ." He hunted for a word. "Unsympathetic."

"What's that supposed to mean?"

"This is a place of contradictions. The train heading west is a Union train by origin, and most of its passengers and crew are likewise allied in sentiment—though you can be absolutely confident, this is a *civilian* operation and in no way tied to the war effort at all. Not exactly."

"Well, which is it? Not at all, or not exactly?"

He flipped his hands up as if to say *some of each,* and explained. "One of the last cars is transporting dead soldiers back to their homes of origin in Missouri, Kansas, Nebraska, Wyoming, and the like. As far as I know, and as far as I can tell, that's its sole official business, and they're taking passengers along the route as a matter of convenience, and to offset the cost, of course." He shrugged. "Money is money, and theirs is as good as ours. Suffice it to say, they have a refrigerated car full of valued cargo—the human cargo of slain veterans. I'm given to suspect that perhaps it holds a war hero or two, or maybe even General McDowell, whose widow and family have moved out to California. Though the caskets were sealed and unmarked, except by serial numbers, so I'm afraid I can neither confirm nor deny those suspicions." But he smiled broadly, pleased to have guessed at a secret.

"Pretty much what you're telling me is that the fastest, easiest—and you haven't added cheapest, but I'll trust you wouldn't bring it up if it were unaffordable—way I can get myself West is to keep my head down and ride a Union wagon?"

"That's the sum of it—yes. It'll get you there, sure enough. Probably faster and safer than just about anything else we've got headed that way for the next month, truth be told."

"And why's that?" she asked.

He hemmed and hawed again, only momentarily. "There's a bit of a military presence on board. The engine itself is of military vintage, and only the passenger cars are a civilian contribution." His tone lifted into something more optimistic. "Which means that you can expect virtually no trouble at all from the Indians along the way, much less the pirates and highwaymen who trouble trains these days. It'll be quite secure." He stopped, and started again. "And anyway, what of it, if anyone somehow learns that you're from Virginia? This is a civilian task, and a civilian train."

Mercy wasn't sure whom he was trying to convince. "You don't have to sell me on it, Mr. Foote. My trip is likewise unrelated to the war effort. So I believe I'd like to buy a ticket," she said firmly. "As long as the ride is safe and quiet, I'll count my lucky stars that my timing worked out so good."

"As you like, Mrs. Lynch," he said, and he rose from his seat.

She let him make the arrangements, and finally, after she'd handed over almost the very last of her money, he gave her an envelope stuffed with papers, including her boarding pass and itinerary.

"The train'll be boarding down at the end, at gate thirteen." He pointed.

"Down where all those folks are stomping around, making a crowd?"

"That's it. Now have a good day, Mrs. Lynch—and a safe trip as well."

"Thank you, Mr. Foote."

She stared out the window, down at the thirteenth platform.

There wasn't much to see there except for a dense and curious crowd, for the columns between her and the engine blocked the bulk of the view. Even through the obstacles, she could see that the engine was large and dark, as engines went, and an old warning thrummed in her head. Suddenly she knew . . . illogically, and against all sane rejection of undue coincidence . . . that once she got up closer, she'd recognize the machine, by reputation if not by sight.

She drifted dreamlike toward the crowd and then back to the edge of the platform, where the people moved more quickly and with less density. Following the thinner stream, she shifted her satchel to hug it more closely against her belly.

Blue uniformed men with guns pocked the scene, mostly staying close to the engine, to the spot that felt safest to them in this uncertain state of divided loyalties.

The engine's stack rose into view first, between the platform beams that held the shelter aloft. It could've been any freight engine's stack, dark and matte as wool made for mourning. The lamp—which also came into view as she drew nearer—could have been any lamp, rounded and elongated slightly, with a stiff wire mesh to protect the glass.

But then the pilot piece, the cowcatcher, eased into view as two men stepped apart. No longer could it be any engine, from any rail yard or nation. Devilishly long and sharp, the fluted crimson cage drew down to a knife's bleeding, triangular edge, made to stab along a track and perform other vicious duties—that much was apparent from the rows of narrow cannon mounted up and down the slope against the engine's face. In front of the pilot grille, even the rail guards that covered and protected the front wheels were spiked with low scoops and sharp points, just in case something small and deadly should be flung upon the tracks that the pilot might otherwise miss. All the way up the chassis more guns were nestled, as well as elaborate loading systems to feed ammunition

to the devices in a Gatling style. And as she approached yet
closer, squeezing her way through the crowd to get a look for herself, Mercy noted that the boiler was double-, or maybe even
triple-plated, riddled with rows of bolts and rivets.

A water crane swung down low to hang over the engine. Soldiers ordered and shoved the onlookers back, demanding room
for the crew and station workers to do their jobs; and soon the
valves had been turned and the flow was under way. As the engine
took on water for the trip ahead, spilling down the pipes into
the still-warm tanks, the metal creaked and settled with a moan.

The gargantuan machine was nearly twice as large as the ordinary engine huddling two tracks over—not twice as wide, but
longer, and somewhat taller, and appeared thicker and meaner in
every way.

A man beside Mercy—some random gawker in the pressing
crowd—turned to her as if he knew her and said, "My God, it's
enormous! It'll barely fit under the station awnings!"

And behind her came a different voice, slightly familiar and
heavily accented. "But it *did* fit," said the speaker with great
conciseness. The nurse turned around and saw the most recent
Texian to come aboard the *Providence*—the Ranger Horatio Korman. He added, "You can bet they were careful about that," and
he tipped his Stetson to Mercy. "Mrs. Lynch." He nodded.

"Hello," she said, and moved aside, allowing him to scoot one
booted foot closer to the tracks, almost to stand at her side. Together they stared ahead, unable to take their gazes away from it.

Along the engine's side, Mercy could see a few of the letters in
its name, though she could barely parse the sharp silver lettering
with cruel edges and prickling corners that closely matched the
gleaming silver trim on the machine's towering capstack.

The ranger said it first. "*Dreadnought*. God Almighty, I hoped
I'd never see it for myself. But here I am," he said with a sniff. He
looked down at Mercy, and at her hand, which held the envelope

with all her important papers and tickets. Then his gaze returned
to the train. "And I'm going to ride whatever she's pulling. You,
too, ma'am?"

"Me, too." She nodded.

"You nervous?" he asked.

She lied. "No."

"Me neither," he said, but she figured he was probably telling
the truth. He didn't *look* nervous. He looked like a man who had
someplace to be, and didn't much care how he got there. His
two large leather cases still dangled, one at the end of each hand;
and his guns must've chafed against his forearms when he walked,
but he wore them anyway, as casually as a lady would wear a brooch.

Mercy asked, "How far will you ride?"

He glanced at her quickly, as if the question startled him. "Beg
your pardon?"

"How far?" she tried again. "It goes all the way out to Tacoma,
if you ride it long enough. But it stops a bunch of times between
here and there."

He said, "Ah," and his eyes snapped back to the metal train.
"Utah. But I might end up leaving sooner. Remains to be seen," he
said vaguely. Suddenly he turned to her, and he set one of his cases
by his feet so he could take her arm as he bent down to her height.
"Mrs. Lynch," he said, and his breath was warm on her skin.

"Mr. Korman!"

"Please," he said softly. "I can bet old Greeley told you my
job, and my distinction." He looked left and right, and brought
his face so close to her ear that she could feel the tickle of his
mustache against her cheekbone. "And I'd appreciate it if you'd
keep that information to yourself. This being a Union train, I'll
have trouble enough on board as a Texian. They don't need to
know the rest."

She drew back, understanding. "Of course," she said, nodding but not retreating any farther. "I won't say a word."

The press and flow of the crowd shifted closer to the cars upon hearing some instructions. Horatio Korman stuffed his second bag up under his arm and took Mercy's hand. "Will you accompany me, Mrs. Lynch? The two of us being two of a kind, and all . . . or, at least, two folks of similar *sentiments*."

"I suppose I could," she said, but he was already leading her against a current of people waving their bags and reading their tickets instead of watching their steps.

The ranger drew his duster forward over his guns, and adjusted his bag. He took Mercy's envelope of tickets and receipts as boldly as he'd taken her hand. Together they reached the steps to the second car, which was being watched by a man in a crisp uniform in a shade of sky-blue that marked him as a Union underling. But he was an armed underling, and he examined all approaching passengers with the same steady eye.

A porter stood to the other side of the steps, his gloved hand out and ready.

Horatio Korman handed over his own ticket as well as Mercy's. Once they'd been examined, he reclaimed both stamped items and returned the nurse's to her envelope, and the envelope to her hand. Then he picked up his bags once more and led the way inside.

Mercy followed, aware of the implication and a little annoyed, but a little comforted by the ranger's appropriation of her presence. He hadn't wanted to speak with her; he'd wanted her company the way he'd wanted to draw his overcoat forward to cover his firearms. He'd selected her as a reasonably respectable woman of a similar social class, in order to draw less scrutiny as he boarded the train; and because she was a southern girl, he figured he could trust her not to open her big mouth.

Damn the man, he'd been right.

She stood at the entrance to the passenger car's door, blocking the way. She looked back over the platform and the assembled people there, and forward into the car. Horatio Korman was nearly out of sight, almost at the next car back, where he apparently intended to go without her.

On the terrible engine, a whistle the size of a small barrel gulped against its tightened chain, inhaled, and screamed out a note that could be heard for a mile and maybe more. It screeched through the station like a threat or a dare, holding its tune for fifteen seconds that felt like fifteen years.

Even after it'd stopped, it rang in Mercy's ears, loud as a gong.

And behind her, the porter with the clean white gloves called out in a voice that sounded very small in comparison, but must have been quite loud, *"All aboard!"*

 *Eleven*

Mercy's seat was in the fourth passenger car. To the best of her assessment, this meant that the train was lined up thusly: the great and terrible engine, a coal car, a secondary car that probably managed the diesel apparatus or other armaments, a third car whose purpose Mercy could not gather, the seven passenger cars (two Pullman first-class sleeping cars in the lead, the remaining passenger-class cars behind them), then a caboose with full food service, and, finally, an additional caboose that was no caboose at all, but the refrigerated car carrying the remains of the Union war dead. This car was strictly off-limits to all, as was made apparent by the flat bar with a lock the size of a man's fist securing both the front and back doors of the thing, in addition to its painted-over windows that allowed not even the slimmest glimpse inside.

But Mercy could see none of this from inside her compartment in the fourth sleeper car, a square box with a wall of windows and two padded bench seats that faced each other. Each seat could've comfortably sat three women dressed for travel or four men dressed for business, but the nurse had the full length of the bench to herself.

She spent fifteen nervous minutes sorting out her brittle yellow tickets and the papers that ought to accompany her, including both the notes on her husband's passing from the Union Army and her certification from the Robertson Hospital, which said such contradictory and true things about her that she once again thanked heaven she'd kept them in her personal bag, and not stuffed them into the long-lost portmanteau.

The Ranger Horatio Korman was nowhere to be seen or found, but, as the train was being settled, two women came to take the bench that faced Mercy. After polite nods, Mercy watched them closely. She had no idea how long they'd be forced to look at one another or how well she could expect to enjoy their company—if at all.

One woman was quite elderly and small, with a back that was beginning to hunch despite her corsetry's determined stance against this development. Her hair was white, and simply but firmly styled, and her eyes were a watery gray that spotted everything from behind a light wire set of spectacles. She wore black gloves that matched strangely with her pale blue dress, and a little black hat that suited the gloves even if the dress did not. She introduced herself as Norene Butterfield, recently widowed, and her companion as her niece, Miss Theodora Clay.

Miss Theodora Clay was taller than her aunt by a full head, never mind the low gray hat that capped her shiny brown curls. She was younger than the other woman by forty years at least, which might have put her near thirty; she wore a smart but inexpensive lavender suit and gray gloves, plus black boots that peeked their pointed toes from beneath her skirt when she lifted Mrs. Butterfield's luggage to store it in the drop-down berth above.

The sight of her made Mercy feel unkempt, and inclined her to camp in the washroom section of the car—but, she concluded, not until the train was moving and their trip was under way. Besides, the washroom was presently occupied by a tired-looking man with two small children who had trundled inside and shut the door ten minutes previously. He could be heard begging the little boys to finish up and wash their hands, or wash their faces, or fasten their drawers.

She was not particularly comfortable, but she very much wanted the trip to get under way. She could not help but notice how many armed, uniformed men were riding the train . . . particularly for a civilian operation, as had been so vigorously claimed. Mrs. Butterfield spied Mercy watching the enlisted lads and said in a surprisingly hearty voice, "It's a relief to have them aboard, isn't it?"

"A relief? I suppose, yes," she said without committing herself to anything.

"We'll be going through Indian country, after all," she added.

Mercy said, "I guess that's true," even though she didn't have the foggiest idea where Indian country began or ended, except a nebulous sense that it was someplace west.

"I rather like seeing them, the blue boys, with their guns. Makes me feel safer," she said with the certainty of someone who'd heard about the threat, but was fairly certain she'd never meet it in person. It reminded Mercy of Dennis and Larsen from the crash in Tennessee. "And so many of them so young, and unmarried." She turned a keen, squinty eye to her niece, who was reading a newspaper.

Miss Clay did not look up. She said, "No doubt, Aunt Norene."

"And what of you, dear?" she returned her attention to Mercy, who was not wearing her gloves and therefore had her wedding band on display. "Where's your husband?"

"He died," she said, doing her best to moderate an accent that would've given her away anywhere, even underwater. But their chitchat had progressed this far without any commentary upon it, so she hoped for the best.

"In the war?" Mrs. Butterfield asked.

Mercy nodded. "In the war."

The old woman shook her head and said, "Sometimes I wonder that we've got any men left at all, after all this time fighting. I despair for my niece."

Her despaired-for niece turned the newspaper page and said, "I suppose *someone* must." But she added no further objection or encouragement.

Mercy hadn't known and hadn't asked, when the two women joined her, where they might have come from or where their sensibilities might lie; but within the hour she learned that they were from Ohio, and they were headed west to investigate some property left by the late Mr. Butterfield, who'd bequeathed them a mine. However, the details were fuzzy, and his death must've been quite some time ago for Mrs. Butterfield to traipse about in powder blue. Miss Clay had once been engaged to a highly placed and upstanding Union major, but alas, he'd been killed on the field less than a month before their wedding day.

All this information came from Mrs. Butterfield, with Miss Clay declining to annotate the chatter. Indeed, she seemed more predisposed to break into her assortment of papers and novels, even though the journey had not yet started.

Mercy had a feeling that this was her preferred method of ignoring the aunt, for whom she clearly served as nursemaid or assistant. Likewise, the oft-ignored Mrs. Butterfield was more than happy to find a willing ear in Mercy, who didn't much mind the interaction, though she could see how it might grow tiresome over the long haul.

Before long, the sharply dressed conductor came walking through the car to examine tickets and, Mercy gathered, take stock of his charges. He was a man somewhere between the ages of Mrs. Butterfield and Miss Clay, with the ramrod posture of a fellow who'd spent some time in the military himself, but he sported a tall steel brace along one leg. This brace propped him into a standing position and clicked softly when he walked, a mechanical limp that carried him from compartment to compartment. His smile was only a narrow, bent line, impatient to be off and away from what was iffy territory at best. Missouri could not be trusted, not by either side.

Mercy watched him examine paperwork and take questions, answering with haste and pushing ever back, back to the next passengers, and soon to the next car.

A dignified old negro in a freshly pressed Pullman porter's uniform trailed in the conductor's wake, securing luggage and directing passengers to the washroom, explaining the hours during which food would be served in the caboose, and making informed guesses about how much longer it'd be before they left—or before they stopped again. He secured doors, fastened cabinets, checked his pocket watch against some signal from outside, and followed the conductor into the next car, out of sight.

It took Mercy a moment to realize why this felt strange to her, and why she watched him and her fellow passengers with a wary eye as Mrs. Butterfield lectured her on the subject of ice-skating. She looked at the people on the train, one face at a time, and saw old men and old women, and a few younger women like herself; and in the comings and goings of the porters, she saw a few negroes who were young enough to be her brother. But the only young white men were soldiers. Some of these soldiers clustered together in their compartments, and others wandered as if on patrol, or maybe they were only restless. A few were painfully young—teenage boys without any facial hair, and with skinny, concave chests and narrow hips. One or two showed terrible scars across the exposed skin of their necks and hands. Sometimes she could guess with professional precision what had caused the wounds. She recognized close-range shrapnel, artillery burns, and the strange texture of flesh deeply scalded by steam. Mercy privately wondered what her seating companion had so recently wondered aloud—that there were any men left alive at all anymore, on either side.

Finally, after what felt like an interminable delay and an afternoon effectively wasted, the dreadful whistle blew, startling and straightening the backs of everyone inside the seven passenger cars. With a breathtaking hiccup of machinery, the locomotive started forward.

Even Mrs. Butterfield silenced herself as the train's motion began in earnest, crawling through the station and passing crowds, columns, newsstands, parked and boarding freight, and passenger cars still waiting upon other tracks, in other gates. For these few moments, all eyes were on the windows and the panorama spinning slowly by, picking up speed by pumps and puffs, pulling away from the station and then to the fringe of the city itself, past the freight yards, cabins, sheds, warehouses, and cargo lots. And then, much sooner than Mercy might've predicted, they were moving at a steady clip through a no-man's-land of trees, tunnels, tracks, and very little else.

The first few hours were a sedative, lulling the passengers into a contingent of nodding heads, sprawled knees, and open mouths snoring softly. A rotund man with a flask in his vest slipped it up and out, and sipped at the brandy or whiskey he had within it. Within a moment, the wafting fumes told Mercy that the answer was brandy after all.

The world was dull and rocking; the train was a cradle on a track, and even the hardiest travelers were so content to be finally on the move that they grumbled to themselves and slept, even though there were at least another twenty or thirty days of the same routines ahead.

Mercy turned her face to the window, but it was growing February cold—colder here than in Virginia, when she'd left it—and her skin deposited a layer of moistness in the shape of her cheek and the side of her mouth. After all the excitement and fear and uncertainty of learning that she'd be riding on the *Dreadnought,* and after all the frantic scrambling to bring herself all the way from Virginia to Missouri, she was not yet one day into the westernmost leg of her travel and already bored to distraction. Even the reticent Miss Clay was nodding off, her head occasionally tapping against the top of Mrs. Butterfield's as they dozed together.

Just when she thought the trip could not become any more tedious, and that she might surreptitiously snatch one of the tempting dreadfuls that were scattered along Miss Clay's seat, the forward car door opened and two men came strolling through it. They moved single file because the door was so very narrow, and they conversed quietly, though they did not whisper.

The one who was nearest to Mercy was thin, and wearing a Union uniform with a captain's insignia. His hair was snow white, though his face was peculiarly unlined. If he'd been wearing a brown wig or a hat with fuller coverage than a Union cap, she would've guessed him to be around thirty-five.

He said to his companion, "We'll need to keep an eye out," with an accent that came from New England—somewhere north of Pennsylvania.

"Obviously," spit the other man, as if this were the most preposterous thing anyone had ever said aloud in his presence. "Everything is sealed, but that could change in an instant, and then what?" This second speaker, taller and perhaps of a similar rank (Mercy couldn't imagine he'd speak so abruptly to a superior), was wearing a uniform that suggested they served the same government, though maybe a different branch. His hair was a color she'd almost never seen before, except on children: a vivid orange that clashed with the fervent brown of his eyes. His face was strong and attractive, but flustered and a little bit mean.

The captain snapped, "The whole thing makes me *magnificently* nervous. I know what they were saying about it, at the station. And I demand to know—"

"I don't care about your demands—this is not your job! It's—" He stopped himself, having snagged Mercy's gaze with the corner of his eye. He forced a smile that wouldn't have fooled a blind dog, dipped his head, and said, "Pardon me, ma'am." His accent was far more neutral, and she couldn't guess its origins.

She said, "Sure." Mercy was fiercely curious as to what they'd been talking about, but she wouldn't learn now. There was little point in keeping them, but she couldn't bring herself to let the encounter close, so she cleared her throat and said, "I don't mean to sound nosy or nothing, but I was wondering: I've never seen a uniform quite like yours. What work do you do for the Union?"

The first man plastered on a smile that looked somewhat less false than his friend's, and bowed. He said, "Ma'am, please allow me to introduce myself—I'm Captain Warren MacGruder, and my redheaded friend over here"—he winced at the word *friend,* but so slightly that almost no one would've noticed—"is Mr. Malverne Purdue."

She asked, "Mr.?"

"Yes. *Mr.* Purdue is a civilian, and a scientist. He's being paid as a—" He fished for a word, discarded his first choice, and went with the second thing that came to mind. "—consultant." But it clearly left a bad taste in his mouth.

"I see," she said. "My name's Mercy Lynch, and I didn't mean to stop you or bother you; I just wondered, is all. Anyway, I was thinking about heading back to the caboose for a little peck of supper. It's about that time, isn't it?"

Mr. Purdue all but rolled his eyes. The captain dug around in his pocket for a watch, found it, flipped it open, and confirmed. "Yes, it is. We were just heading there ourselves. Would you care to join us?"

"What a coincidence. And how nice," she added, pleased at the prospect of company.

At some point during the conversation, Miss Clay had awakened. She'd been watching the scene unfold as well, and chose this moment to say, "I think I'll join you."

Mercy was surprised, if for no other reason than that Miss

Clay had not seemed very interested in making friends. And it wasn't as if she needed directions or assistance to the caboose; there were only two ways to go on the train—toward the engine or toward the dead men bringing up the rear.

Miss Clay took the lead, underscoring the fact that she had no real need for company. The captain did not offer his arm to Mercy, but he extended his hand, gallantly offering to let her go first—which was much more clever than offering an arm, given the thin aisle.

Mercy reached for Miss Clay's arm and caught it with a soft tap. "Miss Clay, what about your aunt?"

Miss Clay gave her elderly charge a glance and said, "She'll be fine. She's less of an invalid than she'd have you think, and if she needs something, believe me, she won't hesitate to wake someone up and ask for it."

With these assurances, the four of them sidled up to the rear car door and Miss Clay pulled it, mastering the latch immediately—or perhaps she'd spent a great deal of time on trains; Mercy didn't know. Then she stepped out onto the connecting platform and scarcely touched the supporting rails as she took the two or three steps across, and over to the next car.

Out between the cars, the wind was astonishing. It whipped at Mercy's cloak and threatened to peel it off her body, but she gripped the front edges and held it fast with one hand while she felt for the rail with the other one. Malverne Purdue stepped past her with great agility, following in the wake of Theodora Clay; but Captain MacGruder waited behind and put a hand on her elbow, attempting to steady her.

Mercy had no hat handy, for she'd never replaced the one she'd lost in the luggage, so her hair was braided up in a fat button behind her ears. As she crushed her eyes into narrow slits against the cold, fast air, the edges of her cloak's hood flapped like a flag, pulling the braid apart.

"Thank you," she mumbled, arranging her feet and pushing herself forward, trying not to look at the track scrolling beneath her with such speed that it blurred into a wide, solid line. "We must be going quite fast," she said dumbly.

"I believe so," the captain said. He was nearly yelling into her ear, but his words had no sharpness, only genteel agreement. When she reached the other platform, he was immediately behind her; he reached around her to open the door, which had closed behind the two who'd gone before them.

Soon they were safely sealed in the next car back. As they walked, the captain said, "I don't suppose you do much travel by train."

"No sir, I don't," she told him. "This is only my second trip on a train, ever."

"Second trip ever? You've picked quite a machine for your second voyage. May I ask where you're from? I can't quite place you by your speech," he said mildly, but Mercy knew what he meant.

Most Yankees couldn't tell a Tennessean from a southern Indianan, much less a Texan from a Georgian, so she went ahead and lied. "Kentucky." He'd never know the difference, and it was a safe cover for the way she talked.

"Kentucky is a fine state. Bluegrass and horses, as I understand it."

"Yep. We've got plenty of those. The place is lousy with them," she muttered as she turned sideways to scoot past a sleeping child who'd fallen out of his compartment and hung halfway across the aisle, drooling into the main walkway. She'd never actually been to Kentucky. She'd met Phillip in Richmond, and he'd moved to Waterford to be near her before he'd wound up going to war. Not that this stopped her from knowing a thing or two about the place. They'd talked, after all.

"And your husband?" he asked quietly, for many of this car's occupants were likewise asleep.

She glanced down at her wedding band, and said, "He passed. In the war."

"Kentuckian, like yourself?"

"He was from Lexington, yes."

"I hope you'll pardon me if I pry, but I can't help but being curious."

"Pry away," she encouraged him, mumbling "Excuse me" to an old man whose legs had lolled into the aisle.

"Where did you lose your husband? Which front, I mean to ask? I'm friends with a few of your bluegrass cousins myself, and I make a point to look out for them, when I can."

She didn't know if he was telling the truth or not, which wouldn't have stopped her from answering. It was something else that made her hesitate: a sensation of being watched. Mercy looked to the back of the car, and to the right, and met the eyes of Horatio Korman, who had been watching, and no doubt listening, too. He did not blink. She looked away first, down to the floor and then up, for the latch on the door out of the car.

Well within Korman's range of hearing she declared, almost defiantly, "He didn't die on a front. He died in a prisoners' camp, at Andersonville. In Georgia."

"I'm sorry to learn of it."

"So was I, just a week or two ago," she rounded off and up, reluctant to relate the incident with any more proximity. "And I hope you'll forgive me if I leave it at that. I'm still getting the feel of being a widow."

As the wind of the train's motion blasted her in the face once more, she turned her head to see the Texas Ranger watching her still, without any expression. Even the edges of his prodigious mustache did not twitch. His eyebrows gave nothing away.

She turned her attention to the crossing junction over the couplers, and this time navigated with slightly more grace. Captain

MacGruder closed the door behind them both, and followed her into the next car.

Eventually they reached the caboose, a long, narrow thing with tables and chairs established for food and tea service. Miss Clay was already seated with a cup of coffee that smelled strongly of chicory, and Mr. Purdue was still at the tender's counter, deciding on the refreshments that would best suit him. Upon seeing the captain, he selected his meal and came to sit beside Miss Clay, as if this were now the natural order of the universe.

"Could I get you anything?" the captain offered, gesturing at the counter, with its menu composed in chalk on a slate. "I can vouch for the—"

But just then, two men burst through the entrance door, looking breathless and thoroughly disheveled. Both were dressed in their Union blues, and both were blond as angels. They might've been brothers, though the lad on the left held a brass telescoping device in one shaking hand.

"Captain!" they said together. The man with the telescope held it up as if it ought to explain something, but he was nearly out of breath, so his fellow soldier took over.

"From the lookout on the second car," he panted. "We've got trouble coming up from the east!"

"Coming right at us!"

Captain MacGruder whirled away from the counter and acknowledged them with a nod. "Ladies, Mr. Purdue. Stay here in the back. You'll be safer."

Miss Clay opened her mouth to object, but Malverne Purdue beat her to the punch. "Don't lump me in with the women, you yellow mick." He pulled a pistol out of his pocket and made a run for the door.

"Fellas!" said the counterman, but no one answered him.

"Excuse us," said the captain as he pushed the soldiers and

Mr. Purdue through the caboose door and back into the blustery gap between the cars. The door slammed shut behind them and Mercy was left, still standing and confused, with only Miss Clay and the counterman as company. She didn't know which one of them was most likely to know, but she asked aloud, "What's going on?"

Miss Clay realized she'd been sitting with her mouth open. She covered for this oversight by pulling the cup of coffee to her lips and drinking as deeply as the heat would allow. When she was finished, she said, "I'm sure I don't know."

Mercy turned to the counterman, whose uniform was kin to the ones the porters wore. His hair was clipped down close against his scalp, leaving an inky shadow spilling out from underneath his round cap. He said, "Ma'am?" as if he didn't know either, and wasn't sure how to guess. But then a set of shots was fired, somewhere up toward the front of the train, far enough away that they sounded meaningless. He said, "Raiders, I suppose. Here in Missouri, I couldn't say. Bushwhackers, like as not. We're flying a Union flag, after all."

Miss Clay took another ladylike sip from her cup and said, "Filthy raiders. *Stupid* filthy raiders, if they're coming after a train like this. I don't see myself getting terribly worked up about it."

More gunshots popped, and a window broke at the edge of what Mercy could clearly hear. "What about your aunt?" she asked.

At this, Miss Clay's frosty demeanor cracked ever so slightly. "Aunt Norene?" She rose from her seat and carried the cup over to the counterman, who took it from her. "I suppose I *should* look in on her."

"Whether or not *you're* worked up about the train being shot at, I think *she* might be a little concerned," Mercy told Miss Clay. She had also left her satchel on the seat, where she'd assumed it would be quite safe, but she now wished rather hard for her revolvers. She reached for the door and pulled it open, disregarding the captain's instructions as if he'd never given them.

Miss Clay was so close on Mercy's heels that she occasionally trod upon them as they struggled between the cars back into a passenger compartment, where people were ducking down and the shots were more clearly audible. At the moment, all the gunfire seemed to be concentrated at the forward end of the train, but when Mercy leaned across a cowering child to peer out the window, she saw horses running alongside the track at a full gallop, ridden by men who wore masks and many, many guns. She said, "Well, *shit,*" and drew herself back into the aisle with a stumble.

Miss Clay had passed her and was waving back at her. "Hurry up, if you're coming."

"I'm working on it!" Mercy said back, and then the order was reversed, with Miss Clay taking the lead and Mercy all but stumbling over her, trying to reach the next door, the next couplers, the next passenger car.

They flung themselves forward into the fifth passenger car, where Mercy had seen Horatio Korman, but when she looked to the seat where he'd glared at her over that copious mustache, he was nowhere to be seen. She made a mental note of it and pushed forward behind Miss Clay.

In the next car they found the fringes of chaos, and they found Mrs. Butterfield standing in the aisle ordering the other passengers into defensive positions. "You, over there!" she pointed at the man with the two little boys. "Put them into that corner, facing outward. Have you any arms?"

He shook his head no.

She shook her head as if this was absolutely uncivilized and said, "Then stay there with them—hold them in place, don't let them wander. You!" She indicated a pair of older women who were yet young enough to be her daughters. "On the floor, and careful not to flash anything unladylike!"

"Aunt Norene!" Miss Clay exclaimed, reaching her aunt and pulling her back into the compartment.

Mercy followed, scanning the car for the other passengers. Either Mrs. Butterfield had been an excellent director, or baser instincts had shoved every individual into the corners and underneath the windows with great speed and firmness. Seeing nothing else to be done, Mercy ducked into her seat, seized her satchel, and would've interrogated the old lady if Miss Clay hadn't been doing so already.

"Aunt Norene, you must tell us—what's happening?"

"Rebs! Filthy stinking raiders. Leftovers of Bloody Bill, I bet you—nasty things, and brutish! They came riding up and firing, right into the cabins!" she blustered.

Mercy looked around and didn't see any windows shot out, but for all she knew, they'd been playing target practice with them in the cars up ahead. "Is anyone hurt?" she asked, already guessing the answer but not knowing what else to say on the subject.

"In here? Heavens, dear girl. I couldn't say. I should think not, though."

Gunfire came closer this time, and a bullet ricocheted with a startling ping, though Mercy couldn't gather where it'd started or where it'd ended up. She heard it tearing through metal and bouncing, landing with a plop.

Someone in the next car up screamed, and she heard the sound of glass being broken yet again, then the sound of return fire coming from inside the train.

Leaning out her own window this time, Mercy saw more horses and more men—at least half a dozen on her side of the train alone—so she skedaddled across the aisle and pushed past the girl who was sitting there already, lying across the seat with her head covered. On that side, she could almost see . . . but not quite.

She reached for the window's latch, flipped it, and yanked it up so she could get a better look. Craning her face into the wind, Mercy narrowed her eyes against the gusts, and the fierce, cold hurricane of the train's swift passage. On that side of the train she counted six—no, seven—men on horseback, for a total of maybe fifteen.

She let go of the window and it fell with a sliding snick back into place.

Back on her side of the car, Miss Clay was trying to calm her aunt and urge the woman into a position on the floor. "I'll pull down the bags," she was saying. "We'll use them for cover—I'll put them between you and the car's wall, in case of stray bullets."

Mercy thought this was an eminently sensible plan, and if she'd had any suitcases of her own, she would've promptly contributed to the makeshift barricade. In lieu of hard-shelled luggage, she rifled through her bag and felt the chilly heft of the guns. She hesitated, and while she made up her mind, the train picked up speed with a heave. She swayed on her feet and watched out the window as one of the masked men in gray was outpaced. His horse's legs churned, pumping like the engine's pistons, but the beast was losing ground.

He looked up into the window, a rifle slung over his shoulder and a six-shooter bouncing roughly in one of his hands. He pointed it up at her, or at the window, or at the train in general— she had no way of knowing what he saw as he peered up from the rollicking back of his frothing horse. Maybe he saw nothing but a reflection of the sky, or the passing trees. But for a moment she could've sworn they made eye contact. He lowered the gun and flipped it into his holster, while drawing up hard on his horse's reins and letting it veer off with a bucking skid.

Mercy realized she had been holding her breath. She released it, and she released her grip on her own chest.

Sensing someone standing nearby, she spun about and found

herself face-to-face with Horatio Korman, who was standing so close, he might've been sniffing at her hair. The thought fired through her head—*So, I'm not the only one the bushwhacker saw in the window*—and she said breathlessly, "Mr. Korman! You've startled me!"

The ranger said, "You need to get down. Take some cover like a sane woman, Mrs. Lynch."

"Mr. Korman, tell me what's going on!"

"How should I know?" he asked without a shrug. "I'm just a passenger here, myself."

"Guess," she ordered him.

"All right, I'd guess raiders, then. They look like Rebs to me, so it's safe to say they're sworn enemies of yours, and all that." If there was an accusation buried there, he let it lie deep, and left the surface of the statement sounding blank. "I'm sure the militia boys on board will make short work of them."

From up front, a riotous wave of artillery cut through the popping blips of gunfire. The difference between the *Dreadnought*'s cannon and the bushwhacker rifles sounded like the difference between a lone whistler and a church choir.

The engine kicked and leaned, whipping the cars behind it so they swayed on their tracks, back and forth, harder than before, more violently than normal.

"They'll be blown to bits!" Mrs. Butterfield declared with naked glee.

But the ranger said, "I wouldn't bet on it. Look at that, can you see? They're peeling away, heading back into the woods."

"Maybe they know what's good for them after all," the old woman said smugly.

"I reckon they've got a pretty fair idea," said Horatio Korman. "That was just about the fastest raid I ever saw in my life. Look. It's already over."

A final spray of Gatling-string bullets spit across the scenery, chasing after the men and horses that Mercy could no longer see through her window. "Wasn't much of a attack," she observed.

Mrs. Butterfield said, "Of course not. Weak and cowardly, the lot of them. But I suppose this will give me something to write letters about. We've certainly had a bit of excitement already!"

"Excitement?" The ranger snorted softly. "They didn't even make it on board." He looked down at the woman, still being squeezed tightly in her niece's arms.

She scowled up at him. "And who are you to comment on the matter? I know by your voice, if not by your rough demeanor, that you must be a Republican, and I daresay it's a shame and a mockery for you to board this vessel, given your *near-certain* sympathies."

He retorted, "My sympathies are none of your goddamn business. Right now they lean toward getting safe and sound to Utah, and I can assure you I don't have any desire to get blown up between here and there. So if they got chased off, *good*. It's all the same to me." He flashed Mercy a look that said he'd like to say more, maybe to her, maybe in private someplace.

As if the ranger had not just spoken so harshly, he tipped the brim of his hat to them in turn and said, "Ladies," as a means of excusing himself and calling the strained conversation to a close.

When he was gone, Miss Clay's frigid glare settled on Mercy. She asked the nurse, "You know that revolting man?"

"I . . ." She shook her head and took her seat slowly. "He was on the ship I rode to St. Louis. He was a passenger, that's all."

"He surely has taken an interest in you."

"We ain't friends."

"Did I hear you tell Captain MacGruder that your husband was from Lexington?"

Mercy told her, "You heard right. And in case you didn't hear the rest, he died down in Plains, at the camp there. I only found out last week."

"I'm not strictly certain I believe you."

"I'm not strictly certain I give a shit," Mercy said, though she was angry with herself for getting angry at this woman, when she had a story handy that was good enough to cover any suspicious guesses. "But if it makes you feel better . . ." She reached for the satchel again, and pushed past the guns into the wad of papers. She pulled out the sheet that Clara Barton had given her and shoved it under Miss Clay's nose. "You like to read? Read *that*. And keep your accusations to yourself."

Theodora Clay's eyes skimmed the lines, noted the official stationery, and read enough to satisfy her curiosity. She did not exactly soften, but the rigid lines across her forehead faded. "All right, then. I guess that means I owe you an apology," she said, but then she didn't offer one.

Mercy retrieved the paper and lovingly put it back into her bag, next to the note from Captain Sally. "Maybe you owe one to Mr. Korman, too, since he didn't do anything except tell you the coast was clear."

Just then, the captain came bursting back through the passenger car with several of his men, including Mr. Purdue and the two blonds who'd first delivered the bad news, who were helping to support an unknown fellow who was bleeding from the shoulder. The captain stopped at Mercy and said, "Mrs. Lynch, you're a nurse, aren't you?"

"That's right. Who told you?"

"A big Texian in the next car up."

She reached for her bag. "But haven't you got a doctor on board?"

"We were supposed to," he said with a note of complaint. "But we don't, and we're not picking one up until the next stop. So for now I've got a man who could use a little attention, if you'd be so kind as to help us wrap him up."

"Of course," she said, happy for the excuse to conclude her awkward talk with Miss Clay.

"Do you have anything useful in that bag of yours?"

"It's all loaded up with useful things," she said, and stepped into the aisle behind them. She could tell at a glance that the man wasn't mortally injured, though his eyes were frantic, like he'd never been hurt this bad before in all his life. But there's a first time for everything, and this first event was scaring him more than it was hurting him. "Where are you taking him?"

"Back to the last passenger car. It's only half full, and we can set him down there."

Mercy followed the small crew back, across the blizzard-wild interchanges between the cars, and into the last compartment of the last passenger sleeper. There, they tried to lay the man down, but he wouldn't have it. He sat up, protesting, until Mercy had shooed all but the white-haired captain away. The car's few occupants were just beginning to rise off the floor and reclaim their seats, as the captain told them, "It's fine, everyone. You can come out again. It was just a weak little attempt at a raid, and it's over now."

So while they rose from their hiding places, they watched curiously as Mercy removed the injured man's shirt down to his waist. The captain took a seat on the other side of the compartment so he could watch the proceedings.

He told the patient, "This is Mrs. Lynch. Her husband died in a camp in Georgia not too long ago. She's a nurse."

"I gathered that last part," the man said. It came out of his chest in a soft gust.

"She's from Kentucky."

She smiled politely as if to confirm this, and prodded at the injury. "Captain, could you scare up some clean rags for me, and some water? I bet they'll have some back in the caboose."

"I'll just be a moment," he said, practically clicking his heels.

The man with the now-naked torso leaned his head against the seat's high back and asked, "Where're you from in Kentucky, Mrs. Lynch? And might I ask, where're you going?"

She didn't mind answering, if for no other reason than it'd take his mind off the wound. "I'm from Lexington. And I'm headed west to meet up with my daddy. He got hurt not so long ago himself. It's a long story. What's your name, sweetheart?"

The loud clap and unclap of the car door announced Captain MacGruder's return. "Here you go, ma'am," he said, handing her a bundle of washrags made for dishes and a pitcher full of water. "I hope these'll work."

"They'll work just fine." She took one of the rags and dunked it into the pitcher, then proceeded to dab away the blood.

"Morris," he answered her question belatedly. "It's Private First Class Morris Comstock."

"Nice to meet you," she said. "Now, lean forward for me, if you would, please."

"Yes ma'am," he said, and struggled to accommodate her.

She wiped the back of his shoulder, too, and said, "Well, Private First Class Morris Comstock, I do believe you'll live to see another day."

"How do you figure that?"

"If it'd stuck you any lower, you'd be losing a lung right now, and if it was any higher, it would've broken your collarbone all to pieces. But as it stands, unless it takes to festering, I think you're going to be just fine." She gave him an honest smile that was a little brighter than her professional version, if for no other reason than his own relief was contagious.

"You mean it?"

"I mean it. Let me clean it up and cover it, and we'll call you all set. This your first time taking lead?"

"Yes ma'am."

She handed him a clean rag and said, "Here. Hold this up against it so it stops bleeding. Now lean forward again"—she shoved another rag behind him—"and we'll plug you up coming and going." She unrolled some bandages and said to the captain, "I hope nobody else was hurt," which was her way of asking if anybody was dead. If anyone else had been hurt, they'd be sitting beside Morris Comstock.

"No ma'am," he answered her. "It was a funny little raid. Didn't get much accomplished."

While the injured soldier was still leaning forward, his face closer to Mercy's, he said quietly, "You know what? I don't think it was really a raid."

"You don't?" she responded quietly in kind.

"I don't." When the rear wound was staunched, he leaned back again. "I think they were just taking a look—just checking us out, to see what the engine could do, and how many men we had in the cars. They didn't even try to board or nothing. They just rode up, fired their guns—mostly into the air, except when they saw fellas in uniform like me—and got a good eyeful."

Mercy said, still softly, since other passengers were watching, "You think they'll be back."

"I sure do. They'll be back—and let 'em come, that's what I say. They may've gotten an idea of how many men we've got, but they didn't even get a *taste* of what we can do."

Twelve

A follow-up raid did not come, not immediately and not even soon. For the next few days, all the soldiers were in the very highest state of tense alertness, jumping at each click in the tracks, and leaping into readiness any time the whistle blew. Mercy became almost accustomed to it, as she became accustomed to her seatmates—even as Miss Clay continued to be both aloof to her and, in the nurse's estimation, a tad too friendly with the young soldiers, if *friendly* was the right word. She tolerated their company better than anyone else's, at least, and much to her aunt's glee, she spent a fair bit of time being escorted to and from the dining car by whoever was on duty, or passing through.

"You never know," burbled Mrs. Butterfield. "She might take to a husband yet! It's not too late for her, after all. There's still time for a few children, if the Lord sees fit to have her matched."

Mercy nodded like always. And when Mrs. Butterfield nodded off, and Miss Clay had wandered back to the caboose (or wherever it was she went when she was gone), Mercy fondled the guns she now wore underneath her cloak. They fit there quite nicely, and no one noticed so long as she didn't do too much wiggling around. Though the cars were heated by steam heat siphoned off the boilers, the windows were thin and they sometimes rattled, and the cars were never quite so toasty as she would've liked. So it wasn't strange that she wore the concealing cloak almost all the time. She rather doubted that anyone would notice or care, even if she was spotted sporting weapons; but she enjoyed keeping them a secret, close and unseen up against her body.

At night she settled into the seat that transformed to a bed, nestling into her semi-private space with the divider separating her from even her compartment-mates, for all the difference it made. The divider stifled nothing, and every noise of the train's daily and nightly motion filtered into the strained sleep she managed to catch. But by the end of the first week, she had a system down: She excused herself to the washroom to unfasten her day corset and remove her shoes, then, covered by her ever-present cloak, returned to the compartment to coil beneath a blanket in her narrow sleeping space, where she listened to Mrs. Butterfield snore and to the nocturnal comings and goings of Miss Clay, who slept even more infrequently than Mercy.

In the mornings, she repeated the system in reverse, beginning in the wash area once more and reassuming her personal attire for daylight hours. She also washed her face, brushed her teeth, and combed her hair back into a bun—or sometimes, if she felt particularly inspired, into braids that she pinned into a more elaborate and secure updo. The braids held their position better when she stepped back and forth between the cars—a procedure that was becoming almost unremarkable, though the February wind still clapped her in the face with the force of an irate schoolmarm every time she flipped a lever to let herself out of the Pullman.

She wondered after the men who conducted the train, and wondered how they slept—in shifts, she assumed—and how odd it must be to live and work in constant motion. She supposed that eventually they must become accustomed to it, just as she'd become accustomed to the smell of the Robertson Hospital; and she came to trust them as they kept the train moving, always moving, through daylight and darkness, and save for the occasional short stop that never lasted longer than an hour or two, however long it took the boilers to be refilled and the stash of diesel and coal to be replenished.

Until Kansas City.

Shortly before the Kansas City stop, which was meant to be an all-afternoon intermission from the grind of the tracks, the coupler that connected the fifth and sixth passenger cars broke as they whipped around a bend.

It was reported almost immediately, and there were few ways to handle it other than to force a stop and let the disconnected cars catch up. This maneuver was undertaken with no small degree of trepidation from the passengers and crew. In addition to the general suspense of being halted on the tracks and waiting for the train's rear compartments to roll up and collide, there was also a terrific sense of vulnerability. Only a few miles outside the station, the *Dreadnought* sat parked on its track as if waiting for a wayward duckling to retrieve its position in line. All the passengers, crew, and soldiers sat or stood at attention, watching every window for a hint of danger. No one had forgotten the abortive raid, and no one wanted to see it repeated while they were sitting like those aforementioned ducks.

Miss Clay clutched at her portmanteau and Mrs. Butterfield sat rigid, upright, and propped into a position of defiance as the now-slowed rear cars caught up foot by foot, unstoppable even in their tedious approach.

"Ladies and gentlemen," announced one of the blond soldiers, whose name had turned out to be Cyrus Berry. "Kindly brace yourselves," he urged. "The back cars are going to bump us any second—"

And indeed, soon enough on the heel of those words that it almost interrupted them, the back cars collided with the front cars, smacking together in the place where the coupler had failed, and battering against the forward spaces so that luggage toppled down from storage, hats were knocked off of heads, and more than a few people were thrown to their hands and knees on the floor.

Pierce Tankersly, the other blond soldier, came through the front door, asking, "Is everyone all right?" His query was a bit premature, for no one was yet certain of personal allrightness, and the two little boys by the front window had only just begun to cry.

Mrs. Butterfield answered for the group. "I believe we'll all survive. But tell me, dear lad, what happens now?"

"Now, we fix it," he said firmly and with a determined expression that told everyone he didn't have the slightest idea how this might be accomplished, but he had every faith that someone, somewhere, had a handle on the situation.

True to his assumptions, a pair of porters and one of the conductor's men came along shortly, and while the nervous soldiers kept their arms at the ready and their eyes on the windows, the rail men began a hasty job of affixing the cars together in a temporary manner. Mercy didn't see the whole of their endeavors, but she gathered it had something to do with bolting a new joint into place and praying it'd hold until Kansas City. In order to better guarantee this outcome, the *Dreadnought* pulled rather slowly into town.

Almost immediately after their arrival, Cyrus Berry departed the car and returned to it, passing along a message that was undoubtedly running the length of the train. "Ladies and gentlemen," he began again, his arms held out in a bid to command the whole car's attention. "Due to the coupler issues between the fifth and sixth car, we're going to be spending the night here in town. To make up for the inconvenience and delay, the Union will provide everyone with money enough for a hotel room and supper here in town while repairs are being made. Please see the conductor or one of the porters for details and information about the hotel in question, and how to collect your fees. We'll be leaving the West Bottoms Station tomorrow morning at ten o'clock, or that's the plan as it stands right now."

Then he tipped his hat to the passengers and moved on to the next car.

Mrs. Butterfield was delighted, and even Theodora Clay seemed pleased. "I'm forced to admit, I like the sound of a proper bed. These folding jobbies are hard on the neck, don't you think?" she asked no one in particular.

Her aunt made murmuring noises of assent.

"Absolutely. And to think, it's only been a week. Maybe we'll get lucky and something else will break along the way," Mercy suggested as she gathered her satchel and slipped her head through the strap, so it would hang across her chest.

"I don't know if we should hope for that," Miss Clay said. "We were fortunate to see the coupler fail so close to town. I don't know about you, but I'd be immensely nervous if the train were to limp much farther. We were only going a quarter of our usual speed, these last few miles. Unless, of course, you aren't particularly worried about meeting any southern raiders."

Mercy pretended not to hear the implication and said primly, "I'm certainly not looking forward to any such thing." Then, upon seeing Pierce Tankersly helping the widower and his children find their way to the door, she added a bit more loudly, "Though we've got plenty of good company on this train, and I'm pretty confident that the boys on board will hold 'em off just fine, if they do come sniffing back around. Now, if you'll excuse me," she said to her seatmates. She stepped out into the aisle behind the two little boys, who were thrilled silly at the prospect of getting off the train, even if only for the night.

She made her way to the exit with baby steps, halting occasionally to allow others to slip in front of her, and finally descended the short iron stairs onto terra firma once more. She bounced on her heels to stretch her legs, and turned her head hard left to right, which resulted in a satisfying crack.

Upon locating the conductor, she collected an envelope that contained an address and some Union bills to cover the afternoon and evening. A porter from the West Bottoms Station pointed her and a few of the other passengers to a nearby street, and they found their way to an unornamented brick establishment in the city's heart as a small herd. The smell of stockyards wafted on every breeze, accompanied by the scent of oil, burning coal, and the hot stink of steel being soldered and pounded.

Mercy looked around and did not see Mrs. Butterfield or Miss Clay, but she smirked to imagine their reaction to the lowbrow quarters they'd be directed to. While she was taking visual stock of her fellow travelers, she spied the back end of Horatio Korman slinking away from the crowd and into a side street. Her eyes followed him around a corner until they could track him no farther.

Wondering what he was up to, she decided to follow him.

The neighborhood smelled no worse than the hospital, and this was only the stench of animals, after all: sheep, cattle, and hogs being shuffled about between markets before they headed for plates. Mercy had grown up around these smells, and could effortlessly ignore them. She walked past the Kansas City Live Stock Exchange with its immense gates and ranch-style signs, back around the station, and then past another stockyard she'd somehow missed on the first pass. Much like Fort Chattanooga, most of the people she saw on the street were men, but here and there she saw station passengers or debarkers like herself—mostly in working-class clothing, and mostly white. In fact, that was one of the first things she noticed about the passersby: She didn't see half so many colored people as she did back East.

She spotted one or two, dressed in standard cowboy style with canvas pants, linen shirts, and boots; and she saw one porter on some sort of break from the train station; but that amounted to the whole of the population within her range of vision.

And where had the ranger gone, anyway? Suddenly, she didn't see him.

A hand settled on the small of her back and pushed her forward firmly, but without any violence. "A word with you, ma'am."

"Oh. Mr. Korman, *there* you are. This is getting downright unseemly," she complained as he led her off the main walkway, away from the road, and toward a small sign advertising barbecue that was supplemented by the aroma halo of roast pork and beef.

"It's nothing of the kind. This is just two passengers getting acquainted over supper," he said as he urged her up the step and inside the clapboard structure called the Bar None Saloon and Grill. Just then his hand brushed her waist and found something hard. He paused and looked her in the eye, and for a moment Mercy could've sworn that he almost smiled. "Nice guns," he said, even though he couldn't see them.

She allowed herself to be ushered inside the grill, which was dark and smoky, but so thickly packed with the sweet and sharp aura of simmering food that the stockyards might have been a hundred miles away. They took a seat toward the rear, and Korman positioned himself so his back was to the kitchen wall and he faced the front door. Mercy sat in front of him, and as she adjusted herself on the bench, she realized how cold she'd become as she'd walked the West Bottoms. She peeled off her gloves and felt for her nearly numb ears, then blew into her hands.

"Cold out there," she said, more for the act of saying something than to tell him what he already knew.

"Yup," he agreed, and extracted himself from his overcoat, which he slapped over the back of an unoccupied chair. "You're not lost, are you? You got yourself checked into the Prairie Dog?"

"Not yet. I wanted to stretch my legs."

"You could pick a nicer part of town to do it in."

"This is the only part of town with which I'm acquainted, and nobody's bothered me yet except for *you*."

"Yeah, and I'm about to bother you some more."

"How's that?"

He might've answered, but someone came over and took their order for a pair of sandwiches and home fries, so the conversation stalled briefly, then came back to life. He continued, "A few days ago—that incident with the Rebs."

"The raiders?"

"Raiders," he snorted. "They weren't raiding *shit*." He drawled out the word until it sounded like *sheet*.

She said, "That one man—on the horse, right before they left. I thought he was looking at me, through the window. But he wasn't, was he? He was looking at *you*, behind me. Do you know him? Did you know about the raid?"

The ranger sniffed, a gesture that lifted and tilted one wing of his mustache. "I was pretty sure from the start that they must be some of Bloody Bill's old boys; and when I set eyes on Jesse, that just about cinched it."

"But he was wearing a bandanna over his face."

"Aw, I'd know him anyplace."

Mercy wasn't sure what to make of this information, so she said, "But Bill's dead, ain't he? He's been dead for years."

"And it's never stopped his bushwhackers from chasing blue all over Missouri, has it? That was his old band. And though I called 'em boys, Jesse's a little older than me. The rest of them, though. They're probably just backwoods kids with nothing better to do, and no intention of wearing a uniform or following orders."

"Sounds like you think real highly of them."

"The James brothers aren't too bad, if you get to know them. But that's beside the point. It wasn't a raid, because Jesse and Frank are too damn smart to run up against something like the

Dreadnought with a handful of horses, a hoot, and a holler. They're looking for something."

Mercy shook her head. "Lord knows what. Ain't it enough that the thing's a big ol' Union machine? Can't blame them if they want to take it down."

"They can't *take it down,*" he insisted. "They aren't dogs chasing a wagon, though they wouldn't know what to do if they caught it."

"But if you know some of them raiders, can't you ask them?"

He let go of the tiny waxed point of his mustache and asked, "How exactly would you recommend I go about doing that? I can't just hold up the train for a few days and wait on 'em to catch up, now, can I?"

"I don't know. If you were *determined* enough . . ."

"Oh, don't go on like that. I need to get west of here, still—it's my duty and my job to find out what's going on for my own country. That doesn't leave me a fat lot of time to be dickering around in Kansas, just to see what your grays think they require of a Union engine. All I can figure," he continued, "is that there must be something on board that's sparked their interest."

"Like what?"

He shrugged and leaned back against the wall. "I was hoping maybe you had some idea. What do you know about what they're carrying in those extra cars?"

"The one behind the caboose, you mean?"

"That one, sure. And the two behind the engine. Can't be plain old fuel in those two; even a juggernaut like that damn engine don't need half so much to propel it. No, I'm thinking they're bringing something else along."

A pair of sandwiches on hammered metal plates were slapped down in front of them, delaying Mercy's response a few moments more. But when she spoke, after swallowing a mouthful of a very fine barbecue sandwich that was almost too spicy for her taste, she said, "Bodies."

"What?"

"They're carrying bodies—in that back car, anyhow."

Horatio Korman licked his upper lip, which did not remove the full spectrum of sauce that was accumulating on the underside of his facial hair. "Well, sure," he told her. "That's the *official* story."

"You don't believe it?"

"No, I don't believe it. And I don't think your Rebs believe it, either—and I wonder what they know that makes them think chasing the *Dreadnought*'s worth their time and trouble."

"Can't help you there," she told him, and took another bite.

"I don't know why I thought you could," he said with the same accusatory gleam in his eye that Miss Clay had been giving her all week, for exactly the opposite reason.

"Oh, leave it be," she said with irritation and a half-full mouth. When she'd swallowed the whole thing down, she went on. "What do you want me to say? I told the captain the truth, same as I told you the truth—and I didn't rat you out to nobody yet, and I'm hoping you'll treat me the same. My reasons for heading west have nothing to do with the war, and I'm sick of it anyway. I don't want a whole trainful of folks hating me because of where I worked and where I'm from."

"So your sympathies lie not in Virginia?" he asked, with a veneer of false innocence.

"Don't you go putting words in my mouth. I love my country same as you love yours, but I'm not running any mission for my country. I'm no spy, and I'm too tired to fight for anyone but myself right now. Sometimes, I think I don't have the energy for that, either."

"Am I supposed to feel sorry for you?"

"I didn't ask you to," she snapped. "Same as I didn't ask you to pull me off the street and feed me. Just because you and me might be sort of on the same team, that's no excuse for us to hang together." She took another jab at her plate, knowing there was more to it than that. She mumbled, "You're gonna get me in trouble, I swear."

He asked, "And what if I do? What do you think'll happen to you, if they all find out what you're keeping quiet?"

She shrugged. "Not sure. Maybe they dump me off at the next stop, in the middle of noplace. I don't have the money to pay the rest of the way out to Tacoma again. Maybe I get stuck a thousand miles away from where I need to be, with my daddy maybe dying out there. Or, Jesus," she said suddenly, as it had just occurred to her. "Maybe they'll arrest me, and say I'm a spy! I can't prove I'm *not*."

"Don't be ridiculous. They'd arrest *me* before they'd arrest you."

"Why? Because you're doing your job in someplace that ain't Texas?"

"Something like that," he said in a way that made her want to ask more questions. "Fact is, I think there *is* a spy on the train—but I'm not sure who yet. That coupler didn't break all by its lonesome. Someone wants to sabotage the train so the Rebs can catch it, but it sure ain't me. And I can't prove it. But I probably look good for it."

"So what *are* you doing on this train? Knowing that being here is asking for trouble?"

He took a deep breath and the last quarter of his sandwich in one bite, and took his time chewing before answering her. He also took a minute to glance around the room, checking the faces he saw for familiarity or malice. Then he asked, "How much do you keep up with the newspapers, Mrs. Lynch?"

"More lately than usually. They gave me something to read while I was coming west."

"All right. Then maybe you've heard about a little problem Texas has right now, with some Mexican fellas who went missing all in a bunch." He said this conspiratorially, but not so quietly that everyone would try to overhear whatever secret was being told.

"I've seen something about it, here and there. Mr. Cunningham aboard the *Providence*—he gave me the background on the situation."

"Yeah, I'll *bet* he did."

"What's that supposed to mean?"

"Not a damn thing. I imagine he's got opinions on it, and I imagine they're not altogether different from mine. But it's my *job,* not my opinion, to sort out what became of the dirty brown bastards and what they're up to. They went wandering north—"

"To help relocate—"

"They went wandering north," he talked over her, as if he wasn't really interested in political discussion. "And they went wandering right off the edge of the map. I've been chasing every rumor, snippet of gossip, and wild-eyed fable from every cowhand, cowpoke, rancher, settler, and Injun who'll stand still long enough to talk to me, and none of it's making any sense—not at *all.*"

Honestly curious, she asked, "What are they saying?"

He waved his hand as if to dismiss the whole of it, since none of it could be true. "Oh, they're saying crazy things—completely crazy things. First off, if word can be believed, they went off course by a thousand miles or so. And I've got to tell you, Mrs. Lynch, I've known a backwards Mex or two in my time, but I've never heard of one dumb enough to go a thousand miles off course in the span of a few months."

"That *does* sound unlikely."

"It goes well beyond unlikely. And I don't think Mexico knows what's happened to 'em either—that's what really gets me. Likewise—and I'm in a pretty secure position to know—the Republic didn't touch 'em. Whatever happened happened somewhere out in the West Texas desert hill country, and then something sent those men on some other bizarre quest—"

"All the way to Utah?" she interjected.

Derailed, he stopped and said, "Utah? How'd you know that?"

"Because you told me that's how far you were riding the other day. The Utah territory's a long piece away from West Texas, I'd think."

"Amazingly far," he confessed. "But that's what the intelligence is telling us. Something strange happened, and the group shifted direction, drifting north and west. The last reports of Mexican soldiers have come from the Mormon settlements out there— you know, them folks who have all the wives and whatnot. The Mormons may be swamp-rat crazy themselves, for all I know, but they're scared to death."

"Of a legion of soldiers? Can't say as I blame them. Lord knows it'd give me a start to find them in my backyard."

"That's not all there is to it, though," he said, and he shook his head some more, as if there was simply no believing what he was about to say. "Reports say these Mexis have gone completely off their rockers. I heard," and he finally leaned forward, willing to whisper, "that they've started *eating people*."

"You shut your mouth!" Mercy exclaimed.

"But that's what people say—that they're just mad as hatters, and that something's gone awful wrong with them. They act senseless, like their brains have leaked right out of their heads, and they don't talk—they don't respond to anything, English or Spanish. Mrs. Lynch, people are going to *panic* if word gets out and nothing gets done about it!"

"Well . . ." Mercy tried to process the information and wasn't sure how to go about it, so she racked her brain and tried to think of something logical. "Do you think it's some kind of sickness, like rabies or something? People with rabies will do that, sometimes; bite people—" And she cut herself short, because saying so out loud reminded her of the Salvation Army hostel.

The ranger said, "If these fellas have some kind of disease, and it's so catching that a whole legion of 'em came down with it and went insane, that's not exactly a comforting thought. Whatever's going on, we need to contain it, and maybe . . . investigate it. Figure out what's wrong, and figure out if we can do something about it. But I'll be damned right to hell if I have the faintest idea what's going on," he said before stuffing bread and potatoes into his mouth.

She said, "I wonder if it's got something to do with sap."

"What, like tree sap? Oh, wait, no. You mean that stupid drug the boys on the front are using these days? I don't see how."

"I wouldn't have believed it either, till I wound up in Memphis. I saw some fellas there, some addicts who'd used the stuff almost to death. They looked . . . well, like you said. Like corpses. And one of 'em tried to bite me."

"An addict trying to bite a nurse ain't quite the same as cannibalism."

She frowned and said, "I'm not saying it *is*. I'm only saying it looks the same, a little bit. Or maybe I'm just crackers." Then she abruptly changed the subject, asking before she had time to forget, "Say, you don't know anyplace around here where I could send a telegram, do you?"

"I'd be surprised if there wasn't a Western Union office at the station. You could ask around. Why? Who're you reporting to, anyway?"

"Nobody but my mother. And the sheriff out in Tacoma, I

guess. I'm just trying to let folks know that I'm still alive, and I'm still on my way."

When the meal was over, she thanked him for it and went walking back to the station, where she did indeed find a Western Union and a friendly telegraph operator named Mabel. Mabel was a tiny woman with an eye-patch, and she could work a tap at the speed of lightning.

Mercy sent two messages, precisely as she'd told the ranger.

The first went to Washington, and the second went to Virginia.

SHERIFF WILKES I AM WESTBOUND AND PRESENTLY
IN KANSAS CITY STOP EXPECT ME WITHIN A FEW
WEEKS STOP WILL SEND MORE WORD WHEN I GET
CLOSER STOP HOPE ALL IS WELL WITH MY FATHER
STOP

DEAR MOMMA PLEASE DO NOT BE ANGRY STOP I'M
GOING WEST TO VISIT MY DADDY WHO MAY BE
DYING STOP IT IS A LONG STORY AND I'LL TELL IT
TO YOU SOMETIME STOP DO NOT WORRY I HAVE
MONEY AND TRAIN TICKETS AND ALL IS FINE STOP
EXCEPT FOR I GUESS I SHOULD TELL YOU PHILLIP
DIED AND I GOT THE WORD AT THE HOSPITAL STOP
GO AHEAD AND PRAY FOR ME STOP I COULD
PROBABLY USE IT STOP

After she'd paid her fees, Mercy turned to leave, but Mabel stopped her. "Mrs. Lynch? I hope you don't mind my asking, but are you riding on the big Union train?"

"Yes, I am. That's right."

"Could I bother you for a small favor?" she asked.

Mercy said, "Certainly."

Mabel gathered a small stack of paper and stuffed it into a

brown folder. "Would you mind dropping these off at the conductor's window for me?" She gestured down at her left leg, which Mercy only then noticed was missing from the knee down. "I've got a case of the aches today, and the stairs give me real trouble."

"Sure, I'll take them," Mercy said, wondering what terrible accident had so badly injured the woman's body, if not her spirit. She took the telegrams and left the office with Mabel's thanks echoing in her ears, heading down to the station agent's office and the window where the conductors collected their itineraries, directions, and other notes.

Down at that window, two men were arguing over tracks and lights. Mercy didn't want to interrupt, so she stood to the side, not quite out of their line of sight but distant enough that she didn't appear to be eavesdropping. And while she waited for them to finish, she did something she really shouldn't have. She knew it was wrong even as she ran her finger along the brown folder, and she knew it was a bad idea as she peeled the cover aside to take a peek within it. But she nonetheless lifted a corner of the folder and glanced at the sheets there, realizing that they weren't all notes for the conductor: some were telegrams intended for passengers.

Right there on top, as if Heaven itself had ordained that she read it, she saw a most unusual message. At first it made no sense whatsoever, but she read it, and she puzzled over it, and she slapped the folder shut when the men at the window ceased their bickering and went their separate ways.

It said,

CB ALERT STOP STALL AT KC AS LONG AS POSSIBLE STOP SHENANDOAH APPROACHING FROM OC TOP SPEED STOP SHOULD CATCH TRAIN BEFORE ROCKIES STOP CONFIRM OR DENY CABOOSE BY TOPEKA IF POSSIBLE STOP SEND WORD FROM THERE STOP

Alas, her workmanlike reading skills moved too slowly to give it a second, more through inspection before the conductor spotted her. Once he did, she approached him, to keep from looking too guilty. She handed the folder to the man, bid him good evening, and returned to her hotel room feeling deeply perplexed and revisiting the message in her mind.

By the time she undressed for bed, she'd guessed that "OC" might be Oklahoma City, since "KC" was so obviously Kansas City. She didn't know what the "Shenandoah" was, but if it was traveling at top speed, and trying to "catch" the *Dreadnought,* she was forced to assume that it must be a mighty piece of machinery indeed. And what did "CB" mean? Was it someone's initials? A code name? A sign-off?

"Shenandoah," she whispered to herself. A southern name, for southern places and southern things. "Could be a unit or something." She turned over, unable to get very comfortable on the cheap bed, yet grateful enough for it that she wanted to stay awake and enjoy the fact that it wasn't moving. So she stayed up and asked the washbasin against the wall. "Or another train?"

The last thing that rolled through Mercy's mind before her eyes closed and stayed that way was that Ranger Korman was right.

Someone on board was a Rebel spy.

It wasn't her, and she didn't think—based on their conversation over supper—that it was the ranger, either. So whom did that leave?

She sighed, and said, "Could be almost anyone, really."

And then she fell asleep.

Thirteen

Come morning, Mercy stood on the train station platform with her fellow passengers, waiting for the opportunity to board once more. She noticed a few absences, not out of nosiness, but simply because she'd become accustomed to seeing the same people day in and out for the previous week. Now she saw new faces, too, looking curiously at the awe-inspiring engine and discussing amongst themselves why the train required such an elaborate thing.

The conductor overheard the questions, and Mercy listened to his answer, though she didn't know how much of it to believe. "True enough, this is a war engine," he said, patting at the boiler's side with one gloved hand. "But that doesn't mean this is a war operation. We're sending some bodies of boys from the western territories back home, and while we're at it, we're bringing this engine out to Tacoma to retrofit it with a different sort of power system."

One curious man asked, "Whatever do you mean?"

"At present, she's running on a two-fuel system: diesel and coal steam. She's the only Union engine of her kind, though I understand the Rebs use diesel engines pretty regularly. In Tacoma, we're going to see if we can retool her to use straight diesel, like theirs. It'll give us more power, better speed, and a lighter payload if we can work it out."

Mercy had a hard time figuring how a liquid fuel would be any lighter than coal, but she was predisposed to disbelieving him, since his story was different from the St. Louis station agent's—and now that she'd talked to the ranger, and now that she'd seen the telegram that wasn't meant for her eyes. She'd never quite bought that the war engine was on a peaceful mission, and the longer she looked at it, the more deeply she felt that the train's backstory was a lie.

Then something dawned on her, seeming so obvious that she should've thought of it before. She did her best not to draw anyone's attention by dashing. Instead, she shuffled back toward the rear end of the train, to the caboose, and the bonus car that trailed bleakly behind with all its windows painted over. There was a guard standing on the platform that connected it to the caboose, but no one else was paying it any mind.

Mercy had no means of telling whether or not anything had come or gone, or been loaded or unloaded. But she spied an older negro porter, and she quietly accosted him. "Excuse me," she said, turning her body to keep her face and her voice away from the guard, who wasn't watching her, but might've been listening.

"Yes ma'am. How can I help you?"

"I was wondering . . . have those fellows opened that car at all? Taken anything off it, or put anything inside it?"

"Oh *no* ma'am," he said with a low, serious voice. He shook his head. "None of us are to go anyplace near it; we was told as soon as it stopped that nobody touches the last car. I even heard-tell that some of the soldiers got a talking-to for getting too close or peeking in the windows. That thing's sealed up *good*."

She said, "Ah," and thanked him for his time before wandering back to the passenger cars, turning this information over in her mind as she went. If the train was transporting war dead home to rest, why weren't any of them ever dropped off? She wondered who on earth she could possibly share her suspicions with, then saw the ranger leaning up against one of the pillars supporting the station overhang, an expression on his face like he'd been licking lemons.

"Mr. Korman," she said. He must have heard her, but he didn't look at her until she was standing in front of him.

"What?" he asked.

"And a fine morning to you, too, sir," she said.

"No, it isn't."

She asked, "How's that?"

He spit a gob of tobacco juice in an expert line that ended with a splatter at the foot of the next pillar over. He didn't point, but he nodded his head toward a spot by the train where two dark-haired men were chatting quietly, their backs to Mercy and Horatio Korman. "You see that?"

"See what? Those two?" The moment she said this, one of them pivoted on a sharp-booted heel, casting a wary glance across the crowd before returning to his soft conversation. His face had a shape to it that might've been part Indian, with a strong profile and skin that was a shade or two darker than her own. He had thick black eyebrows that had been groomed or combed, or merely grew in an unlikely but flattering shape. He and his companion were not speaking English, Mercy could tell, even though she couldn't make out any of their particular words. Their chatter had a different rhythm, and flowed faster—or maybe it only sounded faster, since the individual syllables meant nothing to her.

"Mexicans."

Temporarily knocked off topic, Mercy asked, "Really? What are they doing here? They're going to ride the train with us?"

"Looks like it."

She thought about this, and then said, "Maybe you ought to talk to them. Maybe they're here for the same reason as you."

"Don't be ridiculous."

"What's so ridiculous about that? You want to know what

happened to their troops; maybe *they* want to know what happened to them, too. Look at them: they're wearing suits, or uniforms of some sort. Maybe they're military men themselves." She squinted, not making out any insignia.

"They ain't no soldiers. They're some kind of government policemen or somesuch. You're probably right about what they're after, but there's nothing they can contribute to the search."

She demanded, "How do you figure that?"

"Like I told you the other night, they don't know any more about it than we do. I've got all the best information at hand, and I've busted tail and greased palms to get it. I'm closer to learning the truth than anybody on the continent, and that includes the emperor's cowpokes."

She gave a half shrug and said, "Well, they've gotten this far, same as you. They can't be all useless."

"Hush up, woman. They're trouble, is what they are. And I don't like trouble."

"Something tells me that's not altogether true."

His mustache twitched in an almost-smile, like when he'd discovered the guns under her cloak. "You might have me there. But I don't like seeing them. No good can come of it."

"I don't think I've ever met any Mexicans before."

"They're tyrants, and imperialists, every last one of them." If he'd been holding any more tobacco in his lip, he no doubt would've used it to chase the sentence out of his mouth.

"And I guess you've talked to every last one of them, to be so sure of that."

The ranger reached for his hat to tip it sarcastically and, no doubt, walk away from the conversation, but Mercy stopped him by saying, "Hey, let me ask you something. You know anything about a . . . a train?" She went with her best guess. "Called the *Shenandoah*?"

"Yeah, I've heard of it."

"Is it . . ." She wasn't sure where she was headed, but she fished regardless. "Is it a particularly *fast* train?"

"As far as I've heard. Rolls for you Rebs, I think. Supposed to be pretty much the swiftest of the swifties," he said, meaning the lightweight hybrid engines that were notorious for their speed. They'd been designed and mostly built in Texas, some of them experimental, as the Texians had searched for more ways to make use of their oil.

She stood there, nodding slowly and wondering how much she should tell him. He'd already made plain that he didn't care what the Rebs wanted with the train. Then again, he might've been lying, or he might care if he thought there were spies on board. Anyway, it wasn't like she had anybody else to tell.

While she was still pondering, he said, "What makes you ask, anyway?"

She would've answered, too, if the whistle hadn't chosen that precise moment to blow, causing the few children present to cover their ears and grimace, and the milling adults to cluster tighter together, pressing forward to the passenger cars in anticipation of boarding or reboarding.

"Never mind," she said instead. "We can talk about it later."

She walked away from him and joined the press of people. As the crowd thickened, she was more and more likely to be spotted conspiring with the ranger; and although she was the only one who *knew* he was a ranger, everyone had already gathered that he was a Texian, and she didn't want to join him as a pariah. She understood why he would prefer to keep his status as a law enforcer quiet, though: military men like to have a hierarchy. They wouldn't have liked to think that someone outside that hierarchy was hanging around, wearing guns, and from a strictly legal standpoint, they wouldn't have any authority over him. But they could make his life difficult, especially in such a confined mode of transport.

Back on board the train, Mercy was surprised to note that

Mrs. Butterfield and Miss Clay had beaten her to the compartment. She was even more surprised, and openly curious, to note that the two Mexican men had been assigned to her own car. The two ladies opposite her were not whispering, just conversing about the newcomers in their normal voices.

"I heard them speaking Spanish," said Mrs. Butterfield. "Obviously I don't understand a word of it, but that one fellow there, the taller one, he looks almost white, doesn't he?"

"He might *be* white," Theodora Clay pointed out. "There are still plenty of Spaniards in Mexico."

"Why? Wasn't there some kind of . . . I don't know . . . revolution?" Mrs. Butterfield asked vaguely.

Her niece replied, "Several of them. But I wonder why they're on board, heading north and west? That sounds like the wrong direction altogether, don't you think? They aren't dressed for the weather, I can tell you that much."

Mercy suggested, "Why don't you ask them, if you really want to know?"

Mrs. Butterfield shuddered, and gave Mercy a look that all but said, *Good heavens, girl. I thought I knew you!* Instead, she told the nurse, "I'm sure I'm not interested in making any strange new friends on this occasion. Besides, they probably don't speak English. And they're all Catholics anyway."

"I bet they *do* speak English," Mercy argued. "It's pretty hard to find your way around if you don't speak the language, and they've made it this far north all right."

Miss Clay arched an eyebrow, lifting it like a dare. "Why don't *you* go chat them up, then?"

Mercy leaned back in her seat and said, "You're the one who's dying to know. I was only saying that if you were *that* desperate, you could just *ask*."

"Why?" Miss Clay asked.

Mercy didn't understand. "Why what?"

"Why aren't you interested? I think interest is positively *natural*."

She narrowed her eyes and replied, "I'm inclined to mind my own business, is all."

But later on that day, nearly up to evening, Mercy found her way back to the caboose in search of supper, and there she found the two Mexicans seated at a table with Captain MacGruder and the injured (but relatively able-bodied) Morris Comstock. Morris smiled and waved, and the captain dipped his hat at her, which gave her the perfect excuse to join them. She ordered a cup of tea and some biscuits with a tiny pot of jam and carried them over to the seat the men had cleared in her behalf.

"Gentlemen," she said, settling herself. She made a point of making eye contact with the two Mexicans, for the sheer novelty if nothing else. They seemed to find her presence peculiar, but they behaved like the gentlemen she'd accused them of being, and murmured greetings in response.

"Mrs. Lynch," said the captain. "Good to see you again. We were just having a little talk with these two fellows here. They're from Mexico."

Morris said, "We were giving them a friendly warning, too. About that Texian riding in the sixth car. He's a mean-looking bastard, and I hope he don't make problems for these folks." However, he said it with a gleam that implied he might not be too disappointed at the chance to reprimand the ranger.

MacGruder cleared his throat and said more diplomatically, "I understand you're acquainted with the Republican in question. Came out on the same riverboat, to St. Louis, is that right?"

"Yes, that's right. I don't believe it's come up before, though. How did you know?"

"Miss Clay might have mentioned it, in passing."

"I see."

"Señora," said the darker of the two men, the one she'd seen at the station with the uncommonly tidy eyebrows. "Please allow me to introduce myself: I am Javier Tomás Ignacio Galeano." He said the names in one long string that sounded like music. "And this is my associate, Frederico Maria Gonsalez Portilla. We are . . . inspectors. From the Empire of Mexico. We do not intend to cause a stir aboard this train; we are only in the process of discovering what has happened to a lost legion of our nation's soldiers."

Mercy was glad his English was so good. She didn't need to strain to understand him, and she didn't feel that idiotic compulsion to speak loudly. She said, "I've heard about that—it's in the newspapers, you know."

His fellow inspector said, "Yes, we are aware that it has made your papers. It is a great mystery, is it not?"

"A great mystery indeed," she agreed, feeling a tiny thrill over the conversation with a foreigner. She'd known plenty of northerners and southerners, but she'd never met anybody who was from a-whole-nother *country* before. Except Gordon Rand, and he didn't hardly count.

Inspector Galeano fretted with his napkin and said, "If only we knew what had happened, out in the west of *Tejas*." He called the Republic by the name it'd worn as a Mexican state.

"What do you mean?" she asked.

He told her, "Something occurred, and it sent them off course, up past the low, hot country and north into the mountains. We have learned that they made it as far as the territory of the . . . of the . . ." He searched his English vocabulary for a word, but failed to find it.

"Utah," Morris Comstock provided. "Where the Mormons live, with all them wives."

"Mormons, yes. The religious people. Some of them have made reports . . . *terrible* reports."

Mercy almost forgot that she wasn't supposed to know any of this, but managed to stop herself from exclaiming about the cannibalism before anyone could ask her how she'd come by the information. Instead, she said, "I'm sorry to hear that. Do you have any idea what happened? Do you think the Texians did something . . . rash?"

Inspector Portilla's forehead crinkled at the use of *rash,* but he gleaned the context and said, "It's always possible. But we do not think that is the case. We have had reports that some Texians are implicated as well."

"What kind of reports? *Terrible* reports?" she asked.

"Equally terrible, yes. We believe"—he exchanged a glance with Inspector Galeano, who nodded to affirm that this was safe to share—"that there may be an illness of some sort."

"That's possible," Mercy said sagely. "Or a . . . a poison, or something." Then, to forestall any questions about her undue interest, she said, "I'm a nurse. This stuff's interesting to me."

"A nurse?" said Inspector Galeano. "We were told there would be a doctor on the train, but we've heard of no such—"

Morris Comstock interrupted. "We were supposed to pick one up in Kansas City, but he never showed. So now we're supposed to have one in Topeka, maybe. I swear, I think they're just telling us tales."

The captain crossed his arms, leaned back, and said to the Mexicans, "Mrs. Lynch is the one who patched up poor Morris here, when he got winged during that raid."

Inspector Galeano wore a look of intense interest. He bent forward, laid one arm on the table, and gestured with the other hand. "We only developed this idea very recently, from *inteligencia* that found us in Missouri. But perhaps I can ask you this question— and I hope you will not consider me . . ." He shuffled through his vocabulary for a word, then found it. "Rude."

"Fire away," she told him, hoping that she looked the very picture of enthusiastic innocence.

He said, "Very good. These are the facts as we understand them: A partial force of soldiers was sent from a presidio in Saltillo. They met with commanders and acquired more personnel in El Paso. At the time, their numbers were approximately six hundred and fifty. They traveled east, toward the middle of the old state, near Abilene. From there they were to march on to Lubbock, and up to the settlement at Oneida—called *Amarillo* by your people. By then they had added another hundred settlers to their number. But they never reached Lubbock."

She observed, "That many people don't just vanish into thin air."

"Nor did these," he agreed. "They've been glimpsed, and there are signs of their passing, but the signs are . . ." He retreated to his original description, finding none other that suited the gravity of the situation. "*Terrible*. They wander, driven by the weather or whatever boundaries they encounter, bouncing from place to place, and . . . and . . . it is like a herd of starving goats, everywhere they go! They leave nothing behind—they consume all food, all plants and crops, all animals . . . and possibly . . . all the *people* they meet!"

"People!" Mercy gasped for dramatic effect, and squeezed one of her biscuits until it fragmented in her hand. She let its crumbs fall to the plate, and left them unattended.

"Yes, people! The few who have escaped tell such *stories*. The missing soldiers and settlers have taken on an awful appearance, thin and hungry. Their skin has turned gray, and they no longer speak except to groan or scream. They pay no attention to their clothing, or their bodies; and some of them bear signs of violent injuries. But these wounded men—and women: as I said, there are settlers among them—they do not fall down or die, though they *look* like they are dead. Now, tell me, Nurse Lynch, do you know of any poison or illness that can cause such a thing?"

Her instinct was to blurt, *Yes!* but she gave it half a minute of measured consideration while she nibbled one of the intact biscuits. After all, Ranger Korman hadn't taken her seriously, and she didn't know these men *half* so well. Finally, she said, "Well, I've known of men poisoned by putrid foods, canned goods and the like, from battlefield stores. Sometimes those men go a bit senseless. But this sounds to me more like like sap-poisoning."

Inspector Galeano asked, "Sap-poisoning?" and Captain Mac-Gruder looked like he was next in line with questions.

"There's this drug that the boys use out on the front. Gotten real popular in the last three or four years. When the addicts came into my old hospital, we called 'em 'wheezers' because they breathed all funny. And those fellas who use too much of it . . . they go crazy. I never saw any as crazy as what you're talking about, but I've seen close." Memphis. The Salvation Army. Irvin, who bites.

Captain MacGruder said, "I've seen a few sap-heads in my time, but never as bad as that." He tapped his fingers on the edge of the table. "They make it out of a gas, you know."

"I *didn't* know."

"Nasty yellow stuff. They get it from somewhere out west— I'm not sure where, but someplace so far west, they've got volcanoes. That's all I know. They bring it in by dirigible. Pirates run the whole operation, I think. Can't think of anyone else nutty enough to tangle with it."

The inspectors sat upright with a snap. "Really?" said Inspector Galeano. "You must tell us more! Señora Lynch, you said you'd seen it make men *loco*?"

She hesitated, but they looked at her with such an eager air of expectation that she had to say *something*. "You have to understand, this was a long way from West Texas. And Mexico, for that matter."

"That's fine," Inspector Portilla insisted. "Go on, *por favor*."

Mercy spoke not a word of Spanish, but she knew a "please" when she heard it, so she told them the truth. "There was a mission, a place for veterans there. And upstairs were men who'd been separated out from the rest. They were . . . they were like you said." She nodded at Inspector Galeano. "Thin, and their skin wasn't the right color, and they were starting to look like . . . like corpses." The rest came out in a burst. "And one of them tried to bite my hand. I thought he was only trying to lash out at me, 'cause he was mad that I was poking him and prodding him, but . . . no." She shook her head side to side with fervor. "He wasn't trying to eat me, or anything. He was just—"

"Trying to chew on your flesh? Señora," Inspector Portilla pleaded. Then he turned to Captain MacGruder. "You said this was made from gas? Flown in by dirigibles?"

"That's my understanding," he replied.

"Then perhaps we can solve two mysteries at once!" the inspector exclaimed. Then he dropped his voice and told them, "A large unregistered dirigible crashed out in West Texas, right around the same time—and the same place—that our forces first disappeared. We believe it originated on the northwest coast, but we can't be certain."

Mercy gasped. "You don't think—"

He went on, "I don't know *what* to think. But what if this airship was carrying sap?"

The captain presented another possibility. "Or a load of gas to be processed *into* sap."

Everyone fell silent, astonished by the prospect of it—and, frankly, not believing it. Mercy said slowly, "Surely . . . surely if it's just gas, it would just . . . go away? Rise up into the air? Or maybe blow up, like hydrogen does."

Captain MacGruder agreed. "Surely it wouldn't be concentrated enough to . . . to . . . contaminate all those *people*."

Inspector Portilla sighed. "You are probably right. But still, it is something to think about," he told them. Then he excused himself from the table, and his fellow inspector left as well.

Left alone with the Union men, Mercy said, "Damn, I hope that's not right. I can't *imagine* it's right. Can you? You've been on the fronts, haven't you? Have you seen the men who lie around and look like corpses?"

"I've seen sap-heads, but nothing as bad as what they're describing—or what you described, either. I don't like to put it this way, but men who dull their senses with drugs or drink or anything else . . . they don't live too long on a battlefield. But I've seen the glassy eyes, and the skin that starts to look like it's drying out and going a funny color. Don't hate me for saying so, but men like that are virtually no good to me, not out on the field. If they make themselves into cannon fodder, that's probably the best use to be made of 'em."

"Oh, I understand," she said. "You've got a job to do out there."

"Yes ma'am," he said. He might've been on the verge of saying more, but the caboose door opened and Malverne Purdue entered with a disgusted look that blossomed into a fake smile. "Men. Mrs. Lynch. So good to find you here."

Morris Comstock said it first. "Actually, we was just leaving. Sorry. Have yourself a fine supper, though," he added. Then he pulled himself up out of the chair and followed the captain back through the same door, holding it open for Mercy, in case she wanted to follow.

She said, "Thanks, but I'll be along in a bit. I might ask for another cup of tea, something to settle my stomach."

The captain nodded as if to say, *Suit yourself.* The door smacked shut behind him.

Mercy finished the last few sips of her now-tepid tea and went for a refresher. When she returned to her seat, she found that the scientist had taken the captain's spot, and he obviously expected her to join him. She smiled tightly.

"Mr. Purdue," she greeted him.

"Mrs. Lynch. Nice to see you, of course."

"Likewise, I'm sure."

He withdrew a flask and poured some of its contents into his coffee. Mercy thought it smelled like whiskey, but that wasn't something she cared about, so she didn't remark it. He said, "Those foreigners who just left the car before I came—I don't suppose you had a chance to talk to them, did you?"

"A little bit," she confirmed. "They were just in here, sitting with Captain MacGruder and Mr. Comstock. They invited me to join them, so I did."

"How very civilized of you," he said. Some nasty sentiment seemed to underlie the statement, but his sharp-featured face remained composed in a very portrait of politeness. "If you don't mind my asking, what was the topic of conversation? I find it difficult to believe that such a diverse group could find much to talk about. Except, perhaps, a mutual dislike of Republicans."

Because it wasn't a secret (Lord knew, it'd made enough newspapers), she said, "We were talking about those missing Mexicans out in Texas. That legion that up and disappeared a few months ago."

"Ah, I see. A relatively safe topic, that."

"What makes you say so?" she asked.

He shrugged. "Politics are funny," he said. "But since that Texian is back in his own seat, I guess it gave the rest of the lads something to bond over, since none of them want him on board. It's a shell game, really. Or, it's like the old logic puzzles, about how to cross a river with a lion, a goat, an elephant, and . . . oh, I don't know. Some other assortment of animals that may or may not want to eat one another." Malverne Purdue took a teaspoon, swirled his mixture of coffee and alcohol, then brought the cup to his lips and took a draft too big to be called a sip.

"I don't follow you," Mercy replied.

He gestured with the teaspoon as he spoke. "It's like this: On board this train we have a great contingent of Union soldiers," he said, tripping over the word *soldiers* as if he would've liked to say something less complimentary. "We also have at least one Texian, a pair of Mexicans, and probably a southern sympathizer or two someplace."

"Sympathizers?" she said. "I'm sure I haven't spotted any."

"You been on the lookout?" he asked. When she didn't answer, he went on. "We might as well assume it, ever since St. Louis. Can't count on anyone in that bloodied-up territory. Bushwhackers, jaywalkers . . . I wouldn't trust any of them as far as I could throw the *Dreadnought*. If there's not a spy or two somewhere on board, I'll eat my hat."

"That's a threat I'm bound to remember."

"Just take it as a warning to watch your words, and keep your eyes open." His own eyes narrowed down to slits, then opened again as if realizing how wicked that expression made him look. He told her, "We're not safe here, Mrs. Lynch. None of us are. We're a target about a dozen cars long, fixed on a track that can be butchered with a few sticks of dynamite. And anything's a possibility. I haven't lived this long by assuming the best of people."

"Spoken like a spy," she said flippantly.

"A spy?" He sniffed a little laugh. "If that's what I was doing with my days, I'd demand a larger paycheck. No, I'm just what was advertised: a scientist, in service to my state and my nation."

In response to this Mercy asked, "How so? What's your job here, on this train?"

The teaspoon went into action again, swerving around in the space in front of him. He wove it like a wand, as if to distract her. "Oh, structural things, you understand. It's my job to see that the train and its engine run steady, and that there aren't any glitches with the mechanics of the operation."

"So the coupler breaking—that was the sort of problem you're meant to catch?"

The scientist sneered. "Problem? Is that what you'd call it?"

"Train bodies aren't my specialty. What would you call it, if not a problem?"

"I'd call it sabotage," he grumbled.

"Sabotage! That's quite a claim."

The teaspoon snapped down with a clack. "It's no claim. It's a *fact*. Someone sprang that coupler, obvious as can be. They break sometimes, sure—I've seen it myself, and I know it's no rare event—but this was altered. Broken. Intended to fail."

"Have you said anything to the captain?" she asked.

"He was the first person I told."

"That's strange," she observed. "I would've thought that if a spy or criminal was on board, the captain would have had all the soldiers out searching the cars, or asking lots of questions."

He made a face and said, "What would be the point? If there's a spy, he—or *she*—isn't going to talk just because someone asks about it, and there probably isn't any proof. All we can do is keep a closer eye on the train itself, and the couplers, and the cars." His voice trailed off.

Mercy had the very acute feeling that he did not actually mean that they should watch the passenger cars. Whatever he cared about was not riding along in a Pullman; it was being towed in one of the other, more mysterious cars—either the hearse in the back (as she'd begun to think of the car that held the corpses), or the cars immediately behind the *Dreadnought* engine itself.

He sat there, temporarily lost in thought. Mercy interrupted his reverie by saying, "You're right. All we can do is keep our eyes open. Watch the cars. Make sure no one—"

"Really," it was his turn to interrupt, "we ought to watch *each other*."

Then he collected his diluted coffee and retreated from the table, back into the next car up.

For all that Mercy instinctively loathed the man, she had to agree with him there. And, as a matter of self-preservation, she suspected she ought to keep a very close eye on Mr. Malverne Purdue *indeed*.

Fourteen

Topeka came and went, and with its passing, the *Dreadnought* acquired the oft-promised physician, an Indianan named Levine Stinchcomb. He was a skeletal man, and less elderly than the slowness of his movements and the stiffness of his speech might lead one to suspect on first glance; Mercy had him figured for a man of fifty, at the outside. His hair was salted with gray, and his hands had a long, lean look to them as if he were born to play piano—though whether or not he did, the nurse never thought to ask.

Dr. Stinchcomb greeted Mercy as a matter of professional courtesy, or possibly because Captain MacGruder made a point of introducing them, in case it proved useful in the future. The good doctor struck her as a man who was generally kind, if slightly detached, and over tea she learned that he'd served the Union as a field doctor in northern Tennessee for over a year. He was not much inclined to conversation, but he was pleasant enough in a quiet way, and Mercy decided that she liked him, and was glad to have him aboard.

This was significant because she'd known more than a few doctors whom she would have been happy to toss off the back of the train. But Stinchcomb, she concluded, might be useful—or, failing usefulness, he was at least unlikely to get in the way.

After tea, he retreated to his compartment in the second passenger car, and she saw little of him thereafter.

Topeka also saw the arrival and departure of a few other passengers, which was to be expected. Along with the doctor, cabin gossip told Mercy that the train had gained a young married couple who had freshly eloped and were on their way to Denver to explain things to the young lady's parents; three cowboys, one of them another Mexican man by birth and blood; and two women who could have best been described as "ladies of ill-repute." Mercy didn't have any particular problem with their profession, and they were friendly enough with everyone, though Theodora Clay took a dim view of their presence and did her best to scowl them along their way any time they passed through on the way to the caboose.

Mercy took it upon herself to befriend them, if only to tweak Miss Clay's nose about it. She found the women to be uneducated but bright, much like herself. Their names were Judith Gilbert and Rowena Winfield, respectively. They, too, would debark in Denver, so they'd be present for only another week.

The ever-changing social climate of the train was well matched with its constant movement, the ever-present jogging back and forth, the incessant lunging and lurching and rattling of the cars as they counted the miles in ties and tracks. It became second nature, after a while, for Mercy to introduce herself to strangers knowing that they'd part still strangers within days; just as it was second nature, after a while, to ballast and balance every time she rose from her seat, working the train's side-to-side momentum into the rhythm of her steps. Even sleeping got easier, though it never became easy. But in time that, too, became a tolerable habit—the perpetual low-grade fatigue brought on by never sleeping enough, and never sleeping well . . . though sleeping quite often, for there was so little else to do.

Though the days rolled together smoothly, if dully, there were hints that things were not perfectly well.

In Topeka, the passengers had not been permitted to leave the train, even to stretch their legs; and there were moments of

tension back around the rear-end hearse. She'd heard men arguing, and Malverne Purdue's voice rising with an attempt at command. No one would tell her what the trouble had been, and
she'd had no good reason to go poking around, but she'd heard
rumors here and there that another coupler had been on the verge
of breaking—whether from sabotage or wear and tear, no one was
inclined to say.

Whatever was being so carefully guarded up front was also
posing a problem. One night she overheard the captain raising
his voice—at Purdue, she'd gathered, though she caught only one
phrase of it, carried on the breeze as she lounged in the second
passenger car with Judith and Rowena, who were teaching her
how to play gin rummy.

". . . and don't worry about that car, it's *my* responsibility—
stick with your own!"

All three of their heads had lifted at that, for it had been
strangely loud, shooting into the window behind them by some
trick of acoustics.

Judith said, "Whatever they're bickering about, I'm siding
with the captain."

She was taller, blonder, and fuller figured than her companion,
with ringlets that never seemed to fail and a porcelain complex-
ion that blushed as pretty as a peach. Rowena was the smaller and
darker of the two, and her form was less impressive; but it was
Mercy's opinion that she was by far the more attractive. Where
Judith had plain features but fine coloring, Rowena had the coal-
colored hair of the black Irish, and the periwinkle eyes to offset it.

Rowena said, "Damn straight," and played a card. "I don't like
the scientist—that is, if he is what he says he is. He's up to something. It's those weasfrom eyes, and that nasty little smile."
She shook her head. "The captain, though, he's a looker, with that
frosty hair and the face of a boy. The uniform don't hurt him none,
either."

Mercy said, "It's funny what they say about men in uniform—how people think women just can't resist 'em. Fact is, I think we're just pleased to see a man groomed, bathed, and wearing clothes that fit him."

Captain MacGruder selected this moment to come blasting into the car, in the process of passing through it and toward the back of the train. His boyish face was red with rage, and set in a series of angry lines. He did not notice the women—in fact, he seemed not to notice anything but the next door, as he grabbed it, yanked it open, and flung himself through it, as if to put as much distance and as many barriers between himself and Malverne Purdue as humanly possible.

Mercy voiced this last thought aloud, and Judith said, "Can you blame him? Wait for it. Weasel-nose will be along in his wake, any second now."

Sure enough, the forward door opened with somewhat less violence and Malverne Purdue came slinking through it, smoothing his carrot-colored coif and behaving as if he was quite certain that no one had heard him receive the dressing-down. He saw the women and flashed them one of his smarmy grins that always verged on a look of distaste, touched his hat to them, and followed after the captain.

Judith raised both eyebrows behind him and said, "My! I wonder what that was about."

The game continued, and soon they played against the backdrop of a flat Kansas sky that was taking on strips and streaks of gold, pink, and the shade of new bluebonnets. Rowena had a flask filled with apricot-flavored brandy, and she passed it around, making Mercy feel like quite the rebel. Drinking brandy and playing cards with prostitutes was not something she'd ever imagined herself doing . . . but ,well, things changed, didn't they? And given another couple of weeks, she'd never see any of these people again, anyway. She found it difficult to care what her mother would say if she only knew, and even more difficult to care what her father would think, wherever he was, if he was still alive.

Sunset took forever; with no mountains or hills for it to fall behind, the orb only sank lower and lower in the sky, creeping toward a horizon line that never seemed to come. The warm light belied the chill outside, and the passenger cars were bathed in a rose-colored glow even as the riders rubbed their hands together and breathed into their fingers, or gathered over the steam vents.

Porters came through on the heels of the sun's retreating rays, lighting the gas lamps that were placed on either side of each door, protected by reinforced glass so the light wouldn't blow out with the opening and closing of these same portals. The burning yellow and white lights brightened the seating areas even as the sun outside began to set.

"Isn't that something!" Mercy said, leaning her head to see more directly west out the window.

Rowena asked, "The sunset?"

"I don't think I've ever seen a prettier one."

She kept her stare fixed out the window even as the effects of the evening's lovely onset waned. She couldn't quite be certain, but she was almost . . . nearly . . . *just about* positive she could see something shadowed in black leaping and loping up toward the train.

Judith followed her gaze and likewise tried to focus on the dark dots of peculiar shape and size, out to the south and incoming—until, yes, they were both convinced of it. And when Rowena added her eyes to the concentrated staring, she, too, wondered if there wasn't something approaching, and approaching *fast*.

"Mercy—" Judith said her name like a question or a prayer. "Mercy, what on earth is *that*?"

Mercy demurred, "I couldn't say. . . ."

And it didn't matter what she said, or if she said it. Even from her limited view at the window, she could see four . . . no, five . . .

bouncing, *rolling* things coming across the plains at a pace that confounded the three women.

Someone in a seat behind them breathed, "Monstrous!"

Before much else could be added to that assessment, soldiers came running in through the forward door, toward the aft and the next car, shouting, "Everyone stay calm!" at a group of people who were too confused to be very panicked yet. But as order went out, and uniformed men went tearing to and fro in small groups, the passengers experienced earnest concern, followed by excessive fright.

Judith asked, "What do we do?" and no one seemed to know. She and Rowena both looked at Mercy as if the nurse ought to have some idea. She didn't, but she'd learned over long shifts at the hospital that if people looked to you for directions, you gave them some directions, even if all you were doing was getting them out of the way.

Remembering the previous, abortive raid, Mercy pointed up at the luggage bays high overhead, and to the storage blocks to either side of the compartment. "Get all your stuff down," she said. Barricade yourselves in, and keep your head low."

Rowena squeaked, "What about you?"

"I'm going to head back to my compartment," she said. "Stay down. When the shooting starts—"

"*When* the shooting starts?" Judith asked.

"That's right, *when* it starts. You don't want to have your pretty face up like a big old target, now do you?" She stood up straight and stared out the window at the machines, which were definitely rolling, driving up over the uneven plains and bouncing as they approached, popping over the prairie dog mounds and jostling airward after clipping small gullies or ravines.

As the raiders drew closer, Mercy could see that their machines were three-wheeled on triangle-shaped frames, with bodies like beetles and glass windshields that looked as if they might've been scavenged from an airship. The windows were thick and cloudy, revealing little of the men inside except for foggy shapes, at least at their present distance.

She turned away from the window and looked around at the rest of the passengers in the car. "Y'all heard me, too, didn't you? Get all your things out of the luggage bays and make a fort. Do it! All of you!" she barked when some of the men just stared, or the women were sluggish. "We don't have but a few minutes before they're on us!"

Watching the windows with one eye, she began a sideways run for the aft door; and as she made her first steps, she heard a rushing roar, and felt the train surge forward. Someone had thrown on more coal or squeezed more diesel into the engine, and they were definitely moving at a swifter clip.

In the next car she found more soldiers, more passengers, and more restless fear. She didn't see the captain or the Texian or anyone else she might've looked for in case of an emergency, but Malverne Purdue was wrestling into a holster and fiddling with guns, as if he had used them before, but not too often or too expertly.

A little girl in a corner was clinging to the hand of a woman who must be her grandmother, who looked every bit as terrified as the child. The older woman caught Mercy's eyes and asked, "What's going on? Dear, what should we do?"

The soldiers were shouting orders back and forth at one another, or confirming orders, or spreading information up and down the line. Whatever they were doing, they did it loudly, and they did not address the passengers even when directly asked to do so. Mercy understood the necessity, whether she liked it or not, so she reiterated her instructions from the previous car. Then, after a pounding of feet that took most of the soldiers out the forward door, she held up her hands.

"Folks, we're going to need to keep the aisles clear, you

understand me? Did everyone hear what I told this lady here, and this little girl? About getting down your luggage and ducking down behind it?"

Murmurs and nods went around, and some of the faster listeners began opening bays and storage panels; hauling out suitcases, satchels, boxes, bags, and anything else large enough to cover any part of any body; and throwing them into the compartments.

"Everyone, now, you understand? Stay out of the aisles, and don't do any peeking out the windows."

Malverne Purdue, who was now fighting with the buckle of a gunbelt, raised his voice and said, "I want everyone to listen to this lady. She's giving you good advice." Once the belt was secured, and he was wearing no fewer than four guns up front, and one tucked into the back of his pants like a pirate, he said to Mercy, "I know I'm not an officer and it's not your job to obey me, so don't remind me, but: take what you're saying from car to car. Keep these people out of the path; there's going to be plenty of coming and going."

She nodded and they headed off in opposite directions—him to the front, after his fellows, and she to the rear, toward her own compartment.

The wind between the cars was ice on her ears and in her lungs as she breathed one shocked chestful of air that made her eyes water. The train was moving so fast that the tracks underneath the couplers poured past as smoothly as a ribbon of water. If Mercy looked at it for more than a fraction of a second, it made her dizzy.

She gripped the rails and stepped onto the next small platform, then yanked the door open.

By the time she was back in her own car, she was breathless, disheveled, and half frozen. She said, "Excuse me," and pushed past Mrs. Butterfield, who was perched on the edge of her compartment seat and demanding of Miss Clay, "What do you see? What are they doing?"

Theodora Clay had her hands and face pressed against the window, her breath fogging the pane and the tip of her nose going red with the cold. She said, "I see five of those bizarre contraptions. They're gaining ground, but not very quickly."

"How many men, do you think?" asked her aunt.

Mercy knelt down on her seat beside Miss Clay so she could see. Though the question had not been directed at her, she answered. "I can't imagine those things hold more than three at a time."

To which Miss Clay said, "I suspect you're right. Those . . . those . . . carts, or mechanized wagons, or whatever they are . . . they look like they're made for speed, not for military transport."

The nurse added, "And they're made for assault. Look at their guns." She pointed, jamming her knuckle against the breath-slick glass.

Theodora Clay tried to follow the indication and agreed. "Yes, I see two Gatling-form spritzers mounted above each front axle, and small-caliber repeating cannon on the rear axle."

Mercy looked at her with a puzzled frown. "You know something about artillery, do you?"

She said, "A bit," which was such a useless contribution to the conversation that it may as well not have been offered at all.

"All right. Do you think we're in range?"

"Depends on what you mean by that. They could likely hit the side of a barn at this distance, but they couldn't hit it twice in a row, not at the speeds they're coming." Miss Clay looked back down at her aunt and said, "But we should do what Mercy's been telling everyone. Get your luggage, Aunt Norene."

"I'll do no such thing!"

Miss Clay gave the old woman a scowl. She said, in a level,

angry voice, "Then go help *other people* get their luggage out and sorted, if you're too much a soldier to cover your own hide."

Mrs. Butterfield sniffed disdainfully and flounced out of her compartment into the aisle. Once there, she immediately spotted the widower trying to wrangle his two boys, and set to assisting him.

Miss Clay returned her attention to the window and said, almost to herself, "They're gaining. Not by much, but they're gaining."

Mercy was still looking after Mrs. Butterfield and could therefore see out the other side of the train. She said, "And they've got friends, coming at us from the north."

"Goddammit," said Miss Clay. Mercy wasn't sure why the blasphemy surprised her. "How many do you think that makes?"

"I haven't the foggiest. I can't see very far the other way," she said, though she dashed across the aisle and leaned her face against the window. There, she could spot at least three, and a dust trail that might indicate a fourth somewhere just beyond her range of vision. "Maybe the same number?"

She returned to Miss Clay's side and gazed hard at the vehicles.

Theodora said, "They've got a little armor plating, but nothing that could withstand anything like the antiaircraft cannons on our engine."

"They look fast, though. Maybe they think that if they can catch up fast enough, we won't have much time to fire at them."

"Then they're idiots. Jesus, they're coming right for us!"

But Mercy said, "No, not right for *us*." The formation of machines was forking, spreading out and lining up. "Look what they're doing. They're going for the engine and the caboose."

"Whatever for?"

"Well, they know we've got passengers aboard," Mercy pointed out. "And they don't give a shit about the passengers. They want something else. Something at the front, or the rear." She felt like she was stating the obvious, and the longer she watched, the more obvious it became—the machines were deliberately parting to ignore the middle cars.

"You say that like they're reasonable human beings," Miss Clay spit.

"They're every bit as reasonable as the boys aboard this train," she said stubbornly. "Thinking less of them than that'll get you killed."

Theodora looked like she would've loved to argue, but she heard her aunt bullying and bossing out in the aisle and changed her mind, or her tactic, at least. She said, "Leaving room for error, if all the passengers holed up in the middle cars, they might be safest."

"You might be right."

The forward door burst open and Cyrus Berry came squeezing through it, followed by Inspector Galeano and Pierce Tankersly, then Claghorn Myer and Fenwick Durboraw, two other enlisted men whom Mercy had seen coming and going along the train.

Mercy said, "But not yet—we've got to let the soldiers sort themselves out." She cried, "Mr. Tankersly!" and summoned him over.

In a few fast words, she explained her guess and Miss Clay's idea. He nodded. "That's a good plan. I'm going to put you in charge of it."

"What?"

"We've been split into squadrons fore and aft, and we're migrating that way now. Do you have a watch?"

"Not on me," she confessed.

"Does anybody have a watch?" he asked the room. When he was greeted only with mumbles and the frantic mechanizations of people building fortresses out of luggage, Mercy stopped him.

She asked, "How long do you need to get into place?"

"Five minutes," he said. "Give us five minutes. Can you guess that pretty good?"

"Yes," she said, then turned him around and gave him a shove. "Now get moving!"

The whole clot of officials went struggling through the narrow aisle to the back door. Once they were through it, Mercy and Theodora considered the plan.

"There are seven passenger cars," Mercy counted out. "If everyone from the first and seventh can squeeze into the middle five, that'll leave the first and last as buffers and won't crush everyone too badly in the rest."

Miss Clay said, "Yes. And we'll probably even be able to keep the aisles clear, once everyone's settled. Do you want to go up to the first car, or back to the last one?"

"Um . . . I don't know. It doesn't matter."

Theodora Clay made a sound of sublime exasperation and held out a coin as if to flip it. She said, "Last car's closest to where we are, so that'll be easiest. On the count of three, heads or tails . . ."

"Tails," Mercy said, and when heads flashed up, she added, "That's fine. I'll work my way up front: You work your way to the rear, and we'll meet back in the middle."

Miss Clay nodded as crisply as any soldier ever clicked to attention.

Mercy grabbed her satchel and threw off her cloak to make her movements easier—never mind the cold between the cars; she could stand it. She checked her guns, and the two women walked into the aisle, narrowly dodging a second wave of uniformed men brandishing weapons. Then they turned different directions, and ran.

Mercy backtracked the way she'd just come, urging people in the central cars into makeshift shelters and reassuring the hysterical that a plan was in place, though she went out of her way to keep from explaining that it was a feeble plan, consisting

mostly of the order to "Move!" But a plan kept things from going straight to hell, and the soldiers appeared to appreciate it,
going so far as to assist where possible as they polarized themselves
forward and aft, setting up defensive positions and barricades in
the places where the Confederate raiders seemed most likely to
attack.

She met Captain MacGruder back in the first passenger car.
When she'd finished herding its occupants into the second car,
the captain reached for Mercy's arm and lured her back into the
first one, where his soldiers were holing up and readying themselves. He stood there, struggling to ask her something, and not
knowing how to phrase it.

"Can I help you, Captain?" she tried to prompt him.

He said, "It's only . . . I hope we're doing the right thing, leaving the passenger cars unguarded."

She said, "So do I."

"It's placing a great deal of faith in our enemy . . . ," he observed.

Mercy agreed, "Perhaps." Then she looked about. Seeing no
truly unoccupied corners, she led him over to an abandoned compartment and pretended they'd achieved a fragile modicum of
privacy. "Sir, let me ask you something."

"By all means."

"What do they want?"

He said, "I beg your pardon?"

"I may not be an officer, but I'm not an idiot, either. And this
train, this trip . . . it's a big fat pile of horse pucky, and it smells
like it, too."

"I have no idea what you're talking about," he said, with just
enough hesitation to make Mercy quite certain he was lying.

Exasperated, she said, "Look at those machines out there.
They'll be on us at any minute. I've never seen anything like them,
have you?"

"No, I haven't. But why would you—?"

"They're *expensive,* I bet. Probably made in Texas like all the best war toys, and then shipped up here on one of the Republican rail lines that meets up at the Utah pass. That's not a cheap thing to do."

"Madam, I assure you this is purely a civilian mission—"

"Oh, and I'm your mother!" she almost yelled at him. Again she pointed out the window, to a place where the vehicles were shambling at breakneck speed over the low grassy nubs on the prairie. "Look at them. They *know.* They know the passengers are a bluff. They're aiming for the engine and the caboose, or the after-caboose. And I want you to tell me, Captain MacGruder . . . *why?*"

The captain stiffened, and said slowly, "As a civilian, none of this is your concern."

"As a woman stuck on this goddamn train with you and your boys, and someone else's boys getting ready to open fire on us, it sure as hell *is* my concern."

But then a whirring noise up front declared that the *Dread-nought*'s defense systems were winding up, threading strands and coils of bullets up to the Gatling-copies mounted on the engine's sides. Mercy said, "Captain!" She wasn't sure what she'd follow it with, a plea for information or a demand for instructions, but nothing had time to come.

With a jolt that kicked the first couple of passenger cars and made them sway, the *Dreadnought* opened fire, spraying a line of bullets across the sand-colored earth and blasting pits in wavy rows. The mechanized three-wheelers were barely within range, and they dodged, ducking and bucking left to right and back again—unexpectedly stable for such spindly looking creations. In a moment, all of them righted themselves and struck a forward course once more.

"Get back to your car and stay down," the captain commanded, at the exact moment the Rebel craft fired back.

A hail of bullets smashed through the windows that hadn't been opened, sending sprays of glass exploding through the narrow compartment. Everyone ducked and shook their heads, casting shards out of their hair and off their shoulders. Mercy crouched in the compartment, the captain crouching with her.

He said again, "Go, for God's sake!"

More fire from the *Dreadnought* made the cars rock and shake, giving the towed compartments a centrifugal snap every time the larger guns were fired. Mercy retreated as ordered—stopping at the doors and holding her breath, waiting, trying to calculate the incalculable. There was no way to time her steps to a steady roll of the train, because she had no way of knowing when it would fire; so she breathed deeply, yanked at the door, flung herself into the next car, and hoped for the best.

By the time she'd made it back to the third car, one car shy of her goal, a man caught up to her from the first compartment, where half the soldiers were busy fending off the Rebs.

The soldier called out, "Mrs. Lynch!"

When she turned around, he did not wait for confirmation, just wheezed, "Can you come back to the front car? We've got some men hurt."

"Already? But I just left!" she exclaimed, then waved her hands as if to dismiss her own reaction. "Never mind, I'm coming. I'm right behind you."

The sun was more set than not, and its grim yellow glow was the only thing lighting the train. The porters had snuffed the gas lamps and then, no doubt, holed up someplace sensible. Moving up and down the aisles was like crashing through someone else's nightmare, and it was an increasingly dark nightmare, with exponentially more terrors, as the light faded and the confusion mounted.

Just when Mercy thought she couldn't possibly find her way through one more car, she reached her goal, seizing the last frigid handle and clutching it, in order to move herself across the wind-torn space.

"I'm here," she announced with a gasp. "Who needs me?"

The sweep of a nearby three-wheeler was her only answer, not coming close enough to ride alongside the car, but spraying it with enough ammunition to wipe out anyone standing too tall. The whole car stank of gunpowder and ashes, and the sweat of frightened men.

Cyrus Berry turned from his position at his window beside Morris Comstock. He said, "Not here, ma'am. Next car up."

"There ain't no next car up," she griped tiredly.

"Not no passenger car, no. But there is a next car. Go on. The captain's been sniped and I think Fenwick is maybe a goner. Please, will you? Next car up. They'll let you in, I swear it."

The mysterious third car—the one behind the fuel cart and the engine proper—was the very focus of half of this more earnest, better planned raid. She tried to ignore the fact that she might find her answers inside whether or not the captain felt like dishing them out; and she tried to steel herself as she fumbled for the forward door's slick, chilly latch.

"Ma'am!" shouted Morris Comstock without looking away from his window. "Be careful, and move fast!" He pumped the bolt on the rifle and aimed with one eye shut, and one eye narrowed.

She could scarcely see him, for the twilight and the smoke of the guns had made the air all gummy, even as it rushed and swirled through the open windows. "I will," she promised, but she didn't think he could hear her. She seized the slippery latch and gave it a tug, then gave the door a shove with her shoulder.

Almost-night lashed around her. In the few slim feet between passenger car and mystery car, the air was sharp with bullets and loud with the clank of artillery and the grudging, straining pump of the *Dreadnought*'s pistons jamming the wheels over and over and over, drawing the train along the tracks and farther into the sunset—chasing it, doomed never to catch it. Begging for just a few more minutes of light.

Off to her left, so immediate and close that it nearly stopped her heart, Mercy saw one of the three-wheeled monsters leap more intimately into range. She could see, on the other side of the scratched, thick windshield, that there were two men inside, though she could make out nothing but the ovals of their faces and the dark pits of their eyes.

She wondered how they could see at all, then realized that the machines had a murky glow from within. She didn't know if they had lanterns, or some form of electrical light, or something as simple and magical as a jar of fireflies inside the craft. But there was enough for them to see and work the controls; that much was clear.

Mercy stood, paralyzed by the wind and the nearness of the danger, in the spot between the passenger car and the mystery car, and wept from the awful sting of the rushing air and the engine fumes. She gripped the rail above the passenger car's front coupler until her fingers were numb and her knuckles were as white as if they'd succumbed to frost.

The three-wheeler bobbed into view again, and the men within it came close enough that she could see their black eyeholes seeing her—an easy target between the cars—and conferring. It suddenly occurred to her, *They could shoot me. They* might *shoot me. My own fellows might kill me, and never even know. . . .*

But the *Dreadnought* was on watch, and whether or not the three-wheeler had intended to take the easy shot, it did not, for a searing stripe of bullets went scorching along the earth, the live ammunition throwing up sparks and small explosions of light at the edge of the Rebels' line of attack. Off to Mercy's right, out of her line of sight on the other side of the train, something flew into bits with a crash and a ball of fire that temporarily warmed her, even as it horrified her. One of the three-wheelers was down, most definitely.

Off to the left, the three-wheeler that had been very near had gone someplace she couldn't see. She wanted to believe they'd seen she was a woman and had opted to leave her be; but she suspected it was more a fear of the engine, and its guns, and the men in the next car up, who defended the train with the ferocity of lions.

Reaching the mystery car required a literal leap of faith, or at least a few steps of contrition.

Knowing that she'd never get a peaceful moment to make the rushing jump to the other car, Mercy counted to three and threw herself at the other platform, which had not been designed for passengers, and was therefore without the rails, gates, and other safety measures that made crossing these tiny, terrible bridges more manageable on the rest of the train. She wavered as she landed, but caught herself by tangling her hands into the rungs of a ladder that had been welded into place against the car's body. Thusly braced, she used her other hand to grab the latch and jiggle it open.

The door flapped outward into her face, but she dodged it, and swung herself around it, and drew it shut behind her. This motion took fewer than three seconds, and it landed her in the midst of a shuttered car so dark that she could see her own feet only with the aid of a lantern held close to the floor, back in the corner.

She said, "Captain?" since she didn't see him at first. Then she spotted him against the wall, seated, with a rag of some sort held up against his head.

Fenwick Durboraw was lying beside him.

She crouched down low and forced herself to ignore the whistle of ammunition shrieking only feet, or sometimes only inches, above her head. Flinging herself down into the corner, she took the lantern and turned to Durboraw first, since he wasn't moving.

With a flutter and a racket accompanied by renewed fire-power from outside, the rear door opened and a young porter came in carrying two more torches and a box of matches. He said, "I'm real sorry, sirs. Real sorry it took so long."

"Don't worry about it," said Captain MacGruder, his words only slightly muffled by the rag that hung down over his face. He gestured for the man and for the lights, and the colored man brought them forward, setting one beside Mercy and handing the other to the captain.

Then the captain said, "I think we're too late for Fenwick. If he isn't dead yet, he won't last long."

Mercy held the first lamp over him and saw no sign of breath-ing or motion. She opened one of his eyelids and brought the light close, but the pupils didn't contract, and when she turned his head to better feel his pulse, blood came dribbling out of his nose. "What happened to him?" she asked.

"Percussion bombs. Small models, anyway. They're launching them from those meat-baskets," he said. "That's why we threw up the screens, to bounce them back."

She looked up and saw them, silhouetted against the sky from her position down on the floor. They were scarcely any darker, and they looked like old coal screens, which is what they probably were. "But one got through?"

"One got through. He threw himself down on it; look." The captain pointed at the soldier's chest, where the wool overcoat was discolored and strangely frayed, as if he'd caught a cannon-ball to the belly. "Those things, they tear you up on the inside."

Before she could stop herself, she murmured, "And they're called 'clappers,' ain't that right?"

He took a moment to answer her. Finally he said, "That's what the Rebs call them, yes."

Fenwick Durboraw let out a soft, slow breath, and his chest sank beneath Mercy's hand. It didn't rise again. She said, "He's gone, sure enough. Now let me get a look at *you*."

The captain objected, but she pointed at the porter and said, "You there, hold up the light so I can see." Her authority in this world was limited and uncertain, but she knew when to wield it. She forced the captain's rag-filled hand away from his face. At first she saw nothing but blood, sluicing down the side of his head from a deep, long scratch with very sharp edges. She said, "Shrapnel upside the head, Captain. Hold still and let me clean it out."

He did as she told him, wincing against the touch of the rags, which were so damp with his own blood that they scarcely did any good.

She noticed this herself, said, "Hold on. I've got something in my bag," then pulled out a tincture solution and dabbed it on a cloth before giving up and pouring it a drizzle at a time over the wound. "Holy hell, Captain. I've got a shining look at your skull, I don't mind saying. You need a good stitching, and sooner rather than later. Where's the doctor?" she asked suddenly, only just aware of his absence.

"Back car; at the caboose, or behind it," he said. "Purdue commandeered him before I had a chance to, goddamn his soul indefinitely."

"Doesn't matter, I guess." She opened her satchel again. "If he was here, he'd just tell me to do it, anyway," she said casually as she reached for the needles and thread she kept stashed inside. She extracted a curved needle and a spool of thread that was sturdy enough to stitch a couch.

Despite the percussion bombs bouncing off the windows and the occasional ping of a bullet slamming against the car's armored hull, Captain MacGruder's eyes widened at the needle and ignored everything else. "You're going to use that . . ."

"On your head, yes. I'm going to sew your scalp together, and it isn't going to feel good at all, but you'll thank me for it later. Now lie down like a man and put your head on my lap."

"I beg your—"

"I'm not asking for your permission. Do what I tell you, and I'll try to keep your head from splitting open. You don't want your face sliding off your bones, do you?"

He paused. "It could do that?"

"Like warm butter off a pan bottom," she fibbed.

He descended from a sitting position to a lying one, and wiggled weakly until his head was lying atop her thigh, as directed.

"You there." She indicated the porter again. "What's your name?"

He said, "Jasper. Jasper Nichols."

"Pleased to meet you, Jasper Nichols. I'm going to need you to keep holding that, as steady as you can. Bring it near. Closer. I'm not going to bite you, and neither is he." And to the captain, she said, "Close your eyes, if that makes it easier. I ain't going to lie, this is going to hurt. But I think you can take it."

"I'm not going to close my eyes."

"Well, that's up to you," she said. And while the porter Jasper Nichols held the lantern above as steady as humanly possible, given the motion of the train and the kickback from the *Dreadnought*'s weapons, she talked to them both. "Jasper, I figured all you porters were walled up tight in one of the service sections. I'm a little surprised to see you up front. Whatever they're paying you, I expect it doesn't cover military duty."

He kept his eyes on the captain's skin, which was steadily being drawn together and forming a squishing, bloody seam. "Maybe not, ma'am. But I'm from Alabama," he said, as if it explained everything.

It explained enough for Mercy to ask, "Why didn't you enlist?"

Without showing her, he said, "I'm missing a foot. Got it cut off when I was small, for disobeying."

She shook her head slowly, trying to concentrate despite the incessant mechanical movement. "That ain't right."

"Lots ain't right," he said. "Staying back in the 'boose wouldn't be right either, not when these men got to have some light."

"Good call," she told him, temporarily holding the bloody needle in her mouth as she estimated the best way to stitch a particularly uneven stretch of wound. "And I, for one, am glad you made it. What about the men at the other end of the train?"

"My cousin Cole Byron is taking care of them. We didn't put no lights back on in the passenger cars, though."

She said, "That's fine. Leave 'em dark. The folks inside'll be scared, but I bet they'll be safer that way, with nothing to draw attention to them."

The captain mumbled, "They have nothing to gain by going after the passenger cars."

And Mercy replied, "Yes, I believe you and I very recently had a conversation on that subject."

Continuing like he hadn't heard her, he said, "I don't know what they want from the caboose. What would they want with dead bodies?"

"But you *do* know what they want with these front cars, don't you?"

He opened his eyes, which he'd closed after all, once she'd gotten started. He said quietly, "Look around you, woman. Don't you see why their artillery isn't getting through? Except for a little shrapnel and that one percussion bomb . . ." His voice trailed off, then recuperated. "It's not the armor outside that keeps us safe in here."

She paused her stitching long enough to raise her head, and was startled by her own obliviousness. She hadn't noticed, in the wild dance of flinging herself into the darkened car; and she hadn't seen, even now that there were three lanterns casting shadows from corner to corner . . . but how could she have missed it?

From floor to window, and stacked all along the central aisle, the mystery car that trailed behind the *Dreadnought* was packed with bars of gold.

 *Fifteen*

Under her breath, so softly that only the captain and the porter could hear her, Mercy said, "Well, now. I did not see *that* coming. The Union's moving all her money out West? What kind of a crock is that?"

She tied off the last bit of Captain MacGruder's scalp with a knot. Rather than root around for her scissors, she leaned down and bit off the excess thread. And when her mouth was only inches from his ear she said, "So that's what the Rebs want with the train."

He struggled to sit up, wobbled, and found his way upright. "Looks that way. Though how they found out about it, I can't reckon."

"And what about the rear car? What do they want with the noble dead?" she asked. She was almost sarcastic, but the din of bullets beating against the car walls stripped all the subtext out of everyone's words.

"I honestly haven't the foggiest."

"Is there more gold back there?" she asked, wiping off her hands and repacking her satchel.

"Not as far as I know," he swore. And he continued, "But *they* might not know that; and the truth is, I wonder. Malverne Purdue isn't under my command," he said sourly. "The rear compartment is his domain, as decreed by the United States Army. I've been told to mind my own compartment and leave that crooked scientist to his."

Mercy rose up to a kneeling position, her knees popping from having sat too long in a strange tangle with the captain's head atop her lap. This put their eyes at nearly on the same level, for he again leaned on the wall, seated in a loose Indian style. "You don't even know, do you—if there are really bodies back there?"

He said, unsteadily, "I *believe* there are bodies."

"Then there *could* be more gold."

The captain shook his head. "I saw the men loading the caskets, and they didn't seem unnaturally heavy. But they were . . . they were *sealed*. Anyway—" He reached for his hat, which was streaked with a bloody tear. He put it back on with a grimace, and when he spoke again, he sounded stronger. "Purdue's the only man on board this train who knows what's really back there. And unless the Rebs manage to board us against our will, that'll remain the case until we reach Boise."

"Why Boise? I thought those bodies were going all the way to Tacoma."

"So did I, but no one ever tells me anything until the last minute. It turns out they're going to be processed at the army post in Idaho, whatever that means."

Mercy was quiet for a moment. They faced each other that way while the men inside the car fired their rifles loudly and repeatedly. The violent noises were enough to make their ears ring.

She said, "That don't make any sense, not if they're just dead boys being sent home. Maybe the Rebs know something we don't."

"Ma'am," he said, "If the Rebs know something about this train that I don't, I'm going to take that right personal."

She climbed to her feet. The porter Jasper Nichols was already standing, his posture off-kilter due to his false foot. He was peering up through the slits of light where the windows were letting in moonlight, starlight, and flashes of artillery fire. She asked him, "How are we doing?"

He started to reply, but a particularly loud report from the *Dreadnought's* defense system shook the whole train like the roll of a cracked whip snapping from handle to tip. When it had subsided, he said, "I think we're fending 'em off."

But another round of jagged gunshots landed in a bounding roll along the side of the car, as if to contradict him.

Morris Comstock was nearest to Mercy, reloading his repeater with shaking hands. This time she asked him, since he'd been looking outside to aim and fire and might have a better idea about what was going on. "Mr. Comstock, are they retreating? Are they still leaving the passenger cars alone?"

He said, "I don't know," as he slipped another rimfire cartridge into place. "It looks like they're concentrating on us, but I can't see any farther than about two cars back." Then he double-checked his gun, climbed on top of one of the gold-filled crates, and reassumed his position. He said to his commanding officer, "Captain, it might be worth sending someone to check."

"Have we had any word from the back of the train?" Captain MacGruder asked.

"No sir. Not yet. Not unless the porter—"

Jasper Nichols said, "My cousin ain't sent word, so maybe they're doing all right back there."

"Or maybe they're so hard up for help, they can't ask for it. Cyrus?" he called to the private first class.

"Yes sir?"

"You in one piece?"

"Yes sir."

The captain said, "Make a dash back to the rear, and let me know what's going on there. Porter, do you mind going with him?"

"No sir, I don't."

"He might need a light, or something, and I reckon you know the train better than we do. Mrs. Lynch, you go with them, too."

"Me?"

"Yes, you," he ordered, not quite crossly but impatiently. "Since we've got ourselves all reinforced with the—with the contents of this car, we've got better plating than the folks in the rear. It'd take antiaircraft projectiles to put a dent in this car, or cannon of a heavier weight than those meat-baskets will carry. Go make sure the doctor doesn't need any help, and check up on the passengers, while you're at it."

She asked, "Why is it my job to watch the passengers?"

"Because they trust you more than they trust us. They're willing to do what you tell them, anyway, and if they hear it from a soldier, maybe it frightens them more than if they hear it from a nice young woman. Just make sure they're staying low and not doing anything stupid."

"Don't have much faith in civilians, do you now?"

"I don't have much faith in *people*. But right now, I trust you, and Cyrus, and that-there porter to make your way to the rear of this train and bring me back word about what's going on."

He used the interior wall as a brace to shove himself up to a standing position, where he swooned, but held himself upright even against the jostling shove of the train's rocking. As Mercy, Cyrus, and Jasper gathered at the door, ready to take on the next cars, the captain held up his hand and said, "Private First Class!"

"Yes sir?"

"If Purdue is holed up in that back car, you force your way in there, you hear me? Don't you let him pull rank, because he doesn't have one. Tell him I sent you as reinforcements, will you? The time might be coming where I damn well need to know what he's got back there."

"Yes sir, I'll do that," Cyrus replied with a strange gleam in his eye, like he'd just been ordered to do the thing he wanted most in the whole wide world.

"Good. Carry on," he said, giving them a half wave that could've been a dismissive gesture, but was more likely an attempt to balance while maintaining a standing position.

Jasper Nichols took the lead and one of the lanterns, but he shuttered it before opening the door. Cyrus Berry asked him, "What are you doing—trying to get us killed? We need to see, crossing that gap!"

The porter replied, "Just the opposite of that, sir. It's dark as hell out there, and they'll shoot if they see a light. You don't want them to see you, do you?" he asked.

Cyrus looked like he wanted to argue, which Mercy thought was weird. But Jasper Nichols continued, saying, "It's only a couple of steps, and I'll take 'em first, and help you two come over. It won't take a second, if we do it careful."

"He's right," Mercy hissed. "If we're lucky, they won't even see us opening and shutting the doors. Now, come on."

Cyrus took third place in line and the porter opened the door, only to be greeted with a frigid flapping noise and a gust of wind that blew papers around in the compartment like a storm. The captain said, "Goddammit! Who opened that box?" And someone else answered, "Didn't mean to, Captain! Just trying to stand on it!"

Mercy waved her hands to brush the papers away from her face and caught one in the process. She tried to throw it away, but the inrushing air forced it against her fingers, so she wadded it up and stuffed it into her apron pocket. "Let's go, fellows," she said, and then she realized that Jasper Nichols was already across the gap, and opening the other door.

Both doors opened out, so that when they were both open, they offered a small measure of protective cover against anyone scanning the area for something to shoot. But when Mercy put her hands on the door to hold it as she passed, she felt how thin it was, and she imagined that a determined enough bullet would breeze through it as easy as a curtain.

But it was dark—devilishly dark. She wished she hadn't left her cloak in her own compartment, even though it would've weighed her down. Night gave the February wind a keener edge, without the sun to dull its damage. And this wind between the cars was a terror, a banshee, a weapon of its own. The nurse stuck out her feet, reached out her hand for the next rail over, and was grasped instead by the porter, who braced her as she swung the rest of the way across. He helped her to a firmer spot, all but pushed her through the open door, and reached out his hand again to take the private first class in the same manner.

The doors slapped shut, sealing all three of them into the bleak, tubular interior of the next car. They stood somewhat dazed, rattled, and ruffled in the empty car, but then the porter rallied them.

"Stay low!" he said.

"They haven't shot at any of the passengers yet, have they?" Mercy asked.

Jasper Nichols said, "Not as far as I know, but that don't mean they won't start. And anyway, if they're paying any attention, they know we've evacuated this car, and the last one. If they see us moving around in here, they may figure we're up to no good."

Moving forward in single file, in a crouch that was graceful for no one, the three unlikely travelers swiftly found the end of that first passenger car and repeated their half-blind charge across the gap until they were all safely inside the second passenger car.

There, dozens of people—far more than there ought to be—were barricaded, stuffed behind their luggage and between the sleeper compartments, crammed against the floor and alongside the storage bays. All of them were silent as death, and all of them watched with eyes that were too horror-struck to blink. These shiny eyes flickered in the muted rays of the shuttered lantern, watching like foxes from burrows, while the hounds barked in circles outside.

As a matter of professional duty, Mercy asked, in a hard whisper that only just carried above the sounds of the small war beyond the car, "Is everybody all right in here? Does anyone need any help with anything?"

No one answered, so she said, "Good. Y'all stay put and stay low. You're doing it just right. Nobody make a peep, you hear?"

They must have heard, because no one did make a peep, even in polite response.

The three travelers received the same response through the next few cars, until it felt to Mercy like some strange circle of hell—where the floor never stopped moving, the soldiers never stopped shooting, and she was never safe standing up straight. Her back hurt from all the hunkering, and her forearms and elbows took many a hard knock from her passage in the dark, but eventually they reached the last car that ought to be filled with passengers, the sixth sleeper car, and encountered Jasper Nichols's cousin and fellow porter, Cole Byron. The two men nearly knocked heads as they stayed low in the aisle, and the conversation that followed told Mercy little of practical value except that the rearmost passenger car had not been wholly evacuated, which Mercy blamed squarely on Theodora Clay—of whom she'd seen no sign.

Cyrus Berry said, "One more car, then," and convinced Jasper Nichols to lend him the lantern long enough to look. "You stay here," he said to the nurse and to the porter, neither of whom took kindly to the command. But a little girl underneath a fortress of suitcases began to cry about her nose, and the child's mother asked if Mercy would please come take a look.

She sighed and agreed, even though she was suddenly very curious about what precisely was going on in the next car over, since the warfare sounded much louder from where she crouched in the aisle than it had over in the first mystery car. She hesitated before answering the girl's mother, but Cyrus said, "Ma'am, if I need you, I'll call for you," and dashed out the door.

As soon as the soldier was gone, Cole Byron told his cousin, "Something strange is up in that car, man. That crazy Union fellow, the one who ain't the soldier, you know the one I mean?"

"Yeah, I do."

"He's called up a bunch of men from the train, including that big ol' Texian, and he's ordering them around, like he's a man who can tell 'em what to do."

This answered Mercy's other question when it came to the passengers: she hadn't seen Horatio Korman yet, either, and she wondered what he was doing. She was about to ask Cole Byron for details when the man added, "Except for that Texian—he ain't going to shoot no Rebs, but I think he might shoot hisself a Union man or two if he gets half a chance. That's why they done took away his guns."

It made sense, of course, but Mercy didn't like it. She felt umbrage in the ranger's behalf and imagined him holed up in that last passenger car, stripped of his weaponry and seething. Surely he was seething. She couldn't imagine him in any other state.

She did talk to the little girl in the suitcases, and though she had virtually no light to see by, she ascertained by the wet, dark stains down the girl's shirt that she'd bloodied her nose at some point in the melee.

Her mother said, "One of the cases fell down and hit her in the face. Is she all right?"

Examining by feel, Mercy fiddled with the crying child's features until she could declare, "I don't think it's broken, but I can't see to save my life."

"Oh, God," said the mother, aghast.

"No, no, it's not the end of the world even if it's busted,"

Mercy assured her. "She's a little thing still, and a doctor can set it right again. Or I could set it right, if I could see worth a damn," she muttered. "But she'll survive, don't worry. She's made a mess, that's all. You got a rag or something?"

"A handkerchief?"

"That'll work." Mercy took it, and clamped it gently on the child's nose. "You're still bleeding some, aren't you, sweetheart?" she asked the child.

The girl tried to nod, even as the cloth was pressed up against her face. The nurse felt this gesture and said, "That's all right, it'll stop soon enough. Like I told your momma, it's not the end of the world, and you'll be fine. Just hold this like this," she demonstrated, and tipped the child's chin up. "And hold your face up, and back. It'll quit. Don't worry."

An ominous, exceedingly close round of gunshots blasted from very nearby within the train. A few people let out soft screams, or attempted to muffle them, and everyone ducked down lower. The child tried to lean against Mercy's arm for a hug, but the nurse pushed her gently back to her mother's arms and scooted out to the edge of the aisle. The two porters had gone back to the front of the car and were conversing in low tones. Even they had been startled into silence at the terrible proximity of the bullets.

"What's going on in there?" she asked of no one in particular.

She was about to grab the door handle and see for herself when it burst open and Horatio Korman came barreling through, followed by the white-faced doctor Stinchcomb, who appeared to be injured or ill. He slammed the door behind himself. It looked like he would've locked it if he could, but he couldn't see any better than anyone else.

"Crazy goddamn bluebacks!" the ranger swore.

The doctor said, "You must understand, I had no idea—"

"No one gives half a two-ounce sparrow shit if you had any

idea. This is *madness*. This is . . . this is . . ." He picked another word. "This is practically *mutiny*, and you know it same as I do!"

"Mr. Korman! Dr. Stinchcomb!" Mercy hissed from the floor. "Get down, for God's sake!"

Both men dropped like stones, though Korman kept one eye on the rear door as if he expected it to open at any moment. "Mrs. Lynch, what the hell are you doing here?"

"Where's Cyrus Berry? Did he make it back yet?"

"Who, the dumb little private?"

"He's perfectly pleasant, you oaf. Is he still back there?"

The ranger said, "Yes, he's back there, and that's where he'll stay. That lunatic Malverne Purdue shot him dead, not two minutes ago. Surely you must've heard it!"

Someone to the right gasped, and Jasper Nichols came sidling up the aisle with his cousin in tow. He asked, "That red-headed man shot the private?"

"That's right. He accused the kid of some unpleasant activities, and when the boy tried to defend himself that rat-faced, redheaded scientist picked up one of my pistols and shot him dead."

"Berry was following orders," Mercy said, but she said it feebly because she wasn't really sure.

Korman said, "He might've been, but Christ knows whose orders he was answering to. Between you and me, Mrs. Lynch, I'm fairly sure that the boy was a spy."

"Oh, you cannot be serious!" she said, not even bothering to whisper.

"Oh, but I surely *can*. I caught him staring down at those couplers one time too many. I think he's the one who's been trying to snap 'em. If I'd figured it out sooner, I would've shoved him off the train when I had the chance."

Jasper Nichols made a snort that said he thought it wasn't likely to happen, a Texian picking a fight with a southern spy.

Korman only grumbled in response. "It's like I've said all along: I just want to get to Utah. Anyone standing between me and that goal . . . I'm happy to pitch or punch."

Mercy suddenly remembered that the telegram she'd read started with the letters *CB*. Cyrus Berry's initials, but it simply hadn't dawned on her at the time. They could've been lots of people's initials, after all. Could've been Cole Byron's. Could've been nobody's.

"So here's what we're going to do now," the ranger went on, waving the porters closer until their capped heads leaned up to the conversation. They huddled there in the middle of the aisle where no one had any room at all, so everybody's shoulders touched, and everyone could smell everyone else's breath. "You two fellows, can you bolt these doors from the inside? I know they all open out, but there's got to be a good way to fix 'em shut."

They nodded. Cole said, "There's a brace bar to the right. I can fix it."

As if he understood where this was going, Jasper said, "You can fix 'em from the outside, too, if you're serious about keeping those men from coming into this car."

"Excellent. Thinking ahead—I like to see that in a man. You two think you can do that, seal off this car from the last passenger car, the caboose, and the final car?"

"Yes sir. It'll just take us a minute."

"Then do it, and do it now. I'm going to make my way up front. I need to have a talk with the captain," he said, his mouth set in a grim, angry line.

The two porters shifted, begged pardons, and climbed past Mercy and the ranger, who all but crawled their way to the forward doors. Mercy was behind him, and she grabbed his foot in order to seize his attention. "Korman, that captain isn't going to let you anywhere near that car up front."

"Is that where they're holed up? Not in the first sleeper?"

"Yes," she said quickly, still holding on to the instep of his boot. "There's no one in the first passenger car at all, I don't think. But they'll never let you inside their little fort. Hell, I only got inside because the captain got himself hurt."

He reached up for the door latch, gripped it, and looked back down at her. "They let you see it? What's inside?"

"What do you care? You've said so yourself, and more than once, how you don't care what goes on right now between the blues and the grays."

"I said it, and I meant it, and I pretty much mean it still," he said. "But this *does* change things."

"How?"

He turned the latch, and the door cracked open to allow a stream of blistering cold to billow through. It ruffled his mustache and rattled his hat, and he raised his voice so he could be heard over it. "Because until you said that, I was going to tell you to stay here. But now I think you'd better come with me. I need someone they're less likely to shoot."

"Goddammit, Mr. Korman."

"You said it, ma'am," he said, and shoved the door open far enough to rise to a stooped standing position. He dived for the next door and opened it, and Mercy was right behind him, swearing all the way.

Once more, back along the winnowing length of the passenger cars, Mercy's aching back and bent-up legs carried her slowly through the tubes filled with luggage and frightened people. Finally they reached the first passenger car, which was still abandoned, though a few bullet holes in the windows gave the atmosphere a whistling howl that sounded like the singing of the dead.

. Horatio Korman pulled himself into a sleeper compartment and drew Mercy along behind him. He said, "I don't want any surprises in there. You tell me what they've got going on, up in that next car. What are they protecting?"

"Do you really think Cyrus Berry was a spy?" she asked, as if she hadn't heard him.

"Yes, but I don't think it's what got him killed. I think Purdue believed the boy knew what was back there, and he didn't want anyone else to get wind of it. Now, tell me, what's going on up *front*?"

She pointed a finger at his nose and said, "I'm trusting you on this."

"You're a damn fool. For all you know, I could've shot Berry myself."

"But if you *had,*" she said, speaking above the wind and leaning forward, "the doctor or the porter would've said something, and they *didn't*." She looked him in the eyes one more time and then said, "It's gold! Gold! They're moving gold, tons of it."

"Whatever the hell for?" he asked. "Surely they aren't shoring up against a Rebel victory?"

"I don't know why!" she insisted. As she leaned back in the seat, she heard a crumple of paper coming from her apron. She fiddled it out of the place where it'd been riding for half an hour now.

"What's that?"

"I don't know, I found it in that car," she said. "I can't hardly read it, though. Do you have a light?"

He said, "Hang on," and opened up his coat to reveal a vest with many pockets and a holster with a large, shiny six-shooter in it.

She said, "I thought the porter said they'd took your guns."

"Malverne Purdue is an idiot," he said flatly. "He took the two I had out in front, but he didn't search me. He may be some kind of brilliant scientist, but he doesn't know a thing about self-preservation."

Mercy said, "I don't know," for what felt like the hundredth time that day. Then she said, "He shot Cyrus Berry. That must count for something."

"No," said the ranger. "Because he wasn't protecting himself. He was protecting whatever's in that back car. And whatever's there, he thinks it's worth dying or killing over, and shoots like a man who believes that the law is on his side."

"Oh, he does, does he?"

"I know it when I see it." Out from a side vest pocket, he retrieved a device the size of his palm. It was shaped like a cucumber, one half made of metal, the other made out of glass. He pressed a button and the glass end glowed red.

"That's . . . what's that?"

"It's a light for when you want a light that other folks can't see," he explained, taking the paper from her hands. He smoothed the sheet out across his knee and waved his device over it like a conductor's baton. "Red light don't show up very bright, not at a distance."

"Fine, but what does the paper say?" she asked.

"It's a deed."

"Like, a property deed?"

"Yup. Printed up by Uncle Sam."

"Whose deed is it?" she asked.

"Nobody's yet. It's blank. A grant to farm land in the Iowa territory."

She turned it around on his knee and leaned in close, trying to see for herself. "Mr. Korman, there were *scores* of these things, flying around in that car."

"What?"

"There were . . ." She gestured wildly. "Somebody had opened a crate, by accident. The windows are all open in there, and the wind was throwing these papers around like a tornado. This one just stuck to me, that's all."

"And they all looked the same?"

She said, "They were all about the same size and shape."

The ranger fingered the paper, crinkling it and uncrinkling it as he thought. "They're moving money and land deeds west. But why? I don't suppose you were able to sweet-talk that captain out of any useful information."

"Not a thing. Except," she said after a pause, "that he don't know what's in that back car. Whatever Purdue is doing back there, it's coming down from on high. Somebody over the captain's head signed off on it."

"That figures. The captain strikes me as a competent officer, and competent officers are never given enough information to work with. All right, here's what we're going to do: You're going to go into that next car and bring out the captain. Tell him Berry's dead, and I know what happened, and I want to talk to him."

"I thought you were going to go storming the place, guns blazing or somesuch."

"Now, when did I say that? I was going to knock on their door, but now I've got a better idea, and that better idea is *you*. Now, go on. Get him out here."

"I'm not dragging him into a trap, am I?" she said levelly, meeting his eyes above the gleam of the red light, which still burned in his hand.

"No, you're not dragging him into a trap. For God's sake, woman. Just bring him out here."

She got up to do so, but just as she was about to stalk over to the door, a fresh battery of pops and pings reminded her that people were shooting just outside, and she should keep her head down. Stooping a bit, she grasped the latch and swung the door out, propping it there with her own body while she stretched her arm and reached for the other door. Finding it, she hauled herself across the gap, wishing for a helpful porter as she did so. Then she knocked on the door and whipped it open.

As she threw herself inside, letting the door slam shut in her wake, she found herself staring at three drawn rifles and a pistol, all of which lowered upon recognizing her. "Mrs. Lynch," sighed the captain, whose pistol sagged at the end of his hand. "What are you doing back here?"

"I need a word with you," she said. "In private, in the next car over. Please. It's urgent," she emphasized in such a way that she prayed he'd be intrigued and not suspicious. "It's about Cyrus Berry, and the last car. There's a problem, Captain."

They knelt there facing each other at opposite ends of the gold-reinforced car. Most of the stray sheets of paper had been contained, but a few still fluttered wildly, and one got sucked out a window as she waited.

He came to some decision and said, "Fine." He stuffed the gun into his belt and staggered over to meet her, saying, "Hobbes, you're in charge without me." Then he took her by the arm with one hand and opened the door with the other.

Together they navigated the windswept, bone-cold gap with grunts and waves, handholds and curse words. Finally they stood on the passenger car's platform, ready to dive back inside to the relative quiet of that vessel, but she stopped him from opening the door. She put a hand up behind his neck and drew his face down close to hers, so he could hear her and she wouldn't have to shout quite so loudly. "Before we go in there," she said, "Cyrus Berry is dead, and Mr. Purdue has killed him. The Texian saw the whole thing happen, and the doctor did, too."

His eyes widened just as hers narrowed against the wind and darkness.

She continued, "Mr. Korman is just inside this next car. He demanded a word with you. He's on this train on Republic business, not Confederate business, and I think he'll tell you the truth."

The captain made a face that said he feared she overestimated the Texian's purity of motive, but he took the door handle anyway, lifted the latch, and let them both inside.

Horatio Korman was sitting splay-kneed on one of the padded benches, his gun on the seat beside him—not a threat, but a notice that there was absolutely a gun, and simultaneously an advertisement that he was not brandishing this gun. He looked up from under his hat, the shadows from the train windows curling across his face in thick gray squares that offset the black of the car's interior.

"Captain MacGruder," he said. He did not stand as Mercy and the captain slunk over to sit across from him on the compartment bench. "As you know, my name is Horatio Korman. As you don't, I'm a ranger from the Republic of Texas. And you, sir, have one hell of a problem on your hands."

"It's a pleasure," the captain said without looking remotely surprised about either of these revelations. "Now, what the hell is going on?"

"Your sweet blond private is dead and draining in the caboose, shot and killed by Purdue, who you don't appear to have much control over. That little fiend is holed up back there, and I think he's got orders that come down from a higher rank than yours."

In the same unhappy, flat tone, the captain said, "Your assessment of the situation is just about right."

"You've almost got the Rebs run off, now, haven't you?"

The captain didn't answer for a moment. All three of them were holding still and quiet, listening to the reluctant patter of bullets, fewer and fewer, coming from outside. Finally he said, "I believe that situation is under control, yes."

"Good. Because—"

"Good? Now, you wait here a minute, Ranger Korman. I know damn good and well where your sympathies lie, and I want to know—"

"No, you listen to *me,* Captain," the ranger said, escalating the interruptions. "Right now I'm on the side of whoever can get me to Salt Lake City fastest and safest. For all your talk and bluster of this being a civilian train, we both know that ain't the case. I'm here on a duty that doesn't have diddly-squat to do with your war."

The captain said, "I can't say I believe you. Somebody on this train has been sabotaging the ride by bits and pieces, and somebody has been feeding the Rebs information ever since we pulled the civvies on at St. Louis."

"And you think it's me?" Korman asked, patting himself on the chest. "Son," he said, even though the captain was probably older than him, if only by a few years. "I've got better things to do with my time than to slow up a train that I very badly need. And, anyway, you can quit worrying about your spy. He's dead."

"What are you talking about?"

"It was Berry, don't you get it? That boy may have hailed from Ohio, but he had heartstrings that went a lot farther south. You're just lucky he wasn't any better at spying. Blame it on his youth, I suppose. Did he know about the gold you've got in that next car?"

MacGruder flung a glare at Mercy, but she folded her arms and ignored it.

"Of course he knew about it. You saw him in there, propped up on it, shooting out at the meat-baskets and their riders." But something in his voice betrayed an uncertainty. "At least, I thought he was shooting. Maybe he was picking bats out of the sky. Goddamn."

The ranger went on. "Did he know about whatever's in that back car?"

"I doubt it. But to think, I just sent him back there, giving him every excuse in the world to bust it open, find out, and spread the word around."

Mercy said, "You told me you didn't know if it was bodies or something stranger. If you ever said such a thing in front of him, he would've passed it along, don't you think?"

"I'll tell you what I think, Mrs. Lynch," the captain said. "Rumor's had it that you were in league with the Texian all this time. I tried to look the other way—"

Before he could hard-boil his sentiments into an accusation, she blurted out, "I'm from Virginia. I worked at the Robertson Hospital in Richmond. That's the only thing I ever lied to you about. My husband was Phillip Lynch, and he died in the Andersonville camp, and I'm on my way to see my daddy." Though she sat beside him, she slid her legs around so she could face him. "It's the same for me as Mr. Korman. We just need to get west. Neither one of us would've done anything at all to slow this train or harm it. Neither one of us has anything to do with spying."

Her words hung in the night-black air. Between the three of them, they gradually realized that no one was shooting anymore, except far away, and in what could only be described as a retreat.

As one, they rose up and went to the train's south windows and pressed their faces to the panes where the glass hadn't broken. Mercy said, with honest relief, "Look, they're leaving!"

And Korman said, "Thank God." Then he turned to the captain and said, "You, and me, and her—" He indicated Mercy. "We're in this together now."

"How you figure?" he asked.

"Because we're all three being betrayed by somebody. I know my word won't mean much, but let me tell you this: I knew one of the boys who led the early raid that didn't go nowhere. They were just scouting, you knew it the same as I did. But I shot 'im a telegram back in Topeka, trying to get a bead on what's going on here, and I'm hoping for a response in Denver. As a gesture of good faith, I'm willing to share that with you, and send that fellow a warning to leave the train be."

"And why exactly would you do that?"

The ranger gritted his teeth and said, "All I want to do is get to Salt Lake City. This train will get me there faster than any other, and it's in my best interest to see it arrive in one piece. Don't be dense, man. I'm trying to help."

The men stared each other down, until Mercy interjected, "Fellas, listen. All God's children got a job to do here, and all any of us want is to head out west and to mind our own business. But I think we need to mind someone else's business for a bit."

The captain asked, "What do you mean by that?"

And she said, "I mean, I think we should find out what's in the back of this train. Because if it's a bigger secret and something more important than a few tons of gold and a whole passel of land deeds," she let this information slide casually, "then Mr. Purdue is just about the last man on earth I trust to be in charge of it."

"You're suggesting that I disobey orders."

"You were suggesting that Cyrus Berry do the same," she countered, "when you sent him back there. You want to know; you're just afraid to find out. But whatever's back there, Purdue is willing to kill for it—and he'll kill his way up the chain of command, I bet. Whatever it takes to sneak his treasure up to Boise."

In the absence of bullets spitting every which-a-way, the train slowed from its breakneck pace into something more ordinary—not leisurely, but not straining like the engine was gobbling every bit of fuel it could burn, either. The silence that followed, without anyone shooting and without anyone in the passenger car at all, was broken only by the unrelenting wind whistling through the broken patches in the glass.

But off in the distance—terribly far away, so far that they couldn't have seen it clearly even if the sun had been out—a tiny glimmer raced along the horizon line. And from that same position, miles and miles away, the cold prairie air brought a rumor of a tune, one long note held high and loud like the call of one train to another.

Mercy asked, "What's that?" and pointed, even though they were all looking at the same thing, the same minuscule glowing dot that sailed smooth as a marble along some other path, somewhere far away.

Horatio Korman adjusted his hat, jamming it farther down on his head to fight the pull of the rushing air, and said, "Unless I miss my guess, Mrs. Lynch, I'd say that's probably the *Shenandoah*."

Sixteen

The *Dreadnought* pulled into Denver early the next morning and parked a few extra hours for repairs. Most of the passengers debarked, all rattled and some crying, with apologies from the Union and vouchers to take other trains to their destinations. Of the original occupants of Mercy's car, only Theodora Clay and her indomitable aunt Norene Butterfield remained; and of the passengers who'd been present when the meat-baskets made their attack, only about a dozen opted to stick it out. Consequently, the train company would also be abandoning four passenger cars, leaving only three to house the soldiers and remaining scant passengers.

Those who remained were confined to the train while the repairs were made because the captain was insistent that they must get moving at the first possible instant after the repairs were done. The only exception was Horatio Korman, who was let off his car with the captain's tacit approval, much to the astonishment and concern of the other enlisted men.

Purdue had stashed himself in the caboose, where he all but lived now. Like the other passengers, he stayed on board while the Denver crews replaced windows, reloaded ammunition bays, refilled boilers, and patched the most conspicuous bullet holes. He sat at that single portal to the train's very back end and guarded it when he could, and had his right-hand man, Oscar Hayes, keep watch over it when Purdue was occasionally compelled to sleep. Most of the pretense of law and order and chain of command had been abandoned in the last twenty-four hours of the trip, and if Malverne Purdue had ever feigned any respect for the unit's captain, his acting days were over.

While all these situations were simmering and settling, Theodora Clay came back to the second passenger car and sat across the sleeper compartment from Mercy, even though she and her aunt had moved to the other side of the aisle, given the reduction in the passenger load. She placed her hands on top of her knees, firmly gripping the fabric of her skirt as she leaned forward and said, "Things are going from bad to worse."

"Yep," Mercy replied carefully, for she suspected that Miss Clay was not making a social call.

"I've been talking to the captain," she said. "And trying to talk to Mr. Purdue. You must be aware by now that he's a madman. Did you hear he shot Cyrus Berry?"

"Yep."

Her forehead wrinkled, then smoothed. "Oh yes. They said your friend the Texian was there when it occurred. I suppose he passed the information along. Well." She released her grip on the dress and sat up straighter while she sorted out what else she ought to share. "Anyway, as I said. Regarding Mr. Purdue."

"A madman."

"An armed madman, even more delightfully. He won't move, and he won't take tea or coffee, and he just sits, with his chair beside the door and a Winchester lying across his lap and several other guns strapped all over himself. Overkill, I'd call it, but there you go. Sane men take a more moderated approach to these things."

"He's not *really* crazy," Mercy told her. "He's just got a job to do, and he's real excited about doing it."

Miss Clay said, "Be that as it may. Do you have the faintest clue what his job might be? Because no one seems to know what's in the last car, except that it holds the bodies of dead soldiers. And I think we ought to investigate."

"We? You mean, you and me?"

She said, "That's right. You and I. For a brief and maddening minute I almost considered asking your Texian friend if he might be inclined to assist us, but for some reason or another, he seems to have vacated the train. I do pray he won't be joining us again, but that's neither here nor there."

"He'll be back. He's picking up telegrams."

"I'm sorry to hear it. Even so, he might've been just the man to barrel past Mr. Purdue, or to sneak past that other boy who does Mr. Purdue's bidding. If nothing else, I doubt he'd have too many compunctions about shooting past the pair of them. Those Texians. Dreadful lot, the whole breed."

"I've often said the same about Yankee women, but you don't see me going on about it, now, do you?" Mercy retorted.

This shut down Miss Clay momentarily, but she chose not to read too far into the statement. After all, there were class distinctions among the northern regions same as in the southern regions, and everyone knew it. Either Miss Clay was choosing to believe she was being insulted by a Midwesterner, or she'd already concluded she dealt with a gray traitor and had come to terms with it, because she did not call attention to the remark.

Instead she said, "Come now, Mrs. Lynch. There's no need to be rude. I want us to work together."

The nurse asked, "And why is that?"

Theodora Clay leaned forward again, speaking softly enough that her aunt, napping nearby, would not be roused by her words. "Because I want to know what killed those lads."

"I reckon it was a cannonball to the chest, or something similar. Or a missing arm or leg. Like as not, if there are real war veterans dead back there, that's what killed them."

She nodded. "That, or infection, or . . ." She dropped the whisper another degree. "Poison."

"Poison?" Mercy responded, too loudly for Miss Clay's liking.

She shrugged and waved her hands as if she wasn't certain of where she was going, but the plan was forming and she was determined to exposit it. "Poison, or some kind of contamination. I . . . I overheard something."

"Did you?"

"Yes, those Mexican inspectors, they—"

"Are they still on board?"

"Yes," Miss Clay said quickly, eager to get back to her idea. "They've moved to the next car up. They were talking about some kind of illness or poison that they think might've contaminated their missing men. I know you spoke with them."

"They might've mentioned it." Or *she* might've mentioned it, but she didn't say so.

Nearly exasperated, Miss Clay said, "Mr. Purdue was talking to that fellow, that Mr. Hayes."

"About the missing Mexicans?"

"Yes. He was reading a newspaper—while he was back there, like a toad in a hole—and I was only trying to get some breakfast. He was telling Mr. Hayes that something that could alter so many hundreds of people all at once would make a tremendous weapon, if that's what had happened. And before long, if he had his way, the Union would be in a position to produce just such a weapon."

It was Mercy's turn to frown. "Turning a disease or a poison into a weapon? I've never heard of such a thing."

"*I* have," Miss Clay informed her. "During the French and Indian war, the government gave smallpox-infected blankets to hostile tribes. It was cheaper and easier than exterminating them."

"What a gruesome way of looking at it!"

"Gruesome indeed! It's an *army*, Mrs. Lynch, not a schoolyard full of boys. It's their job to destroy things and kill people in the name of their own population. They do what they must, and they do it as inexpensively as they can, and as efficiently as possible. What could be more insidious and efficient than an unseen contagion?"

Mercy lifted a finger to pretend to doodle on the table between them as she responded. "But the problem with an unseen contagion is obvious, ain't it? You're gonna infect your own folks with it, sure as you infect other people."

"Clearly some amount of research and development would be required, but isn't that what Mr. Purdue does on his own time, in order to justify his continued existence as a passenger on this train? He's a *scientist,* and he's guarding a scientific treasure trove. *For the military,*" she emphasized this final point.

"It sounds awful, but I don't guess I'd put it past him."

"Neither would I," Miss Clay said with a set of her mouth that wasn't quite a smile, but conveyed the fact that she thought that now she and the nurse might finally be on the same page. "And that's why we must take this opportunity while the train is stationary, to sneak into that rear car and see what's inside."

Mercy's eyebrows bounced up. "You can't be serious."

"Of course I can. I've even changed my shoes for the occasion."

"Bully for you," Mercy said. "What are you going to do? I've already done my best to persuade the captain to intervene. Shall you seduce your way past Mr. Purdue and—"

"Don't be revolting. And please recall, I've requested your own involvement as well. It'll be disgusting, no doubt. And it wouldn't be necessary if that blasted captain would stand up to the hierarchy and insist for himself that the things under his purview are all known quantities. But alas, I can't convince him to budge on the matter. Ridiculous man, and his ridiculous sense of duty."

"He's all right. You leave him alone."

Miss Clay made a little sniff and said, "If you say so. Now, come on." She changed the subject, rising to her feet. "You and I are going to perform some reconnaissance."

"We're going to do what?"

"We're going to poke around, and let ourselves into that car."

Mercy asked, "How? The doors are sealed and chained. You've seen that yourself, I bet, when we've stopped at stations and stretched our legs. And even if they weren't, Mr. Purdue and his very large gun are standing between us and that car. Or, Mr. Hayes, as the case may be."

"Think bigger. Think *higher*." She pulled on a pair of thin calfskin gloves and fastened their buttons while she said, "We'll go over. There's an emergency hatch on the roof. It's designed to let people out, not *in,* but unless I'm sorely mistaken, it will work both ways." Finished with her gloves, she continued, "Here's what we'll do: We'll go to the last passenger car, take the side ladder up to the roof, and crawl across the top of the caboose, then jump over to the final car."

Mercy said, "You're daft!" but she was already getting excited about the plan.

"I'm daft, and I'm going. And I require your medical . . ." She almost didn't say it, but in the transparent hope that flattery might get her someplace, she finished with, "expertise."

"Oh, for the love of God."

"*Please,* Mrs. Lynch. The repairmen are finished with the rear compartments, and they've moved on to the engine and the broken windows in the first car. We won't be here more than another hour."

Mercy said, "Fine," folded her satchel up, and left it on her seat. She rose and adjusted the gunbelt she now wore more often than not and draped her cloak over her shoulders without raising the hood.

As she followed Theodora Clay out of their passenger car and onto the next one, she did not mention that their errand might prove to be a race against time. She did not tell her companion about the *Shenandoah,* the Confederate engine that had ridden a northwestern track in order to bring those meat-baskets up to the plains and unleash them on the *Dreadnought*. She did not mention that she had indeed been talking to the Texian, and that he believed the *Shenandoah* was still following, tracking to the south and east, but closing ground, despite its defeat. If he was lucky, Horatio Korman was in the process of retrieving a telegram that would inform him of how correct his suspicions were. And if they were *all* lucky, it would say that the *Shenandoah* had given up, turned around, and headed back down to Dallas.

Meanwhile, the engine halted in Denver for only a few hours when it ought to have stayed overnight for an inspection; because a telegram from Union intelligence had been waiting in Denver, no doubt warning of precisely this same possibility and urging haste in any repair work.

While the train sat there, grounded and undergoing the improvements that would keep it rolling the next thousand miles, Mercy Lynch followed Theodora Clay to the spot between the last passenger car and the caboose. It was strange to stand on the junction without the wind putting up a fight, but no stranger than watching Miss Clay scale the external ladder with casual quietness and then, from the top of the car, pivot on her knees and urge Mercy to join her.

When she reached the top rung, Miss Clay whispered, "Move slowly and be quiet. Discretion is the better part of valor in this instance. If we make too much noise, they'll hear us inside."

"Sure," said Mercy, who then pulled herself up on top of the steel-and-tin roof, sliding on her belly like a seal and then climbing to an all-fours position. Her skirts muffled the knocking of her knees, and her wool gloves kept the worst of the frigid surface's chill from getting through to her fingers. But even with the thick layers of clothes, she could feel the cold seeping up through the fabric, and onto her shins, and into her palms.

The nurse had the feeling that Denver was a gray, smoky

place under the best of circumstances, and while the *Dreadnought* was being addressed in its station, a layer of dirty snow hung over everything. It blurred the edges between buildings, sidewalks, streets, and interchanges, and it made the air feel somehow colder. Atop the caboose, which they very slowly traversed in inches that were gained in calculated shifts, slides, and steps, there was little snow except what had fallen since they'd stopped. This snow was a funny color, more like frozen smog than shaved ice. It collected between her fingers and soaked along her legs and elbows where it met her body heat.

Around the train, men hurried back and forth—most of them soldiers or mechanics, bringing sheets of glass and soldering equipment up to the front of the train; but over the edge Mercy could also spy a station manager with stacks of envelopes, folders, ticket stubs, and telegraph reports.

All she could do was pray that no one looked up.

Even if the women flattened themselves down, anyone standing close enough to the caboose could likely stand on tiptoe and see what they were doing. The crawl was torturous and time consuming, but in what felt like hours (but was surely only ten minutes) they had traversed the car and were prepared to lower themselves back down onto the next platform, the one between the caboose and the final car.

On her way down the ladder, Theodora Clay hissed, "Mind your step. And stay clear of the window."

Mercy had every intention of following these suggestions to the letter. She slowly traced Miss Clay's steps down the ladder, across the pass, and then up the next ladder, approximately as silently as a house cat wearing a ball dress. On her way to the top of the final car, she looked over her shoulder to peek through the caboose window, where she saw the back of Malverne Purdue's head bobbing and jiggling. She thought he must be talking to someone she couldn't see, and hoped that she wasn't in the other speaker's line of sight.

By the time she was situated and stable, Theodora Clay was already prodding at the edges of the emergency hatch, or ventilation hatch, or whatever the portal's original purpose might have been. Mercy crept to her side and used the back of her hand to brush the small drifts of snow away from the hinges and seal. Before long, she spotted a latch.

Mercy angled her arm for better leverage and gave the latch a heave and a pull, which Theodora Clay assisted with when the nurse's progress wasn't fast enough to suit her. Between them, they forced the handle around and then heard the seal pop, its rubber fittings gasping open.

Theodora Clay asked, "Why would they seal it with rubber, like a canning jar?"

Mercy was already rocking back on her knees, her hand to her face. "To keep the cold in. Or . . . good *God*. To keep the smell contained! Lord Almighty, that's . . . *Ugh,*" she said, lacking a word with the appropriate heft and reaching instead for a gagging noise.

Her companion didn't do much better. She, too, covered her mouth and nose, then said from behind her hands, "The smell of death, of course. I'd think you'd be accustomed to it, working in a hospital like you have."

"I'll have you to know," Mercy said, her words similarly muffled and choked. "We didn't have *that* many men die on us. It was a very good hospital."

"Must've been. Is there a ladder or anything to let us descend?"

"I don't see one," Mercy said, taking a deep breath of the comparatively fresh air outside, then dipping her head down low to get a better look. "And there's more to that smell than just death."

Inside, she saw only darkness; but as her eyes adjusted, she saw elongated forms that were surely coffins. Her breath fogged when she let it out, casting a small white cloud down into the interior. She sat back up and said, "I see caskets. And some crates. If there's no better way, we could stack them up to climb back out again. But when they open the car in Boise, they'll know someone got inside," she concluded.

"Maybe. But do you really think anyone would believe it was us?"

"You're probably right. And as for getting down . . ." She held her breath again and dropped her head inside for a look around. When she came back up for air, she said, "It's no deeper than a regular car. If we hang from our hands, our feet'll almost touch the floor." Mercy said, "You first."

Miss Clay nodded. "Certainly."

She did not ask for any assistance, and Mercy didn't offer any. It took some wrangling of clothing and some eye-watering adjustments to the interior air, but soon both women were inside, standing on a floor that was as cold as the roof above. The compartment was almost as dark as night, except for a strip of glowing green bulbs, the color of new apples, that lined the floor from end to end. They barely gave off any light at all, and seemed to blow most of their energy merely being present.

But the women used their feeble glow to begin a careful exploration of the narrow car, which was virtually empty except for the crates and the coffins. If the crates were labeled at all, Mercy couldn't detect it; and the coffins themselves did not seem to have any identifying features either. There were no plaques detailing the names or ranks of the men within, only dark leather straps that buckled around each one. Each one also had a rubber seal like the hatch in the roof.

Mercy said, "I'm opening one up."

"Wait." Miss Clay stopped her, even as her hand went to one of the buckles. "What if it *is* some kind of contamination?"

"Then we'll get sick and die. Look, on the floor over there. They're coupler tools, but you can use one as a crowbar, in a pinch. Or you can see about opening some crates, if you're getting cold feet. This was *your* idea, remember?"

"Yes, my idea," Miss Clay said through chattering teeth.

"Ooh. Hang on," Mercy stopped herself. "Before you start, let's stack up a box or two so we can make a hasty exit, if it comes down to it."

Miss Clay sighed heavily, as if this were all a great burden, but then agreed. "Very well. That's the biggest one I see; we can start there. Could you help me? It's awfully heavy."

Mercy obliged, helping to shove the crate under the top portal, and then they man-hauled a smaller box on top of it, creating a brief but apparently sturdy stairway to the ceiling.

Miss Clay said, "There. Are you satisfied?"

"No. But it'll have to do."

Even though she'd been offered the alternative activity of checking the crates nearby, Theodora hung over Mercy's shoulder while she unfastened the buckles and straps and reached for the clasps that would open the coffin.

Mercy said, "Before I lift this, you might wanna cover your mouth and nose."

Miss Clay said, "It does nothing to offset the odor."

"But there may be fumes in there that you don't want to breathe," she said, drawing up her apron and holding it up over her face in an impromptu mask. Then she worked her fingers under the clasps and freed them. They lifted with a burp of release.

More outrageous stench wafted up from the coffin, spilling and pooling as if whoever was lying inside had been breathing all this time, his breath had frozen into mist, and this mist was only now free to ooze tendril-like from the depths of this container. It collected around the women's feet and coiled about their ankles.

Theodora Clay gave the lid a supplementary heave. It slid away from the coffin's top, revealing a body lying within.

Mercy wished with all her might for something like the Texian's small lighted device, but instead she was forced to wait for her eyes to adjust and for the cold fog to clear enough for her to see inside. As the man's features came into focus, she gasped, clapping her apron's corner even more tightly against her face.

Miss Clay did not gasp, but she was clearly intrigued. "He looks just *awful,*" she observed, though what she expected of a man who'd been dead for some weeks and kept in storage, Mercy wasn't prepared to guess. "Is that . . ." She pointed at the loll of his neck and the drag of his skin as it began to droop away from his bones. "Is all that *normal?*"

The nurse's words were muffled when she replied, "No. No, it's not normal at all. But I've seen it before," she added.

"Seen what?"

Mercy had had enough. "Close it! Just close the lid and buckle it up again. I don't need to see any more!"

Theodora Clay frowned, looked back down into the coffin's interior, and said, "But that's ridiculous. You haven't even frisked him for bullet wounds or broken—"

"I said *close it!*" she nearly shrieked, and toppled backwards away from it.

Perhaps out of surprise, or perhaps only to appease her companion, Miss Clay obliged, drawing the lid back into place and pulling the buckles, seals, and clasps into their original positions. "Well, if you got everything you needed to know from a glance—"

"I did. I saw plenty. That man, he didn't die in battle." Mercy turned away and looked longingly at the stack of crates that led to freedom above, and to the light of a dull gray sky. Then she looked back at the crates that took up the places where the coffins had not been placed. She noted the coupler tools, and she picked one of them up.

"Yes," her companion said, and selected another tool that might be used as a prybar. "We should also examine these before we leave."

Mercy was already at work on the nearest one. Since it was placed near the square of light from the open hatch above, she was relatively certain that there were no markings present to be deciphered. She pressed her long metal instrument into the most obvious seam and wedged her arm down hard. This gesture was greeted with the splitting sound of nails being drawn unwillingly out of boards, and the puff of crisp, fragile sawdust being disturbed.

Miss Clay was having more difficulty with her own crate, so she abandoned it to see what Mercy had turned up. "What on earth are *those* things?" she asked.

Mercy reached inside and pulled out a glass mason jar filled with a gritty yellow powder. She shook it and the powder moved like a sludge, as if it had been contaminated by damp. She said, "It must be sap."

"I'm afraid you must be mistaken. That looks nothing at all like—"

"Not *tree* sap," Mercy cut her off. "*Sap.* It's . . . it's a drug that's becoming real common with men on the front. I've heard of it before, and I've seen men who abused it bad, but I've never seen *it*. So I might be wrong, but I bet I'm not."

"Why would you make that bet?"

"Because that man over there—" She used the prybar to point at the coffin. "—he died from this stuff. He's got all the marks of a man who used it too much, right into the grave."

"What about the rest of them?"

"What about them?"

"We should see how they died."

The nurse replaced the jar and plunged her hands down through the sawdust, feeling for anything else. She turned up another jar or two, some labeled samples in scientific tubes, and what looked like the sort of equipment one might use to distill alcohol. She said, "Waste of time. Look at all this equipment."

"I'm looking at it, but I have no idea what any of it does, or what it is."

"It looks like a still, sort of. For brewing up moonshine, only not exactly. I think the army's trying to figure out what makes the drug work, and maybe turn it into a poison, or a weapon, like you said. I think they've gotten hold of as much of the yellow sap as they could scare up, and now they're trying to figure out how they can make a whole passel of it." The words came tumbling out of her mouth, quivering with her jaw as she did her best not to shiver. "This is all so *wrong*. We've got to get out of here, before we breathe in too much of this junk. Come on, Miss Clay. Let's go. Me and you, now. We've got to leave this alone."

"Leave it alone?"

"For now, anyway," she said as she spun around and placed her hands on the large base crate that would lead the way up and out. "There's nothing we can do for these men, and right now we don't have proof of anything, just ideas and thoughts. Let's get out of here so we can think. We can talk about it back in the car, if no one catches us and throws us in jail."

"Such an optimist you are," murmured Theodora Clay, who replaced the lid on the crate Mercy had abandoned, then agreeably followed her back up to the ceiling and out onto the car's roof.

Once they were topside, the two women mashed and heaved the hatch back into its sealed position and began their tricky trip back the way they'd come. Mercy grumbled, "That stink is going to stay with me all day. I bet it's all in my clothes, and in my hair."

"Don't be silly. All this fresh wind will blow it right out of you."

"I think I'm going to heave my lunch."

"I pray you'll restrain yourself," Theodora Clay said, urging Mercy back down the first ladder, then up the next.

On top of the caboose, they scooted and dragged themselves forward, working against a soft breeze that came at their faces with more snow and tiny flecks of ice. Their silence was complete enough that they came down on the other side at the last passenger car, climbed inside, and breathlessly stomped their feet to warm them without anyone seeing them.

Relieved and shaken, Mercy escaped her companion and holed up in the washroom, since there were almost no passengers left and no one would be waiting for her to finish. She spent ten minutes unfastening her hair and shaking it, trying to air it enough so that when the locks brushed up against her face she didn't smell the miasma of the rearmost car. Then she washed her hands, face, and neck.

By the time she'd dragged herself back to her seat, the crews were wrapping up the last of their work and the train was being reboarded by the soldiers, porters, and engineers who would carry them the rest of the way west. Outside her window Mercy saw Horatio Korman talking with the captain, their faces leaning together conspiratorially. She also saw two of the captain's underlings shaking their heads as if they couldn't believe that the two men weren't fighting to the death on the spot.

When Mercy saw that the ranger was about to board, she hurried over to the front door, hoping for a chance to ask him what he'd learned at the stop. But when she got there, she found the two Mexican inspectors, who had also been watching the captain and the Texian with a mixture of nervousness and uncertainty.

Inspector Galeano stopped her and asked, "Do you think they'll make us leave the train? We're so close. We only need to make it to the next stop," he said.

She said, "No, nobody's going to make you leave the train.

They're just talking out there, and believe me, they ain't friends. I'm going to try and have a word with the Texian myself in a minute, if you'll excuse me." Then the car door opened and the man in question stepped in.

Ranger Korman paused to see Mercy speaking with the Mexicans. He tipped his hat and said, "Mrs. Lynch," then, to the other men, "Fellas. How about the four of us sit down here for a spell?"

Mercy was so surprised, you could've knocked her over with a feather. The car was otherwise unoccupied, so it took no great feat to seat everyone in one of the sleeper compartments for the illusion of privacy. Mercy sat beside the ranger, and they both faced the inspectors.

She asked him, "Did you get your telegrams? Did you really share them with the captain?"

"I got them, yes. And I shared most of them, just like I promised."

Inspector Portilla said, "I don't understand."

The ranger waved his hand. "We might be on the verge of finding your missing people."

"That is what we hope!" Portilla replied.

Galeano asked, "Was that your mission, too, upon this train? We could've spoken sooner."

Korman said flatly, "No, we couldn't have, but, yes, it pretty much *is* my job to find out what's been happening. Now, you and me," he indicated the pair of them and himself, leaving Mercy out of the equation for the moment, "we're all men working for our governments. *My* government didn't have anything to do with what happened to your men, and *your* government didn't have anything to do with it. So we've got a problem on our hands: the kind that can blow up into open war, because everybody's pointing fingers. And if there's one thing Texas don't need right now, it's another front to keep track of, do you hear me?"

The inspectors exchanged a glance and nodded. "Your support of the southern cause—"

"Is irrelevant to this conversation," he interjected. "Except for how those stubborn jackasses are still bound and determined to take this train. You and me, we don't want them to take this train. We want them to leave this train alone, so that we can all find our ways to our destinations. Can we agree on that much?"

Everyone nodded, and Inspector Galeano asked, "Why are they so determined to stop this train? I know that the engine is a war device, but we are nowhere near any of the war fronts."

"Gold," said the ranger. "Tons of it. *She's* seen it," he said, cocking a thumb at Mercy.

Somewhere outside, the conductor made the formal declaration that all should come aboard, and the engine's whistle belted out its piercing note, punctuating the conversation strangely. They sat together in awkward silence as soldiers and porters followed directions and came back onto the train, bustling back and forth through the aisles as they came and went to their stations.

When the train finally jerked itself forward in the first tentative steps toward moving, Inspector Portilla spoke again. "The army won't part with the gold. We cannot suggest that they leave it behind so the Rebels will leave the train alone."

The ranger pointed a finger at him and said, "You're right. I thought of that myself. I don't mind telling you that I even thought of *doing* it myself—if everything important was tied up in that rear car, I might have cut the thing's couplers and ditched it along the track, somewhere before we hit the mountain pass. I don't mean to disrespect anybody's war dead, but in this instance, the problems of the living ought to take precedence."

Mercy said, "But the gold's up front, and they're still coming, aren't they?"

To which the ranger replied, "Yeah, they're still coming. The

Shenandoah is burning up track, trying to beat this machine to the pass."

"The . . ." Inspector Galeano struggled to wrap his English skills around the word. *"Shenandoah?"*

"It's a train. Or it's an engine," Horatio Korman explained. "It's a damn fast one, too—one of the fastest the 'federates have pulling for them. We designed it and outfitted it in Houston a couple of years ago, and it's been running the cracker line back and forth through Louisiana, Alabama, and Georgia ever since. She's a V-Twin runner; the first of her kind, but not the last. And the engine system gives the thing a real boost, sending her gliding along the tracks like she's barely touching them."

"Can it catch us?" Mercy asked.

"In my opinion?" The ranger lifted his hat up with one finger and scratched a spot under its rim. *"Maybe.* And if they beat us to the pass, they'll dynamite the tracks to keep us. They know that most of the civilians are off the train now, and they figure anyone left is fair game. That's the friendly warning Jesse gave me, anyhow. They're going to come at us hard."

"For money," she said, as if she could hardly believe it of her own kinsmen.

To her surprise, Horatio Korman said, "No. That's not the whole of it. There's plenty your captain friend left out of his story. There's more going on in that front car than plain old money. That deed you pulled, do you remember it?"

"Sure I do."

"It was blank, and you know why? Because they don't know who they're going to give it to yet. They're taking this load along the coast and down through California, recruiting all the way."

Inspector Portilla asked with a frown, "They are going to buy soldiers?"

"They're gonna *try."*

"But folks out West," Mercy said, "they don't give a damn

about what's going on back East. Who in their right mind, all settled someplace quiet and safe, would go to war for a few dollars and a few acres of land?"

The ranger brightened, pointing at her now, because she'd asked exactly the right question. "I'll tell you who: Chinamen."

Mercy and the inspectors sat up and back in surprise. "Chinamen?" she asked.

"Chinamen," he confirmed. "Out on the West Coast, they've got 'em by the thousands. By the tens of thousands, and counting—and they don't want them there, that's a sure fact. Some places even done passed laws to keep them from bringing their women and children here, *that's* how much they want to be rid of them."

Inspector Galeano leaned forward again, steepling his fingers as he braced his elbows on his knees. He said, "The West doesn't want its Chinamen, and the East wants more soldiers. The Chinamen want to stay here as citizens, and the Union can make them citizens."

"They're the only folks on the coast who might be able to be bought," the ranger said. "And there's a surplus of 'em, and they'll do just about anything for a little respect. That's what the Union's offering them. Thirty acres and start-up capital for farming, out in the middle of noplace where they won't bother no one but the Indians. Once they're out there, they can fight each other or make best friends, for all the shit the Union gives. I don't expect the government has thought that far ahead, to tell you the truth."

"You're probably right," Mercy mused. "It's a bold plan, though. If it works."

"As you can guess, the Rebs would just as soon it *doesn't* work. I can hardly blame them; and I sympathize with their plight, I really do; but I don't know what to tell them."

"What will you do if they take the train?" Mercy asked. "You're not going to fight them, are you?"

He said, "No," and then, as casually as if he were telling her what he had for breakfast, he said, "If they blow up the tracks and we don't stop, I'll die like everybody else, like as not. But if they cut us off and we're able to halt ourselves in time, well . . . I sent word along to Bloody Bill's old crew that I was still riding the train. I also mentioned that there was a woman here who they ought to look out for. I meant *you,* but I wasn't real specific." The ranger gave her a look that implied he'd told them she was a Confederate nurse, but he wasn't going to air that extra bit in front of the inspectors. "As for you fellas, I don't think they'd bother you none. You're obviously not Yankees, so if you keep your head low and wait out the trouble, I bet you'll mostly be all right, no matter how it falls."

Mercy said, "Thank you, I think."

"You're welcome. Anyway, here's why you boys are in on this talk," he said to the inspectors. "The Rebs have told me they think they've seen your troops, and they're scared just plain shitless, if you catch my speaking."

The inspectors made noises indicating that yes, they got the unpleasant gist of *shitless.*

"They've made it way far north, fellas. They're well outside of everybody's jurisdiction now—mine, yours, the U.S. government's. We're so far gone from Texas, or any part of any state that might have been Texas, or might be Texas one day, that it's just plain ludicrous. Nobody but those oddball Mormons are in charge out there, and they're just barely afloat. But those troops are definitely working their way through Utah. When we leave this train, you fellas and me, I want us to make some kind of arrangement."

"What kind of arrangement?" asked Inspector Portilla.

"A *gentleman's* arrangement. Which is to say: I don't like you, and I don't want to be your friend any more than you want to be mine. But somebody's got to vouch for each of us, you get me? When we find out what's going on, I can't have you accusing my government of something it didn't do, and you won't have me accusing your government of something it didn't do, either. We'll sort this out, make a statement, agree on it, and present it to both sides so nobody gets all up in arms about it, however the cards fall."

After a few brief seconds of consultation in Spanish, the inspectors decided they were amenable to this and offered their hands. They shook on it. Then Horatio Korman told them, "I've got the latest rough estimate of the mob's position. When we get off the train at Salt Lake City, we'll go out there together and see what we can find out. It looks to me like they're too damn close for comfort, if they're . . ." He hesitated, then said, ". . . sick, or whatever they are. They're coming up on cities, and people. Bigger places than they met out in West Texas."

Inspector Galeano said, "And the more people they meet, the more the trouble grows. Yes, Ranger Korman," he said, using the formal title like he'd known it all along. "Your terms are reasonable. And you are right: If we do not sort this out together, there could be more war, based on misunderstanding. And I will not have it on my watch."

"Nor I on mine," said the Texian. "Now, if you'll excuse me, I need to have a little chat with the nurse here in private."

The inspectors made polite excuses and withdrew, ostensibly to the caboose, leaving Mercy and Horatio Korman alone in the deserted sleeper car. She rose and took the seat across from him, so they could face each other more directly.

He said, "This is the part where you tell me what you were up to an hour ago, when I saw the edge of your pretty blue cloak fluttering on top of the caboose. Gave me a hell of a start."

"Mr. Korman!" she exclaimed."

"Don't play dumb with me; it's too late for that. What'd you turn up back there? What did you and . . . Was it that uppity Yankee woman? That Clay woman, riding with her auntie?"

Mercy sighed and did not argue, which he took for a yes.

"What were the two of you doing up there, if not heading up and over, into that rear car? What did you find?"

"It was *her* idea. And we found bodies," she told him. "And drugs."

"Bodies? Drugs? Well, I guess I already knew about the bodies—"

"No, Ranger Korman, I don't think you understand. All of this is tied up together. Your missing Mexicans; the dead men in the back of the train; the army scientist who's off his rocker, scaring everyone away from the caboose exit with his Winchester . . . All of this is part of the same thing; I can feel it in my bones," she said.

And then she told him the rest.

Seventeen

The first few days of the ride to Salt Lake City were tense and dark, overshadowed by a cluster of clouds that never quite dropped snow but never quite went away, either. The train rolled, darkened and patched, along the rails and out of the prairies and plains of the Midwest, climbing in and around the edges of the Rockies, and then up, and around, and through the narrow places and the frightening black tunnels. Gradually the train took on elevation. Sometimes the going was easy and the train chugged with something like merriment, as if it were a dog being taken for a swift sprint around a yard. But sometimes when the sky hung low and the train's course took it higher up against the clouds, every firing of every piston felt like a horrendous chore that it didn't wish to perform.

In Denver, the *Dreadnought* had experienced the addition of a piece of equipment that looked like it'd been forged in hell.

This new addition was a snowplow fixture as large as a small cabin, designed to replace the pilot piece in case of a storm—or, worse yet, in case of an avalanche across the tracks. The snowplow was circular and made of reinforced steel and cast iron, of such a size that four or five people could've stood within its opening. But inside the circular frame it was fitted with hundreds of interlocking and overlaying blades, angled to move snow, rocks, or anything else that was unfortunate enough to land within its

path. It looked less like something made to move snow than
something designed to bore tunnels in rocks . . . or process entire
herds of cows into ground beef.

Every once in a while, often in the very deepest part of the
night when things were the quietest, Mercy could hear something
whistle or whisper among the mountain peaks and across the wide,
blue lakes that met between them. So far away, and she could
hear it faintly but sharply. It made her think of the prick of a pin
left inside a dress after alterations: sudden, bright, and small, but
faintly alarming.

One time, upon seeing that her car-mate was still awake,
Theodora Clay blinked sleepily and asked out loud, "What on
earth is that noise?"—but not so loudly that any of the few travelers around her, all the remaining civilians, would awaken.

Mercy murmured, "I couldn't say."

"It sounds like another train."

"It might be, someplace far off. There are other tracks, here
through the mountains. Other paths."

Miss Clay yawned and said, "Yes, I suppose. They must all
feed together for a while, until the pass at Provo."

"What's so special about the pass at Provo?" Mercy asked.

Miss Clay said, "Supposedly it's the only spot where the mountains are passable for hundreds of miles in either direction. All
the railroads have made bargains, deals, arrangements; however it
works. Everything going west goes through that pass, except the
rails that run from Chicago to the coast, and the ones that go
through New Orleans, through Texas. I expect it will be impressive. All those tracks, side by side. Crowded into one stretch like
that. I wonder how long it runs."

And then they slept. In the morning, there was breakfast in the
caboose with the inspectors, who never seemed to sleep, but always seemed very, very watchful. After the inspectors had retired
with their coffee, Miss Clay put in an appearance. She seemed to

have a special sense for when the foreign men would be absent, so she could "eat in peace," as she put it.

Mercy privately thought that it was very like a Yankee, to go to war over the rights of people whom you'd rather die than join for tea. But in the name of peace, she kept this to herself.

Malverne Purdue also kept to himself, in that corner beside the caboose's rear exit. He'd become a fixture there, a signpost of a man whose duty was only to declare, "No trespassing," and threaten to enforce it with the Winchester across his knees. By and large, he was ignored, except when one of the porters would ask him about a meal, or Oscar Hayes would arrive to relieve him for a few hours of sleep.

Mercy could see him from the corner of her eye while she sipped her coffee, which she liked a bit better than the tea, all things being equal.

Theodora Clay could see Purdue, too, though she went to great and chilly pains to pretend otherwise. If ever she'd once looked at him with a kindly eye, the world wouldn't have known it now. A reasonable observer might've assumed that there had been some kind of falling out between them, but Mercy figured that Miss Clay was only keeping her gaze clear lest her eyes reveal something of their adventure in the rearmost car.

Tea came and went, and with it the dull daily routine of life aboard the train rolled on, every bit as monotonous as the tracks beneath the wheels. Mercy missed the two easy virtue girls who'd taught her how to play gin rummy; but they were gone, and even if Miss Theodora Clay had owned a deck of playing cards, Mercy wasn't entirely sure she would've liked to play.

Soldiers patrolled the three remaining passenger cars, from the gold-filled car up behind the fuel cars to the caboose, where a scowl from Malverne Purdue ended the circuit before it could reach the refrigerated compartment. Down to a man, they were tense and unhappy, all of them listening, always listening, for the hoot of a train whistle coming up along the tracks to meet them—trying to beat them—to the pass, beyond which there was no reasonable way for one train to sabotage another. On the far side of the pass, the rails went their separate ways once more; so if they weren't caught before sprinting that span (which Captain Mac-Gruder had told her was nearly thirty miles long), the odds of them being affected by the engine of southern origin were virtually none. If the *Shenandoah* didn't blow up the tracks by then, the Rebs would be out of luck.

Mercy didn't think to wonder what had happened to the doctor until someone mentioned that he'd debarked in Denver, same as almost everyone else. This peeved Mercy greatly. No military regiment, legion, group, or gathering ever went anyplace near danger without a medical professional in their midst, or at least that's how it ought to go. And the truth was, even if Mercy had been a proper doctor with a proper doctor's training and experience, she had only her small satchel filled with basic equipment at her disposal. Anything much more serious than a broken bone or a bad cut could only be managed, not treated.

She felt alone, in the middle of everybody—even the other civilians who hunkered in the center passenger car and read books or played cards or sipped out of flasks to pass the time. She was the only medical professional of any sort on board, which meant that every stubbed toe, every rheumy eye, and every cough gravitated her way for analysis and treatment. It was the nature of the beast, she supposed, but even these small ailments did little to punctuate the wary boredom.

No one ever really nodded off anymore.

No one ever really paid full attention to the books, or the cards, or the vest-hidden flasks; no one enjoyed the passing scenery as the black-and-white mountains scrolled past and the freezing waterfalls hung along the dynamited cliffs like icicles off a gutter. No one listened with both ears to any of the chatter, or the rolling,

pattering passage of the train. Everyone kept one ear peeled for
the sound of another whistle splitting the icy air.

And finally, on the fourth day, they heard it.

It squealed high and sharp.

The whistle blew again, and the echo bounded around between
the boulders and the tiny glaciers that slipped with monumental
slowness down the perilous slopes.

And everyone seized up tight, hearts clenching and unclench-
ing. One by one, everyone rose and went to the south side of the
train, from whence the noise had come. And soon, all the faces on
board—except perhaps the determined and devilish Malverne
Purdue, and maybe the conductor, up front and invisible—were
pressed up against windows that could not have been colder
if they'd been sheets of ice instead of glass. Everyone breathed
freezing fog against the panes, wiping it away with gloved hands
or jacketed elbows. Everyone strained to hear it again, hoping
and praying the first shriek had been a mistake, or had only been
a friendly train, passing on some other track on the approach to
the pass at Provo.

Norene Butterfield groped at her niece's arm and asked,
"How far are we from the pass?"

And Miss Clay said, without taking her eyes off the smudged,
chilled window, "Not far. We can't be far."

"And once we get to the pass, we're safe, aren't we?"

But Miss Clay did not answer that part. She didn't exchange the
knowing glance Mercy shot her either, even though both of them
knew good and well that the pass was a death trap if both trains
were penned within it simultaneously. Only on the far side would
they find anything like safety.

Mercy climbed down from the seat upon which she'd been
kneeling, and whirled into the aisle. Horatio Korman had been
hanging about in the third passenger car, and the captain had
been hanging about in the first one—or else, in the car with the

gold, from which she'd been specifically forbidden from entering again unless directly ordered otherwise. With this in mind, she turned to the right and headed for the rearmost door, opening the latch and dousing the steam-warmed car with a torrent of frigid wind. She shut the door as fast as possible, tugging her cloak up around her head and pulling it tight over her ears, trying to filter out the worst of the blizzard as she felt about for the rail and the platform space over the coupler. She moved to the next car easily, despite the temperature and the wind that felt strangely dry, as if it belonged someplace hellishly hot and not this winter place covered in snow.

In the third car, she found a sight similar to the one in the second, where she'd left Miss Clay and Mrs. Butterfield—except here, most of the faces pressed to the windows belonged to men in uniforms. Horatio Korman stood against the far wall alone, arms folded. He glanced up at Mercy when she came blasting in, accompanied by the weather, and he gave her a frown that told her to shut the door, already.

She did so and approached him, cheeks flushed from even that brief exposure, and hands shaking despite her gloves. She said, "Is it them, do you think?"

"Yeah, I think it is."

"Can they catch us?" she asked for what must've been the hundredth time.

He sucked on his lower lip, or on the gobbet of tobacco he undoubtedly stored within it. Then he reached for a window, lowered it, and spit quickly before closing it again. His mustache ruffled and his hat pushed back by the wind, he shook his head slowly and said, "Not 'can they?' but 'when will they?' We're less than five miles from the pass, and once we're in, it's cliff face straight up and down, on both sides of the rails—an expanse that runs maybe a quarter mile wide, with about twelve sets of tracks running through it."

Mercy tried to imagine it: a frozen corridor like a tremendous wagon track in the snow, with no way up or out to the left or right, no way to back up and go around, and a race to get through to the other side.

He said, "If we're lucky, they'll only trail us. They can shoot at the train's rear car all day—ain't nobody inside there gonna give a shit. Or if we're lucky another way, they'll be stuck on some track far over to the south, far enough that they'll be hard-pressed to do us too much damage, because they won't be close enough, even if they manage to pull up alongside us."

Pierce Tankersly turned away from his window and asked the ranger, "And what if we're *not* lucky? What then, Texian? What will they do?"

"If we're not lucky?" He adjusted his hat, bringing it back down low enough that he could've grazed it if he'd lifted his eyebrows in surprise. "They'll overtake us, and muck up the tracks, just like they promised." Tankersly gave him a quizzical look implying the soldier knew precious little about trains, so the ranger clarified. "If they blow the tracks up there, this train will go off the rails. Literally. Most of us'll probably die on impact. Some of us might live to get shot, or freeze to death."

The private said, "Then what are you standing over here for, man? They may be your allies on the map, but you'll get killed same as us if they manage to undo the *Dreadnought*! Take up a position—hell, go find the captain and see where he'd like an extra man."

But Korman said, "No. I can't do that. I won't shoot at my own fellows, or fellows that *might* be mine. I wouldn't do it even if I thought it'd make a lick of difference to whether or not they take this train. That just ain't how it works, junior. And if the shoe were on the other foot, you'd probably treat the situation just the same."

"It doesn't matter what foot what shoe is on. I'd fight for my life, regardless!" the young man said.

The ranger replied, "Well, all right, maybe I'm wrong. But I'm *not* fighting for my life. There's nothing I could do to slow down that train, and not much you could, unless you want to go up to our front cars and run those weapons she's pulling down. Otherwise, best I could hope to do is keep them out of the passenger car. I don't know how many of them are dumb enough to try to board us like a pirate ship moving at ninety miles an hour, but I'm willing to bet the answer is none too many."

Closer, definitely closer, the whistle blew again—shaking the sheets of ice that hung off the mountain.

Tankersly said, "What the hell is wrong with you, man? What if they do board us? What if, somehow, they stop us and you survive it—then what?"

"Then nothing," he replied, as easy as thanking the porter for a cup of coffee. "They know I'm on board, and they won't shoot me."

"Then maybe someone should!" The private swung his revolvers around and pointed both at the ranger, who didn't move a muscle.

He only said, "You? You want to shoot me? I guess you could, and I could even see where it might make sense to you. But keep this in mind: I could've taken you down one by one, throwing your corpses overboard without thinking twice about it. For the last five minutes I've had a nice fat shot at a whole row of you dumb sons of bitches, all of you with your backsides ripe for the aiming at. But I didn't shoot you, because I ain't got no problem with you. I'd like to see you succeed. I'd like to make it to Salt Lake City in one piece, and killing you off won't do anything to help me reach that goal."

He looked like he wanted to spit again, but maybe he was out of tobacco, or maybe he didn't want to pull down the window and get another blast of cold air in the face. "Hell," he said instead. "I've said it since I got on board, and I'll keep saying it until I get let off or get thrown off: *I'm not here to fight against you,* on behalf of the Confederacy or the Republic or anybody else. Y'all leave me alone, and I'll leave you alone, like I've left you alone all this time. And that's the best offer you're going to get from *me.*"

Somewhere beyond the window, the whistle blew again. Even Tankersly looked over his shoulder, sensing it was close. And since the ranger hadn't drawn, and hadn't budged, the private reluctantly turned away. But he said, "I'm watching you, Korman."

To which the ranger said, "Knock yourself out. Maybe I'll do a little dance."

Mercy turned away from the conversation and went to a spare square of window in order to see outside. At first she thought the glass was going opaque from too many eager breaths being puffed upon it, but then she realized that the visibility was shrinking from outside, not within. A dusting of snow billowed down through the pass—which she could see, just barely, because of the way the track bent ahead and showed her the curve of the train.

There it was: a gap cut between the mountains. At this distance, it looked immense, though she knew that the ranger must be right, and it couldn't be any wider than a quarter of a mile. Feeding into it were about a dozen tracks, all lined up side by side so they made a pattern of stripes squeezed into the narrow corridor.

And off to the south, she could see it now: the *Shenandoah.*

It streaked up to meet them, a bullet of a machine, drawing only four cars as opposed to the *Dreadnought*'s eight (if she included the snowplow fixture, which was of such terrific size and weight that she might as well). It was behind them, yes, and coming up from an arcing track that surely added more distance to their flight. But even from her spot on board the Union train, Mercy could see that the other engine was flying like lightning. Surely it was difficult to judge, but it couldn't be her imagination that the *Shenandoah* was gaining ground, and as her eyes tracked the gap and the other engine's path, she could've sworn that the ranger was right—it wasn't a matter of if, but of *when*.

The foremost door on the third passenger car blew open and Captain MacGruder came shoving through it, with Inspector Galeano at his side. The captain pointed out a spot on the defensive line and told the Mexican, "There. And we'll put your partner at the first car so we can make use of you both."

The inspector pulled a gleaming, silver-wheeled pistol out of a carved-leather holster and let it spin as he twisted it with his wrist and up into his hand. "*Sí, señor.* Wherever you need me."

Then the captain turned his attention to Horatio Korman and said, "You, come with me."

To Mercy's mild surprise, the ranger did not object. Instead, he immediately stepped into the aisle and replied, "I thought you'd never come around."

The nurse saw where they both meant to go and she asked, "Come around to what? Where are you two going?" Instead of answering, they moved to the rearmost door and opened it. She followed, even though she had a feeling that one or both of them was on the verge of ordering her not to. Before the wind had died down from their crossing of the couplers and the gap, she had entered the caboose behind them and drawn the door shut, clipping off the wild, freezing air and sealing them into something like a very uncomfortable vacuum.

She turned around just in time to see Captain MacGruder level his service revolver at Malverne Purdue and tell him, "Out of the way, Purdue."

But Purdue was already on his feet, Winchester in hand and aiming right back at him. He said, "No."

The caboose was empty except for the five of them: Mercy, the ranger, the captain, Purdue, and the loyal Oscar Hayes, who looked like he'd rather be almost anywhere else at that particular moment. The silence that fell in the wake of the *no* was thick and muddled with the ambient roar of the train and the wind, and the occasional whistle of the incoming train and the *Dreadnought* itself, which finally saw fit to answer the *Shenandoah*.

The ranger had not yet drawn either of his visible guns, which had been returned to him after the last stop. But one hand hovered in a warning, prompting Mercy to wonder how she'd not yet noticed that he favored the left.

Without lowering his gun or so much as blinking, the captain said evenly, "Purdue, I know you've heard it. Have you seen it, out the window here?"

"Nope."

"They're gaining on us, and soon they're going to catch us. If they beat us to the pass, we might be done for. Do you understand me?"

With equal deadpan delivery, the scientist said, "I do, but I believe my experiments are more important than a few casualties."

"Believe what you want. That engine is moving four cars, and it's pumping on a new draw—the same kind as our engine, but lighter and more powerful. That's not fear, that's a fact—isn't that right, Ranger Korman?"

"That's right. The V-Twin system will move that engine with almost twice the power of the one we're riding now, and they're pulling half the weight."

"The *Dreadnought* can outrun them."

"The *Dreadnought* is towing too much to outrun that Rebel sprinter," the Texian insisted.

"Then we'll shoot her off the tracks. I remain unconcerned," said Malverne Purdue, who also remained ready to fire at the drop of a hat.

Horatio Korman said, "Maybe, maybe not. But if she gets ahead of us, and gets any lead on us—as she almost certainly will—they'll take out the tracks and then we're all of us dead."

"We'll blow it off the tracks before it passes us."

His patience running thin, Captain MacGruder said, "It's not going to get a chance to pass us, Purdue. We're going to drop some weight and outrun it. We'll beat it to the punch if we can shake some of our load; but we can't let them get ahead. We're all done for, if we do."

Purdue said, "Well then, I guess we're all shit out of luck, because you're not unfastening this car," he said, indicating with a thrust of his shoulder the rearmost vehicle, the hearse. "You wouldn't do that, would you? You wouldn't disrespect the war dead like that, would you, Captain?"

"Right now the needs of the living come first. Now, get out of the way, Purdue, and let us have a go at those couplers."

"Over my dead body."

"I'm not afraid to arrange it," said the ranger, his hand still vibrating an inch over the butt of his gun where it jutted out of his belt.

The captain said, "The dead will have a lot of company if we don't let that car go."

Oscar Hayes had his gun out, but he didn't know where to point it. He wouldn't shoot the captain, surely, but his wrist was sagging in the direction of the ranger, just in case he needed to shoot *someone*. Purdue hadn't budged. The captain and the Texian were so tense, they could've twanged like harp strings.

And the *Dreadnought* pulled them all closer to the pass with every second.

"What have you got back there?" asked the captain. "What have you *really* got, that's what I want to know."

"Dead people. That's all."

Mercy decided it was finally time to jump in. She said, "He's moving a drug called yellow sap. He wants make a weapon out of it."

Most of the eyes in the caboose and at least one gun shifted focus to aim right at her.

The ranger's didn't. He didn't take his glare away from the scientist, because he already knew what was in the caboose. He added his right hand to his left, and now both palms dangled over both butts of both his guns.

She blurted out the rest. "The dead men back there didn't die in war. They died from too much sap. But the stuff the sap's made of—it does a whole lot worse! It makes people crazy, so they eat each other!"

The captain's gaze whipped back and forth between them. He demanded of Purdue, "Is she telling the truth? Is she?"

Not quite rattled, but taken off guard, Purdue grumbled, "She doesn't know a damn thing."

Mercy thought maybe Horatio Korman would back her up, but he didn't—perhaps because he wanted the scientist and his assistant to forget about him, and fight with the captain instead. So she defended herself, saying, "I *do,* Captain—please, you have to believe me! And you," she said to Purdue, "if you want to prove me wrong, then show him what you're hoarding back there!"

"I want to see your papers again," the captain said to the scientist. "I want to see who processed them, and who signed them, and—"

"What difference does it make?" demanded Purdue, changing his approach. "Yes, we're making weapons—that's what armies *do*! What's carried in the last car is important to our program—more important than anything we've ever been able to create so far. The *potential,*" he said, pleading now, almost. "You have no idea what *potential.*"

Mercy said, "Just this once, Mr. Purdue's right, Captain. You have no idea of the potential. You have no idea what it does to people—what it could do to the South, yes, but what it could do to anyone. *Anywhere*. The gas that makes the sap, it kills without caring what uniform anybody's got on."

The captain weighed this, even letting his guns lower a fraction of an inch while he thought. He said, "I have my orders, too, Purdue. And I have my men to protect, and *you're* not one of my men. Those dead fellows in the back, there's nothing I can do for them now—and if the Union wants its weapon, the Union can send somebody back here for that cargo. They can forgive me later, or court-martial me if they'd rather, because by God, we're—"

Purdue's posture changed ever so slightly, and at the same time his fingers made the slightest jerking motion. But before he could interrupt the captain with a bullet through the heart, Horatio Korman's guns were in his hands—both of them, faster than a gasp. He fired them both, one at Oscar Hayes, and one at Malverne Purdue.

Hayes went down without a sound, and Purdue's rifle muzzle flew skyward, firing one outstandingly loud bullet straight through the ceiling.

Before Purdue could fall all the way to the floor, the captain was on him, kicking the big gun away and pushing his booted foot up against the injured man's chest. Korman's bullet had caught Purdue through the shoulder, up near the junction where it met his neck. He was bleeding obscenely; it gushed over his torso as he flailed to stop it, but he failed to push the captain's boot off his chest.

He burbled, "You can't. You can't do it. Everything depends on it! My career depends on it, and maybe the Union—the whole Union!"

Horatio Korman said, "Your Union can go to hell." And he sheathed his guns with a spin that put them down gentle into the holsters.

"I'd rather it didn't," the captain said. He discerned with a glance that Hayes was dead, then checked Purdue. "This bastard might live, at least long enough for me to have him tried. You would've shot me."

"You're going . . . ," he gagged. "To cost us . . . *everything*."

"No, *you* were going to cost us everything, and now you aren't. Ranger, do you know how to undo these couplers?"

"I'm sure one of us can figure it out. If not—" He turned to Mercy. "Mrs. Lynch, how about you run and grab us the nearest porter?"

She nodded and stumbled away, wondering if she should patch Mr. Purdue or leave him, as she suspected that, with prompt and thorough attention, he might well survive the wound.

By the time she returned with Jasper Nichols, the ranger and the captain had managed to disengage the coupler all by themselves, and the rearmost hearse was disappearing slowly into the distance. The *Dreadnought* put on an extra burst of power to match the ones it'd made in its flight from the defeated meat-baskets; and, less the weight of the missing car in the rear, the whole train lurched forward with renewed vigor.

Mercy turned to the porter and asked, "What about the caboose? Can we get rid of that, too?"

With a look out the window, he said, "Ma'am, we could, but it might not do us no good. Look." He pointed, and she saw that he was right.

The *Shenandoah* was coming up around the curve, wending up the arc of its own track, closing in on the pass. There was a gap of maybe a hundred yards between the end of the *Dreadnought* and the beginning of the next engine.

Mercy breathed, "Oh God." And at the same time the captain said, "God help us." Horatio Korman said nothing.

The porter said, "We're already too late. Here they come, and here's the pass. We're right up on it."

Besides, as the porter explained, the real weight on the train

came from the forward cars and the snowplow attachment—
which was to say, the fuel and ammunition car . . . and, as Mercy,
the captain, and the ranger privately assumed, the car stuffed
with gold bars. But a lighter train meant a faster train, never mind
the food stores or the stoves or the cooking units in the caboose.
It had to go. All of it had to go. They could grab a new one of
everything in Salt Lake City, provided they ever arrived there.

Mercy shoved one arm up underneath Malverne Purdue just
as the captain ordered her to do so. She lifted him like an unhappy calf, and heaved him across the couplers into the third passenger car. "Come on, now," she told him. "And if we get a free
minute or two, I'll do what I can to close up that wound."

The scientist didn't object, but he didn't help her much, either. She dropped him into a seat and patted him down quickly
for guns or other weapons. Finding only a small derringer and a
boot knife, she took them both and pocketed them. And when
she was reasonably confident that blood loss and lack of agency
would keep Mr. Purdue out of trouble, she stood up and went
back into the aisle.

There, she nearly collided with Captain MacGruder, who said,
"Get the inspector over there to help you get him to the next car."

"What?" she asked, but Inspector Galeano was already at her
side, taking the man's other arm and lifting him back up again.
"We're moving him again?"

"I'll help," the inspector said.

"All right," she replied dubiously, and grabbed the stray, flop-
ping arm of the scientist, who was becoming more rag doll–like
by the moment. "If we don't set him down someplace soon, and
for good, we'll lose him yet."

Captain MacGruder overheard this, and he said, "Now ask
me if I care. Move him up to the second passenger car, and set
him down there. If he lives, he lives. If he doesn't, I'll shed a little
tear and move on with my afternoon."

He continued to shout orders up and down the line, though since it was he and the ranger who had worked out the coupler disconnects, these two men returned to the gap. In less than a minute, the caboose unhitched and sadly, slowly, slipped away into the *Dreadnought*'s wake.

The two men flung themselves back inside right before Mercy and the inspector opened the forward door, and she heard him delivering more orders every which-a-way behind her. Then she understood. They weren't just leaving the caboose and the rear-most hearse car; they were leaving this last passenger car, too.

"Everyone, forward!" she heard the Texian cry, and between herself and Inspector Galeano, they wrestled the inert Malverne Purdue into the second car.

Mrs. Butterfield and Miss Clay were startled by the sight of the bleeding man, though neither seemed moved to help settle him someplace. Mercy took care of that herself, lying him down in a sleeper car and feeling at his neck for a pulse, which came more faintly with every breath. The man's skin had gone white, with a bluish gray around the creases at his eyes and mouth; but the nurse stood by her original assessment that he could yet be saved . . . even if it was only for a court-martial and hanging.

Mercy stuffed a handkerchief against the wound and dashed to her seat for her satchel, from which she grabbed gauze and wrappings. She applied them to the best of her ability while the inspector served as a silent assistant—taking what she discarded, holding what she needed, and generally doing a damn fine job of staying out of her way. She thanked him with murmurs and tried to ignore the frantic hollers of the passengers, soldiers, and porters as the train lost one more segment and the third passenger car drifted away behind them.

"It's madness!" Mrs. Butterfield declared. "Where will all of us sleep?"

To which the Texian said, "Out in the snow, with the coyotes and the mountain lions—if we don't keep *this* train ahead of *that* one," and he pointed out the window.

The old woman gasped like she might faint, and Theodora Clay stepped up and slapped the ranger across the face. "How dare you!" she exclaimed, not really asking a question but making an accusation. "Trying to frighten an elderly lady like that!"

"I'll frighten her and *worse,* if it gets her out of my way," he said, unmoved and apparently unstartled by the prim but sharp attack. "Now look out that window and tell me you think we're going to beat them through Provo."

As he said it, the pass loomed up and swallowed the train, car by car in quick succession. The shadows from its immense walls were cut sharply up, and as high as the sky to the right . . . and up to the clouds on the left, where the *Shenandoah* was not gaining as swiftly as before, but remained close on their tail.

"Everything that can go, *is going,*" the captain chimed in. "Now make room."

Though three passenger cars had made for a fairly spacious arrangement for two dozen military men and half that number of civilians (plus the conductor, rail men, and assorted porters), reducing that number down to two cars made for cramped quarters, and Mrs. Butterfield had a point: only one of these cars was a proper sleeper. Mercy couldn't imagine anyone being so narrowly focused as to be worried about that fact right this second; but a glance at the matron, with her sour face and her arms crossed and clenched around her bosoms, told the nurse that she still had a whole lot to learn about people.

With much more shouting, ordering, and cramming of people up and forward—and into the next car up, where there was temporarily more room—the *Dreadnought* shed the third passenger car as smoothly and strangely as the previous two and picked up speed.

Mrs. Butterfield complained as she looked out the back window, "Soon you'll have the lot of us sleeping in the coal car."

Horatio Korman said, "No ma'am—just you." Then he immediately returned his attention to something the captain was saying, and to the window beyond the captain's shoulder, where the *Shenandoah* was drawing up nearer, ever nearer, clawing up to the *Dreadnought*'s pace by feet—not by great leaping yards, not anymore, but still coming. The ranger said, "It's not a bad idea, actually."

Captain MacGruder said, "Are you kidding me?"

"No, I'm not. And I'm not just talking about her. I think we could fit the lot of them into that car just past the fuel car. The one with the *special armor* inside," he said, flashing a meaningful look at the captain.

Mercy caught it, too. She said, "Yes, Captain. There's only—" She did a quick count. "Eight civilians—or ten if you count the inspectors, but I don't think you should. I don't know about Mr. Portilla, but Mr. Galeano looks like he knows his way around a gunfight, and he has his own pistol."

"Nine, if we count you," he pointed out.

"So count me. You might need me, and there's nobody else, if anybody gets hurt. But you can stack these eight folks up inside the—" She almost said *the gold car,* but stopped just in time. "The car up there. They'll be safer there than anyplace else. Who cares if they see what it's carrying?"

This perked ears all around, and loudly voiced questions of, "What's it carrying?"

The ranger said, "There ain't much time. Get them out of the way, and the rest of y'all can fight your war like civilized killers."

Mercy almost expected MacGruder to keep fighting, but he decided in a snap, "Fine. Do it. Comstock, Tankersly, Howson— get these folks up to that car. You know the one."

"What? *Now* where are we going?" Theodora Clay demanded.

"Someplace safe," Mercy said. "Safer, anyhow. Just go. Take your aunt and hunker down."

"I think *not*."

"Think whatever you want, but would you at least get Mrs. Butterfield up front? I doubt she'll let anyone else take her."

Miss Clay hesitated, but she flashed a glance out the window at the onrushing train, and recognized the truth of their words. "Fine. But I'm coming right back."

Hastily the handful of leftover civilians was loaded, shoved, and urgently led to the front of the train, where the former car of mystery was waiting. It had been cleared out by the time they arrived, so that something like an aisle was open in the middle of the floor. Seeing the arrangement as she helped with the last of the evacuation, Mercy was glad for the quick improvisation of the soldiers.

Morris Comstock asked her, "Are you coming?"

She realized she and Miss Clay were the last civilians there. "Yes," she said.

Miss Clay said, "I'm coming, too."

But Mercy beat her to the door and slammed it shut, closing herself and Comstock out onto the coupler passageway. She drew a bar down and fixed it, effectively locking the whole group into the car. She took a deep breath, turned to the private first class, and said, "I hope I'm doing the right thing."

Morris Comstock looked at the irate face of Theodora Clay, her gloved hands beating against the window as she screamed, and he said, "The best thing that can be done, I expect. They'll be safe in there," he added, speaking loudly so that he'd be heard over the wind.

"I hope."

"If they aren't, there's not much we'll be able to do for them, anyway."

Together, as if they'd had the same idea at the very same instant, they each gripped the vibrating iron rail and leaned out
to see how close the front of the other train was. It was staring
straight ahead up the track, coming right for them.

The far side of the pass was a cliff as cutting and certain as the
one to their immediate right—so close that, sometimes, Mercy
was quite positive, she could've reached out a hand and dragged
it along the icy boulders if she wanted to lose a few fingers. But
the sides of this astonishing pass rose up so high that they shut
out the sun and cast the whole man-made valley into shadow, and
through the veil of this shadow the face of the *Shenandoah* was an
angry thing. She could make out its round front with the stream-
lined pilot piece and its billowing stacks. And when a faint curve
of the track allowed for something less than a head-on view, she
could also see one side of the pistons, which pumped the thing
faster, harder, and with greater efficiency than the engine that drew
her own train forward.

Morris Comstock said, "This is going to be bad," as if Mercy
didn't already know it.

"Hurry," she said, opening the next door and letting them both
back into the first passenger car.

Morris Comstock spotted Lieutenant Hobbes and said, "Sir,
the civilians are secured in the forward car," with a snappy salute.

"Glad to hear it. You—" He pointed at Mercy. "—the captain
wants you back in the next car."

"I'm going," she told him, pushing sideways past Morris and
shuffling through the narrow aisle, alongside the rows of men setting up for trouble—lining up by the windows, lowering them as
far as they'd go, and breaking them out if they'd frozen shut.
They ducked down low behind the passenger car's protective
steel walls and waited for someone over *there,* on the other track,
sidling up close, to fire the first shot.

In the second car, Mercy seized her poor, battered satchel and slung it across her chest, where it bumped against the gunbelt she'd been wearing all morning. Until the bag bounced and reminded her, she'd completely forgotten about it. But whom was she going to shoot? The Rebels, if they got close enough? No, of course not. No sooner than Horatio Korman would've shot at them. The Union lads on the train? No, not them either.

But given the havoc and the horror of the moment, being dragged along a track at impossible speeds, and chased and harried around every bend and up every craggy plateau, she wore them. They were loaded, but they remained unfired for the time being.

"Captain MacGruder?" she called, not seeing him immediately.

He stood up from behind one of the sleeper compartments, where he'd been hovering over Malverne Purdue. "Over here, Mrs. Lynch. Tell me, do you think you can fix him?"

"Jesus couldn't fix him," she said under her breath. "And I don't know if I can patch him up, if that's what you're asking. I wonder why Ranger Korman didn't just go for the heart."

"There's no telling. Or, I don't know." The captain shrugged, using his foot to nudge at Purdue's limp leg. "He moved real sudden with that gun. The ranger's good, but there were two men to shoot. In all fairness, the bastards both went down."

Mercy said, "I'll make him comfortable. That's all I can do."

"I didn't ask you to make him comfortable. Put him on a bed of nails if we've got one. But I'd like to see him survive long enough to explain himself."

"I've done my best," she said. The captain went away, back to the front lines on the southern side of the train, where the windows were all open now—wind pouring through them, blowing everything that wasn't nailed down all over the place. And snow came inside with the wind: it had begun as a faint, spitting bluster of tiny shards of ice, but it was becoming something denser, something with more volume and sting when it slapped against faces and into eyes.

Convinced there was nothing more she could do for the unconscious Purdue, she left him, drew the curtain to close him into
the compartment, and stood up so she could see what was going
on. It was almost enough to make her want to dive back inside
and join the scientist in a defensive huddle.

The *Shenandoah* was so close she could see it now, its engine
straining and speeding along, the pistons churning and pumping.
She could also see faces—that's how close it had come—faint but
definite, lining the windows in a mirror of the men on the *Dreadnought*. Men also dashed to and fro along the Rebel engine and its
scant number of cars, climbing with the certainty of sailors on
masts or cats along cupboard shelves. It was strange and awful,
the feeling of pride combined with horror Mercy felt as she kept
her eyes on them, tracking one after another like ants on a hill.

While she stared, and while the mountain shadows flickered
and flew across the pass and across the trains, a tense pall settled
upon the men and women of the *Dreadnought*. Maybe, Mercy
thought, the same moment of hesitance was making the *Shenandoah* quiet, too. It was one final moment when things might possibly go another way, and the confrontation might end in some
other fashion—or never occur at all.

And then, with the sound of a planet exploding, the moment
passed and the battle came crashing down upon them.

Eighteen

Mercy could not be certain, but she believed the first blow happened simultaneously, as if both trains' patience simply exhausted itself, and everyone shot at once—taking a chance on starting something awful, rather than receiving something awful without kicking back.

Or maybe the *Dreadnought* fired first.

And why shouldn't it? The Union train had the most to lose, being stuffed with gold and paperwork and soldiers, and being an expensive piece of war machinery to boot. Heavier, slower, and more valuable, the *Dreadnought* had one primary thing going for it: immense firepower. As Mercy scanned the cars of the *Shenandoah,* tugged behind one another like sausage links, she saw only one fuel car and only one vehicle that looked remotely prepared to move armaments and artillery. The engine itself was armored and reinforced, yes, but its gunnery lacked the forethought and sophistication of the *Dreadnought*'s assault-oriented design.

So the *Dreadnought*'s strategy was simple. It had to be simple, for the options were so strictly limited.

Stay ahead of the *Shenandoah*. Don't let it outpace us.

Blow it off the tracks if you can, or if you have to.

Fire.

The nurse would play the moment over and over in her head,

on an infinite loop that would surprise her sometimes, startling her out of a reverie or out of her sleep, for the rest of her life.

And she would listen to it, watch it, scrutinize it through the windowpane of her memory and wonder if it mattered. Surely it didn't matter who fired the first shot, or what small action caused the event to begin. But merely knowing that it might not matter did not make it bother her any less, not at the time and certainly not in retrospect, and it did not keep that moment out of her waking nightmares.

Her terrified and very human reaction was to duck down, to dodge, to lie on the floor and pray.

Ears ringing, she staggered to her feet and tried to hold that position—upright, still crouched, out of the line of fire. But the train was reeling. It rocked on the track even as it hauled itself forward, keeping that pace, not letting the *Shenandoah* come up too close but throwing everything it had at the other train. The recoil from the engine's cannon, the unevenness of the track, the gathering clumps of snow that must surely have knocked the balance here and there . . . these things made it hard to stand and hard to concentrate, never mind how the sound of war and windows breaking compressed and reverberated within the steel and cast-iron tubes.

Gunpowder smoke accumulated despite the errant wind, and driving snow collected inside the car—dusting the seats and the corners, and drifting wherever it found a relatively quiet eddy in the raucous, rattling mayhem.

It was hard to breathe and even harder to see, but one of the sharpshooters was sharp-shot, and he tumbled backwards off the seat where he'd braced himself. Mercy ran to his side. She knew the soldier on sight, but didn't recall his name. His face was surprised, and stuck that way.

Someone shouted. Mercy couldn't make it out; but someone

tripped over the corpse and nearly kicked her in the shoulder, all by accident, all in the calamity of the moment. Sensing a way in which she could be useful, she drove her arms up underneath the dead shooter and man-hauled him backwards across the aisle and against the far wall beneath a window that faced the sheer cliff.

The forward door burst open and Horatio Korman stood framed within it, holding it ajar and fighting with the wind to keep it from flapping him in the face. "Mrs. Lynch!" he hollered.

"Over here!"

"Next car up! Come on now, we need you!"

"Coming!" she said as loud as she could, but no one could have heard her over the din. "I'm coming," she said again, and even if the ranger hadn't caught the words, he caught the sentiment. He extended a hand to her, and only then did she realize she was still half crawling in the aisle.

"Hang on," he told her. He seized one of her wrists and lifted her bodily up, into the doorway, and then he pressed her against the wall to the side of it—outside in the frozen storm of rushing air—as he jammed the door shut behind himself. Together they stood on the place above the couplers, the platform that shifted back and forth as if deliberately designed to keep anyone from standing upon it—while the train was shaking so badly, and snapping like the sharp end of a whip every time a new cannon volley was fired from the engine up front.

"Hang on," the ranger urged again. He took her hand and placed it on the rail.

She squeezed it, feeling the iron leech a sucking chill up through her gloves. It was a skinny thing, made only to guide, not to support. Certainly it'd never been made to support a wayward passenger under circumstances such as these.

"Hurry. We're wide open. If they see us, and if they get a shot, they can take us."

She wanted to believe they wouldn't—just like before, maybe, when they'd seen a woman on the train, and maybe since they knew Ranger Korman was present . . . maybe they'd know him by his hat and his posture. But then she realized something astonishing: His hat was gone, either blown out into the Utah mountains or stashed someplace in one of the cars, she didn't know which. His dark hair whipped wildly, with the one white stripe flickering down the middle like a candle's flame.

"I'm coming," she said, and the act of opening her mouth to tell him let the winter into her mouth and down her throat. She choked on the words and squinted against the wind, though it cut tears out of her eyes and froze them on her skin.

Blindly she groped for the door—and, still more on her knees than on her feet, she found it. The ranger braced her, using his body to give her as much cover as he could; and when the door opened, they toppled inside together.

Mercy hit the floor hands-first and sorted herself out enough to ask, "Who needs me?" only to see Private Howson holding his hands over some gaping bit of bloody flesh at his throat. "Let me see it," she commanded, approaching him on hands and knees, and none too steadily even at that.

Something bright and loud exploded very close.

The windows splintered and blew inward. Soldiers screamed with dismay or pain, and the day was bright with a split second of terror and chaos. When it had passed, there was blood—much more blood—and the powder and slivers of glass joined the blowing snow within the passenger car.

"Nurse!" someone cried.

She said, "One at a time!" but she looked over her shoulder anyway, and saw Pierce Tankersly wearing a long slash of red across his forehead and one shoulder, and a shard of glass sticking out of one hand. It was bad, but not as bad as Private Howson's gushing throat wound, so she gestured and said, "Over there, Mr. Tankersly. Against that wall. Anyone who needs help, against the far wall!"

Only one other soldier joined Tankersly. In the swirl of the moment, Mercy couldn't see who it was—but if he was strong enough to shift himself to a new position, he could wait for her attention.

She pried Howson's hands away from his throat and saw what looked like a bullet wound scarcely to the left of his windpipe, low enough that it had probably clipped his collarbone, too. "You," she said. "Let's get you over here," and she half led him, half towed him over to the nearest bench in the car that wasn't a sleeper. She stole a cushion off a seat and put it under his head, trying to estimate if he was breathing his own blood, and determining that he wasn't.

"Sorry about this," she said preemptively. She lifted his head up with one hand. Though it must've hurt him, he didn't make a sound, and only clenched his jaw and ground his teeth. Then she said, "Good news. Bullet bounced a little, probably off this bone"—she pointed to the spot beside his sternum—"and it went right on out the back of your neck." She tried to keep her mouth down close to his head so he could hear her when she reassured him, "At least I don't have to do any digging."

While she was wiping, checking, and stuffing gauze, the porter Cole Byron appeared at her side. He asked, "Ma'am, can I help you here? I don't have a gun, but I want to help!"

"Help!" she echoed. "Absolutely. I'd love some help. Hold this fellow's shoulders up for me, will you? I'm trying to tack up the exit wound."

With the porter's assistance, she stabilized Mr. Howson as well as he was likely to be stabilized. Then she turned back to Mr. Howson and said, "You're not bleeding anymore, or not much anyway. Will you be all right here for a few minutes? You're not going to up and die on me if I go pull some glass out of your fellows over there, will you?"

He squeaked, "No ma'am, I won't."

"Good. You hold tight. God*damn* this glass is everywhere!"

Mercy turned her attention to the two men who sat quietly beside the far wall, just as she'd ordered them to. Doing her best to keep her hands and knees and elbows off the shard-covered floor, she hunkered and scooted over to Pierce Tankersly and the other fellow, who was named Enoch Washington. "Mr. Tankersly," she began, but he cut her off.

"I think you're too late for Enoch," he said.

Another explosion pounded the car and it rocked, leaned, and settled again on the tracks, nearly flinging half the car's occupants to the floor or into some unhappy position. "I'm sure he's—," she started to say, but one look at him, now flopped over onto the carpet, told her otherwise. She pulled him over onto his back and exclaimed, "How did he get cut *there*?"

She pointed at his thigh, where there was a gash long enough for her to jam both thumbs inside. In the dead man's hand, she saw the shard covered in gore.

"He pulled it out. Oh, sweetheart," she told him uselessly, "you shouldn't have pulled it out!" Not that it would've made much difference if he'd left it in. The big artery had been cut and he'd bled out fast. All the needles and thread in all the world couldn't have saved him, unless maybe he'd gotten cut lying on an operating table. But probably not then, either.

Tankersly said, "Ma'am?"

"Be right with you," she told him, and she pulled Enoch Washington's body out of the way, back behind the last row of seats where he wouldn't trip or distract anyone. Then she returned to Pierce Tankersly and said, "I'm here, I'm here," in a breathless voice that he certainly couldn't have heard very well. "Let me look," she said. "Let me see."

"Is it bad?" he asked. "When the window blew"—his lip was trembling, maybe with cold, maybe with fear—"it caught me in the face."

"Can you see all right? Blink your eyes," she told him.

He obliged and she said, "Already I can tell it's not so bad. Both eyes look fine."

"Then why can't I see? Everything's all blurry!"

"It's blood, you daft fellow. The cut's along your forehead and—no, put your hand down. I'll take care of it in a minute. Head wounds, they bleed something awful, but your eyes aren't hurt and you're not bleeding to death, and those are the big things right now." She began patting and cleaning him where she could, and she gave his good hand a rag to hold up to his forehead. "Lean back," she requested. "Lean your head back against the wall so you're looking straight up at the ceiling, will you do that for me?"

"Yes ma'am," he said, "But how come?"

She said, "Because . . ." at precisely the moment she whipped the long piece of glass out of his palm. "I didn't want you to watch me do *that*."

He squealed and gasped at the same moment, giving himself hiccups.

"I knew it'd smart."

"It's gushing! Like Enoch!" he said with panic.

"No, not like Enoch. There's nothing in your hand that will make you bleed like he did," she promised. But she did not add that he'd cut some muscles, and surely some tendons, too, and the odds were better than fair he'd never have the correct and proper use of all the fingers ever again. "This isn't so bad," she said it like a mantra. "Not so bad at all. I want you to do something for me," she said as she took a rag and balled it up, then stuck it in his hand and wrapped some gauze around it.

"Yes ma'am."

"Sit on it. Put it under your thigh, right there. The pressure'll make the bleeding stop."

"You're sure the bleeding'll stop?"

"I'm sure the bleeding'll stop," she said firmly. "But it might take a few minutes, and I don't want you to get all scared on me. That knock on your head needs some pressure, too, and that's what your good hand is for, just like you're doing now. Keep your head up, and keep that rag held on it just like that. When it's dry, I'll stitch it up for you. You just sit here, and stay out of trouble. I'm going to check on Mr. Howson."

"He going to be all right?"

"Hope so," she said, but that was all she said, and she didn't make him any more promises.

She didn't make it back to Mr. Howson either, though she could see him reach up with one hand to scratch a spot behind his ear, so he was clearly still breathing and kicking. Someone called out, "Nurse!" She didn't recognize the voice, but when she turned around, she saw Morris Comstock holding up one of his fellows by the shoulder and one arm.

"Coming!" she said, and she scurried forward, only noticing when she did not hear the crunch of glass that there was far less underfoot. Over at the far end of the car, Cole Byron was scooping and scraping the floors with a set of burlap bags, collecting the glass and shoving it into the rear corner where the body of Enoch Washington rested.

She approved, and would've said as much except that Morris Comstock was calling for her again, and whomever he was holding was utterly slack. She helped the soldier lower his comrade down onto a row of seats, but she shook her head. "He's dead, Mr. Comstock. I'm very sorry."

"He might not be!" Morris shouted, and there were tears at the edges of his eyes, either from the wind or from the situation, she couldn't say.

She said, "He took a bullet in the eye, see? I'm sorry. I'm sorry, I'm sorry," she repeated, even as she felt at the man's neck to make doubly sure that all the life was gone from him. "Help me move him, over there with poor Mr. Washington."

"You want to just toss him in a corner?"

"Should we leave him here, taking up space and getting in the way? I'm sorry," she said yet again. "But he's gone. Help me, help me take him over there and we'll remember him later."

The *Dreadnought* accented her sentiment with a round of volleys that rocked the *Shenandoah,* sending it swaying on the tracks at such a tremendous degree that as Mercy stood in the corner beside the corpses, she could see the holes that had been blown in the other train's side. And she could also see that still, yes, again, and more, it had gained on them.

Risking her own neck, eyes, and hands, she went to a window by the rearmost door, and she looked out over the tracks between the trains and counted them. "One, two, three," she breathed aloud. "Four. Just four sets."

"Maybe eighty feet, at the outside," Horatio Korman said. He'd been sitting there beside the door, on the other side of the aisle. "Maybe eighty feet between us and them. They won't try to cross it," he assured her.

She noted that his hat was back. It jerked and fluttered despite its firm grip around his skull. "You think?"

"They ain't stupid," he said, reclining and putting his booted feet up onto the seat beside him.

"They're chasing this train," she said; as if she could think of no dumber course.

"Again I say, they ain't stupid. They need the gold, and they want the deeds so they can burn them. Last thing the Rebs need is fresh bodies to fight, when they don't have any fresh bodies themselves. All they have to do is get ahead of us."

She tore her gaze back and forth, between the *Shenandoah* and the Texas Ranger, one in frantic motion and the other the very picture of forced calm and resignation.

Mercy asked, "You think they're going to do it? You think we're all going to die?"

"I think they're going to do it. And I'm pretty sure *some* of us are going to die. Fat lot of nothing I can do about it, though," he said, settling his back against the northern wall of the passenger car. The cliffs zipped past behind him, only feet from his head, throwing off shadows and sparkles of light that glanced off the ice that made his face look old, then young, then old again.

"So you just . . . you give up?"

"I'm not giving up anything. I'm just being patient, that's all. Now get yourself away from the window, woman. You dying won't do anybody any good, either."

She said, "I should go back to the other car, see how they're doing."

"I wouldn't recommend it. Look out there; look at that train. They're right up on us. Side by side, neither one of us with anyplace to make a retreat. Just these goddamned cliffs, and just this goddamn ice and snow in these goddamned mountains."

Suddenly, Mercy did not care very much at all what the ranger recommended. She grabbed the door's handle, since she was so close to it already, and she gave it a tug and threw herself outside, all alone, into the space between the cars. She pulled the door shut and half expected Horatio Korman to follow after her, trying to stop her, but he only stood—she could see him through the window. The way his arm moved, she thought he, too, was reaching for the latch, but either she was wrong or he changed his mind.

He mouthed, *Be careful,* and turned away.

She was careful, and it was a jerky shuffle from one car to the next, but she made it—faster this time, even faster than when he'd been pushing her along, helping her find the handholds.

She stepped inside the next car, and the wind came billowing up behind her, shoving her cloak over her face and flapping it up around her arms until she closed the door and leaned against it, catching her breath. "How's everybody in here?" she asked in a hoarse shout.

Half a dozen voices answered, and she couldn't sort out any given one of them. But she saw two men lying haphazardly over the seats, and half inside the sleeper cars. She immediately went to the fallen soldiers.

One was dead, with most of his face missing—and what was left was frozen in such a state of shock that Mercy wished to God she had something left to cover him. She pulled his body off the seats and drew him back to the corner to leave him there, just like she'd been leaving the bodies in the next car up. Then she reached for one of the sleeper car curtains and yanked it down, popping all the tiny rings that held it up in one long, zippered chain. She dropped the makeshift shroud down over him and went back to the second man, who was in much better shape, if unconscious.

It was Inspector Galeano, with a large red mark in the shape of a windowpane across his face. She didn't know if he'd fallen or if the window had blown inward, but he was only coldcocked, and not otherwise in serious peril, or so Mercy ascertained as she pulled him onto one of the sleeper beds and gave him the once-over. His prominent, stately nose was broken, but his pulse was strong and his pupils reacted in a satisfactory fashion to light and shade.

Mercy took a moment to wipe the drying blood off his upper lip, and then she slapped at his face, not quite hard enough to sting. "Inspector? Inspector?"

After a few seconds, he answered with a string of words muttered in Spanish. Mercy had no idea about a bit of it, but he was talking, and that was progress.

"Inspector Galeano? Can you hear me?"

"*Sí.*"

"Inspector?"

"Yes," he said this time. "Yes. I'm—" He sat up and swooned slightly, but recovered and patted himself all over. "Where is my gun?"

"Can't help you there," she told him. "How's your head?"

"My face . . . hurts," he said, trying to frown, stretch his cheeks, and wrinkle his nose all at once.

"You've busted your nose, but if that's the worst you get out of the day, we'll call it good, all right?"

"All right," he said, but he repeated the phrase as if he wasn't sure what it meant. His eyes were scanning the glass-covered floor.

"Your gun," she said, guessing what worried him. "Is that it, over there, under the—?"

He saw the spot she indicated and said, "Yes!" before she could finish. And he threw himself up and off the recliner before she could stop him.

"Watch for the glass!" she yelled, but she'd already lost his attention. He was crawling back up to the window, checking his ammunition and readying himself for more. "Watch for the glass," she said again, uselessly. It was everywhere, and it wouldn't do anyone to watch out for it, because there was simply no avoiding it.

Mercy scanned the car for a porter and didn't see one. She had her backside to the forward door when it opened and Morris Comstock stood in its frame, calling, "Mrs. Lynch!" at the top of his lungs.

"Coming!" she said, rather than ask what precisely he needed. No one ever hollered her name without needing something.

When she rose, she was nearly sick to her stomach, from the incessant motion and the blood all over her hands—with powdered glass sticking to her skin and drying there—but also from the sight of the *Shenandoah,* because she could now see that she was looking at its two rearmost cars and the engine was pulling ahead of the *Dreadnought.* On her way to assist Mr. Comstock, she leaned her head around and saw that, yes, the southern engine had passed the northern one; and as she watched, the Rebel craft leaped on the tracks with a burst of speed, as if some final gear had been engaged and this . . . *this* was the fastest it could move. Even if it couldn't keep it up long, it didn't have to.

She said, "Oh God," and Mr. Comstock took her by the elbow and said, "I know!"

Back once more through the windswept breach, and back once again into the first passenger car, she came face-to-face with the captain, whose old head wound was bleeding again—or else he'd come by a new one, near the same spot. He said, "The inspector!"

He meant Inspector Portilla, who was facedown and being addressed by Lieutenant Hobbes, who was trying to turn him over and wipe away whatever blood he found. Mercy said, "Let me see him!" and rushed to his side. His uniform was scorched, cut, and tattered, and a large hole was pulsating just above his heart, toward the center of his chest.

All the wounds had been like this so far—all the men were firing out the windows, which gave them cover below the shoulders . . . and gave the men on the other train an open target at everything above them.

"Inspector!" she said, and drew him almost into her lap. "Inspector!"

He didn't answer, and his eyes were rolling, not fixing on anything. "Help me," she said to Morris Comstock, but suddenly he wasn't there—so she looked around and saw Cole Byron, who met her eyes and darted to her side. "Help me," she said. "Gently; we have to move him gently."

Together they did so, retreating to another sleeper compartment and stretching him out. She tore at his shirt, popping the buttons and revealing a chest with a smattering of salt-and-pepper hair and a hole the size of her fist. "Jesus Christ!" she exclaimed. "What hit him?"

Cole Byron said, "I think they're mounting antiaircraft over on the *Shenandoah*."

"If they aren't, they might as well be," she said. Upon fishing around in her satchel, she realized she was out of rags. Undaunted, she reached for another curtain, yanked it down, and tore it up. The porter followed her lead and helped with the tearing. As she stuffed one wad of thick wool fabric into the wound, she tried to talk to the inspector, even as she was increasingly convinced that the cause was lost and they were about to be short one tall, light-skinned Mexican.

The wound's pulsing became erratic and jerky. She could feel it ebb and surrender under her hand, where she held the balled-up curtain rag firmly in the wound, just in case there was some miracle imminent and the bleeding might be contained. But no miracle was forthcoming. The heart stopped altogether.

More antiaircraft shells went splitting through the car, and a splatter of someone's blood shot across her face in a red, hot streak.

"God Almighty!" she shrieked, and came up to her knees shouting, "Who's next? Who just took that hit?"

"Ma'am!" someone made a weak response, and it was Morris Comstock again—the first man she'd treated on board the train. He was clutching at a place on the side of his chest, and his hand was soaked with blood, and so was his shirt.

"Mr. Comstock!" She ran up underneath him, catching him as he came down from the window like a sack of potatoes. "Good heavens, look at you. Here we are again," she said, right into his ear, since his head was slumping just above her breasts. "We've got to quit meeting this way. Tongues will begin to wag."

He gave her a pathetic grin, and his eyes rolled back in his head.

She shook him, and lowered him to the ground—once more summoning the Pullman porter. Together they moved this man, too, to the sleeper car where the Mexican inspector had died, though Mercy noted that his corpse had been moved over to the corner . . . presumably by Cole Byron, though she hadn't seen him do it.

"Mr. Comstock, please stay with me now," she begged. He mumbled in response, but his words came out in no particular order.

The chest wound was bad, but not so bad as she feared; and when she looked back to the car wall where the private had been hunkered, she understood why. The steel on the car's exterior had taken the brunt of some shell, but that shell had penetrated by at least half a foot, bashing into the torso of Mr. Comstock.

Mercy put her head down over his chest and stared, and listened—straining to hear the faint sounds of a ruptured lung over the sounds of a battle and a rampaging train all around her—but she didn't catch any whispers of air coming and going in a deadly leak, so she almost felt a tiny bit optimistic.

She looked up and smiled frantically at the porter. "The wind's knocked out of him, but he's not shot!" The flesh around the tear was beginning to bruise, and it would be a nasty one, nearly the size of his head when all was blossomed and rosy. It was likely that a couple of his ribs were broken as well. She went to work covering the gash, cleaning it, and trying to hold enough weight down on it to make the bleeding stop.

A great pulse of fire came from the front cars of the *Dreadnought;* she heard it and felt it in every bone, in every muscle. She felt it in the veins that throbbed behind her eyeballs, and she clutched at the nearest seat back, squeezing Morris Comstock's limp hand because it was something to hold, and the horror and the noise and the gunsmoke were more than she could bear alone. Even the porter had left her—she didn't know where he'd gone, but at this point, she trusted that he had a good excuse. She only patted at Comstock's sweat-drenched hair, which was melting, having frozen into tiny, fluttering icicles while his face had been near the window.

And then. Like that.

As quickly as the shelling had begun, it ended.

Then there was no more firing at all, from either train, though the near silence that remained in its wake was no silence at all. It was the pounding of heads and the ringing of ears that had too long heard bombastic artillery fire, and could no longer process its absence.

Strangely, Mercy found this almost more frightening than the onslaught. She asked, "What's going on? Captain MacGruder?" She looked for him and didn't see him immediately, so she asked, "Lieutenant Hobbes, what's happening?" Hobbes gave her a look that said he had no better idea than she did.

Then she noticed that the ranger had joined them. Even he looked confused. She asked him, too—"Ranger Korman?"—but he shook his head.

Then the forward door opened, and through it burst Mrs. Butterfield; and Mr. Abernathy, the blacksmith from Cincinnati; and Miss Greensleeves, lately of Springfield, Illinois; and Mr. Potts from Philadelphia; and Miss Theodora Clay, who looked exactly as homicidal as a soaking wet cat; all of whom were supposed to be fastened into the gold-filled car as a matter of safety.

Mrs. Butterfield began screaming something about her rights as a paying passenger, but Mercy didn't hear most of her tirade, because the conductor came shoving his way past the lot of them. Then she understood. He'd had the gold car opened (by force, no doubt) so that he could pass through it, temporarily leaving his attendants to guide the train. He was red faced and panting, and his expression was grim but rushed.

He said, "Look!" and he pointed out the window, and everyone saw—the *Shenandoah* had completely overtaken them and was quickly leaving them behind.

Captain MacGruder sized up the situation fastest, and asked, "What do we do?"

The conductor said, "There's a tunnel ahead—about two miles up—and I must assume—"

"We have to stop the train," said Lieutenant Hobbes, who had heretofore not led any charges, but had done an admirable job of following orders. This was the first time Mercy had seen him come to the front of the line.

Not caring who'd said it first, or who was in charge, the conductor said, "The ranger said it, and I believe it: they'll blow the tracks, or whatever they're going to do, as soon as they get enough of a lead on us to make it happen. So we're stopping the train. We'll defend it from a standing position, if we have to!"

"That's madness!" cried Mrs. Butterfield, who forced her way through the crowd. "You can't stop the train! We'll all freeze to death out here, or those filthy Rebels will come back and finish us off!"

"It's better than barreling forward into a trap!" the conductor cried right back at her. "I've given the order to throw the brakes, and preparations are being made in every car. I've told the porters to ready themselves—"

"Every car?" Mercy asked.

"Yes—there's a brake on every car. There has to be. We can't stop otherwise," he explained hastily.

The ranger stepped up to join the conversation and said, "Two miles, is that what you said? Can we stop this snake in that kind of time?"

The conductor said, "We're going to try," as he spun on his heels and went barging back toward the *Dreadnought,* assuming that the message would find its way along the cars that were left.

"Everybody's going to have to brace," the captain said. "Find a spot and settle down. Help the fellows who are hurt. Someone go to the next car—you, Ranger, will you do it? Head to that next car and tell them. Pass it down."

Horatio Korman gave him a head dip that was as good as a salute, and went for the rearward door. He was scarcely on the other side of it when the slowdown began—not in a jerk or a lurch, but with a drop in speed that made those on their feet sway, and grasp instinctively for something solid.

A shout went up from the front of the train, and a quick piping of the whistle—not a full-blown blast, but a series of short peeps that must be some sort of signal. Then a great squeal screamed from a dozen points along the cars as the brakes were applied, and leaned on, and struggled against, and the great, terrible, foreshortened and battered train began to grind to a ghastly, troubling stop that could not possibly come fast enough.

Whatever luggage had thus far remained in the storage bins fell in a patter that bounced off heads, backs, and shoulders. People squawked; Mrs. Butterfield wailed. Mercy staggered and tried to grab the edge of a sleeper car wall in order to steady herself, but she failed and fell backwards. The captain caught her and pulled her down into the aisle, where bits of glass were still sparkling, sliding, collapsing into dust beneath boots and shoes, and cutting into hands, forearms, and knees.

"Captain," she asked him, not shouting anymore, even over the grinding howl of metal tearing against metal and fighting for traction. She could only spit out her question in a choked gasp, but his head was close to hers, so he could hear her anyway. "What will happen, when we stop? Can we back up, and go the way we came?"

He shook his head, and his wind-tousled hair brushed up against her ear. "I don't know, Mrs. Lynch. I don't know much about trains."

After another series of notes from the whistle, the brakes were tested yet further, jammed yet harder, and pulled with another synchronized arrangement of men leaning on poles and posts. They prayed for the immense machine to slow down, end the push, and stop the forward clawing; and the *Dreadnought* responded.

Sluggish and huge and heavy, it weighed the commands of the brakes against the pure inertia that fought like a tiger to keep it rolling along the snow-dusted tracks.

But down, and down, and down dropped the speed. Down, but not enough.

Mercy clambered to her feet, clutching at the captain, at the seats, at the frames of the sleeper compartments. She raised her head enough to see that the end of the pass—the immense, coal black tunnel—was right upon them, and despite all efforts to the contrary, they were going to slip right inside it—right into darkness; right into a stretch that was surely a trap.

And there was nothing to be done about it.

Nineteen

The tunnel gaped and yawned, and devoured the great train slowly—incrementally—like one snake swallowing another. The *Dreadnought* was not moving very fast, but it was moving with great determination and immense willpower against the frantic thrusts of the brakes; the squealing of metal against wheels against tracks against stopping mechanisms retreated until it was a dull whine that echoed in the darkness. And this darkness slipped over the train with the sharp, demarcating smoothness of a curtain lowering. As if the tunnel were a tomb or some ancient crypt, the veil of false midnight smothered the nervously chattering or whimpering voices within the passenger cars.

This tunnel, and this darkness, ate the length of the train from the engine to the second passenger car, which was now the last car.

And when the whole strand was as black as the bottom of a well, every breath was held and every heart was perched on the verge of stopping.

They waited.

All of them waited, eyes upturned and glancing about, casting from the front to the back of every car, seeking some glimmer of light or information. All of them sat in hushed and worried poses.

Everyone waited, wondering how the end was going to come.

All backs and arms and fists were clenched, ready for the

explosion that would bring the tunnel down atop them, or the dynamite blast beyond the tunnel that would mark the end of their tracks.

But it never came.

And finally, in the dark, Mercy heard the voice of Cole Byron say, "Maybe they overshot us. Maybe they got too far, past the end of the tunnel. They were going awful fast; it would've been hard for them to stop."

This weak hint of optimism prompted someone else—she couldn't tell who—to say, "Maybe we hurt 'em worse than we thought. Maybe they derailed, or their engine blew."

The train gave a small jump, and continued to roll forward under its own habit, not from any power from the boilers or the hydrogen. The engine struggled against the track, and everyone on board cringed, wondering when they'd see the light on the other side—not knowing how long the tunnel would last, or how long they could linger like this in darkness, in silence, in hideous anticipation.

As the train continued to squeeze through the compression of darkness, no one on board spoke again, even to bring up more maybes, or to offer hope, or to whisper prayers. No one asked any more questions. No one moved, except to adjust a tired knee—or lift a skirt out of the glass litterings on the floor and feel about for a more comfortable position.

Someone coughed, and someone sniffled.

One of the injured men moaned in a half-conscious grunt of pain. Mercy hoped that whoever it was, he didn't come around while the blackness of the tunnel crushed them all into blindness. How awful it'd be, she thought, to awaken from injury to pain and darkness, wondering if you hadn't lived at all, but died and gone someplace underground.

Minutes passed, and then blocks of minutes. It must have added up to a mile, maybe even more. Everyone counted the distance, or tried to, but it was difficult without any light, and without the swiftly moving cliffs rushing by to gauge their progress.

Then something winked up ahead, casting a tiny sliver of light off something and into the car's interior, but it lasted only for an instant so brief that anyone who blinked would have missed it.

Someone's shadow moved, and another flickering light bounced off the tunnel walls. This time it left enough of a glow for Mercy to see that it was one of the porters; but their dark skins and dark uniforms and the darkness of the car's interior made it impossible for her to guess which one until he spoke. It was then that she realized Jasper Nichols had joined his cousin in the car—when, she didn't know for certain.

He leaned his head out the window and said, "We're almost out. We're going to be coming out real soon."

But no one knew whether to cheer or to cry at that news, so everybody flinched instead, tightening inside their clothing— tightening their grips on one another, if they were so inclined. Everyone hunkered, and ducked, and made instinctive gestures to cover their heads and faces against the unknown perils that the light would reveal.

More slowly than it had consumed the train, the tunnel expelled the nearly stopped *Dreadnought* and its charges back into glaring sun that reflected off ice and snow to create a world of shocking brilliance.

This brilliance infected the cars as the train inched forward; but there was momentum enough to bring them all to the other side of the mountain tunnel, and there was momentum enough that the whole length of the train shuddered when it hit a fresh carpet of accumulated snow, there on the other side.

The train chugged, and sluggishly leaned forward against the fluffy white obstacle, which would have meant little to it had they been going faster. The snow accomplished what the men with the lever brakes could not.

It stopped the *Dreadnought*.

Anguished silence preserved the moment while people stared anxiously about. Then Jasper Nichols, who was closest to the window, leaned out from it once more and said, "Good Lord help me, but I'll be damned."

Captain MacGruder was the second to pull himself up and dust the glass fragments from his pants. "What is it, man?" he asked, even as he went to the window to see for himself. His motion startled the rest of the car into action. One at a time, he was joined by everyone present, or at least those who were able to haul themselves up on the seats and lean their faces into the white outdoors.

It wasn't snowing here, on this side of Provo.

The sun beat down from directly above, uncut or dimmed by any shadows, anywhere. The air was cold enough to preserve meat, and the snow was thick enough on the ground to swallow ankles—with a crystalline crust on every surface, giving all of it a mirrorlike sheen that made the afternoon blaze all the brighter.

Hands rose to foreheads, shading squinting eyes against the unexpected light.

The captain said, "Is that them up there?"

And the lieutenant joined him, also shadowing his eyes against the glare. "It's the *Shenandoah*. They passed us by a ways, it looks like."

"Half a mile or more. More, I think," he said.

Mercy could see it then. The back end of the Rebel vessel and the curve of its length on a track, motionless, and distant enough that it looked small.

"They didn't blow the tracks," she said. "They could've blown the tracks, but they didn't."

Jasper Nichols said, "Maybe they tried. Maybe they couldn't."

"I didn't hear any explosions," said Theodora Clay, who was suddenly right beside Mercy, her head and shoulders out the window, straining to see, same as everyone else. "Look at them. They've just . . . *stopped*."

The captain murmured, "I wish I had a glass. I can't see a damn thing, between the sun and the snow. It's all so bright, I can't . . . it's giving me a headache already."

Mercy said, "Maybe Ranger Korman—" But she cut herself off and said, "Wait a minute. Where'd he go?" because it'd be just as simple to go get him herself.

The Texian was easy to find, because he'd been on his way to rejoin the first car when Mercy opened the rearmost door and stepped onto the platform. It struck her as odd to find the train stationary, but she was pleased to walk so easily; and when she saw Korman's face on the other side of the second car's window, she smiled at him with relief.

"Ranger Korman!" she said when he opened the door to join her on the coupler.

He did not greet her back, but said, "What's going on up there? Can't you see the train?"

"Yes and no," she told him. "You seem to be carrying all sorts of interesting toys; you got anything like a spyglass hidden in that waistcoat of yours?"

"Yup," he told her.

"Well then, bring it out if you've got one," she said. "There's something funny about the *Shenandoah*. Just sitting there on the track. They aren't stuck in the snow, are they?"

"I can't imagine," he replied, and he reached for the ladder that rose beside the rearmost door of the first passenger car. As he climbed, he added, "This isn't enough snow to bog down anything with the power to move that fast. Though now that we're stopped, it'll be a pain in the ass to get started again."

"I'm coming with you," she said, understanding that he meant to get a better look from the roof.

"Suit yourself," he told her without looking back, and without offering to help her.

Within seconds, she was standing beside him on top of the first passenger car roof. Lieutenant Hobbes called out from below them, "Hey, up there. Is that you, Mrs. Lynch?"

She called back down, "Me and Ranger Korman. We're just taking a better look. Hold your horses, we'll tell you what we see."

The ranger pulled out a long brass tube, and while fiddling with the adjusting screws, he pointed it at the *Shenandoah*.

After perhaps twenty seconds of examining the scene in this manner, he switched the device to the other eye. Mercy couldn't imagine that this would make any difference, but she didn't say anything; she only stood there and shivered, holding her cloak up around her shoulders tightly, and breathing in air so brittle and cold that it made her chest hurt.

Then he made a noise that sounded like, "Hmm."

It was the sound a doctor made when he found that things were undoubtedly worse than suspected, but knew that it wouldn't do anyone any good to worry the patient. Mercy knew that sound, and she didn't like it one little bit.

"What do you mean by *that*?" she asked.

He did not move the glass. Only upon shifting to get up into his personal space did she realize he was holding it half an inch away from his eye, surely to keep the metal from freezing to the soft spots around it. He only said again, "Hmm."

She liked it even less the second time. "What is it? What do you see?"

"Well," he said. He stuck a *p* on the end so it came out as, *Whelp*.

"Oh, for Pete's sake, give me that thing," she said.

He let her take it.

Through the gloves she wore, she could feel the chill of the exposed brass. She took the ranger's lead and held it very slightly away from her face. It took her a bit to find the spot she was seeking. Then the rear of the Rebel train slipped into the magnifying circle, and she followed it with the lens all the way up to the engine. And she froze, as still and breathless as the jagged mountains on either side of her.

"You see them, too?" Korman asked.

"I see . . . *someone*. Something."

"Do those look like uniforms to you?"

"On the Confederates? No, wait, I see what you mean. Yes, they look like . . . like light-colored uniforms. On some of them, not on all of them. And they're . . . they're *attacking* the *Shenandoah*!"

"That's what it looks like," he said. "And I hate to say it," he breathed roughly, as if he *truly did* hate to say it, "but I think we've found our missing Mexicans."

She pressed the lens as close as she dared against her own eye, searing her skin with the burning ice that collected on the spyglass's metal rim. Yes, she could see them, pounding their hands against the engine, and against the railcars, and trying to crawl up onto the train. A handful of men were treed atop the back of the engine and the fuel cart, kicking at the invaders and using the butts of long guns to bash them back to the snow.

"Why aren't they shooting?" she asked.

"Might be out of ammunition by now."

She shifted the glass enough to scan the area better and then gasped, sucking in more of the icy air and choking on it with a little cough.

"What?"

"Jesus," she said, handing him the lens. "Jesus, Korman. Look out past the engine. There's more coming." She turned and stumbled for the nearest ladder, reversing herself back down it. "They're coming, and there's . . . Jesus," she said again, and now she was down on the platform, shoving the door open. Behind her, she could hear the ranger following in her footsteps, lowering himself with a couple of quick steps that had him right on her heels.

She flung open the car door. Panting, she confronted the captain. "They're coming!"

"Who's coming?" he asked, clearly frightened by her fear and trying to contain it, but requiring more information.

The ranger pushed his way past the door and answered. "The Mexicans. The missing ones, all seven or eight hundred of them, or however many there are—but it looks like more than that to me. Where's that inspector you folks had up in here? Can't keep their names straight."

"Portilla's dead," Mercy told him without looking over her shoulder at the corpse. "And those men out there—something horrible's wrong with them, just like all of us have been talking about. Just like the papers said, and just like the inspectors told us. Speaking of who . . . Cole?"

"Ma'am?"

"Please, you or Jasper. Go get Inspector Galeano."

"Yes ma'am," he said, and was out the back door in exactly the kind of rush she wanted to see.

A volley of shots fired from the *Shenandoah;* they rang back to the *Dreadnought* like distant firecrackers, shocking everyone on board into defensive positions and gasps.

But Mercy said, "No! No, they're not shooting at us now. They're shooting at those other people—only they aren't people anymore, not really. Someone must've found some more bullets. Oh, God help them!"

"God help *them*?" Theodora Clay gasped. "Have you even been *present* on this train for the last hour?"

"Present and working like hell to stay alive on it, same as you!

But those are *men* on that train—real ordinary men, alive and sane, same as you and me! And those other things, the things that are overrunning them . . . they aren't human. I swear," she said, almost gagging with despair. "They've been poisoned—poisoned into monsters!"

The rear door burst open, and Cole Byron came through it with Inspector Galeano, who was wild eyed and full to bursting with questions. The first one out of his mouth was, "Portilla?"

Mercy replied, "I'm real sorry, Inspector. I did what I could to save him, but I—"

"Please, where is he?"

"He's there. And I'm sorry; I'm real sorry—"

Something big fired from the *Shenandoah,* something more like the antiaircraft artillery they'd used to pepper the *Dreadnought* before.

Mrs. Butterfield cried, "They're shooting at us again!"

But this time the captain said, "No." He was holding the ranger's glass, leaning out the window. "No, Mercy's right. Those men aren't shooting at us. Holy Christ, what . . . what are those . . . they aren't . . . they can't be . . . *people?*"

"It's the missing Mexicans," the ranger said again. "Give him the glass," he told the captain, indicating the inspector. "Let him look. He'll tell you."

The captain came fully back into the car and handed the looking glass to Inspector Galeano. "They're attacking!" he said with wonder.

Theodora Clay threw her hands in the air. "Why would Mexicans attack a southern train? And furthermore, what do we care? Let's fire up our own boilers and get moving, the Rebels be damned!"

The conductor came bustling through the forward door in a stomping rattle of cold feet and clutched shoulders. "What's

going on up there? Can you see it? I've got a scope up front."
Then he saw the inspector hanging out the window, staring through
the looking glass. "Who are all those people?"

"The missing Mexicans," the ranger said yet again.

Inspector Galeano drew himself back inside, his breath blowing white in the car's interior, wafting about in the breeze. "They've
been poisoned, and they . . . they look . . . it's as if they are walking corpses!"

"There are hundreds of them," said the captain. His hands
were trembling, but Mercy did not call any attention to it. "Hundreds, maybe a thousand or more. Swarming like *bees*."

The ranger took his glass back from the inspector, and, as if it
was the rule that whoever held it had to look through it, he positioned himself on the seat and put himself back out into the open
air again, gazing with that long, gleaming eye at the pandemo-
nium on the tracks ahead.

He said, "And they're coming."

Theodora Clay said, "What?"

As the exclamation made the rounds, the ranger came back inside, swiftly, nicking his arm on a triangle of unloosed glass from
the window frame. He snapped the looking glass shut and jammed
it into his pocket. "They're coming!" he said again. "A huge goddamned wave of them! You—" He seized the conductor by the
vest. "You get this thing moving! You make it move right now!"

"Let me see the glass!" Mercy demanded.

But he said, "If we don't get out of here, and fast, you're not
going to need it." And he shoved past her to the rear door, saying
over his shoulder, "Get those civilians back in that car—get
everyone in there who's hurt, or who can't shoot. Everyone else,
up front! We need people who can shoot!"

The soldiers were disinclined to take orders from the ranger,
but the captain gave the view from the window another steady
gaze and reiterated them. "Out!" he shouted. "Everyone without

a gun, get out! Get back into the forward car; you'll be safer there," he continued, beginning to herd them backwards the way they'd come.

The conductor was already gone, having obeyed the order to flee sooner—perhaps because he had his own glass, and was able to judge for himself that nothing good was coming his way. Mercy could not hear him or see him, but before long, she could hear the *Dreadnought* rising again, awakening from its temporary pause and firing up, blowing its whistle in a long, piercing, hawk-like scream.

As the few remaining civilians were ushered away, Theodora Clay said, "No. No, I won't go, not this time. Take my aunt and stuff her in that car if you must, but I'm staying. Someone give me a gun."

"Ma'am," said Lieutenant Hobbes. "Ma'am, you have to leave."

"I don't, and I won't. Someone—arm me, immediately."

"That isn't going to happen," the captain told her.

But she held her ground and continued to fuss and fight as the rest were sent away. The ranger returned to check the first car's progress. He asked, "How are we doing? Where's that conductor? He'd damned well better be up front, lighting the damn engine or whatever it is he does. We haven't got another minute!"

At which point, Miss Clay spotted an opening. She flung herself at the ranger, who appeared half horrified, half repulsed, and wholly suspicious of the gesture. She pressed her well-dressed bosom up against his chest and whined, "Oh, Ranger, you wouldn't believe it—they're trying to send me away, up into that first car!"

He replied, "Get off me, woman. We have bigger problems to attend to!"

But she didn't get off him; she clung to him like a barnacle and wheedled, "They say everyone without a gun has to go back up front—stuffed there, useless—and I won't have it."

On the verge of seizing her wrists and flinging her away, he wanted to know, "Why's that?"

She dropped away from him, as cold and prim as if she'd never touched him, except this time she was holding one of his Colts. "Because now I have a gun."

"Woman!"

"Oh, you've got plenty of others," she said dismissively. "I felt at least three. Shoot with those, and let a lady defend herself." She turned away from him, concluding the conversation. She flipped the gun's wheel open, inspected the contents, and spun it shut again. She let it swing from her fingers and held it out in her hand, testing its weight, before throwing it into her palm with an easy tip.

Even the ranger paused, though she wasn't aiming anything at him. "Where'd you learn to swing one of those?"

She glanced at him sideways, then returned her attention to her inspection of the firearm. "My father's a gunsmith. He does quite a lot of work for the government. A lady can learn plenty if she's paying attention. Now, can I talk you out of a handful of bullets, or will I have to content myself with these?"

The ranger shrugged, dipped into a pouch on one of his gunbelts, and pulled out a fistful of the requested ammunition. He clapped it into her open palm and said, "Maybe you're not perfectly useless after all."

"And maybe you're not a perfect barbarian. I'm always willing to be surprised by such things."

"Y'all two stop flirtin' over there," Mercy groused. "We've got trouble."

"Worse than that," said the lieutenant. "We're about to have company."

Captain MacGruder said, as quickly as he could force the words out of his mouth, "There's no way to barricade ourselves inside, not really. The best shots will have a better chance up on the rooftop. We'll split our ranks, abandon the second passenger car, and concentrate on defending the smallest space possible."

Theodora Clay was already out the door and climbing the ladder, and Ranger Korman was behind her.

The captain pointed out half a dozen others, saying, "But keep in mind, you're on your own when the train gets moving again!"

As if to underscore the point, the *Dreadnought*'s boilers let off a keening sound, followed by the rattling of metal that was cooling and is being warmed once again. And behind that sound came the clatter and noise of something else—something inhuman, but not at all mechanical. It approached in a horrid wave, a cry unlike anything a living man or woman might make, coming from a thousand men and women, sickeningly nearer every moment.

Mercy said, "The injured! Get all the injured out of that second car!" Suddenly she couldn't remember who was back there anyway, if anyone at all who was still alive. No one seemed to answer her, so she ran for the rear door. But Jasper Nichols and Cole Byron stopped her.

Byron said, "We'll get them, ma'am."

She saw that Jasper had a gun and wondered where he'd gotten it. Byron might have had one, too, but he had already turned away from her and headed out through the door. Soldiers came charging in around them and past them, and suddenly the first passenger car was immensely crowded.

The captain was standing on one of the seats, directing the crowd like a symphony, sending some men forward and some men up. Lieutenant Hobbes and two of his nearest fellows were sent to the conductor to help protect the front of the train and work the *Dreadnought*'s defense systems.

When the captain paused to take a breath, Mercy stood beneath him and said, "What about me, Captain? Where can you use me?"

He looked her up and down, his eyes stopping on the gunbelt she wore and the pieces she'd picked up on the battlefield. He pointed at her waist and asked, "Do you know how to use those?"

"Well enough."

He hesitated and stepped down off the chair, to face her directly. They made a little island in the swirling bustle of frantic men seeking positions. He told her then, "Get up to the engine and help them there. That's the most important thing right now, really. We've got to protect that engine. If we can't get the engine moving again, none of us are leaving this pass alive."

She drew up to her full height, took a deep breath, and said, "You're right. I know you're right. I'm going. And I'm going to do my best."

Mercy Lynch had seen enough salutes in her time to feign a pretty good one, and she did so then, snapping her heels together.

A peculiar look crossed the captain's face. Mercy couldn't place it. She didn't know what it meant, and there wasn't time to ask him.

"Inspector Galeano!" the captain called.

"Here," he answered.

"Accompany Mrs. Lynch, please. We need people up front, protecting the engine. And I've seen you shoot."

"Absolutely," the Mexican replied, and he hurried to her side, checking his ammunition.

The *Dreadnought*'s whistle blew.

The nurse turned and ran, the inspector beside her. They ran out through the forward door and shoved their way through the gold car, using their elbows to clear a path. When they finally pushed into the gleaming brightness of the snowy afternoon, they were both startled—very startled—to find that there was no snowplow attachment between them and the next car.

Mercy couldn't imagine where on earth something so enormous

could've possibly gone, but then she saw it being winched around on a cart. The wheeled platform it had been attached to had been levered off the track, and was being worked toward the front of the engine with a pulley system that defied description.

The sight made her pause, marveling at the smoothness of it. Three porters and two rail hands, whom she'd seen once or twice in the caboose over coffee—that's all it took to maneuver the thing. It hardly seemed possible, yet there they were . . . and there it went.

The conductor shouted something to someone, and Lieutenant Hobbes's voice rose up over the snow. Mercy caught only the last words, and they weren't meant for her, but the inspector said, "Señora Lynch!" and spurred her forward, over the gap with a leap. There they met another soldier and another porter, who was carrying a tool that was nearly as long as he was tall.

"Ma'am," he said to her in passing. "Inspector."

The porter dropped the tool like a hook over to the other platform and, with the help of the soldier, began cranking the two cars together, closing the spot left by the snowplow attachment's absence.

They pushed farther forward, into the fuel car with its stink of iron and condensed steam, and copper tubes and charcoal and smoke. Between the two sections of this car, there was a walkway, and on either side were the great reservoirs of coal and the immense processing equipment that produced and delivered the hydrogen. It loomed up above them, tall enough to close out the gleaming white sky and white cliffs. But through it they ran, and up into the next car, which wasn't really a car so much as a wagon piled with crated ammunition that was affixed to the *Dreadnought* itself.

"Go on, you first," Mercy told Inspector Galeano, who nodded at her and made the leap to the engine.

"I'm right behind you!" she said. And there, at the edge of

the engine, Mercy Lynch eyed the ledge between herself and the machine. She crossed it with two short steps—grabbing the handrails on either side of four stubby stairs that led into the engine's pilot chamber—as she watched the retreating feet of the Mexican inspector climbing above her and disappearing over the side.

Behind her, something screamed.

It didn't sound like a woman, or a man either. The scream was parched and broken, and it was god-awful close.

Mercy turned around and saw—right behind her, nearly on her heels, in the spot between the ammunition cart and the back edge of the *Dreadnought*—a man who was not a man any longer.

She saw his face and it reminded her of other faces. The wheezers in the Robertson Hospital. The dying men in Memphis, lying strapped to cots and begging for the very thing that was killing them. The bodies in the sealed-up caskets that had been in the rearmost compartment of the train only hours before.

This face was the same.

It was grayish, with yellow pus and sores around the edges of every membrane. Its eyes were sunken and dry, withering in its skull like raisins. It sat atop a body with flesh that was beginning to slough off, wearing clothes that were only mostly intact, missing buttons, patches, pockets, and other pieces that could be snagged and removed.

But *this* face.

This face was snarling, and approaching her.

The corpse-man reached for the handrails, just as Mercy had done. While it grabbed, its mouth tried to grab, too—it gnawed at the air in the space between them and snapped at her shoes.

And although she'd spent her adulthood saving lives . . . and although she'd never, not even accidentally, killed a man . . . she seized one of her guns and she fired at the wrinkled space between the corpse-man's eyes.

He was so close that when his skull exploded, bits of his brain and face splattered across everything, including Mercy's cloak and dress. Pieces of him slid down slowly off the hem of her skirt, dripping and plopping down between the tracks.

The rolling noise of grunts and screams and groans was all around her now, closing in and pinning her down like a tangible pressure. But she shook it off, and she turned and she climbed— up into the engine, where the inspector was holding his hand down to her, calling, "Here! Climb up!"

She scrambled and seized his hand, and let him help her up over the side, where Lieutenant Hobbes and the conductor were frantically throwing levers, pressing buttons, and shouting directions to the men who were trying to affix the snowplow to the front of the train.

But the swarm was upon them, as if that first corpse Mercy had shot down was only the scout, and the rest were right on its heels. She climbed up on a bin and saw the men out front trying to move the snowplow into place draw their guns and begin shooting, trying to clear a big enough patch that they could work those last latches, bolts, and pulleys and get the train moving.

Behind her, the boiler was coughing and straining its way to full power once more. The stretch of the superhot metal made ghastly whimpers, as if it, too, understood the necessity of leaving, and leaving *now*.

Lieutenant Hobbes leaped to the foremost edge of the western wall, leaning forward and aiming outward. He fired, providing cover for the men below.

Mercy positioned herself on the east side, and Galeano climbed up to stand with his feet planted apart atop the conductor's shed. He flexed his wrists, checked his bullets, picked his targets below, and with an anguished shout, opened fire on his undead countrymen.

The nurse followed suit.

She fired off one shot, then two. Aiming down, hitting them in the heads and necks. Exploding their skulls away from their bodies, leaving their arms and legs to splay and sprawl and collapse to the ground. She refused to look past the circle where five men were ratcheting the snowplow into place. Right there, in that circle, the undead were sweeping down on the workers in ones and twos. But beyond that circle, appallingly close, they were coming in fives and tens. In dozens. In hundreds.

But she had only two hands, and only so much ammunition. The satchel she wore was slung across her back, freeing up her arms and elbows so she could aim and shoot, sometimes hitting and sometimes missing. One head. Two heads. A puff of snow like dust, right in the place where a corpse had only just been running. She missed another one, and couldn't recall how many shots she'd fired.

Below her, the five men were dividing their time between self-defense and the task at hand, and the task at hand was losing ground. Above her, Inspector Galeano was still shouting, still shooting; and beside her, Lieutenant Hobbes was reloading.

Mercy's right gun ran out of bullets. She whipped her satchel front and center, dug around hastily, and filled both wheels of both guns with quivering fingers gone numb from cold and recoil and fear.

Lieutenant Hobbes said, "Mrs. Lynch!"

And she said back, "I'm reloading!"

"Hurry!" And he fired again, and again.

She clapped the wheel of her left handgun into place, fully stocked once more. Mercy dared a glance up ahead at the *Shenandoah*. Her heart constricted as she saw the Confederate men holding their position with prybars and long-barreled guns that were long empty. They used them like bats, swinging and swatting the attackers away as long as their arms could stand it.

"Mrs. Lynch!" It was the conductor this time. She'd never

caught his name, and didn't know where he'd picked up hers, except from standing around and listening to people shout it.

She responded by aiming and firing again, as the wave kept coming and the men below kept working.

A dead woman was running in fast, her full skirts in bright colors and patterns layered up together. Her arms were bare, despite the frigid temperatures, and her hair was as wild as a squirrel's nest. This dead woman's face was contorted, her lips drawn back and her jaw thrust forward; she was reaching with her teeth.

Mercy aimed carefully. She waited until the woman's eyes looked wet and near, and her scream could be discerned as an individual cry above the echoing cacophony of the bizarre battle.

And she fired. She pulled the trigger once, and watched the top of the dead woman's head shatter. Her legs kept moving, only for a few steps more; then she stumbled to her knees, and then forward into the snow. But at least the corpse hadn't reached the porter, who was beginning to climb up the side of the snowplow; and it hadn't reached the rail-yard man, who was hot on the porter's trail.

The rest of them, though. They were still coming.

Inspector Galeano screamed, "*Ay, Dios mío!* Keep it clear!" He fired the last three bullets in his barrel and seized at his own ammunition bags, hunting for more. "They are coming! They are still coming!"

The conductor hollered something down at the men on the snowplow, but Mercy didn't catch it. She was focused on following directions, on keeping the spot in front of the train clear of the climbing, clamoring bodies with their clamping teeth and corpses' eyes.

Right under her arms, the first porter rose up so that she was shooting past him, over his head. She was surely giving his ears a terrible thrashing, but he didn't complain. He said at the top of his lungs, "Clear! Fire and start!"

This startled Mercy into looking over at the lieutenant. She saw two of the other rail men coming up over the edge beside him; and then she understood that the men on the ground in front of the train were finished, and the snowplow was readied, and they could leave, if only they could barrel through the barriers before them. She holstered her guns and they sizzled hot against the leather, smoldering warm patches against her hip.

"Here," she said to the porter, who struggled to lift himself over the edge. She took him by the shoulder, under the arm. "Here, come on. Get up here."

He fell down past her, into the *Dreadnought*'s interior, and she reached for the rail man.

The rail man gazed up at her in terror. He kicked hard, knocking away a corpse's teeth as they nipped and chomped at his boots. He was struggling, his striped shirt ripped and the jacket he wore over it hanging from one arm.

Mercy braced her feet around a pipe that was down by her knees, reached over the edge, and seized his forearms even as he grasped at her wrists. He was heavy, but she was strong. She'd lifted a pony once or twice, and plenty of men at the Robertson Hospital, when it'd come to that. She could lift him, too.

She heaved him backwards, and up, and with an awkward sideways slide over the rim, he toppled down into the interior, gasping for breath like a freshly caught fish in the bottom of a boat.

The conductor was moving, a man with a mission and maybe— God willing—a plan. "Help me!" he said to the lieutenant, who was still firing potshots as the uniformed dead began to climb, using their fallen brethren as ladders and stepstools on their way ever higher, trying desperately to make it up to the living folks inside the iron giant.

Lieutenant Hobbes holstered everything, leaped off the bin, and joined the conductor beside a pair of metal levers that were as long as a tall man's thigh.

"On the count of three—pull that one!" the conductor said as he pointed.

"Count of three," the lieutenant repeated.

"One, two, three—" And the levers both came down, not easily, but with the strain of both men's backs cranking and pulling with all their weight.

A snapping latch cracked almost as loud as the guns, and the balance of the engine shifted; Mercy felt it as a slight leaning forward, where before the engine had seemed to point up just a touch.

"It's on!" said the rail man. His observation was picked up and echoed around the narrow space. "It's on! It's on!"

The conductor's mouth was a line as hard as a riveted seam. He said, "Let's go." He drew down on the whistle, and the edge of his gray mustache twitched with determination, or rage, or desperation, or something else Mercy couldn't quite read.

As he pulled the whistle, he used his other arm to flip another switch, and pull a knob. He ordered the rail men and the porters to take up shovels, check the hydrogen lines, and make sure the stuff was being made and sent up from the fuel car.

There was no room to maneuver, or even to get out of the way—not with the lieutenant and his two soldiers, the five rail men and porters, the conductor, and Inspector Galeano still firing from his bird's-eye perch.

Mercy gripped the edge of the nearest bin, and the *Dreadnought* lunged. It didn't move forward; not quite, not yet, but it gave a shove and a lean, like a man bracing himself to break down a door, and its next lean and shove drew the whole train forward with a rattle as the cars clacked together, flexing on the track, knocking against one another from the sudden pull.

"The plow!" hollered the conductor. "Start it up!"

The nearest porter reached for a lever built into the floor; it had a squeezable handle, and when this handle was drawn back down and the lever was jammed into the necessary position, a new hum joined the fray.

The hum started slow, and low; it began distant, and thundering, and rough. A cloud clearing its throat, or a mountain shrugging off a small avalanche. A windmill caught in a gale, shuddering and flapping. The conductor called for it, saying, "More hydrogen! Divert it from the secondary boiler! Just power the plow first—we won't move without it!" With more fuel, the hum came louder, and steadier. It went from the crooked fan blade, unbalanced and wobbling, to a smooth and vocal growl that rose up so loud that it almost (not quite, but almost) dampened the sound of Theodora Clay and the men in the passenger car firing; the Mexican inspector, still upright, still shooting, and now openly crying; and the undead hordes oncoming.

Mercy covered her ears. She could see the lieutenant gesturing, the porters shoveling coal, the rail men adjusting gauges, and the whole lot of them—their mouths open, and then their hands signing as if they were all deaf, like her—communicating over the astounding volume.

She couldn't stand there and hear it, hands over ears or no.

The situation was as under control as it was going to get, and when the *Dreadnought* gave another heave, combined with the devouring hum as the snowplow sucked up the snow, cut it, and threw it away from the tracks . . . she could've sobbed with relief. She choked on the sob, forced it down, and looked away. As the engine got moving again, she clung to whatever solid and un-crowded bits of the bin she could hold, and worked her way back to the steps leading off the engine, then back through the fuel car and down its stairs to the gap.

Shaking and eyes watering from the smoke and the snow-plow's ravenous roar, she wobbled to the steps and saw two of the corpse-men. They moved as one and came toward her, but not fast enough to dodge her bullets. It took her three shots to take them down, but she pulled the trigger once on her right gun, and twice on her left and did just that. She didn't even remember unholstering them. She couldn't imagine how it had happened, how she'd been holding on to the rail, and then holding on to the guns, and shooting them into the faces of the men in the light-colored uniforms.

The *Dreadnought* picked up speed until it was running at a jerky, pitiful crawl.

Snow began to spray, commensurate with the pace: up a few feet, and out a few feet, feeding dunes on either side of the tracks as the rotary blades dug in and churned.

The engine followed its snow-gobbling plow. As Mercy stood there on the bottom of the fuel car's steps, relieved to see the tracks moving under her feet once more, she caught a glimpse of the pilot piece sliding past—abandoned beside the tracks when the men had unhitched it and cast it aside.

Mercy crossed the space between the fuel car and the passenger car, leaping to the passenger car's platform, throwing open the door, and tossing herself inside.

Malverne Purdue was standing there, his skin whiter than his shirt with loss of blood and the stress of standing when he should've been lying down. His blood soaked everything near his wound and seeped down into his pants. He looked through Mercy, registering her only as something that stood between him and something he wanted.

He staggered forward, through the door and out onto the platform again. She stumbled after him and he shoved her back.

She considered her guns and reached for one of them. "Mr. Purdue, get back inside and—"

He swung his arm back and struck her. He was holding something in his hand, and she couldn't see it clearly enough to know for certain, but it looked like it might've been one of the ceramic mugs from the caboose's stash. It was heavy, anyway, and it knocked her back and almost over the slender rail.

She caught herself on it, folding over it and latching her feet under its bottommost edge. Gasping, she stood upright again and felt at her face. When she pulled her hand back from her mouth, there was blood on her glove. She didn't think it'd been there before, but she might've been wrong.

No, she wasn't wrong. In a moment she could taste it, and feel it smearing along her teeth.

Malverne Purdue was rambling loudly. "This!" he said. "This, all of this—it could've been harnessed, don't you see? Don't you understand!"

Mercy pulled herself off the rail and faced him, only to see that he'd turned and was looking over the other short rail at the corpses who were coming at them from every direction at once.

His back to her, he continued. "We could've *used* this. We could've ended the war. And you would've lost; of course you would've. You're going to lose—you know that, don't you?"

"Me?" she asked, as if it were a personal accusation.

"Yes, of course *you*. You and that ranger, and those Rebels." He sneered at the *Shenandoah,* getting closer off to their left. He sniffed at the men on it, still holding their own. "I knew. I always knew. That's not a Kentucky accent, you ridiculous woman. I can tell the difference. I'm from Ohio, myself."

He gave her his full attention again, in a way that was wholly unpleasant and sinister. "And it was *your* fault, in a way. You were the one who drew them together, and who made them stand against me. They wouldn't have done it, if you hadn't goaded them!"

"Me?" Mercy wondered where the other soldiers were, where the captain was, where the ranger was—where anybody was. Still shooting, she presumed. She could hear them, above her and in-side the passenger car. She said, "You can call it my fault, if you want to. And that's fine. If it's my fault that you didn't get to do this"—she waved her hand in the direction of the undead—"then, fine, I'll take credit!"

"We could've controlled it!"

Was it madness or a last-minute surge of strength before death that made him sound so powerful, so fiercely insane? She didn't know, and she didn't care to know, but she again reached her right hand for her gun as he came closer.

"This has to end someday. There has to be a winner and a loser. That's the nature of war!"

"This isn't *nature,*" she told him, clinging to her gun and holding it between them. "That, over there, those people," she said. "That's not *nature.*" She didn't shout it. She didn't have to. His face was as near to hers as a groom before a kiss.

Pressing her gun up against his stomach she said, "I'm warning you, Mr. Purdue—I'm warning you!"

He said, "Warning me? That you're going to shoot me?" His breath frosted toward her face, but the cloud was drawn away by the motion of the train. Behind him, a panorama of horror unfolded—a horde, mostly men and a handful of women, running as if they'd only just learned how. All of them dead. All of them hungry. All of them coming, and chasing the train, and howling their morbid despair.

"I *will* shoot you," she promised. "If I have to. And maybe even if I *don't.*"

His laugh was a barking, nasty sound filled with phlegm and blood, and it was the last noise he ever made.

Surrounded by gunfire on all sides, Mercy couldn't tell—not at first—where the killing shot had come from. For a moment she thought it'd been her own gun, and she gasped as Malverne Purdue toppled back from her, falling away in a shuffling slump. But there was no new blood at his belly; it was on his head, and pouring down from it. As his body spiraled in a pirouette of death, she saw that the top of his skull had been struck and the crown was all but gone.

His eyes were blank as he hit the rail, and his body buckled over it, falling off the train and into a pack of dead men and women who fell upon it like wild dogs on a deer.

Mercy looked up. She still held the one gun, still pointing toward the place where the scientist had stood. She squinted against the white cliffs and the sparkling of the sun off the ice, and realized she was looking up at Theodora Clay.

Miss Clay was hanging on to the edge of the roof with one hand, her shoulders shaking with every rumbling roll of the rail ties. Her other hand held the gun she'd taken from Ranger Korman.

She shouted down, "For such an educated man, he was never very . . . *civilized*!"

Twenty

Back inside the passenger car, Mercy was nearly numb.

Miss Clay joined her momentarily, and from the other door at the other end of the car, Ranger Korman entered, looking ruffled but unscathed. A few others trickled in behind him, until there were no more footsteps on the steel roof and everyone was crowded into the sleeper car.

Above the car and all around it, the snow was blowing now—billowing harder and faster than any blizzard could've tossed it. Flung by the spinning blades of the plow, the snow gushed up, out, back, and around the passenger cars until it almost felt like riding through another tunnel, this one white and flecked with ice.

It was flecked with other things, too.

Here and there, a streak of bright brown blood went slapping across the side of the train, splattering into a window. A few fingers flipped inside. Chunks of hair. Bits of clothing, and a shoe that—upon inspection—still had most of a decomposing foot inside it. The rotary plow took the undead attackers and treated them no differently from the ice and snow that had clustered on the tracks, chopping them up and tossing them, shoveling them out of the way with its rows of biting blades.

Mrs. Butterfield was crying in a corner; her legs were drawn up beneath her, and her skirts billowed mightily, though she patted at them, trying to push them down, between sobs.

Theodora Clay was not at her side.

Instead, Miss Clay was a row away, reloading. And when she finished reloading, she was hanging out the broken window and picking off more living corpses one by one if they were able to reach the train and cling to it. Next to her, Ranger Korman was doing the same, and on the other side of him, Inspector Galeano did likewise.

Mercy looked to her right and saw the captain, grim-faced and soot- or gunpowder-covered, glaring out at the *Shenandoah*. Upon it, the surviving men were waving desperately—she could see that much even without a glass, they'd come so close. Some of the undead had wandered away from the Rebel engine in search of the louder, more glittering prey of the *Dreadnought;* and now it seemed almost possible that the distant soldiers might make a break for it. But where would they go?

As if he'd heard her thinking, the captain said, "We aren't going very fast. Barely staggering. A live, running man could catch us, easier than these dead things."

Lieutenant Hobbes shoved his way past the first passenger car door. His timing was almost perfect. He, too, had been looking at the other train and calculating the odds with his eyes. He pointed over at the other engine, now not even a quarter of a mile away, and said, "They're men, sir. Same as us. Soldiers, is all."

"I know," said the captain.

One of the soldiers down the line opened his mouth to object, but the captain cut him off by saying, "Don't. If it were us out there, we'd hope the other men would lend a hand, wouldn't we?"

It was Morris Comstock who weakly said what several others were no doubt thinking. The blood loss must've made him insubordinate, or maybe he was only too tired to restrain himself. "They're *dogs,* sir. Look what they've done to us. Look what they've done to the *Dreadnought,* and to the train! And to me! And to—" He looked around at the wounded. "All of us, sir!"

"Dogs?" Captain MacGruder whipped around, pulling himself out the window and glaring beneath eyebrows that were covered in frost. He sniffed, and rubbed his nose along his sleeve to either warm it or dab it. "Dogs did this to you? A man who fights dogs is something even lower. I fight *men*, Comstock. I fight them for the same reason they fight us: mostly because someone told them to, and because this is just the way the lines drew up, us on one side, them on the other."

He held his position, breathing hard and thinking. One leg on the seat of a lounger and one knee raised up, braced against the interior trim. His elbow holding him steady, his gun still partly aimed out the window, at the sky.

Nobody said a word, until he went on. "Those things"—he waved the barrel of his gun down at the screeching hordes—"they aren't men. They aren't even dogs. And I won't leave anybody to 'em. No—" He cut off Comstock with a syllable. "Not anybody."

Ranger Korman, who had not budged this whole time, said, "I like the way you think, Captain. But what precisely are we going to do for those boys over there?"

Inspector Galeano tried, "We could . . . clear a path for them. Maybe?"

"That'll be just about the best we can swing, I think." The ranger nodded. "We'll have to get up front, use the engine's defense systems, and line up inside here, too, and take down as many as we can. If we're lucky, at least some of those fellows on the *Shenandoah* might make it to a car."

Theodora Clay, of all people, mused, "If only we had some way to reach them—to let them know we mean to help."

Lieutenant Hobbes said, "The engineer has an electric speaking trumpet. I saw it, up front."

"Go get it," the captain said. "And fast. We don't have long. All right, folks. Who has ammunition left?"

Most of the soldiers grudgingly admitted that they still had some, and the ranger was still well stocked, but Mercy was out. She said to the captain, "I'll do it."

"You'll do what?"

"I'll go on top of the car, and I'll holler to 'em with the speaking trumpet. You men with the ammunition, you clear the way if you can."

"Now, don't be ridiculous, Mrs. Lynch. We'll get one of the porters to—"

"No. I'll do it," she told him. "I'm out of bullets, and most of you soldiers are better shots than me, anyway."

When Lieutenant Hobbes returned with the speaking trumpet, she swiped it out of his hand and took off.

Out on the passenger car platform, the world was white and in motion.

Still moving at a crawl, still throwing chunks of dead bodies left and right, the *Dreadnought*'s plow cast every flake into a canopy of glittering ice and frothy pale coldness. It arced overhead and off both sides, wings made of snow, twenty feet long and high. Mercy wondered how much faster the engine could pull and how much higher the wings would stretch. But there wasn't time to wonder much, and the ladder was slicker than ever, covered with pureed ice and freezing gore.

Her gloves tried to stick, for they were also damp and willing to harden.

She pulled them off with her teeth, shoved them into the pockets of her cloak, and then put her bare skin on the frigid metal. Every rung burned, and at least one took small, ragged strips from her fingers, but she climbed and climbed, and then she stood on top of the car, upright and blasted by the wind and the flying snow.

Mercy hoped her cloak was blue enough to signal with. She hoped that the large red cross on her satchel might show across the yards between her and her countrymen, stranded on their engine island.

She waved her arms, stretching them wide and flapping her hands; and when it appeared that they saw her, she lifted the speaking trumpet to her mouth and pulled the lever that said ON. A squeal of feedback was loud enough to pierce her eardrums, even over the roar of the wind and the plow and the tracks clattering past, but she steadied herself—spreading her legs and bending them, just enough to give herself some balance and some leverage. When she was at her full height, the black cloud of coal smoke went streaming over her head, mixing with the snow and covering her with smears the color of pitch and dogwood blossoms.

"Shenandoah!" she hollered as loud as she could. The machine picked up her voice and threw it even farther, as hard as the plow threw the snow. "When the *Dreadnought* starts shooting, make a run for these cars!"

Her mouth hurt. Her lips were freezing and numb and the words sounded slurred, but she said them anyway, screaming into the cold. "We mean to cover you!"

At first she couldn't tell if they'd understood, so she lifted the speaking trumpet again to repeat herself. But they nodded, and were drawing closer with every moment, so that new details about their appearance became apparent every second.

They huddled together, then separated again and readied themselves to jump or slide down off the engine at a moment's notice.

She didn't know what ought to happen next.

They were ready. She was finished.

The *Dreadnought* surged, or perhaps its plow snagged on something particularly juicy, and the car upon which Mercy stood shuddered. She dropped to her hands and knees, crushing the speaking trumpet. She clung to the roof, pinching it by the rim and pulling it up against her body as she shuffled along, trying to reach the nearest ladder.

The *Dreadnought*'s whistle blew.

It was no code of beeps and chimes, and no warning this time, either. It was a declaration of readiness. Everyone was ready. The moment was approaching, and the narrowest point between the two trains was imminent.

Now or never.

She held her breath and waited.

Now or never.

Now.

A volley of shots rang out as timed as a firing squad. Not the nearest undead, but the remaining corpses that stormed the *Shenandoah*—these dead men fell to the ground, clearing the way for the Rebels to jump, slide, or climb. Not the sort to look a gift horse in the mouth, they jumped, slid, and climbed down to the snow, and after a moment's confused milling, they ran toward the *Dreadnought*.

Another round, another pounding volley cut through another small clot of the raging dead. Most of their fellows did not seem to notice that anyone living was coming up behind them.

Another round, another pounding volley.

Mercy thought of the British during the Revolution and how they'd lined up in rows, all firing at once, and then replacing one row with another. That's what it sounded like, just underneath her. And when she looked over the edge, she could see their guns sticking out the windows, all in a row, just as she'd imagined. When they fired, it was on someone's signal—she could hear the one-word order even over the blustering wind.

"*Fire!*"

Another round, another pounding volley, and another cluster of dead men (plus at least one dead woman) fell to the ground. One or two struggled to rise, but were down enough to stay down when the living men ran past.

Mercy counted five. Five souls left, from the entire crew of the Shenandoah, however many that might've been.

But they looked like five sturdy men. The strongest, always. Who else makes it out alive? No one, of course. None but the men with the thighs that could pump in time with a train's pistons, moving their legs toward the enemy train because it was the only thing that could save them now. They were out of bullets and options and ideas, so here they came—hats flying off heads, jackets flapping behind them, boots weighed down with snow and snowmelt as they pushed through the stuff, which was not knee high but at times drifted up to their shins.

Mercy clung to the roof of the passenger car, peering over the edge and cheering the men on with every breath. She prayed little prayers that puffed out in tiny clouds, all of them whisked away on the wind with the snow and the churned-up bodies of the undead who'd stayed on the tracks, charging forward, everyone wanting to catch the train.

Three more volleys, violent rounds of organized fire and gunpowder coughing out the windows, and another hole was blown in the crowd.

"Come on . . . ," Mercy said under her breath. Then, as one man stumbled, fell, and was shortly covered by the monstrous creatures, she shouted it. "Come on!" she ordered the remaining four. "Come on, goddamn you, *come on*! You're almost here!"

Her hood was blown back and full of filthy snow, and her hands were absolutely senseless. They could've frozen to the edge of the roof, for all she knew, and for all she was letting go. She cheered the runners until she was hoarse. At some point, one last gap was blown in the thinning circle of undead, and the four men sprinted through, as red-faced and dirty as the nurse atop the train.

"Almost here!" she cried.

And they *were* almost there, yes, coming up to run alongside the train. Winding down, though. All of them, from trudging through the snow. They were weakening. They were so close, and it might not be enough.

Mercy prised her hands off the edge. Scrambling, knees and elbows and hands and boot-toes doing everything possible to hold to the roof, she hauled herself to its edge, just above the gap where one of the Rebels was losing steam, not quite close enough to heave himself on board.

She missed the last three ladder rungs and landed on the platform with a thud. Her knees ached, but her feet couldn't feel the impact, as they were already deadened from the icy air and the freeze-and-refreeze of dampness.

"You!" she said, as if there were anyone else she might be talking to.

He gasped something in response, but it was unintelligible.

"Stay with me!" she commanded, and began the process of unbuckling the gunbelt from around her waist. It might work. Then again, it might not. The man alongside the train was a large fellow, brunet and heavyset but not so much fat as beefy. Regardless, he looked heavy.

Sending up a heartfelt prayer for the strength of the leather, she used the belt to lash herself to the platform rail—and she gave off a prayer for the railing, too. Then she ducked around the pole, held on tight with one still-ungloved hand, and held out the other one.

"Take my hand!"

He replied, "Mmmph!" as he tried to follow her instructions, flinging himself forward and grabbing, but she remained barely out of reach.

So she lowered herself, sliding down along the pole. She leaned like she'd never leaned before, stretching herself out as if she could gain a few inches in height by pure willpower. Her hand trailed farther from the gap, nearer to the man.

It wasn't enough.

But all she had to do was let go with the hand that braced her. Let go of the rail. Gain that extra half a foot.

Yes.

"On the count of three!" she told him, since that was what worked for everyone else.

He nodded, and beads of sweat on his face went scattering as he jogged forward, still forward, almost spent—she could see it in his eyes.

"One . . . two . . . *three!*"

She released the pole and trusted the gunbelt to hold her, and the pole to hold the gunbelt, and the platform to hold the pole. She threw both arms out this time, leaning at her hips and straining. He gave one last surge—probably the last surge that was left in him—and closed the space between them.

Their hands met.

She seized his. He tried to seize back, but there wasn't much strength for him to lend, so she did most of the work.

He stumbled.

She said, "God help me!" as she pulled him briefly off his feet. Then his knees were coming down against the tracks, and he was hanging in midair—supported just by her and the gunbelt. He was trying to help her help him, but it was hard, and he was almost gone, really. She'd asked too much of him, she could see that now; but she still had something of herself left, so she wrenched him up a joint at a time.

She had him by the wrists, and then the forearms.

Then the elbows.

Then the pole was beginning to bend and her arms were threatening to unhinge from their sockets, and the belt was straining as if the buckles might go at any minute.

The Rebel's eyes went wide.

She knew what he was thinking, as plain as if it were written on his forehead. She growled, "No. Don't. Don't let go. *Hang on.*"

And then a pair of strong hands was on her shoulder, on both shoulders. Someone was pulling her up, and back, and drawing the Confederate with her.

She didn't fight it, but pushed back into the utilitarian embrace. Soon the arms were around her waist, and then one was loose and reaching over her arms, to the Rebel, who took the hand that was offered him.

In a matter of moments, the three of them were on the platform. The Rebel, lying splayed there, threw up. Mercy, trussed to the bent pole, unbuckled herself with hands that shuddered with exhaustion. Inspector Galeano leaned against the wall of the car, holding his stomach and gasping.

"Thank you," she told him.

The Rebel tried to say thank you as well, but instead threw up again.

Mercy asked, "You got the rest of them?"

He didn't nod, but made a tired shrug and said between gulps of air, "Two of them. Another did not reach the train."

The Rebel drew himself up to his quaking, bruised, scraped knees, and using the rail, pulled himself to his feet. He mustered a salute, and the inspector saluted back, parroting the unfamiliar gesture.

Mercy put a hand out and behind the Rebel, who might yet require a bit of steadying, in her professional opinion. But he held himself straight and wiped off his mouth with one sleeve, using the other to wipe his brow and cheeks as he followed the Mexican inspector into the passenger car.

They were greeted by Horatio Korman and Captain Mac-Gruder, who were assisting the other two men who'd made it on board.

Lieutenant Hobbes was bent over one of the wounded Union men, offering comfort or bandaging. Mrs. Butterfield had stopped crying, and Miss Clay was still on point at the window nearby. Cole Byron stood by the forward doors, his dark skin shining with perspiration, and another porter crouched just beyond him, repairing a loosened connector. Morris Comstock was on his feet, and, like several of the other soldiers, was still picking off the undead here and there, though they could see fewer and fewer as the train gathered speed.

As the pace improved, the snow blew higher and harder around them, and this, too, helped wash the teeming undead away from the battered train and the passengers within it.

Everything was ice and soot, and gunpowder and snow, and a few dozen heartbeats spread along the train's length. Most of the windows were gone, and the wind blew mercilessly inside, whipping hair into faces and clothing against bones.

For a while, no one spoke. Everyone was afraid to talk until the train was moving determinedly enough and the snowplow was kicking the debris high enough that not even the speediest of the monsters could catch them.

And then, after a few cleared throats, there were words of greeting.

Shortly thereafter, it was learned that Sergeant Elmer Pope, Private Steiner Monroe, and Corporal Warwick Cunningham were now in their midst, and all three men were exceedingly grateful for the assistance. They made no pretense of bluster. When things might have become awkward, given the circumstances, there instead came a moment of great camaraderie when the three Confederate men stood alongside the Union men and everyone looked out the windows at the retreating, ferocious, thinning hordes of the living dead.

The sergeant said, "I want you to know, we'd have done the same. Shoe being on the other foot, and all. Whether command liked it or not. We would've dealt with that later, but we wouldn't have left you."

And Captain MacGruder said, "I'd hope so." He didn't take his eyes away from the window until Inspector Galeano spoke.

As softly as the atmosphere would allow, the inspector said,

"We're all together in this." Galeano was a ragged figure, his own uniform singed and seared with gunpowder, and bloodied here and there. His hat was missing and his wild, dark hair was more wild and dark than it should have been, but so was everyone else's. They were northern and southern, Texan and Mexican, colored and white, officers and enlisted fellows . . . and, come to that, men and women. But the snow and the coal-smoke were finished with them now, and the wind had gotten its way. Their eyes were bloodshot and their faces were blanched tight with cold; and they were all bleak inside with the knowledge of something awful.

It was a train full of strangers, and they were all the same.

Inspector Galeano spoke again, and he was hoarse from the blizzard and the shouting. The Spanish consonants were filed sharp in his mouth. He said, "There will be questions. From everyone, everywhere. All our nations will want to know what happened here. And we are the only ones who can tell them."

Captain MacGruder nodded. "There'll be inquiries, that's for damn sure."

Sergeant Pope said, "We were after your gold, and you were after the Chinamen out West. We had a fight between us, fair as can be."

"But we won't get our Chinamen now," said the lieutenant. "The deeds all went sucking out into the pass someplace when that crazy woman busted out the gold car's window with a prybar." He pointed at Theodora Clay, who stood utterly unapologetic. "And the gold . . . I don't know. I expect there are better uses for it."

Corporal Cunningham said, "And Lord knows we're in no position to take it from you now." He gave a rueful little smile.

"We both had our reasons," said the captain. "Civilized reasons. Disagreements between men. But *those* things . . ."

"Those things" was repeated in muttering utterances around the car.

The Southern sergeant said, "I want all of y'all to know, we didn't do that. Whatever was done to them . . . we didn't do it. I've never seen anything like it in my life, and I don't mind telling you, I near shit myself when they started eating my soldiers."

"Us either," said Lieutenant Hobbes.

And Captain MacGruder clarified, "They aren't our work either. I'll swear to it on my father's grave."

General murmurs of agreement and reinforcement made the rounds.

"As a representative of the government that once . . ," Inspector Galeano sought a word, and didn't find it. So he tried again. "Those people—those things that aren't people anymore—they were my countrymen. I can assure you that whatever became of them was no work of ours."

The ranger said, "Nor Texas, and that's a goddamned *fact*."

Anyone could've argued, but nobody did.

But everyone's innocence having been established, a great round of speculation got under way. If not the North, and if not the South, and if not Texas or Mexico . . . then who? Or, God help them all, what if it were a disease—and there was no one at fault, and no one they could demand an explanation from?

All the way to Salt Lake City, the passengers and crew of the *Dreadnought* huddled and whispered, periodically checking themselves in the lavatories for any signs of drying eyes, graying skin, or yellowing membranes.

And no one found any.

So Mercy told them everything she knew about the yellow sap, and Inspector Galeano told them about a northwestern dirigible that had crashed in West *Tejas,* carrying a load of poisonous gas.

Twenty-one

The next morning, the *Dreadnought* pulled what was left of its cargo and passengers into the station at Salt Lake City. Everyone on board looked and smelled like a war refugee.

All the occupants, including the conductor, his crew, and all the porters, stumbled down from the metal steps and onto terra firma in the Utah territory with a sense of relief that prompted several of the remaining civilians to burst into tears. Chilled beyond the bone, with many of them sporting injuries large and small that Mercy had done her best to patch, everyone was dazed. The train's boilers cooled and clacked, but its hydrogen valves were all tightened into silence. Its interior was littered with broken glass, bullet casings, and blood. There it sat on the line, abandoned and silent, a husk that—for all its mighty power—looked forlorn.

Mercy sat on a bench inside the station's great hall with Ranger Korman, Inspector Galeano, and the three Rebel soldiers. All in a row they watched the people bustle by, coming and going, taking notes and asking the inevitable questions.

Though they received a few strange glances, no one stopped them to ask why three Confederates had been aboard or why they were being permitted to simply *leave;* and no one demanded to know what a Mexican inspector was doing there; and no one wondered aloud why a Texas Ranger was this far north and west of his home turf.

This was not America, after all. Nor the Confederacy, or Texas, or Mexico either. So if anybody cared, nobody said anything. There was no war here, Utah's or anybody else's.

Paperwork was sorted.

New trains were offered.

All the rattled civilians were sent to their original destinations.

Theodora Clay and her aunt Norene vanished without a good-bye. Mercy wondered if Horatio Korman ever got his gun back, but she didn't ask. She was pretty sure that if he'd wanted it, he would've seen about retrieving it. Captain MacGruder and Lieutenant Hobbes were assigned to another train and other duties before Mercy ever got a chance to tell them how much she'd appreciated their presence. But she liked to think they knew, and understood.

In time, someone approached the three southern men and gave them envelopes with tickets, back east and south, Mercy assumed. The soldiers offered quiet parting salutations and tips of their hats and were gone. Inspector Galeano left next, taking his tickets and claiming his seat on a train that would eventually take him to his homeland, where he would have a most amazing story to tell.

Then it was the ranger's turn. Horatio Korman stood, touched the rim of his hat, and said, "Ma'am." And that was all.

He, too, left her seated on the wide wooden bench, all alone and not quite certain if she was glad for the sudden privacy after so many weeks of being cooped up and crowded . . . or if she was very, very lonely.

But finally it was her turn, and the conductor of her own train was crying, "All aboard!" on the tracks outside. She squeezed her tickets, climbed to her feet, and met her train.

It was called the *Rose Marie,* and it looked nothing like the *Dreadnought,* which was somehow both reassuring and disappointing. By comparison, the *Rose Marie* looked like a fragile thing, something that could not possibly make the remainder of the journey—over mountains or around them, across plains and along rivers, for another thousand miles.

But the little engine with its pristine sleeper cars and shiny steel trim carried her swiftly—at times even more swiftly than the *Dreadnought* ever did, which was no surprise, since its load was lighter and it was not dragged down with a militia's fortune in arms and ammunition.

The rest of the mountain chain passed with a panorama of epic scenery sometimes covered in snow, and sometimes glittering with sky blue lakes of melted ice.

Mercy did not talk to her fellow passengers much. What would she say?

Beyond the most necessary pleasantries, she ignored and avoided them, and she was likewise ignored and avoided. Even though she'd cleaned her cloak and dress to the best of her abilities, they still showed bloodstains and tears, and—as she discovered in the washroom one morning—two bullet holes. Her hands were bandaged, a task she'd undertaken by herself and upon which she'd performed a decent job, if not a great one; but her fingers ached all the time as they healed, and the new skin stretched tight and itchy across the places where she'd lost the old.

The last thousand miles, between Salt Lake City and Tacoma, were exactly as uneventful as the first two thousand had been action filled.

Sometimes, when she thought she'd go stark raving mad with boredom, she'd remember lying atop the roof of the *Dreadnought*'s passenger car, the skin of her throat sticking to the freezing metal and her hands all but glued together by ice. She'd recall watching the southern soldiers as they ran, dodging, ducking, between the ranks of the hungry dead, running for their lives. And she imagined the smoke and snow in her hair, and then she considered picking up a penny dreadful or two at the next stop.

She picked up a total of three, using almost the very last of her cash.

She even read them. Well, she had the time. And nothing else to do.

And people tended not to bother a woman with a book.

After a few days, she checked the newspapers at every stop, looking for some sign that someone—anyone—had made it back and begun to explain what had happened at Provo . . . and the *Dreadnought,* and the people who'd ridden upon it. But she never spied any mention of any of these things, so she told herself that it must be too soon. Inspector Galeano could've never made it back to Mexico yet; Ranger Korman wouldn't have even hit Amarillo yet; and Captain MacGruder wouldn't be back at the Mississippi River yet. So she'd be patient, and wait. Eventually, the world would know. Eventually, a newspaper somewhere would have to announce the story and tell it whole, and true.

Eventually.

But not while Mercy Swakhammer Lynch made her way to the West Coast.

In a dull fog of fatigue and apathy she rode through Twin Falls, Boise, and Pendleton. She spent the night in Walla Walla, and in the morning boarded another train, one called the *City of Santa Fe.* Then, on to Yakima, from whence she sent her final telegram to her final destination, in hopes that the sheriff would be there to collect her, because if he wasn't, Mercy had no earthly idea what she'd do next.

Cedar Falls. Kanaskat.

Auburn. Federal Way.

Tacoma.

Mercy exited the train with an upset stomach and a nervous headache.

She stepped into an afternoon covered with low gray clouds, but the world felt bright compared to the relative shade of the train's interiors. It was cold, but not exceptionally so. The air was humid and tasted strange—a little tangy, and a little sour with a scent she couldn't quite place.

The station was a big compound, but the tracks were not very crowded, and the *City of Santa Fe* was the only train debarking. Only a few people milled around the station's edges—the station managers, the engineers, the railmen who worked the water pumps and inspected the valve connections, and the ubiquitous porters . . . though she noticed that they weren't all black. Some were Oriental, in the same sharp porter uniforms but with hair that was long and braided, and sometimes shaved back from their faces.

Mercy tried not to stare, but the sight of so many at once amazed and distracted her.

Her curiosity about the men did not distract her from the unsettling truth of her situation. She was three thousand miles from home, absolutely broke, and possessing virtually nothing but the clothes on her back and the contents of her medical satchel, which had become much depleted over the weeks.

She stood beside the station agent's door and tried not to fret about the circumstances. She scanned the face and vest of every passing man, hoping to spot a badge or some other mark that would identify a sheriff.

So she was rather unprepared to hear, "Vinita Swakhammer?" Because in order to reply, she was compelled to address a smallish woman in her mid- to late thirties. This smallish woman wore pants that were tucked into the tops of her boots and a fitted waistcoat with a badge clipped to the watch pocket. Her jacket was frankly too large, and her brown slouch hat was held aloft by a curly tangle of dark brown hair that was streaked with orange the shade of cheap gold.

"Sh . . . ," Mercy began. She gave it another shot. "Sheriff—?"

"Briar Wilkes," the other woman said. She stuck out her hand.

"And you're . . . you're the sheriff?"

She shrugged. "If there's law in Seattle, I guess it's me as much as anybody."

"I never heard of a woman sheriff before."

"Well, now you have," Briar said, but she didn't seem to take any offense.

Mercy imagined it was the sort of thing she answered questions about all the time. She said, "I suppose so. I didn't mean to be rude."

"Don't worry about it. Anyway, do you have any . . . bags or anything?"

"No. This is it," Mercy said. Then she asked quickly, "How did you know it was me?"

Briar Wilkes cocked her head toward the station's exit and led the way out. "For starters, you were the most lost-looking person on the landing. You must've had a real long trip, coming all the way from Virginia. You ever been out this far west?"

"No ma'am," she said. "First time."

"That's what I figured. And anyway, you're about the right age, and traveling alone. I didn't know you were a nurse, though. That's what the cross on your bag means, right?"

"Right. I worked in a hospital in Richmond."

The sheriff's interest was piqued. "Smack in the middle of the war, huh?"

"Yes ma'am. Smack in the middle."

"That must have been . . . hard." Sheriff Wilkes led the way back outside, which put them in front of the enormous building. "We're going over there, just so you know." She pointed down the street, where a set of docks were playing host to a small multitude of airships. "I hope you don't have any trouble flying. I know some folks are afraid of it."

"That'll be fine. How far away is Seattle from here?"

"Oh, not far. It's maybe thirty miles to where we're going. And

I can't believe I didn't think to tell you right away, but your pa's doing all right. For a while there, we really thought he wasn't going to make it, but he pulled through."

"Really?" said Mercy, who likewise couldn't believe she hadn't thought to ask. It was the whole point of her trip, wasn't it, finding her father, and seeing him?

Sheriff Wilkes nodded. "Really. He's just about the toughest son of a gun I ever did know. Or he's in the running for that title, that's for damn sure. I say that, because you're about to meet one of the other toughest sons of a gun I know. You see that dirigible right there?"

She indicated a patchwork metal monster that bobbed lazily above a pipe dock.

Mercy could see the top of it, but not much of the bottom. That bit was blocked out by the dockyard gate, and another, smaller ship. "I see it."

"That's the *Naamah Darling*. Her captain, Andan Cly, is a friend of mine and your daddy's."

"I didn't know my daddy had any friends," she said, then caught herself. "I mean . . . Oh hell, I don't know what I mean. I haven't seen him, you know? Not in years. Not since I was a little girl."

Briar Wilkes said, "That's what he told me, and he feels real bad about it. Worse probably than he's willing to say. But when he thought he was dying, and we didn't know how much longer we could keep him alive, the one thing he kept asking for, over and over, was to see his little girl." She gave an ironic laugh. "Course, he was delirious as could be, and I finally figured out that his little girl had to be a grown woman now. And it took us a while to get enough details out of him to track you down. I won't lie to you, it was a pain in the ass."

"I bet."

"We sent out word with air captains in every direction,

especially those who went pirating along the cracker lines, or who had connections back East. He said last he knew of you, you'd been in some town called Waterford."

"That's right," she said.

"But we couldn't find it, and could hardly find anyone who'd heard of it. But one of Crog's old buddies—Crog, he's . . . he's another one of the air captains out here, one of Captain Cly's good friends—anyway, Crog's buddy said it wasn't too awful far from Richmond." She caught herself, or caught Mercy looking overwhelmed and uncertain. So she changed direction and said, "But I won't bore you with the details. Suffice it to say, it took some doing, tracking you down."

"Well, it took some doing, getting myself out here," she said softly.

It was Sheriff Wilkes's turn to say, "I bet."

They walked in silence for the rest of the block, until they reached the gates. Then the sheriff paused and turned to her charge. "Listen, there are some things I ought to tell you, before we get to Seattle."

Mercy got the distinct impression that Briar Wilkes was going to continue right then and there, on the very spot, telling her whatever things she had to say, but someone hailed her from over by the pipe docks.

"Wilkes!"

"I'm coming, I'm coming. Keep your shirt on, Captain."

Rather than declare further impatience, the speaker emerged from underneath the *Naamah Darling,* stepping slowly into the wide gravel aisle next to his ship. The captain—for this surely must be him—looked up and down at Mercy and said, "So this is Jeremiah's girl?"

"Sure is," said the sheriff.

"Damn sight prettier than her old man, I'll give her that," he said with a crooked grin that was surely meant to be disarming.

Mercy didn't realize for a moment that she'd stopped in her tracks upon catching sight of Captain Cly. And then she understood his attempt to disarm, and why he seemed to move carefully, as if he thought he might frighten her.

She was staring at the single largest man she'd seen in all her life.

And Mercy Lynch had seen plenty of men in her time— soldiers, big fighting lads, strapping old boxers and wrestlers, blacksmiths and rail-yard workers with shoulders like sides of beef. But she'd never seen anyone who was quite the sheer *size* of Andan Cly, captain of the *Naamah Darling*. Seven feet and change, surely, the captain hulked in the center of the lane, holding still and keeping that crooked smile firmly in place, though now he was aiming it at the sheriff. He was an awesomely constructed fellow, with rippling arms and a long torso that boasted muscles like railroad ties under snow, showing through his thin undershirt. The captain was not particularly good-looking—he was bald as an apple with jutting ears—but his face wore lines of sharp intelligence and his eyes hinted at a warmth that might be friendly.

She thought he must be chilly, running around like that, but he didn't look cold. Maybe he was so big that the cold couldn't touch him.

Mercy Lynch gave his cautious smile a tentative return, and followed Briar Wilkes up to greet him. She shook his hand when he offered it to her, and she said, "It's nice to meet you."

"Likewise, I'm sure. I hope you had a pleasant trip."

She opened her mouth to reply, but didn't know what to say. So she closed it again, then responded, "It was an adventure. I'll tell you about it on the way, if you want."

"Can't wait to hear it," he said, and he scratched at the back of his neck—a nervous gesture, one that was holding something back. "But while we're flying, I think we probably ought to tell you a few things about Seattle—before you see it for yourself, I mean. I expect Briar here told you about your father—that he's doing okay after all?"

"She told me," Mercy said.

He nodded, and quit scratching at his neck. "Right, right. But I don't guess she got around to telling you about . . . *where* he lives?"

"It hadn't come up yet," the nurse responded.

"I was working my way to it," Briar Wilkes said.

Mercy was forced to wonder, "Is it . . . is he . . . is it bad? Is there something wrong, like he's in a jail, or a poorhouse, or something?"

The sheriff shook her head. "Oh no. Nothing like that. For what it's worth, we live in the same place. Me and my son, we live in the same building as your dad. It's just . . . well, see . . . it's just . . ."

The captain took over. "Why don't you come on up inside, and we'll give you the whole story, all right?" He put a hand on her shoulder and guided her toward the ship. "It's a *long* story, but we'll try to keep it short. And there's no shame on your dad in any of it. We just have a peculiar situation, is all."

Beneath the *Naamah Darling* was a set of retractable stairs not altogether different from the ones that led up into a train's passenger car, but longer by two or three measures. She followed the sheriff up inside the belly of the airship. The captain brought up the rear, drawing the steps behind himself and shutting them all inside.

The ship's cockpit was all rounded edges and levers, all buttons and steering columns and switches in a curved display with three seats bolted into place. The center seat was oversized and vacant, marking it as the captain's chair. The other two were occupied, and both swiveled so their occupants could see the newcomer.

In the left seat was a slender Oriental man about twenty-five or thirty years old. He wore a loose-fitting shirt over ordinary pants and boots, and a pair of aviator's goggles was pushed up onto his bare forehead.

The captain pointed one long finger at him and said, "That's Fang. He understands you just fine, but he doesn't talk. Right now he's pulling double duty as first mate and engineer."

To which the occupant of the other chair said, "Hey!" in a tone of half-joking objection. The objector was a teenager still, and skinny as a rail with brown hair that hosted a nest of cowlicks.

Andan Cly pointed at him next, saying, "That's Zeke, and . . . and where's Houjin?"

An equally young head popped out of the storage bay at the rear of the craft. "Over here." The head vanished.

"Over there, yeah. Of course he is. Anyway, that's Zeke, like I said, and the other one's Houjin—sometimes called Huey, sometimes not."

Briar Wilkes pointed at the boy in the third seat and said, "Zeke's my son. Huey"—she cocked her head toward the place where Huey had briefly appeared—"is his buddy. I guess they think they're going to see the world together or something, if they can talk the captain into teaching them how to fly."

The captain made a grumbling noise, but he didn't put much weight behind it. "They're both sharp enough, when they pay attention," he said. It wasn't high praise, but it made Zeke beam, and it brought Huey up out of the cargo bay.

The Oriental boy was Zeke's age and approximate size. He had a keen, smart face and a long top braid like Fang's, but he was dressed almost identically to Zeke, as if the two of them had coordinated this semblance of a uniform, and were determined to play at being crew.

The captain said, "All right, everyone. You've had your chance to stare. This here is Jeremiah's girl, Miss Vinita Swakhammer."

Mercy said, "Hello, um, everyone. And just so you know,

I'm . . . well, I *was* married, so it's Vinita Lynch. But y'all can call me Mercy if you like. It's just a nickname, but it's stuck." Before anyone could ask, she added quickly, "My husband died. That's why I'm out here alone."

Andan Cly said, "I'm real sorry to hear that, ma'am," and the sheriff mumbled something similar.

Standing in the center of the bridge, she felt large and awkward in their midst; and now they felt sorry for her, which made her feel even more conspicuous. She was taller and heavier than everyone present except for the gigantic captain, and her summer coloring stood out against the dark hair and eyes of everyone else. Unaccustomed to feeling quite so out of place, and a little uncomfortable at being the object of everyone's attention, she nonetheless continued, "Well. Thanks a whole bunch for picking me up and giving me a ride out to my daddy. I appreciate it."

Briar Wilkes assured her, "We're happy to do it. And now that the captain's finally welded in some extra seating, we've even got the space to transport you without making you sit on the floor."

"Or stand up against the cargo nets," the captain said under his breath, like it was a private joke.

The sheriff didn't pay any attention to him; she just showed Mercy over to the wall beside the cargo hold, where a wide net was hanging behind a bench that had straps attached to it. "You and me, and either Huey or Zeke—depending on who loses that argument—will sit right over here. You just buckle one of these harnesses over you, and it'll keep you from sliding around too much if we hit rough air."

Mercy took a look at the apparatus, generally understood it, and sat down to fasten herself into place. Briar Wilkes took a seat beside her, and immediately the two boys bickered over who got to sit in the engineer's chair. Zeke lost the ensuing battle and was subjected to the indignity of sitting beside his mother.

The boy asked Mercy, "You ever flown before?"

And she said, "Once. A few weeks ago. I flew from Richmond to . . . to Chattanooga, sort of."

"Sort of?" his mother asked.

"Long story," Mercy summed up.

As the steam thrusters hissed themselves to full power, the captain gave the order to unhook from the pipe. He pressed various buttons, and the ship drifted upward in a lazy rise.

No one spoke while the *Naamah Darling* launched—the quiet was an easygoing superstition, until the craft was tipping its crown up against the low, heavy clouds above Tacoma. Then the captain took the steering column and moved it smoothly, thoughtlessly, to swivel the craft to face the north. The thrusters were fired, and the hydrogen vessel began a leisurely flight.

Once these things were under way and there seemed little chance of distracting the captain from something important, Briar Wilkes cleared her throat. "Speaking of long stories," she began, even though no one had spoken of such things for several minutes. "Now's the time, I guess, to ask you what you might've heard about Seattle."

"Seattle?" Mercy wrinkled her forehead. "Well, I guess I don't know much. There was a gold rush up north, and it went through it, isn't that right?"

Zeke muttered, "Something like that."

His mother elbowed him. She said, "Go on. What else?"

She thought about it, and answered slowly. "I thought there was an earthquake or something, a long time ago. I had it in my head that the town was pretty much torn down, or just abandoned. To tell you the truth, I didn't know anybody lived there, much less that my dad called it home."

Briar nodded. "You're more right than wrong. There was an earthquake; that's a fact. But it was made by a big mining machine, and it tore up the city but *good*. A lot of people died, and a bunch of buildings were destroyed, but most of the city proper is intact." She hesitated, as if that was not the correct spot to end her commentary. So she added, "In a sense."

The captain chimed in, talking over his shoulder while he stared out the big glass wraparound windscreen. "It's all still there," he said. "Everything that didn't go down with the Boneshaker is still standing."

"The what-now?"

The sheriff said, "The mining machine."

"Oh."

He went on. "That's right. But whatever that machine did, tearing up the foundation like that, under the mountains . . . it stirred up a real nasty gas. The gas makes people sick as hell, and it kills them. In a sense," he concluded with Briar's qualifying remark.

"In a . . . sense?" the nurse repeated. She felt something warm and awful in her stomach and she could almost imagine where this was going, but she wanted to be wrong, so she went ahead and asked. "How does something kill somebody, but only in a sense?"

Briar Wilkes cleared her throat. "I hate to say you'll have to see it for yourself, but I'm afraid that if I tell you, you won't believe me and you'll think I'm out of my mind."

"It might surprise you, the things I might believe."

"All right, then. The gas—we call it Blight—turns people all rotty, like they're dead and walking, decomposing even though they're still moving. And still," she paused, "hungry."

Mercy nodded. She had spent so many nights wondering where the gas had come from—the stuff from which the sap was made—and now, inexplicably and horribly, she was fairly certain she had her answer.

The captain said from his chair, "Anyway, that's the sum of it."

Inside the *Naamah Darling,* all was silent except for the whistle and clack of the ship's inner workings. Then Mercy asked, "So this gas, it just comes up from the ground in this city?"

The sheriff said, "Yup. And there's not a damn thing anybody can do about it." She hemmed and hawed. "Except for the wall they built."

"A wall?"

"A wall. All the way around the city, holding the gas inside."

Mercy's eyes narrowed. "And holding all the dead folks inside, too?"

"That's right. I'm not saying it's a perfect solution. I'm just saying nobody knew what else to do, so that's what they did. And the thing is, inside the wall, where the city's all dead and full of gas . . . some folks live inside down there."

"How?" she asked, wondering wildly if her father weren't one of the undead, living down inside the gas like that.

Briar waved her hands like she was using them to weigh how much information she ought to dish out. "I ain't going to lie—it's complicated. You'll get the hang of it real quick, though. You'll see. Mostly it's a matter of pumping fresh air down from outside the city, down to the underground where everybody lives, in the sealed-up parts."

"In the . . . sealed-up parts. All right," Mercy mused, calmer at having an explanation. "That sounds like a righteous mess to me, but I think I see where you're going with it. And my daddy lives down there? Down in this walled-up city?"

The sheriff nodded with tremendous relief. "Yes. That's it. He lives down inside the poisoned city. A bunch of us do. Me and Zeke here, and Houjin, and maybe a few hundred others, all told. The captain and Mr. Fang come and go—they don't live there, but they know their way around. That's the story of it, at least the hard parts."

Mercy bobbed her head, considering all this, and matching it against what she'd seen on her trip out West. But she did not say anything to the sheriff or the captain. Not yet. There'd be time for it later—time for examinations and explanations, and questions and deductions. It could wait. She could sit on it for another few miles, maybe another few hours. Maybe another few days, just until she was certain and she understood more about how this strange northwestern world worked.

And when the *Naamah Darling* arrived at the Sound, and the walled city rose up underneath the dirigible like some dark, immense castle from a fairy tale that never knew a happy ending, Mercy knew that this world would be strange indeed.

Briar Wilkes unhooked herself from the harness and said, "I'll get you a mask."

"A mask?"

"A gas mask, yes. It's not safe to breathe in there until you get underground, into the sealed-off quarters. But those quarters aren't equipped to handle an airship landing, so we put down at the old fort and head underground from there. And until we get underside, you'll need a mask."

Mercy watched as the captain and Fang donned their equipment. The boys also pulled out masks made of leather and glass, affixing them to their faces until everyone looked insectlike. Briar retrieved one from the cargo hold and gave it to the nurse, who'd never seen anything like it and wasn't positive how she ought to wear it.

The sheriff saw her confusion and sat down beside her on the edge of the seat so she could almost face her. She pulled out her own mask and held it up, showing how the straps and seals were the same as the one in Mercy's hand. "Like this," she said, taking off her hat and stretching the mask's straps to fit around her skull. "The seals need to be real fitted around your face, so it's airtight. Make sure you don't get your hair caught in them, or the ties from your cloak."

"All right, I see. I think."

And with a little help, Mercy matched the rest of them—her face turned buggy by the contraption she wore. It was uncomfortable and strange, and it smelled odd. Inside the rubber thing with its charcoal filters and thick glass lenses, everything tasted like medical tubing and the *Dreadnought*'s smokestacks.

"Everybody ready?" asked the captain. When he'd received a positive response from absolutely everyone on board, he said, "Good. Here we go. Dropping altitude and setting down at Fort Decatur. Approximate arrival time is, oh, I don't know. Three or four minutes. Wind's calm, and Petey's got his flare showing all's well. Ladies and gentlemen, we are now landing in the city of Seattle, such as she is."

Mercy strained her neck but didn't see what the captain was talking about, so she took his words on faith. When the ship began its dipping drift downward, she held on to her stomach and was very faintly glad that no one could see her face very well. She wasn't going to be sick, not from the ride, at least. But the weight of the last month settled on her with a vengeance, now that she was very nearly at her destination.

She was *there,* in the place where the yellow sap came from— she was virtually certain of it, even before she could see the smoggy air smearing itself across the windscreen, leaving nasty wet smudges the color of boiled yolks.

She was there, in the town where her father had disappeared to all those years ago.

As the ship dropped lower, deeper into the thick, awful air, she struggled to remember the flashes of her childhood that had come to her throughout the trip. The way he'd taught her to shoot. The smell of his beard when he'd come inside from the farm. The bulk of his arms and the plaid of a shirt he wore more days than not.

None of it sparked to life. None of it gave her the sweet ping of nostalgia she was hoping for. All of it felt foreign and dream-like, as if it had happened to someone else and she'd heard about it only secondhand.

But here she was.

The ship came to rest with a thud, jarring her bottom against the metal bench. Then it came back up a few feet to hover, and the whole thing shook softly as the anchoring chains were detached and affixed to something outside. Finally, all was still.

Through the small lenses of her mask and through the great lens of the windscreens she could see lights strung together. The lights were steadier than mere torches, but they were fuzzy bubbles without too much definition, and she couldn't discern their actual nature. They showed a sickly yellow-tinted world, and a wall made of logs that must've come from enormous trees—bigger than anything she'd ever seen down South. The wall disappeared in each direction, but that might've meant nothing. Through the fog, she could see perhaps only twenty yards, and those yards were none too clear.

Her chest hurt, and she felt quite distinctly breathless, as if she'd been running. She reached up to the mask to adjust it, or move it, but the sheriff stopped her hand.

She said, "Don't. I know it takes some getting used to, but we're down in the thick now. Once the anchor claws have been deployed, you can't trust the air in here." A pop and a sigh interrupted her. When they'd faded, she said, "And that was the sound of the bottom hatch opening."

Mercy shook her head. "It just . . . it feels . . . I can't . . ."

"I know, and I understand, but you *can*. You have to. Wear it or die, at least for now. But I promise, not for long." Briar's eyes behind her own mask tried to convey reassurance, and a lift to her cheeks implied a smile.

Mercy tried to smile back, and failed. Against her expectations and her will, her eyes filled up.

The sheriff leaned forward and all but whispered, "It's all right, darling, I promise. Pull yourself together if you can, not because there's anything wrong with crying, but because having a stuffy nose in one of these things is a goddamn nightmare." She patted the young nurse's arm, then squeezed it gently. "There's time for crying later. All the crying you like, and all the crying you can stand. Come on now, though. Let's get you unlatched. It's time to go see your daddy."

Mercy fumbled with her harness and extracted herself with difficulty. By the time she was finished, she noticed that the captain and the boys had already disappeared down the hatch, down into the fort.

Briar helped, untangling the last canvas strap and setting it back in place against the ship's interior wall. She stood up straight and urged Mercy to do likewise, and she brushed a stray bit of travel dust off the taller woman's shoulders. "You're going to be just fine."

"I don't know. It's been so long, and he's never said a thing. We ain't been close. I ain't never heard from him, not since I was little."

The sheriff nodded at all of this. She said, "I'm not sure what it's worth to hear me say so, but he saved my life, when I first came down here. He's got a reputation for it—for looking after newcomers and helping people learn their way. This is a dangerous place, but, your pa . . . he makes it *less* dangerous. People love him because he looks out for them. He looks out for all of us. When people thought he was dying, they moved heaven and earth to give him the last thing he wanted. The last thing he asked for."

"Me."

"You. And I know you figure that I don't understand, and that maybe I'm just being nice to you. And that's true, partly. I *am* trying to be nice to you. But you ought to know: I lost a husband too, a long time ago, before Zeke was even born. I also lost my father; and, like you and yours, we weren't none too close. It's a world of widows and orphans down here." The sheriff looked away, out the massive windscreen, as if she could see past the fog, and past the log walls.

Then she finished, "But all the things we think we know about the folks who spawned us or raised us . . . well . . . sometimes they're wrong, and sometimes what we've seen isn't all there is to know."

Twenty-two

By the time Mercy had unloaded herself from the *Naamah Darling,* Zeke and Huey were nowhere to be seen. The captain was talking with a man—Petey, presumably—who was holding a flare on a pike. All around her, the world was latticed with lights that hummed and buzzed against the fog; and above them she could see the glittering eyes of birds—long rows of them, seated atop the sharpened ends of the log walls that were clearly failing to deter them from sitting there.

Briar Wilkes saw her looking at them and said, "Don't pay 'em no mind. People get funny about the crows in here, but they don't ever bother anybody."

"I thought nobody could live in here, breathing this air?"

The sheriff shrugged. "Somehow, the birds manage. But I couldn't explain it. Come on now, I want to introduce you to somebody."

Somebody proved to be another woman, somewhere between Mercy's height and Briar's, and wider than the both of them without appearing fat. Her hair was dark but tipped with gray, and one sleeve of her dress was pinned up to her chest so it wouldn't flutter emptily. She had only one arm, and that arm moved strangely. It was covered in one long leather glove.

"Vinita—I mean, Mercy—this is Lucy O'Gunning. She's one

of your father's oldest friends, and she's been helping Mr. Chow nurse him back to health."

"Hello, Mrs. O'Gunning."

"Missus! Don't you bother with that, you darling you. I'm Lucy and you're . . . Mercy, is that what she said?"

"It's a nickname, but I think I'm keeping it."

"Works for me!" she declared. "Come on back, now. Jeremiah's going to be tickled pink!"

Mercy murmured, "Really?"

And although Lucy had already turned, ready to lead the way down and under, she stopped and laughed. "Oh, I don't know. Tickled pink's probably not the right way to put it. I think he's as nervous as can be, now that he knows he's going to hang around awhile. The idea of saying a quick good-bye looked good to him, but . . ." She trailed off, then waved her one arm to draw Mercy and Briar forward, back into the fog and into a corridor leading to a long set of stairs that led down into a very black darkness. Her voice echoed around in the stairwell. "He's not much of a talker, your dad. And now I guess he's figured out that there's a whole passel of stuff he should tell you. Since there's time, and all."

The nurse was almost glad to hear it, that she wasn't the only one with a belly full of rocks.

Lucy O'Gunning led Mercy and Briar down to a door with a rubber seal around it, which she opened with a latch that was built into the wall beside it. "Be quick, now," she said. She led the way; then they both dashed inside behind her. The door closed with a sucking snap, and a glowing green light along the floor showed another portal immediately ahead. Lucy told Mercy, "One more door, and then we get to the filters. The more barriers we can put between ourselves and that air up topside, the better."

So the next door opened and closed, and so did the subsequent two, which had panting filters made of sturdy cloth and seals of wax or rubber around all the edges. The underside breathed in long, hard gusts that came and went, inhaling and exhaling. Off in the distance, Mercy could hear the rolling, mechanical thunder of machinery working hard.

Briar told her, "Those are the pumps. They keep the air moving from up over the wall and down to us. They don't run all the time, though. Just a few hours, most days. Did you see the air tubes, when we were coming in? The yellow ones? They're propped all over the city, up past the wall so they can grab the good air."

"No, I didn't see them," Mercy replied. She wondered what else she'd missed, but kept such wonderings to herself as she followed down the tunnels, hallways, and unfinished paths that wound through the underground.

"Once we get on the other side of the next seal, you can take the mask off," Lucy informed her. And, indeed, in a moment they all peeled the things off their faces, stashing them under arms or in bags, except for Mercy, who wasn't sure what to do with hers.

"Keep it," Briar told her. "Put it in your bag. We've got plenty more, and you'll be needing it later. We'll get you some extra filters for it, too."

"How much farther are we going?"

Lucy said, "Not much. We're going down into Chinatown, because that's where the only decent doctor is for a hundred miles. And yes," she snapped before anyone could contradict her, in case they'd been planning on it, "I'd count Tacoma in that, too. Anyway, we don't have much farther."

Seattle was a great rabbit warren of a city, there under the earth. In some places it looked almost normal: Mercy walked wide-eyed past rows of apartments and rooms filled with cargo, all of them perfectly ordinary except for the lack of windows and the persistent use of false lights and candles stashed in every corner.

The whole underground smelled damp and mossy, like a hole dug in a yard, since that's what it was.

They passed curious men and no other women, which Mercy noticed right away. But all the other residents nodded, dipped their hats, and offered friendly greetings. When Mercy looked perplexed at this, Lucy explained that everyone knew who Mercy was, and why she was coming. Mercy didn't know how to feel about this, but she tried to be polite back, even as she was ushered along. Always down stairs and up steps with rails, or no rails, and down corridors with floors of polished marble or no floors at all—just damp earth like a root cellar.

She found herself imagining what it looked like, up there in the city itself. She occupied her thoughts with speculation about the roving dead who she'd been warned roamed the streets, and considered that they very likely looked much like the afflicted Mexicans who'd nearly brought down two trains in the Utah pass. And just about the time she was out of things to wonder about, she became aware that all the men she was passing were Chinamen like Fang, and they also wore their hair in ponytails or braids shaved back away from their foreheads. They regarded her with curiosity but no malice, and they did not speak to her, though some of them hailed Lucy with a few quick words that she didn't understand.

Finally. Inevitably.

They arrived at a door at the very moment an aged Chinaman was exiting from it, trailed by gruff swearwords and a general air of aggravation in the room beyond. "And I don't need that goddamn potion. It tastes like shit, and I'm just not going to drink it anymore!"

The old man rolled his eyes, making Mercy think that everyone everywhere who had ever had a grouchy patient must make that same face. He said something to Lucy, who nodded.

The one-armed woman lowered her voice and said, "Don't

judge him too harsh. He's lived hard, and nearly died to save the lives of strangers. And you were the only thing he wanted, when we would've done anything to make him happy. So I want you to know that I'm glad you came, and even *impressed* that you came. Because not every daughter would've done it, and I think it speaks well of you. Briar, honey?"

"Lucy?"

"It's time for us to go."

Mercy wanted to argue with them, to demand that they accompany her, to accuse them bitterly of leaving her just when she needed them most.

But she didn't.

And they didn't stay.

They slipped away, and back, these two women whom she'd known for not even a day. One old enough to be her mother; one an older sister, or a young aunt. Her only connection to anything above, and her only way out if she refused to step through that cracked-open door.

She put a hand on it. Took a deep breath of air that smelled and tasted stale, and faintly like sulfur. Pushed the door an inch, then stalled. Recovered her willpower. Pushed it far enough to admit her.

She stepped into the doorway of a room with all the fixtures of a hotel. A basin stood against a far wall; a dresser with a mirror squatted beside it. The walls themselves had been painted with cheerful stripes in a bright red that was almost orange, and a deep blue that was almost purple. These were illuminated by a pair of gas lanterns on the end tables on either side of the bed.

On this bed was a man half-propped up against a mountain of pillows, and looking quite peevish about it.

He lounged there with one leg braced up and reinforced in a cast composed of wood stays and canvas. Around his torso was a similar set of stays, nearly corsetlike, and Mercy understood at a glance that some of those ribs had been broken, and that his chest had been carefully immobilized to keep the pointed bits of bone from doing damage to his lungs or other organs. She took all this in and admired it, even approving of the partial hat he wore over an otherwise shaven and naked head. She understood that this, too, was a bandage, and that some head wound must've rendered the covering a requirement.

It was easier for her to see him that way, as a patient.

She'd dealt with many patients on many beds, and there were a handful of types, but no real mysteries to any of them. She could look him up and down and gather that he'd survived some hideous trauma, and even glean the nature of if she looked closely enough: A badly broken leg; compound fracture, no doubt. An assortment of broken ribs. A head wound that must've gone down to the bone and might even have splintered the hard bits beneath the skin. The telltale pockmarks and seams that showed where stitches had been removed, and where a cut or a puncture had conclusively agreed to remain closed.

But it was harder to look at the man and know she hadn't seen him in so very long. It was tough to see that battered face with the flattened nose (broken long ago, she could tell, as easily as if he wore a sign) and the broad cheekbones that she'd inherited, giving her the same wide face that looked almost square in the right light. And it was a struggle to meet his eyes, which were watching her back from underneath fluffy eyebrows shot through with the first threads of silver. One had a scar that cut across it, healed years ago, by the look of it.

She took all this in, and she stood in the doorway without knowing what to say, or how to move, or if she should take up the chair that his physician had used to examine him, there beside the bed.

He took her in, too, and did not say anything either, did not seem to know if he should invite her inside or ask her to leave.

His stubbly face was turned on the pillow, pressing against it so he could get a look at her. He cleared his throat with a wet, weak sound that probably wasn't the noise he'd meant to make.

Finally, he said, "Nita?" Both syllables cracked against his uncertainty.

She clutched the door's latch and stood in its frame as if it were a magical space that would protect her from whatever happened next. But she replied: "Daddy?"